THE PLEDGE

Dr Sarah Yarwood-Lovett is currently an established professional sustainability expert tackling some of the biggest global challenges in tech. Having spent 16 years as an ecologist, as she crawled through undergrowth and studied the nocturnal habits of animals (and people), her mind naturally turned to murder.

Forensically studying environmental clues has seen Sarah surveying sites all over the UK and around the world. She's rediscovered a British species thought to be extinct during her PhD, with her record held in London's Natural History Museum; debated that important question – do bats wee on their faces? – at school workshops; survived a hurricane on a coral atoll while scuba-diving to conduct marine surveys; advised parliament, given evidence as an expert witness and set (and met) industry-leading sustainability targets.

Her unusual career has provided the perfect inspiration for the Dr Nell Ward series – murder mysteries with an ecological twist – and, more recently, suspenseful thrillers where nothing is more ruthless than nature.

Also by Sarah Yarwood-Lovett

Dr Nell Ward series
A Murder of Crows
A Cast of Falcons
A Mischief of Rats
A Generation of Vipers
A Trace of Hares
A Swarm of Butterflies
An Ambush of Tigers

THE PLEDGE

SARAH YARWOOD-LOVETT

ZAFFRE

First published in the UK in 2026 by
ZAFFRE
An imprint of Bonnier Books UK
5th Floor, HYLO, 105 Bunhill Row,
London, EC1Y 8LZ

This is a work of fiction. Names, places, events and
incidents are either the products of the author's
imagination or used fictitiously. Any resemblance to
actual persons, living or dead, or actual
events is purely coincidental.

A CIP catalogue record for this book is
available from the British Library.

ISBN: 978-1-78512-330-6

Also available as an ebook and an audiobook

1 3 5 7 9 10 8 6 4 2

Typeset by IDSUK (Data Connection) Ltd
Printed and bound in Great Britain by CPI (UK) Ltd, Croydon CR0 4YY

The authorised representative in the EEA is
Bonnier Books UK (Ireland) Limited.
Registered office address: Block B, The Crescent Building
Northwood, Santry, Dublin 9
D09 C6X8, Ireland
compliance@bonnierbooks.ie
www.bonnierbooks.co.uk

For Ian.
For being wicked and golden and brilliant.

Chapter 1

Friday 11th April

OK, BE HONEST: HOW CONTENT are you with your life, right now? How would you score it, on a scale of one to ten? Do you think your answer puts you in the majority, or the minority?

I was *horrified* when I read the Life Satisfaction survey results: most people, allowing for some global variation, are *happy* with their lot! That was mystifying to me a week ago. In fairness, it didn't reflect my world. *Didn't*: past tense. A lot's changed in a week …

The survey described how satisfaction scores are linked to education, income, health, nature … yada yada. How banal, how *limiting*, I thought.

In my universe, it's status, power, influence. You might display it with your property portfolio, the elite fleet in the pristine garage, staff to run it all, and holidays on private islands orbited by superyachts. Or you might be more covert – conspiracies and secrets whispered in corners of exclusive clubs, weaponised knowledge wielded with fatal precision. One thing is constant: it's never enough. You scramble onto the next plane of privilege, only to catch a glimpse of a higher level, just out of reach. Any joy at an achievement, any fulfilment, is slain in seconds by that insatiable craving.

Many vow they'd kill for such exclusiveness – few are joking.

I said all this was past tense. Because now I've climbed that slippery slope myself, higher than I ever expected, I've come to see that power plays aren't games.

When I saw who, at that illustrious altitude, I was rubbing shoulders with – what the untouchable are truly capable of, with no one to hold them to account – I had to ask, 'Is this really what I want?' And I was shocked to see how clawing my way up had caused my downfall.

It took nothing less than murder to change my course.

As King's Counsel, such things are naturally in my peripheral experience, so I should have seen the truth much sooner. But some things are too close for perspective. In the 'warts and all' case of Harrington v. Life – and death – maybe you'll see the truth before I did . . .

One week ago – Friday 4ᵗʰ April – 3.30 p.m.

I emerge into grave, grey London light, on the courtroom steps, blinking at the flashing wall of photographers and TV crews, all rabid to capture my comment on the verdict. The rumour has already rushed from the courtroom, beating the clipped stride of my brogues from the bench.

Marcus sidles up beside me, oozing obsequiousness. 'Knew we'd nail them.'

'You didn't,' I murmur, fixing a smile in place for the photographers. 'I hope you're not losing your mental faculties, Marcus, because your *exact* words were that you "wouldn't touch this if you were on a melting icecap and this case was your only life raft." My arched eyebrow reminds him that I'm famous in our chambers for recalling quotes verbatim – handy for a KC, *and* for when your colleagues try to steal your thunder by rewriting history.

I catch the BBC interviewer's eye and she nods, then begins her introduction to camera. 'In today's radical verdict, the government was found *not guilty* of violating their agreement with the Climate Change Commission. Defending accusations of failing to meet their renewable energy commitments through a lack of investment, they claimed that changing impacts and opportunities require regular revisions of practical solutions. Those upheld claims were presented forcefully by Thea Harrington KC, who joins me now.'

As the camera swings towards me I smooth my hair, having removed my wig, and straighten my jacket. I've worn men's shoes and suits since realising how well they're designed to disguise a figure enjoying the spoils of a successful career. I reject the female enslavement of bodycon dresses and pencil skirts, which demand increasing discipline and self-restraint, just as you can afford to indulge – *and* just as biology turns against you. *No, thanks.* My tailor's adept at hiding my peri-meno pounds, so I don't have to deny myself the finer things in life.

I'm not vain: the nicest compliment I can expect is that my six feet make me statuesque, though I'm usually called intimidating. But the compliments I *value* are about my intelligence. I lift my head, channelling that as I face the camera and the crowing crowd.

From the shockwave of widening eyes, gaping mouths, I can see the wall of journalists still can't believe today's result.

I compose my modest smile to convey magnanimity in victory – so much more effective, more *galling* to those defeated, than gloating.

Especially as this win – *my* win – is against significant odds: the kind of high-profile, precedent-setting case that changes the course of the law. *And* it will deliver my coveted senior partnership; better late than never, but long overdue, so I won't look too grateful, given how Marcus shrank from this case. I couldn't afford to: the only way to smash the glass ceiling is to take on those riskier cases. So there's no *way* Marcus is going to steal my glory now, even though he's inching into shot.

The interviewer's bias pulsates off of her, and she can't quite hide the smirk when the jeering rises. The activists beyond the cameras press forward, holding up signs and chanting – and I am the sole focus of their impotent anger.

We'd expected this: when we'd arrived at the courthouse and seen the demonstrators brandishing their banners behind the police barrier, Arthur, our Managing Partner, had given me a knowing wink and murmured, 'Best publicity money can't buy. You show your trademark grace under pressure, Thea, and we'll do very well out of this.'

But as the crowd swells, I see how vastly we've underestimated their animosity. It's a cacophony of fury. My stomach churns at the ocean of desperate, fierce protestors, surging like a tsunami. The human barrier of uniformed police staggers back, unable to hold the tide.

My swallow is dry as a desert as I stare down the lens. My voice better not crack. I smile, injecting confidence into my tone. 'Today's verdict will no doubt stir emotions, but this is a *just* result. While we're *all* concerned about the impact of climate change, we must be realistic. A responsible government has many things to balance, and needs the freedom to make appropriate decisions, without the imposition of impractical idealism.'

The interviewer hides a sly grin. 'Of course, one of the things *you've* had to balance is your potential conflict of interest, since your husband is the Energy Minister.'

'We are professionally independent.' My reply is velvet with practise. 'Governments, advisors and MPs have to be adept practitioners of pragmatism.'

Yells from the protestors drown me out. 'Your pragmatism is killing the planet!' 'How about barristers and MPs give up the extra homes they never use? Save us having to build more for a growing population? How pragmatic would *that* be?'

At the jeers, Marcus slithers away. Out of the corner of my eye, I see him back-slapping Arthur, who'd promised my promotion if I pulled off this coup. I feel my magnanimous smile wither on my lips. Arthur had assigned reluctant, slippery Marcus as my co-counsel. Marcus didn't do any actual *work*, so he had plenty of time for long lunches with the boss. His connections are lofty enough to pique even Arthur's ambitions. The implication hits me as they shake hands. Has Marcus scored a promotion off the back of this? Or has *mine* been parlayed to *him*?

The rising roar of the crowd makes me rip my gaze from my colleagues. Turning, I lock eyes with a young protestor, beyond the interviewer. Her appearance makes me gasp. It's like looking in a mirror, twenty years ago – when I'd have been standing there.

Her intense hazel eyes burn with ferocious indignation. That confidence that you're on the right side of justice, with no complicated compromises, feels like a lifetime ago.

But then her arm swings up and she *hurls* something right at me.

As I flinch, a deafening cheer rises. Her peers follow suit: missiles shoot past my ear.

Trembling, I duck, my heartbeat galloping. A hard *thud* on my neck makes me stagger. I touch the spot and feel wet, sticky . . . blood? I stare at my shaking hands and my fingertips ooze with . . . *something*, but not blood.

A volley smashes into my chest, my face – and I feel the shivery shock of gelatinous ooze down my cheek, my throat, my chest and – *ew!* – into my bra. I shudder at the cold slither of egg sliming down my skin.

Fighting back disgust, I hold my shirt away from my body, relief avalanching through me that my waistcoat will prevent anything being see-through on camera. Whoops erupt around the woman, her fellows high-fiving her. *Rise above it. Rise above it.*

As photo flashes strobe around me, recording the disintegration of my dignity, my stomach knots. My vision tilts as I look for the most elegant exit, for escape. There's no route through this roaring protest.

Then I catch sight of them, in the distance, beyond the chaos: Marcus in his pristine, egg-slime-free suit, strolling round the corner, head bent towards Arthur's.

I'm their bloody decoy! With a sharp nod at the interviewer, I force my way around the courthouse, praying my assertive stride and sheer outrage will keep me upright on my shaking legs. My chauffeur-driven Bentley is waiting for me, engine running, ready for the getaway. As I slide into the quilted rear seat, my driver asks, 'Where to, Ms Harrington?'

'Fawsey Hall.' I can hardly go for celebratory drinks with actual egg on my face. *Unlike Marcus.* But I still have to pin down Arthur. Before I can call him, my phone rings.

Charles. As if I need another irritant. 'Darling, sorry.' His Eton-accented, faux apology grates. I know that tone, and what's coming. 'I'm staying in town this weekend.'

Uh huh. No prizes for guessing what Charles is doing tonight. He'll come home on Sunday night, reeking of another woman's perfume – then grab his phone like a lifeline whenever I leave the room.

My twenty-year marriage is transactional – I'm not naive – but divorce means forsaking the pros of our merger: the social status, the lifestyle, which, as he constantly reminds me, are all due to his precious network.

'I see victory is yours again. Clever girl.' It's the same tone he'd use to a labrador that's retrieved a stick, and it needles me instantly.

'Must you?'

'Must I what?'

'Talk to me like that.'

'What, *congratulate* you?'

'No, *patronise* me. You don't need to be so reductive with the "clever girl" nonsense. I'm a woman, who's just had a landmark success. You wouldn't congratulate a man for something as seismic as this by saying "clever boy."'

'Oh, here we fucking go. *Congratulations*.' His sarcasm drips spite. 'Felicitations. A thousand commen-fucking-dations. And, while we're chucking praise around, how about a modicum of gratitude for the man who *put* you in this position, eh? You don't get into chambers like Arthur's easily. You *know* I pulled some strings—'

I stab the 'end call' with force, feeling like I could hurl the phone out of the window – but it buzzes in my hand. Seeing it's Arthur, I answer it, fighting to regain my composure.

'Thea. Our woman of the hour.'

'Glad you noticed. I trust you're confirming that this win secures my promotion.'

At his discouraging silence, I add, 'You'll recall our agreement, or shall I quote you?'

'As *you'll* recall, Thea, the agreement noted that promotions need to be ratified with all partners. And I'll be transparent, some partners have made the very fair point that it was Marcus's connections who brought us the case—'

God. The connection fixation again. Yes, they may be vital – Charles has made sure I shaped my life around the tyranny of them and those who wield them – but you still need the talent and the guts to follow up. And Marcus doesn't have either. I should have expected Arthur to put me and Marcus in competition. And Charles has just put that fire in my belly to fight for *myself*, for once.

'You're right that Marcus's contact approached *us*. You'll also recall Marcus *refused* the case. We share today's victory because *I* accepted it.' I pause for a beat. 'Then *won* it.'

'But Marcus's network has an undoubted value—'

Ugh. 'I'm glad you're interested in the company he keeps, Arthur. I could share an incriminating photo with you now, showing him with the opposition. My hunch is he was taking a bribe, to sabotage this case – the case he'd advised us against taking.'

Arthur's pause makes me smile. It means he's appraising the risk, considering the likelihood of it. 'I'd have to see the photo, Thea.'

I knew he'd call my bluff. If I had any evidence against Marcus, I'd have used it long ago. 'I'd send it – if I could. But that would compromise me, *and* our win, so I can't. *My* loyalty is to our reputation. Which is exactly what you need in your senior partners. Wouldn't scorning that loyalty – by rewarding someone who's actively harming our chambers instead – be counter to everything you've worked for, Arthur?'

'Oh, Thea.' He chuckles. 'That's quite the front.'

'Make an assessment on the balance of probabilities, then.' I shrug. 'After this case, I'll be in demand, Arthur. Whatever chambers I'm at. So, if you can't decide now, then—'

I can almost hear cogs turning as he calculates his options. 'Fine. Consider it done.'

'I just want what we agreed.' I pause again, for just one beat. 'Plus twenty per cent.'

Arthur splutters, then clears his throat.

'I've got another call coming in, Arthur, so I'll have to—'

'I'll send the contract tonight.'

'Good. And Arthur, due to his misconduct, Marcus can't be part of our inner circle. I trust I can leave it to you, to ensure I won't see him on Monday?' I hang up, but I don't have the glow of satisfaction I expected. Maybe it's marred by the sticky egg starching my shirt. Maybe it's because my phone *isn't* beeping non-stop with offers. At least it shows me that I've probably negotiated my best offer. It won't do for Arthur to ever realise that.

Arthur, Marcus, Charles: they're all the same. All cut from the same private-school cloth, sharing opportunities and a single brain cell dedicated to self-preservation.

I hate to admit it, but Charles did accelerate my career. Like a spider in a web, he could tweak a contact with deadly accuracy, accelerating the right jobs, firms, cases . . .

These days, my talent, my reputation, speak for themselves, *thanks*. But I'm so entangled that it's impossible to see how to free myself without life unravelling.

I stare out of the window, watching London flash past. I hate how Charles always makes me feel like I owe him, like I haven't earned my place or don't have my own value. I hate that he's ruined this moment for me. And I think . . . I *think* I'm starting to hate *him*.

The rebel in me rises: I'll enjoy tonight. No Chateau Lafite Rothschild, with a chef-prepared dinner over lacklustre conversation then a dull box set. No. My evening, my way.

Finally, the Bentley sweeps into the gated drive. This glimpse of the manor at the end of the avenue was Charles's trump card when I considered his proposal. True, breathtaking grandeur. Signifying a family of power, old money. Now, with its Cotswold stone gilded by the setting sun, it couldn't look more idyllic. I've got used to a life like this.

Once the driver's left, I traipse around the house, filing away my work in my panelled study, lined with tomes and framed awards. I draw a bergamot-scented bath in my spa-like en suite, throw my egg-splattered clothes into the laundry, order an illicit Wagas on DoorDash, then sink into the fragrant foam with a strong negroni and a *Strike* audiobook. *Bliss.*

Half an hour later, I don silk pyjamas, mix another cocktail, then settle on the sofa beside the crackling fire as I tuck into gyoza and teppanyaki noodles.

If we divorced, I'd be urged to leave here, to keep the Kensington townhouse rather than Charles's ancestral home. The thought of leaving this place – my home – makes my stomach churn. Maybe I could negotiate to keep it. Charles may be grateful that I want to take it on. He inherited the estate, but it's *my* underrated talent – that runs it. I'm the one who makes all the upkeep decisions, who organises the never-ending maintenance – and pays for it. I *deserve* to own it.

My heart thumps with fear – of the unknown, of what life will be like – and also a sense of freedom. I feel like a defiant Oxford student again – and that protestor's face flashes into my mind. Mellowed by sips of spicy gin, I see she was just railing against the system, believing you can steer the juggernaut course of economy onto ethical tracks.

As a shiny-faced intern, I'd had those ideals, the desire to use my powers for good – chambers are saturated with pro bono work for worthy causes. But I'd deferred taking any of those on, justifying that I needed to amass the influence, the *status*, to do real good. Once you start that climb, no peak is high enough.

My phone beeps with my new contract. *Finally*, I've reached those heady heights. Yet now I'm here, I'm too ensnared by the lifestyle to divert my energies into pro bono cases at the expense of high-profile work. Deferring good intentions is really the erosion of them, isn't it? My conscience stings.

But one's worldview matures, doesn't it? That student will have the same epiphany, that money always wins. Any idealism, hoping for better, will be trampled out of her, too.

I head to the sideboard to pour another cocktail, and my gaze is arrested by our wedding photo in the antique frame. It wasn't one of the many posed, rictus-smile pictures, but a candid snap: Charles is turned to me, our bodies close, intimate, even. He's plucking confetti out of my hair, wisping from the frothing veil that's swept back over the glittering family tiara. My face tilts up to his like a flower towards the sun. Our smiles are radiant and teasing, as if we're sharing a secret. He's leaning in towards me, his eyes full of desire – and the captured moment holds us forever on the brink of a kiss . . .

When I look at this picture, it hits me like a sucker punch. It transports me straight back to how I felt at the time. The drunk-on-life excitement of knowing that I'd been more than a rebellious fling for Charles; that our ideals matched and that we wanted to really *do* something with all the potential we were fizzing with.

And *this* is where it brought me . . . The sick, hollow feeling makes me dizzy.

Turning, I take in the room. I mean, this is a wonderful place to be. I have a successful career. I have a fabulous lifestyle. What have I really got to complain about?

Charles, I guess. And general . . . *disappointment*. That it all feels so empty. I wish he still had that spark. Could still subvert opinion, confound expectations. I loved that he made me look at issues from other angles, how he always had a counter-argument ready. Our sparring made me a far sharper barrister, I can at least credit him with that.

Maybe we can resurrect that? Maybe we've both just been too busy, too consumed with work to have time for each other. Maybe it just takes a few dates, some real attention.

I head to the kitchen for more ice, and notice a small wrapped box on the kitchen island. Guessing it's a delivery left by the housekeeper, I seize the chef's knife from the block, snick the tape and draw out the contents.

Huh. A timepiece, like an antique pocket watch, ticking but showing the wrong time: 1.30 p.m. One of Charles's gifts? It's well-chosen. It'll go well with my pinstripe.

The clock's back is engraved: an irregular shape around an etched 'OneT'. *Should I know what OneT means?* Once my curiosity is roused, it must be satisfied. So, I search on, opening the casing, shaking the box – and jump when a thick card falls out.

Thea Harrington, your success today has earned you this invitation to join us – the world's most exclusive group, the OneT Club – at our summit. Go to London Airport's private lounge at the right time, on the right day, with your passport. The recognition you deserve awaits.

Chapter 2

Friday 4ᵗʰ April – 5.30 p.m.

THE MORE I EXAMINE THE fascinating gift, the odder it seems, and now I'm laughing at myself. What am I doing, trying to crack some cryptic message? What is this OneT Club, anyway? There's nothing online about it … which makes it, what? Suspicious? Alluring?

I can never resist solving a mystery, so this puzzle, together with the seduction of arriving at a private airport lounge to be whisked off to a summit, sounds … amazing!

It must be a scam. Yet the romance of it calls to me. I examine the card, peer at the writing, turn it over. Tracing my fingers across it, I find an indent. Yanking open the kitchen drawer, I grab a pencil and lightly run it over the hidden letters:

BC.DE.D.D

BC? Is this a date reference? DE? D.D? Is that meant to sound like a name? Or are they initials? Then why the full stops? Google gives me nothing to work with. In my tipsy state, I count out – slowly – on my fingers what numbers the letters would equate to: 23.45.4.4.

I blink through the alcoholic fug. Is 23.45 a time? So, is 4.4 a date?

I stare at it. That's *today's* date. In six hours' time. *Holy* … Am I supposed to be there at quarter to midnight? Urgency grips me. I stand, looking towards my bedroom, wondering what to pack. '*Be prepared for anything*,' it said …

What am I doing? I sit again. I'm not rushing off, with no idea of why – or who's behind it. I'm not at anyone's beck and call. When I don't even know where I'm flying to …

I glance at the watch, my eyes fixing on the odd shape again. Could it be a country? I open Google Maps on my phone, comparing shapes of countries, islands, continents …

There are so many. I roll my shoulders – and pour a drink. There must be a way to cut this down. I check the watch again – and register the actual time: 2 p.m.

If this is an island, then it's either four hours behind or eight hours ahead. A search by time zone would focus things a lot …

I look up what falls in those bands. Eight hours ahead is the Philippines. I scour Indonesia, scanning between Australia and China – but I can't find a match.

Taking a long drink, I see where four hours behind would take me: skimming the east of Canada and the USA, and down through the Caribbean islands …

And there it is. I gasp at the island that's a perfect match for the shape etched on the watch, nestled near Barbados: the island of St Innocent. *Yes! I'm on to something!*

Googling the name of the island, I discover that it's privately owned. Is that a surprise? I can't even tell. I have another long sip of my cocktail. Can't hurt.

I keep searching, and finally find an article about the island's purchase by a company: Innocent Holdings, part of Iðunn Luxury Brands. I've heard of it, of course, and I look it up.

Owned by Olga Helgesdotter ... *Where have I heard her name?* I scan the pages. She tops the *Forbes Rich List* as the owner of a parent company of super luxe fashion, beauty, travel, devices and homeware brands. I scan the other names in the top five, and their mini-bios, and see that tech is mainly responsible for the world's great wealth.

Now I *am* intrigued by the invitation. I'd think it was a hoax, if it wasn't for the watch.

I'm interrupted by my phone ringing. As I answer it, I see Charles has sent a text. I don't care what he has to say so I don't open it. But the phone call *isn't* him, so I answer it.

'Thea?' my paralegal hisses through the phone. 'If you're at home, you need to leave. *Now.* You've been doxxed. Your home addresses are all over social media.'

'Whaaat?' I respond, at negroni-speed. As I tap my name into Google, it blows up with threats and photos of my homes, with addresses. Vitriol and hatred spews off the screen.

'Do you have somewhere to go?' my paralegal asks. 'Family? A trusted friend?'

I nearly laugh at the idea of a friend you can turn to when the world is against you.

'Anywhere at all?' she insists.

I glance at my strange set of clues. *What the hell.* How bad could a weekend in the Caribbean be? Better than trying to hide from climate activists. And I have to admit – whoever this is, their cryptic approach intrigues me. 'You know what, I think I do.'

Friday 4th April – 11.30 p.m.

A few hours later, my Cristal champagne is being topped up by my personal concierge while I wait in the private lounge to board a bloody *private jet*.

The thought of Charles pulling his burning-with-envy-but-can't-show-it face thrills me more than the adventure ahead. He's flown private once, with the PM. All his eagerness over it was deflated with the instant media backlash, calling for the Minister for Energy to fly cattle class, or go by Eurostar – not take the 'one rule for them, one rule for me' approach.

I feel mean for wanting to make him jealous. It seems too easy these days for it to be a fair fight. A wave of sadness like *mourning* hits me. At uni, Charles was driven, provocative. I knew, when we met at a party, that we wanted the same from life. He wasn't handsome, but he reeked of money. *Power.* The right background, the PPE degree, success written in his stars. It was addictive. Beautiful women flocked – so I kept my distance. I was aloof, with just a hint of sparky eye contact, a suggestion of interest, aiming to intrigue – then ensured I was never available. The chase piqued his curiosity. He pursued with more focus than a hound on his family-led hunts. Back then, a contrary remark ignited debate; these days, it just prompts a sneer.

I redouble my intention to try to reinvigorate that part of him. The next time we're together, I'm going to *really* try. I make the pledge to myself, but a small voice inside me is adding a caveat: that the next time we're together will also be a test. There has to be some hope of life; you can't revive something that's dead. The next time I see him, I'll know: we'll either be back on course, or heading for divorce.

I take a deep breath, affirming the decision to myself, and spot the young woman sitting opposite me. She's handling this luxury with indifference, studying the screen of her open laptop, typing rapidly while she listens to something on her earbuds, and nods at the concierge's offer of champagne.

As I assess her, I wander over to the table of magazines behind her and flip noisily through one, in case the earbuds are a ruse. I squint at her screen, and – with a sinking heart – I see myself. She clicks on the Mail's article and replays the Egg Incident. *Great*.

Returning to my seat, I nod at her screen. 'My day's improved. How about yours?'

She snaps it shut, eyeing me warily. 'Can't tell yet.' A hint of a London accent. For all her casual demeanour, she doesn't look wealthy. She seems bookish, like a nerd at school who grew into her confidence at uni. There's an air of gritty determination in her sharp, appraising gaze – which now lingers on the chain of my pocket watch.

I spot the delicate Fizili Ultra-Thin glinting on her wrist, set to island time. I recall how well-chosen my timepiece was. While the sleek black watch seems at odds with this mid-thirties woman in jeans, green Kickers and Nike hoodie, I realise it's understated, mysterious. The choice speaks of hidden depths, and that makes me smile.

Seeing my glance at her wrist, she smiles back, tapping her waist, mirroring where my pocket watch sits. 'The great summons from Olga Helgesdotter?'

'Ah, you too, then.' I nod, helping myself to the fruit platter beside me.

'Does it feel like you're entering the dragon's lair?' she asks.

I laugh, mid-chew of a strawberry that tastes of carefree summer. 'It *is* a bit like that!' I extend my hand, inviting her formal introduction. 'You already know I'm Thea Harrington.'

'Asha Sani.' Her handshake is accompanied by a flicker of a grin.

'So now you have an ally in the dragon's lair.' I pause to let the sense of comfort, of conspiracy, breathe – then, 'So, do you know what this is all about?'

'Not . . . exactly. I know she's been number one on the *Forbes Rich List* for years as the owner of Iðunn Luxury Brands, and I know she's got . . . something *important* planned.'

I have a million questions for her, but the concierge murmurs, 'May I invite you to step this way? Your aircraft is ready to depart.'

Asha goes ahead as I hunt for my bag, before I'm assured it's been taken aboard for me. On the jet, I'm impressed by the luxe leather seats, the walnut veneer, the *space*. Even the air is fragrant. Other passengers have appeared from apparently nowhere. *V* VIPs, of course. Yet again, I'm reminded there's always another level to climb. *Never enough.*

Oh my God. The young woman slouching in a front seat is only bloody *Zyra*. Most influential musician on the planet. Her tours sell out so fast, she changes a country's GDP. I'm fascinated to see that she isn't behaving like a diva; she's achingly cool in artfully ripped jeans and a vintage Stones T-shirt under a tailored military-style blazer. She plugs in her earbuds, the message clear.

The earbuds aren't for me, they're her defence against the middle-aged guy ogling her. Fat, balding, oily, a face only a mother could love. But his name made up for a lot, if you were swayed by such things. It's certainly weathered him a few UK-taxpayer-funded sex scandals. Prince Hubert – Hugh – Duke of Clarence. The monarch's expectations aren't high, judging by how frequently bailouts, palaces, security and honours are bestowed.

My heart sinks as Hugh squints at me, then oozes over. 'Thea? Charles didn't say you'd be here.' Seizing my hand, he presses it against his moistened lips, a gesture he thinks is gallant but is totally *ick*. I'm too surprised at the mention of my husband to pull away.

As Hugh turns, I shudder and wipe the back of my hand. At uni, Charles's set orbited his, with Charles finally ingratiating himself in our second year. Despite my ambition, I kept my distance from Hugh's sleazy entitlement. Whenever I saw him, drunk and coked up at parties, alarm bells shrieked in my head like a forest full of clamouring birds, like my skull would shatter.

Then I see who Hugh's beckoning. *Charles! With the VVIPs!* As my husband's eyes meet mine, his sycophantic smile dies on his lips as shock flickers. *Ha!* I nod, like I was expecting him, ensuring that it appears to him that I'm one step ahead there, at least.

I lean in to kiss him like any delighted wife. 'Darling! You made it! *So* glad.' My smile's serene, but my mouth is so dry that my lips catch on my teeth. I sip my champagne.

He blinks rapidly. 'Likewise. Darling.' A lie. His neck turns puce, his trademark tell.

'I've been looking forward to this for quite a while,' I add, wondering if he had been.

But the hint of a frown suggests that he, too, was only summoned at the last minute. 'Indeed,' he manages, and I hold in a laugh at the stock reply he uses when he doesn't have a clue.

My seat is annoyingly near his. 'I didn't know that you knew Olga,' he probes as we fasten seatbelts. But he's looking at me with the intrigue of his younger self.

'I know you didn't.' I'm enjoying . . . what? His interest? Or his vulnerability?

Olga . . . Ah . . . yes. Hearing him say her name reminds me of when he returned from COP30 with a severe case of mentionitis: *Olga says, 'Your ideal future is the gift of your present.' Olga says, 'Envision your desires, and they'll find you,'* as if your life goals were lost car keys. I'd rolled my eyes until I'd given myself a headache, but I'd noted his new crush.

Now, though, doubt flickers. Have I been invited not because of my talent, but his connections? *Again?* Or *worse*, as a marital gooseberry while Olga 'envisions' her latest desire?

'I should never underestimate you, should I?' Charles shoots me a sidelong, secret smile, and it sweeps me up into his orbit again. But I need to know more about our host and why she wants us – and I won't ask him, or I'll sacrifice the intrigue currency I'm accruing.

Once we're airborne, I follow Asha to the bar, ask for a Manhattan, and resume our chat. 'So, what *is* Olga's club all about? What's the "something important" she's planned?'

'I couldn't say. But take note of the guest list,' Asha whispers. 'Everyone here, plus a few more, are all carefully selected, for a specific reason. Strictly no entourages, managers, assistants or equerries.'

Warning prickles my neck. 'So all of us are Olga's guests? How can she get a crowd like this together at her whim? Without their team? An MP, a prince, a popstar, and you?' I frown at her. 'What do you do, Asha?'

'Journalist. Olga's included me to help oversee comms and announcements.'

'*Announcements*? Jeez. She's confident we'll fall in with her plans, isn't she?'

Asha laughs. 'You reckon you can refuse a request from someone with untouchable, rules-don't-apply levels of power? Word to the wise, Thea – don't even *think* about it.'

Saturday 5th April – 5 a.m. local time

The massage, nap, fine dining and cocktails while watching the skimming clouds keep me occupied during the flight – and away from Charles as much as possible, so I can strategise. I'm still wondering what Olga wants of us as we land in Bridgetown, Barbados, at 5 a.m.

Even pre-dawn, the wave of heat hits me like a wall, and I'm glad of my layered outfit in holiday jewel tones. I bite back a grin at Charles, still in suit trousers, who looks surprised, then worried, that I'm equipped for the climate. I don't even think about transferring my luggage; oh, how quickly one adjusts.

Under the red-edged sky, we're scooped towards the inviting twinkling lights of the port. As I inhale the fresh ocean breeze that whips loose strands of hair around my face, I find myself staring up at a sleek, towering superyacht. I manage not to gape.

We're all personally greeted by young, tanned crew members. Mine is a young man with a friendly smile. 'Welcome aboard, Ms Harrington. We are your home from home for the next twelve hours, our journey time to St Innocent. Let me show you to your suite, in case you want some sleep. I'm Drew. If you need anything at all, please just ask.'

Charles and I have separate suites – and I'm not sure if I'm encouraged by that (if it means that we're here in our own rights, rather than as a couple) or worried (if it means that Olga knows more about our marriage than she should). Maybe I'm overthinking it; maybe she's just a woman who demands her own space, and thinks others do, too.

Despite my whirling mind, the motion of water and the sheer cosseting luxury of the yacht lulls me. I sink into a deep, restful sleep until mid-morning. My request for coffee is exceeded by a cheerful Drew who brings a richly aromatic cafetiere and a platter of delicious, freshly baked pastries. I indulge: I should enjoy this, right?

I take a book to the pool on the main deck. I'm glad my sunglasses hide my wide eyes as I take in the view of our foaming wake, carving through endless sapphire sea past emerald islands, with wheeling gulls overhead. Drew offers me a mimosa and I beam and accept.

Angling my broad-brimmed hat low against the dazzling sun, I notice that Charles now wears crisp, tailored pale chinos and a short-sleeved shirt that I don't recognise. I wonder if everyone's closets have been filled with designer holiday wear. I should check mine.

I wander over. 'Morning. Did you sleep?' I kiss his head and he catches my hand.

'Yes, a little. You?'

'Yes.' My gaze flicks over his face, seeking giveaway micro-expressions that may warn me if his latest mistress is about to host me on her own bloody private island.

He gives nothing away, but there's always been a tacit understanding between us about affairs. Our only rule is that we're discreet. If Olga *is* his mistress, then she's flouting that rule, and I wonder if he's angry at her putting him in this position.

I attempt nonchalance, and lean back, staring up at the bluest sky I've ever seen, soaking up the heat. 'How long has it been since we had a holiday, Charles?'

'About eight months. Mustique—'

'No, I don't mean staying at someone's villa, on best behaviour all the time, networking from breakfast to nightcaps. I mean a real holiday. Just us.'

His brow furrows. 'Honeymoon probably. Except for a few weekends in Europe.'

'Huh. I think you're right. We could be better at prioritising each other, couldn't we?' I let the observation hang. I wait to see if he also thinks we need time together.

'God, I'm an arse.' He sits up, waves for Drew to bring over a bottle of champagne – 'Bollinger, '88,' he specifies – and turns to me. 'I know you're waiting for me to say something. So I should at least do it in style.'

I sit up, wondering if he's already got a break somewhere planned. God, will we enjoy each other's company in close proximity for over a week? I know in my heart that's why he's had affairs; I'm always busy. Charles might be great at pulling in contacts, but a legal career takes long, lonely hours to build. We'd both made choices in how we directed our time. But if Charles agrees that time together would be important, maybe there is hope …

Drew pours fizzing champagne into coupes and Charles takes his glass, facing me.

'Thea. Congratulations on your victory.'

'My … what?' He's not thinking about a holiday together? Taking time together?

'Your landmark win. I didn't make a fuss because I never doubted you'd prevail. But it's a significant moment and we should celebrate.' He raises his glass. 'The thing I've always liked most about you is your brain, that you're an original thinker. To your little grey cells.'

My heart swells at his compliment to my intelligence. Charles knows that matters to me. I don't suppress my smile as I tilt my glass towards his. As I sip, the bubbles fire against my lips, yet … somehow … I still feel hollow. It's that we'd both forgotten about my case; he'd had to make an effort to recall it and say something. And by that time, I was already thinking about something else altogether. We're not on the same wavelength anymore …

I look for distractions. Luckily, this opulent floating palace is crammed with them. Zyra – who's American, with a small-town rags-to-riches story – has ditched her jeans for a swimsuit, to drink a mimosa at the poolside. It's no coincidence that Hugh chose a shady seat on the deck, with the exclusive single malts and the view of the young woman in swimwear.

I have to wonder if she's assessing him right back, behind her oversized shades.

I turn to greet Asha as she sets up her laptop on the intricate marquetry of an antique desk just inside the state room. As she's offered a platter of fruit, pastries and any drink she can think of, I pick up my *Strike* book and settle on deck as Charles wanders over to Hugh. The hours – and nautical miles – speed by.

The lunch is amazing, the company less so. I sense everyone is uncertain about what lies ahead, but doesn't want to blink first, so conversation is limited to chitchat. The prince rolls out a tired repertoire of weak anecdotes that he expects us all to laugh along with. Charles slips in every story he has about Olga – and my hackles rise. Zyra mentions her latest album. Asha, by contrast, just listens to everyone. No comments, no responses.

Zyra shows me footage of her shows. 'I'm so lucky to work with the best team. Just *look*.' Shots of glittering stadium shows with fans holding adoring messages and Zyra blowing kisses are spliced with slick lifestyle posts and behind-the-scenes montages. Just enough glimpses of her elevated life to give the sense of a personal connection to a global phenomenon.

'How do you decide what to post?' Social media is an alien animal to me.

'Oh, *I* don't post. I'm so lucky, I have just the best team in the world for that. They capture all these little moments, you know? And then they curate the cutest stories to share. It's a lifesaver, because I really wanna connect with my fans, you know? But I have *so much* to balance. I delegate all my promotional work to my great team who get to unleash their *own* creativity. They're just the *best*. I couldn't be prouder of them.'

'Great.' I don't know what to say to the gushing LA-esque positivity, but Zyra smiles and takes another mimosa back to the pool, like I'm a tricky interviewer she's won over.

I wonder if she always talks in interview-ready soundbites, if she can ever say what she really thinks. Her brand is built on being her 'authentic self', and even I know that's social media code for 'totally fake', but you'd think that the advantage to being so much of a powerhouse that you're invulnerable to cancel culture would mean you could actually be genuine. Occasionally.

As I settle down to read, I glimpse the view beyond my pages: islands glide by, their golden sands and verdant palm trees bright against the azure ocean.

Asha is still busy with her computer. *Is she preparing the announcement she mentioned? About what?* It's clearly keeping her busy as she taps at her laptop inside.

The sea spray is refreshing in the baking sun. Dolphins frolic in the wake, then dive to the azure depths. I treasure the sight, not pointing it out to Charles or Hugh, who are working their way through the single malts on the top deck, their laughter louder and looser with every glass. We all have the same chance to observe things. Whether we do or not, is up to us.

I observe something else, too, from my discreet vantage point: a glass nudged out of reach, so the female member of staff has to lean over to collect it, getting groped in the process.

'Hey!' The pretty young crew member, in tailored tee and shorts, glares at Hugh.

'Everything OK?' Drew darts over, shooting anxious glances at the prince. 'Please, allow me to refresh your drink, sir. What'll it be?'

'It'll *be* Your Royal Highness,' Hugh snaps.

'I'm s-s-sorry, sir?'

'You should be. I'm Your Royal Highness or Your Grace. Save the 'sir' for the plebs.' Hugh glares at Drew. 'Are you some stinking supporter of a republic?'

'Hugh.' Charles's laconic tone tells me he knows what's coming. 'This isn't uni.'

But Hugh circles the flinching man. 'I bet you'd take the glory of an MBE or a knighthood, given the chance. I'd better convert you.' His mouth twists into a sneer. 'Kneel.'

'Wh-what?'

'If you want a knighthood, you have to kneel.'

'I don't … I'm *American*! I don't—'

'I said *kneel*,' Hugh roars, his face like a beetroot.

Flicking nervous glances at his colleague, Drew shivers to one knee.

'Both knees.' Approval smooths Hugh's voice. 'You must supplicate yourself to me.'

Drew's face flames. His leg shakes as he lowers his other knee to the floor.

I stare at Charles, wondering when he'll step in and stop whatever Hugh has in mind. Charles is too nonchalant, swirling his whisky, to *not* know what Hugh has planned.

'Now, hold out your hands,' Hugh goads. 'Like you're begging me.'

My heart is hammering. I'm leaning forward, silently urging Charles to intervene. My sick, churning gut knows that this is our watershed moment. Charles is the only person I know who can dissuade Hugh from his more stupid ideas. He alone has the power to steer this moment – and I need to see if he's man enough to.

Drew cups his hands but stares at the ground. His body is rigid, like he's willing this to be over. Hugh's gaze is triumphant. 'If only I had a sword. Have you a sword, Charles?'

I stare at Charles, willing him to flex his well-oiled diplomacy.

'No, Hugh,' Charles replies like this is well-rehearsed, and fever-heat flashes over me. 'I don't have a sword.' His tone is *encouraging*, and my stomach roils.

Zyra passes me, pauses, then notices the unfolding scene.

'Lucky I'm the Prince of Improv, then,' Hugh announces, as he unzips his fly.

I shrink back into my seat, and freeze.

Drew recoils, looking up in horror, and beside me, Zyra gasps. 'What the fuck?' She glares at me, like the men's behaviour is my fault, like I should intervene. *Then* she takes out her phone and starts filming them, and I thaw enough to cheer on the inside.

'Don't move,' Hugh soothes the young man as he starts urinating on him. 'Oh, no, I said *don't* move,' he repeats as Drew recoils. 'Not if you want to keep your job. And not if you want to learn the real order of the world. You'll thank me for this.'

Hugh's urine streams over Drew's hands, his head, his face, as Drew flinches. I glare at Charles, who refills his whisky, unperturbed. Sick grief washes over me as I stare at him in pure disgust. Any respect for him, any regard at all, has withered away. It's the end of us. It's the end of life as I know it. Uncertainty, anger and fear *surge* and I hate that the one certainty I'm clinging to is that I have to capsize my life. I feel like I'm drowning.

'What the fuck are you doing?' Zyra charges in, leaping over the seating in her rush, holding up her phone as she films. 'Move away, Drew. It's OK. You can move away.'

Drew shuffles off, out of range, dry-sobbing outraged shuddering breaths. His colleague joins him, offering a towel, and an apology that isn't hers to give.

'What the *hell* are you thinking?' Zyra challenges Hugh, still filming him as he finishes over the luxe sofa, then zips his trousers, ignoring her as Charles tops up his drink.

Zyra taps her phone, to unleash the video to the world via social media. Before she can, Hugh slaps it out of her hand with so much force that it spins high in the air. With her face contorted in outrage, Zyra leaps for it, agile as a cat, her arms outstretched. I watch her reach, then just *clip*, the edge of the phone – tipping it overboard into the sea.

'You *asshole*! Look what you've *done*! You can't throw my belongings overboard! That's *theft* and *assault*!' Zyra leans on the railings, staring down at the foaming ocean, then spins round, raising her hands in despair. 'Everything's on there! *Everything*! My songs, my contacts, my whole goddamn *life*!' She stops short, perhaps realising she has everything backed up on the Cloud – and that her other devices mean she can access everything. *Including that video.*

Hugh's smug smile flickers. I recognise his expression from our uni days and I shiver. He's like a moral black hole, sucking the energy out of everything around him. Without an equerry to advise him, I wonder if Hugh knows Zyra can still access, and *use*, that film?

Undaunted, Zyra stares him down. 'You *vile* waste of oxygen. You'll regret this.'

I note the authority in Zyra's voice. She's used to giving instructions that are followed immediately, and I know she won't drop this. But Hugh is too entitled to be ruffled. His expression is unimpressed, as blank as a shark's is when it slides around easy prey.

I give her a conspiratorial smile but she glares back, like I was conspiring with *them*.

That show of disapproval, the second in as many days from young women who are fearless enough to openly challenge the wrongs they see, seeps into my heart like black rot.

Chapter 3

Saturday 5th April – 4.30 p.m.

As ZYRA WALKS OFF, I spot Asha regarding the assembled company; she's clearly watched the whole scene. She doesn't speak, and her controlled, neutral gaze travels across the shallowing ocean, jading and foaming with surf, to our destination: the looming island of *St Innocent*.

My breath catches at the sight. Emerald volcanic peaks tower dramatically from scattered islands, fringed with jungle. There's a wildness, an impenetrability, to the nature here, and I'm intrigued and overawed by it.

As the anchor drops, we bob on water so clear I can see the darting shoals of fish investigating, then shimmering away from our vessel. I soak up the view of our home for the next few days. A luxury glass-fronted lodge with azure infinity pools extends from one side of the two-storey house that glints amongst the forest's palm trees, and three cabins dot the beach on the other.

The bay is wide, flanked by two curving peninsulas that reach out like a welcoming embrace. Climbing aboard the tender to speed us to the wooden jetty, we're squashed in uncomfortable proximity, buffeted over the surf, spritzed with sea spray.

It's easier to avoid Charles once we're ashore, met with soft music and liveried staff who press delicious drinks into our clammy hands.

I sip, scanning our new environment. I spot a gleaming tail rotor of a helicopter on the roof of the house; the only other way to get here, I guess. Around the house and pools, lush gardens of exotic tropical blooms lead towards the spa to the right and the jungle beyond, the shaggy denseness of it showing the wildness beyond the manicured luxury of tamed nature.

The edge of the bay forms a lagoon with craggy rocks for diving off into the sparkling, turquoise waves. In the centre of the bay, a circular bar ensures you don't have to choose between cocktails and a swim.

The pristine golden sand is warm as it seeps into my sandals. Along the foam-lapped shore, shaded daybeds invite you to lounge after taking a dip. The nearest daybed is occupied: a mature woman with a tanned, suspiciously taut body cinched inside a tight white Gucci swimsuit peers through oversized sunglasses. She waves, and only then do the waiting staff invite us to approach. *Holy . . . is this . . . Olga?*

As she stands, tying a sarong over flat abs, she looks like she drips money. Rocks like knuckledusters adorn several fingers while her little finger bears a crested signet ring. A Patek Philippe Grandmaster dangles off one slender wrist, and a diamond bracelet winds around the other. Her skin is flawless – even her neck, which usually adds a decade of truth to the tweaked bare face's lie. She must have a plastic surgeon on speed-dial. I wonder if she'd stoop to an affair with Charles, and I'm annoyed – now I've decided on divorce – that the idea still stings.

'Welcome.' Her Nordic accent is clipped. 'Come, enjoy some refreshments, and meet the rest of your cohort. Tonight, we will feast and enjoy a private concert' – here she smiles at Zyra – 'and then we will get down to business.' She seizes the end of a glittering lead and an animal that had been lying at her side lumbers to its feet.

Holy crap. It's a massive black cat. I don't mean a fat moggy, I mean a real, actual big cat. What are the pure black ones called? A panther, isn't it?

Diamonds glint around its neck and Olga hands the lead to who I presume is the handler. Dear God, his day job must be a nightmare. I wonder if the cat is kept sedated, to avoid the obvious professional hazard. As it's steered away, its slow gait suggests it is.

With a sly smile, Olga stalks inside, calling over her shoulder, 'Thea, I'm glad you solved the puzzle to get here. I need sharp brains for what I have in mind.'

I preen at the compliment – then shudder at being so easily seduced. As Olga strides indoors, we follow like ducklings. Or lambs to the slaughter.

Inside, this cool oasis overlooks the ocean, a vista of blue infinity, with sapphire waves cresting below us. An incredible glass sculpture chandelier that looks like a coral reef dominates the ceiling, soaring over a lavish layout of textured neutrals, with casually placed art. This is elevated sophistication.

A familiar-looking man and a woman sit on low, sleek sofas around a marble table, conspiring. Another man looks restless as he checks the corner bar for snacks.

While staff silently refresh drinks, Asha nudges me, tilting her head towards the trio. 'Spotted what the extra group have in common?'

They all have impressive timepieces gleaming on their wrists, which may or may not show that Olga invited them the same way as me; because the one thing that's obvious about this group is their comfort in such opulence. It marks wealth more surely than head-to-toe designer gear. They're not gaping at a view served up by ambitious billion-dollar architecture, or at the exclusive materials used for every fitting, or the breathtaking art: they're used to it.

They might find the surroundings unremarkable, but they stiffen as our host approaches. Even the twitchy guy at the bar stands still. As I scan them, recognition sparks, but their names aren't coming yet.

Once everyone's comfortable, Olga beams at us. 'Welcome, the OneT Club! You are my esteemed, chosen few – because together I believe we can make significant changes.'

I frown. *Is that a hint of what's to come? What changes does she mean?*

Olga's eyebrows flash and she gestures towards my group. 'Hugh and Zyra need no introduction, of course. But indulge me. It's a great honour to have both royalty and a celebrated artiste here. We're also joined by Asha Sani, a dynamic journalist with great socio-eco credentials; UK Energy Minister Charles Harrington; and one of the tougher environmental lawyers on the circuit, Thea Harrington, KC.'

Olga gestures to the trio. 'And I'm honoured to be united with my respected colleagues in business. Kali Huang, leading the way in biotechnology, for all our benefits.'

Ah ... I recall her description from that Forbes list ... Olga might call it biotech, I'd call it Big Pharma. Apparently, Kali has a ruthless reputation for sheer negotiation grit. I'd guess she's a well-preserved early fifties, who works hard to appear ageless. She doesn't speak but scans us like a hunting cat seeking weakness, smelling blood.

'Uri Cato, innovator extraordinaire in AI.' Olga turns to the restless guy, the youngest of the business cohort – probably early forties – in a gym shirt and basketball shorts. From *Forbes*, I know he's streaking ahead in the AI race, which is a more cut-throat world than his disarming appearance would lead you to believe.

'Next!' With the energy of a contained firework, Uri rearranges the garnishes on the bar. I imagine his restlessness contributes to his continual inventions: his start-ups become billion-dollar companies, then he moves on to the next big idea. His critics say he's erratic, others praise his track record of success: he *is* the world's third richest individual, after all.

'And Magnus Black III, political influencer, financier and Wall Street royalty.'

I nearly choke on seeing Hugh's scowl at the regal description of the older man. Charles's nod of recognition is wary, not warm, towards the Republican party supporter. They must have crossed paths, so it's interesting to see the cool reception from men used to glossing over personal feelings for the gain of a network.

The ultimate nepo baby, Magnus has lost more millions than his detractors can reliably count, yet he's still one of *Forbes'* top five wealthiest in the world. His bloated frame reveals a taste for excess and indulgence over nearly six decades, yet his expression is one of permanent dissatisfaction.

Hold on. I scan them, then lean in to whisper an answer to Asha's earlier question. 'These three, plus Olga, are four out of the five richest people in the world.'

'Bingo.' Asha looks at me like that explains everything. But I don't understand.

This may just be normal company for people like Olga – but this set-up has to be deliberate, surely? These aren't the type of people who can attend a last-minute summit, without assistants. So what's the catch? How has Olga lured them in?

'Why am I here?' I whisper.

'I only know *the question* you'll all be presented with. After that, it's up to all of you.'

'What question?'

Asha doesn't have a chance to answer as Olga turns to us. 'All of you – plus one more guest who's yet to arrive – are here for reasons which will become apparent. For now, please relax or freshen up for a banquet on the beach, with a very special private concert.' She beams, again, at Zyra. 'And *then* we'll get down to business.'

While Zyra and Uri are led outside to their lodges, I note the walkways are covered and air-conditioned to ensure constant, convenient control of the natural environment.

I don't follow because I'm steered up the curving marble staircase and shown to the Hibiscus Suite. My bed's acreage is piled with fine cotton, linens and pillows, facing the verdant forest that rings with birdsong and glints with waterfalls. After Asha's and Olga's cryptic comments, I'm grateful for the calming effect of the lush view. The walls are clad with raw silk which reflects the light so finely that its tone changes when a lone cloud drifts across the blazing sun. The heavenly scented oils and treatments beside the rainfall shower are too tempting to resist. In a mist of jasmine, I let the water ripple over me, then wrap myself in a fine robe.

When I open my wardrobes, I find my luggage unpacked and exquisitely arranged – with a couple of additional outfits, too. I gape at the seamless, silent efficiency. Recalling Olga's warning of getting down to business, I select my armour: navy linen palazzo pants and a kimono wrap top, the closest item to a jacket, but loose enough to be bearable in this heat.

I check my phone and iPad to see if I have any emails. No signal. And the Wi-Fi is … *ugh* … password-protected. I search the room in case it's been provided on a note like in a hotel, impatient to be granted the instant worldwide access I'm used to. No such luck.

There is, however, a bar that seems to be curated with my favourite cocktails, snacks and – my weakness – Belgian chocolates. Plus, a gift, in the signature navy quilted box of Iðunn Luxury Brands. Inside is a gold bracelet, with delicate square links.

Holding it up to the light, I wonder why Olga chose this, when all her other gifts have been exceptionally well informed. I'd never wear a bracelet. They're too . . . faffy.

And then I realise what it is. The square links aren't *links*. They're *rungs*. It's designed to look like a ladder. A ladder that doesn't lead anywhere, because it takes you back to the start. My deepest fear: that I can never climb high enough.

Heat flashes over me. Shoving it back in the box, I step back, darting glances all around the room, like there are cameras, like she can see into my soul.

Olga's generosity is more than barbed: it's *knowing*. She knows my weakness, and she's showing me that with an expensive gift, which she *also* knows I'd never wear. It's a power move, to impress upon me that *she* knows everything about me, and where my levers are, while *I* know nothing about her. Unease lurches. Especially given the changes she alluded to. Is this to show me I'll have no choice when the question Asha referred to is asked?

I linger on the galleried landing, hoping someone will appear to walk downstairs with, wanting to gauge if anyone else here is as unsettled as me. The landing leads to more bedroom suites with their views of the forest, like mine, or the ocean. I don't know who has what suite yet.

When no one emerges, I take a deep breath, apprehensive at the evening ahead, and head downstairs. I'm ushered outside with the rest of the group to a table overlooking the bay.

'I invite you all to feast!' Olga declares.

I'm not sure what her idea of a feast is, but I suspect it's not the same as mine. The woman clearly has no idea what a carb even smells like.

I can barely register our host's forced bonhomie over dinner. No one else seems to be sharing my agony. The four tycoons are at one end of the table, the rest of us at the other. I'm the bridge, in the middle, opposite Hugh – though I can't bring myself to look at him.

Despite my studious avoidance, I can't help overhearing Hugh as he talks to Kali. 'It sounds like your work encounters a lot of regulation roadblocks, then?'

'Too many. It gets very onerous to continually hit delays.'

'Then you must chat with Charles. He's a whizz at navigating those pitfalls.' He gives an ingratiating smile. I have to admit, he's always been brilliant at linking the right people. It might be the only skill he has, but he also knows how to leverage it. 'No one would be *more* delighted than me if *my* connection offers you even a little advantage.'

Olga sits in an actual throne at the head of the table, her stance making her look uncomfortably disciplined. I want to imagine her on a rollercoaster, screaming her head off, but I bet she'd still maintain her ramrod posture.

'It's an honour to welcome you to my new, remodelled eco-retreat. I want to challenge you all to think about our impact on the world. In every sense.' Her gleam scans the table. Even small talk feels like a challenge.

If this is an eco-retreat, it's logical that our meal is seafood, even if it *is* gold-leaf-garnished sushi and caviar. I presume this is Olga's low-food-mile solution, until Uri comments, 'Loving this Washoku. I've only ever had this in Osaka.'

Magnus looks put out, and I realise he'd leaned in to speak to Uri just as Uri turned to Olga with the compliment.

'Precisely.' Olga nods at the recognition of quality. 'Caught fresh this morning.'

As she and Uri discuss the merits of sushi, I look around the table to see if anyone realises – or cares – that it means she'd had it flown in. No one's surprised, despite all the eco-credential top trumps, and I realise this isn't extreme for people who live like this. Only Asha notices, and she catches my eye with a smirk.

Once we've eaten, Zyra slips away and Magnus slides into her seat, opposite the prince. 'Great to see ya again.' His Texan drawl is a badge of honour, faithful to his roots, despite his New York and Hamptons residences.

Magnus spots Hugh's fleeting grimace before the prince can force a smile and his eyes narrow, making him look like a pudgy child about to tantrum that his favourite toy has been taken away. 'How's tricks? Hope you're not getting into any more . . . situations. Pays to keep your friends close, don't it?'

I wonder what he's referring to. There were rumours of Hugh being financially bailed out a while ago, but no investigation uncovered why.

'Worldly-wise, as always, Magnus.' Hugh emphasises his own cut-glass accent in response, like his class is his defence. Or rather, his offence.

Hugh gave a controversial interview a year or so back, trying to defend some of his more unsavoury decisions. Asha wasn't the journo who quizzed him, but now *something* about her name is reaching into my memory. Sani . . . *Sani* . . . Was she the researcher? The one who broke the scandal? Behind the scenes, but lethal?

A blast of fireworks makes me jump. I turn to see a stage in the centre of the ocean bay, beside the bar. Zyra, striking a pose, is spotlit in the centre as music builds.

I have to hand it to her: she plays the set like she's performing to a packed stadium. Her music fills the night as lasers and lights dazzle the clear sky. It's a bit mainstream pop for me; but I guess that's why she has such broad appeal, and an army of adoring fans. Her Zylots.

The finale builds to a terrific crescendo of fireworks, drone lights and lasers – and from the white-hot heart of the light, another silhouette struts forward. The unmistakable walk – coltish, clipping, torso angled, copied by hundreds of models – of Estelle Abimbola.

She's impossible in every way, if you believe the rumours. Impossibly long and lean – that much is obvious – but also impossible to work with. Her asymmetric gown – presumably by Olga's fashion house, since Estelle's their brand ambassador – shimmers in the light, and her hair sheens down her back. The stage is running out, but she's still catwalking onwards, until she's strutting over the languid ocean towards us. Of course, there's a platform just under the surface, but I still gasp. The walking-on-water effect is mesmerising.

The sand doesn't slow her stride up the beach to greet Olga, then Zyra, with air kisses.

'You are both amazing as always,' Olga beams. 'And I do so love to start my retreats in style.' She stretches out her arms. 'But now, we turn to business. So I must invoke the digital detox rule.' A member of staff steps forward with a foam-lined case as Olga says, 'Your phones, please. To protect our privacy, given the confidentiality of this summit.'

What, now? Before I can protest, the tycoons and Hugh all comply, like this is *normal.*

'Thank you for your advance agreement, and for making yourselves available for these four days.' Olga encourages our compliance with a nod towards the case.

Four days? Her colleagues aren't surprised. So, if you're not a tycoon, your schedule isn't important enough to matter.

My outrage must show as I shift, steely-faced, and Olga turns to me with a disarming smile. 'It's only temporary, and your phone will be quite secure. It will become clear why this is so important – so, for now, I'm asking you to trust the process.'

'What if someone needs to reach me? Or I need to get hold of someone?'

'Your every need will be taken care of,' Olga assures me. 'And I'm sure if someone needs you, you're worth the wait.'

'I meant in an emergency …' My voice trails off as I recognise the unlikelihood. That strikes a sombre note in my heart, and Olga realises my protest has withered.

Zyra shrugs, holding up her hands. 'My phone's in the ocean. If you can get it, you're welcome to hang onto it for a few days before returning it to me.'

Seeing my hesitation, Uri winks at me. 'You haven't attended an exclusive symposium like this before? Don't worry. It's standard practice. I was at a defence strategy meeting last month where we were locked in a SCIF, no personal electronics allowed and fully shielded from all radio frequencies for maximum security. At least here, we're free to roam.'

That's why the Wi-Fi's inaccessible, then, and why no one's surprised at that. Even so, I don't like the intrusion and lack of trust. *It shouldn't be necessary … should it?* I side-eye my companions, to see what they do. Meekly, Asha drops hers into the case, then Charles checks his phone and, with a pained sigh, hands it over. Reluctantly, I follow suit.

As the staff member hurries off to the house with the full case, Olga crooks her finger, inviting us back inside. As I follow, I see Olga's staff file along the jetty to board the tender, then wait for the team member who'd taken our phones. Once he's hastened to join them, now with a bag, the little boat zips towards the yacht.

'Hold on!' I blurt out. 'Are the staff *leaving*?' I turn to Olga, unsettled. 'Is that all of them?'

'Naturally.' Olga smiles. 'I made that clear, didn't I? *Total* privacy. I need this group's undivided attention so we can reach a focused decision. There cannot be any external forces intruding for the next four days.'

The back of my neck prickles in warning. This feels … all wrong, like Olga is manipulating us all in some way. It does not bode well. What the hell are we walking – no, *sleep*walking – into?

I gaze around at the group. There is not the universal concern I expect to see. Kali and Estelle look surprised, at least, but no one else seems remotely worried.

'Does that mean you're actually allowing your team a vacation?' Kali asks, her tone pointed.

'Of course. Not usually all at once, but they've made provision for us, so we'll be comfortable in their absence. And I do like to take good care of my team. I treat them like family, really.'

Estelle coughs, and turns to stare out at the ocean. I follow her gaze and see the harbour arms closing behind the tender that speeds towards the yacht. The harbour gate's spotlights highlight the riffling water as the curving ends meet.

The gate shuts, enclosing the bay, shielding this island idyll from the outside world.

Locking us away.

My gut lurches. This isn't right. This cannot be right.

Still no one speaks up. We follow as Olga leads all of us – including Zyra, exhilarated from her performance, with a hoodie over her sequinned playsuit – into the main house. We continue through the great room and down wide marble stairs, through a cool corridor which is ablaze with abalone uplighters. We're being led towards the ocean – or maybe under it? My heart pounds at the oddness, the lack of explanation, the alienness of it.

Yet, around me, there's easy chatter: compliments on Zyra's set, the island, the food, questions for Olga about the gathering. It's just Uri who looks around in alert silence. I follow his lead, noting the cooling air as gooseflesh makes the hairs on my arms shiver.

We're led into a plush, dimly lit meeting room; the hush the deepest I have ever felt. The only windows are a continual strip around the top of the walls, but outside there's inky darkness.

'An under-ocean lair?' Uri asks approvingly as he takes an ergonomic seat.

'A naturally cooled, secure business centre,' Olga counters. 'Please, sit comfortably. I have an alternative to dessert. Better than empty calories.'

I frown as Kali pulls on a medical coat then wheels an IV drip over to Olga's seat at the head of the long, polished table. *Is Olga ill?*

As Kali inserts the IV into Olga's hand, our host explains, 'Youth blood plasma. One of Kali's company's elite treatments. She's kindly arranged for you all to benefit from an anti-ageing treatment to revitalise organs, skin, brain. And she's administering it herself so that we have total privacy for our meeting.' Her smile is sinister. 'So essential, I'm sure you agree.'

I try not to recoil in horror as Kali squints at the trickling liquid seeping down the drip, into Olga's vein.

'We'll need some revitalised thinking,' Olga says, 'as we'll be spending the next few hours together addressing the most serious question we face.'

Kali attaches an IV to Magnus and I'm panicking now, because I'll be next. What the hell is this? I don't want some teenager's blood transfused into mine.

No one else is freaked out. Not even Zyra, Estelle or Asha. I'd regard them as too young, in their early to mid-thirties, to need it. They look so youthful. *Ah. Maybe this is why!* Appeasing the fickle spotlight of fame's notorious intolerance of maturity.

Estelle taps the vein in her hand in readiness. Maybe this is just routine for models. Her acceptance makes my heart *race*. It seems too intimate and sinister to be OK.

My unease makes my betraying gaze move to Charles. He's regarding me with a hint of challenge. He expects me to refuse? Kali's hand on my arm makes me jump. This can't be risky, can it? Not for people like this. Olga would have checked everything carefully, surely?

My swallow is dry as the back of my hand is sprayed numb, the canular pushed in, the tube inserted. I stare at the packet of clear plasma on the hook, wondering who it's from, why they gave it, what effect it will have on me … And then it's done, and Kali's already moving on to Uri, who just nods and complies.

How is this normal? Do the uber-wealthy usually sit in near darkness, being flooded by the blood of the young in the vain hope of clinging on to youth? It's … vampiric.

I'm so disturbed, I can't concentrate on what Olga is saying. As I drag my focus back to her, she says, 'Thank you for your interest in my plan. Our future now lies in your hands.'

Has Olga just revealed the question Asha hinted at earlier? Her expectant gaze, to see who'll respond first, is predatory.

The room around me, so drenched in darkness, with undulating water at the window, makes me feel disorientated and rolling, like I'm still on the superyacht. Flashes from bioluminescent fish in the black ocean feel like robbers prowling at the window. I feel hunted. And this creepy drip, pulsing into my vein, has me tethered – like a goat in a lion enclosure.

As Kali connects Charles's drip, and then her own, Olga's sinister smile flickers. Now that we are – very literally – a captive audience, everyone shifts, uneasy at what's coming.

'Success is often met with challenges. And we're facing the largest yet. I need you *all* to join me in a commitment. *You*,' she turns to Zyra, Estelle, Asha, Charles, Hugh and me, 'to share your skills, your influence, the *passion* you inspire, to give our venture *profile*.'

She turns to the billionaires. 'And I'm giving *you* the opportunity to future-proof your businesses, by funding our endeavour – with half of your fortunes.'

'Hold on, *what*?' Uproar rolls around the table as the tycoons protest.

Olga's blood-red lips stretch into a wide smile. 'But *first*, I'm going to show you why you can't *afford* to refuse. Welcome, ladies and gentlemen, to *The Pledge*.'

Chapter 4

Saturday 5th April – 9.30 p.m.

THE DISSENT IS DROWNED OUT as a soundtrack swells. Olga smiles; she has stirring words to go along with the stirring music. '*You* are the elite group I've selected to face this quest with.'

She turns to the tycoons. '*We* are the OneT Club. "T" since our joint wealth is *one trillion* dollars. That's one per cent of the *entire* world's wealth. *We* are the powerful few whose decisions change the course of history. *We* leave *legacies*.'

Uri's smile flickers like he's a cat waking up to a mouse dancing before him. But I'm prickling with unease, waiting to see what this means for the rest of us. We're all riveted.

Olga sits back. 'The press call me the phoenix: my business and my ethics resurrected and rebranded from the ashes of a scorched reputation. I can share my success with you – you three who also own multi-billion-dollar companies – who face these public gauntlets every day. Increasingly, we're asked to prove our sustainable credentials, our ethical approaches—'

'And you have proven success in that area, do you?' Estelle asks. I don't expect Olga's brand ambassador to question her, and I'm avidly attentive.

'Court of public opinion says so,' Olga states. 'More crucially, my *share price* does.'

'Oh, I'm glad to hear it.' Estelle gives a warm smile. Then I remember that she's a model, in professional control of her micro-expressions. I can't take her at face value. 'All helped, I'm sure, by careful press coverage.' Estelle nods at Asha.

'Indeed.' Olga smiles. '*And* the consultancy I hired to solve the issues.'

Ah . . . now I know what Estelle's referring to. It would have been a landmark court case – had it ever got that far. Estelle was Olga's shield in the huge scandal of Iðunn profiting off unethical labour. As brand ambassador, Estelle was the face of Olga's outreach campaign, visiting factories, holding hands with exploited women as she listened to their stories, assuring them of Olga's promises. The press hadn't seen such tragic, stricken beauty since Lady Di, and Estelle's photogenic, glamourous image was everywhere. But the product line folded. So much for promised improvements. Somehow, throughout it all, Olga's name was barely mentioned, until she was reinvented as a visionary, having learned the hard way.

'It gave me *focus*,' Olga says, as Estelle shoots daggers across the polished table. 'It showed me a life needs a legacy like success needs a successor. Now I know what mine is.'

Why did Estelle respond to Olga's summons, if she feels so strongly opposed to her? Is she contractually bound? Otherwise obligated? Or settling a score . . .?

I wonder why everyone else here – all powerful, wealthy people with busy schedules and not likely to leap at someone's whim – would be marching to Olga's drum, for that matter. Do any of her other guests have an axe to grind? Maybe they all do . . .

'I learned how much the public want to see us act on perceived need,' Olga intones.

'Hooey,' Magnus pronounces. 'You already said it: we're the richest people on the planet. We don't follow public opinion; we *create* it.'

Zyra laughs, and I watch how she flexes her influence. 'Not really, Magnus. *You're* not *leading* anyone. You're just buying off policymakers.'

'That's just the way the world works, honey.'

'Your world, maybe. Not all of us have to resort to that.' She leans back in her seat. 'And if you believe that you're creating public opinion, then the parties you support are interesting choices. Far-right, polarising opinions. Even to the point of inciting violence.'

'If there ain't nothing in the pot, it don't matter how much you stir it,' Magnus rebuts. 'Very few people know what they want. Fewer know how to get it. Visionaries like us gotta take that initiative. And it's *right* we benefit. My time ain't free.' He shrugs. 'Is yours?'

When she doesn't reply, Olga smoothly says, 'You're *so* right, Magnus. *Most* people can't *do* anything. *Individually*, they're meaningless but *en masse* their criticisms can harm us. They don't have any logic or balance: we're either despicable hypocrites on our jets *or* we're the saviours of them and the whole damn planet. *But* if people need visionary leaders, to find sustainable and ethical solutions to steer them out of the climate change disaster before it's too late, then only *we* can be that influential on a *global* scale.'

A frisson flickers around the room as we all shift, glance, frown. *What's coming?*

She leans forward. 'Only people in our position could even *dream* of this legacy: *Saving. The. World.*' She pauses, letting it sink in. 'We won't just be thought-leading titans of industry, we'll be gurus. *Heroes.* The world's perception of us and our values will give our businesses the reputational halo effect of true longevity. *And* . . . it will make us *immortal.*'

'*Is* this just about perception? Showing customers what they want to see?' Uri cuts to the chase. 'Or doing something for real? Because *that's* super complex—'

'Either.' Olga shrugs. 'We set ambitious targets and enjoy the credit that garners. If we meet those targets, then great. But if we can't, no one else will, either. The difference is, *we'll* have stated *intent*. We'll have put our flags right on the summit, leading the way.'

Unease ripples and Olga adds, 'Our targets may be so ambitious that they're impossible. But visionaries like us don't shy away from that. Plenty of companies aren't even *trying*. Just *saying* we have a plan puts us ahead of most. And half a trillion dollars between us, in trust, readily available, gives us credibility without needing to do a thing. Our technical specialists can figure out the details, while *we* announce the goals and *benefit* from the glory.'

'Greenwashing as a business strategy?' Uri summarises. 'What about lawsuits—?'

'Small risks, but toothless.' Olga shrugs. 'Which we fend off by having a *believable* plan. As your mother said, Hugh, a thing has to be *seen* to be believed. We'll be visible and vocal about our Pledge, while acknowledging that the most ambitious north stars are never reached. But the environmental bandwagon is gathering speed. It'll mow us all down if we don't jump aboard.' Her voice has an edge. 'And if I'm on it, I'm taking the reins.'

This is greenwashing on a grand scale. She'd need a shady environmental lawyer to make it look legit … *Shit* … I feel my face drain of blood, even as the plasma pumps into my arm. My murky morals are on the hook to pass this off. Do I … do I *want* to do this?

I squirm under Olga's scrutiny as she weighs my reaction. I see how my professional path has led me here. My recent, victorious case – getting a government off its own ethical hook – was just about the twistiest argument you could find.

'Tell me, Thea,' Olga invites. 'How would you advise positioning this?'

My pulse quickens at the choice: I could avoid saying what she wants to hear, but it won't get me out of this, will it? Or I could advise, and stay on the inside of this select fold.

'I'd position it as a long-term strategy.' My gambit wins a half-smile from Olga.

Oh, what am I doing? Yet I continue. 'You'd sacrifice short-term wins for more meaningful impact, much of which would be too sensitive to disclose in public reports. All ambitious ventures take time to establish. And *truly* groundbreaking work needs to set new methods and global standards – *before* you can measure impact. Meanwhile, this public endeavour positions you all as advisors, winning customer support and loyalty.'

Olga mimes applause. 'And that's why we get the lawyers in. Let me show you why I *know* that customer perception is everything. I'll share what I was sent during what I fondly call my *renaissance* – because if *I* can come under fire, the same can happen to you. *Individually* we can ride this out, as I have. But *together*, we can put up an unassailable defence.'

At her nod, the background music swells. A screen fills with a soaring view of a lush, green, futuristic nirvana, populated by beautiful glossy people in pristine white, every whim met at the touch of an invisible button. The sceptical, irate tycoons, bound by their IVs, have no choice but to sit and watch, unless they want to rip the drips from their hands.

As the music grows sinister, the scene becomes apocalyptic: dry, dusty, barren, a starving, disenfranchised population in rags, looting and shooting. A message scrolls across the screen:

We've seen the films. We're living the reality. Billionaires buy paradise at the cost of people and the planet. Only they can undo the damage. But will they?

Olga purses her lips. 'I was sent this as a warning, when one of my companies produced a line of luxury smart watches.' Poignant chords accompany photos of young children on the screen: first holding sticks of dynamite beside mines, then with missing limbs. It's so stark, so horrific, that I catch my breath. Estelle looks away, biting her lip.

The scrolling writing accuses: *Life and limbs are collateral damage – for things we trash, which poison the earth.*

An extreme close-up of some electronic gadget's guts shows circuits, metal, silicon. The view widens to show piles of discarded devices, becoming foothills of waste, then a mile-wide mountain range. There is movement amongst it all, like ants on an anthill. Then you realise it's people – well, children – picking equipment apart, burning it, and themselves, in their desperation to reclaim the valuable elements.

I *know* about this, of course, but seeing it is different. Unlike the cynics around me, I squirm with guilt at every automatic upgrade. It's not even a treat anymore; it's standard life.

'But that's *scrap*,' Zyra says. 'Why are they hurting themselves like that to collect it?'

Olga glances at me. Another test. So I reply, 'The components are valuable. There's more gold in e-waste than in the equivalent weight of gold ore. Manufacturers are under fire for not reusing or recycling enough. Even reputable recycling schemes can end up illicitly dumping e-waste because recycling is costly and reuse is complex.'

Behind Olga, the warning streaks across the screen: *It's not cheaper to mine virgin minerals if you're held to account for the real costs – to the planet, and to people.*

'You can see this as a challenge, or an opportunity,' Olga says. 'No one here would be truly impacted by any of this. Sure, stories might emerge about our products or services. There'll be a few days of backlash, but they get buried when the next scandal comes along. Share prices may dip, but they recover. Customers have short memories; they forgive us if we have something they want. Which is lucky – because there are more complaints.'

The scene changes to show rainforests being torn down by logging machines, plucking ancient, soaring trees from their soil – hundreds at a time, in seconds – like a child tearing handfuls of grass. *A person dies when you rip out their lungs. Yet that's what we're doing to our planet.*

'This is what biotech looks like.' Olga glances at Kali. 'Depleting habitats for miracle cures. Like lizard venom for Ozempic. Big profits, but not for those origin countries.'

Kali shrugs. 'Miracle cures, or beneficial treatments. And *lifesaving* medication.'

Olga's eyes glitter in the half-light. 'What about drugs that don't live up to their claims? Your responsibilities are greater than anyone else's here, because you're not just selling a product, you're selling *hope*.' As she sits back, I see Kali's jaw clench.

Magnus chuckles. 'We're all here for the mighty dollar, Olga, pure and simple. Ain't one of us here in any place to criticise that.'

'But Magnus, what happens when money undermines your own values?' Olga asks.

'What d'ya mean? We all gotta make our own choices, weigh 'em against the big picture. Even if you're looking to make changes, you don't do that overnight.'

'And are you looking to make changes, Magnus?' Olga asks. 'Are you finally powerful enough to make a stand, or are you still profiting from hypocrisy on your way up?'

Estelle chokes and disguises it with a delicate cough. Guilt twists in my gut as I recognise the same weakness in myself.

'So we'll make a stand *together*,' Olga urges. 'We'll be stronger together. Of course, this is highly confidential. We must treat our plan like a security battleground. We may court attention, but our activities must stay private; un-*hack*-ably so. And who better than Uri to advise us? Your military defence AI software needs Fort Knox-level security, doesn't it?'

Uri meets her arched eyebrow with a level gaze. Something is passing between them, but I cannot decipher it. Then the corner of Uri's mouth tugs into a half-smile, like he's accepting a game of chess from a little sibling whom he expects to enjoy roundly defeating.

Olga doesn't notice as she turns to Zyra. 'It's not just moguls I need, Zyra; I need your profile, your following, and I need to make amends. This is our opportunity. Make your Zylots our *zea*lots. Unleash the passion only you can generate to gain global support for this.'

Zyra tilts her head in acknowledgement, but doesn't answer. Is she wondering what Olga meant by amends? Or is she just too savvy to respond until she has all the facts?

'What *is* it we're gaining support for?' Magnus asks. 'What are you proposing?'

'You're all here because you have a part to play,' Olga explains. '*Mine* is to use my experience to be a global visionary. Since EU sustainability law is always ahead of US law, Charles is well poised to oversee how updates translate to UK law as a test case for US law. He can manage policy to make progress faster – or slower – as needed. He'll make connections with you, Magnus, that extend our influence to international law.'

Charles swells like a toad at her praise. 'I do what I can.'

'My challenge to you, Charles, is to *prove* you can deliver, or you'll be a political deadweight. My plan gives you scope to improve your standing in the polls.'

I almost grin at Olga puncturing his inflated ego, right until she adds, 'Especially as Thea knows only too *intimately* how easily governments can slide off the hook.' Olga's damning side-eye reminds me I'm – possibly literally – the Devil's advocate.

She smiles at Estelle and Zyra. 'The stardust of your glamour will make sustainability sexy, and your worldwide fans will bring us *attention*, which means social pressure.'

Ignoring their grimaces, Olga turns to Hugh. 'And of course, you'll bring special gold dust that only royalty can provide.'

'I . . . I don't . . .' Hugh looks around for his absent equerry to excuse him.

'You need an image overhaul, don't you, Hugh? The risk of being cut off must bite, when it's family. Representing industry leaders at global summits would be timely, publicly and person-ally. Don't downplay how significant your soft power is for us.'

Hugh nods and I see Olga hide a smile at his hubris, while he sits there, obedient as a lapdog to her summons. She doesn't point the paradox out: so she wants the result, not the power play.

She steeples her fingers. 'So, what about the targets I mentioned? Ambitious yet believable. Our *Pledge* is comprised of three goals that will change the world. One: harness renew-able energy with a global working infrastructure. Two: safeguard *all* habitats that need protecting. Three: establish a true circular economy where products are reused and recycled and plastics are banned worldwide.'

A stunned silence falls – then the captive audience erupts with splutters of outrage. *'You must be joking.' 'You haven't thought it through.' 'Everyone will see through this. It isn't possible.' 'If it were possible, it would already be happening.'*

Olga holds up one hand, quelling the protests. 'Quite. It *isn't* happening yet. Because intent comes first. *Then* you can manifest. No one has ever stated ambition like this. Not on this scale. Because no one else could ever credibly achieve it.'

'Including us!' Uri scoffs. 'You're setting us up to fail. And I don't do failure.'

'I'm setting us *up* to be leaders of a brave new world.' She gazes around the table. 'I hear you. I recognise the challenge. And that's why we do this jointly. We collectively support whatever stage we reach. Like our legal advisor said, results can't happen overnight. As long as we state intent, we'll win goodwill. It doesn't matter what we actually achieve.'

She's utterly delusional. This will be a legal nightmare. For everyone.

'You can't make promises that you'll actively break,' Estelle pleads.

'Indeed. If we tried to hide it, that *would* be dangerous.' Olga glances at Kali, Magnus, Uri, and the three of them shift on their seats. 'Hence, our intent has small print.'

'Yeah, and your small print will put us all out of business,' Magnus asserts.

'Not just us,' Kali warns. 'Plastic's everywhere. A ban will ruin almost *every* business overnight. We'll be industry pariahs. Everyone will discredit us, for their own survival.'

Olga shakes her head, undeterred. 'You *know* that scrutiny of these matters is increasing. This isn't a question of *if*, but *when*, you'll be called to account for the actions of your businesses. And *then* you'll be glad of the armour that only my proposal can provide.'

Magnus and Kali tut, and Uri sits back. It's obvious they'll never agree.

Reputation can't compete with capitalism. We'd rather harm ourselves, kill ourselves, than lose a cent. Otherwise, there'd be no opioid crisis; no asbestos in baby talc; no PFAS on our cookware. Everything, including our health and our lives, has a price. It's woefully low.

This team are well aware there's always bad actors in the supply chain, but Olga isn't admitting it. I know enough, like Uri, to see it's complex. It's a proximity paradox: the closer you are to the problem, the more you care and maybe understand. The loftier you are, the less you're affected, the less you understand and – in Olga's case – the more damage you can do.

Yet Olga presses on. 'I expected some resistance. So this is what's going to happen. I'll ask you all to sign a contract, which our lawyer will make watertight.' She nods at me.

Please, I think, *let everyone refuse. And let whatever craziness that snowballs from this melt away.*

'And, as an extra incentive,' she gestures at Asha, 'our journalist here has the exclusive rights to broadcast this – and bring *gravitas*, the right *tone* – to what we're doing. This isn't a backroom deal; we're doing this in the sunlight, under the world's gaze.'

What? Tension ripples around the room, like the muscles of a boa constrictor.

Did Asha know? Her face is neutral. She must have.

'At 10 a.m. tomorrow, we reconvene for you to sign – or decline – my offer.' Olga's voice is danger-edged. 'Be warned: whether you *sign* and declare your intent to save the planet, or you *decline*, an act which will speak for itself – Asha will livestream your decision. To the world.'

At the gasps, she adds, 'I can't force you to turn up so, as insurance, I'll have the recording of this meeting from which to share, let's say, *selected* statements from you instead.'

We freeze in sheer shock. There's no backtracking from this if Olga makes it public.

This is crazy. This is reputational suicide.

Chapter 5

Saturday 5th April – 10.30 p.m.

As soon as Olga makes her threat, with us all still tethered by our plasma drips, the stunned silence becomes a roar of protest.

'What do you mean?' Kali gapes. 'You can't go round recording people without their permission—!'

'True.' Olga punctures Kali's outrage. 'In this deepfake world I don't really *need* to, but genuine recordings do come over as more *authentic*. And that's better for my brand.'

'Yeah, edited, sliced and diced versions. Very authentic,' Magnus growls.

But Estelle shrugs. 'It won't work. You cannot ambush us like this. We will all have the same version of events, only you would be claiming otherwise.'

'Ah.' Olga leans in with a smile. 'The difference is that *I'm* prepared to run the gauntlet of popular opinion. I've survived it, I'm the media's darling now. But you may not feel the same. And I've been *changed* by my experiences. I'm trying to share that with the most influential people on the planet.' Her smile widens. 'Who do *you* think the media will believe?'

'No, Olga,' Kali tries to reason, but there's a twang of panic in her voice. 'Even if we set your methods aside, you know very well that we can't sign up to something at this level, just like that! Let alone in public, without advice. And you can't threaten us with public disgrace if we decline. It's unreasonable. It's . . . *crazy*!'

Uri is the only one who looks contemplative but even he disagrees. 'You *have* to see that this is a flawed concept, Olga. It'll never work.'

Zyra's arms are folded in silent mutiny while she lets everyone else disagree. Hugh is also silent, but he looks out of his depth, gaping like a guppy while not really being sure what he's shocked about.

'Olga, you know what you're suggesting is impossible.' Magnus attempts to reason with her. 'We could never sign over company assets just like that. Even if we *were* inclined to join this enterprise – which is a mighty *big* if – we'd need board approval, legal advice, not to mention the due diligence of transferring investments.'

'Indeed.' Olga smiles, unruffled. 'Which is *precisely* why I'm asking for you to contribute your *personal* wealth – and yes, of course that will be tied up with your stakes in your respective businesses, but there are ways to liquidate these type of investments without destabilising companies. Putting your shares in trusts, for example.'

'Yes, and even those have to go through all the necessary processes, Olga,' Magnus insists. 'You know very well that we can't produce that overnight.'

'And that's exactly why I'm only asking for agreement in principle.' She arches an eyebrow. 'For now.'

Her attitude douses Magnus's goodwill. 'Jeez. There's no reasoning with you. What you're asking for is half our fortunes for something that's gonna derail or even bankrupt our successful businesses, and attach our reputations to something that's gonna blow up in our faces. You're goddamn crazy.' Magnus throws his hands up, the IV line snatching his arm back. 'Get me outta this goddam thing, Kali,' he growls.

As Kali removes her own drip and catheter, then deftly removes Magnus's, pressing a plaster over his oozing vein, everyone holds out their arms, beginning to stand, shaking their heads and muttering dissent.

Olga quietens us by holding up a hand. 'Remember you all have until morning to decide your response. But I'll leave you with this thought: there's a trend amongst our peers for giving away wealth, and we all know the pros and cons of that. My proposal is a unique way to leverage that trend for the good of our collective business; our collective legacies. If we join forces, this offers all of us an unparalleled way to level up, in terms of fame, reputation – and *success*.'

As Kali hands Olga a plaster, our host sweeps off, saying, 'I'll give you time to talk. And maybe some time alone with your *own* thoughts, in your *own* rooms, will be beneficial. I'm *certain* you'll all see your way to appreciating my vision, and the advantages involved.'

I frown at that, wondering if the comment is loaded. I recall my 'gift', and wonder if everyone has received a barbed message. Something to keep us all in check. But Olga's waving and blowing kisses as she waltzes off to her suite.

She either believes everyone has taken her challenge positively, or thinks she wields so much leverage that it doesn't matter; that we'll all do her bidding anyway.

Only that's not quite what happens when you hold billionaires to the ransom of their reputations. Instead, she leaves a maelstrom in her wake.

As we all stride back to the great room, brittle with tension, we catch a glimpse of Olga disappearing past the office, towards the walkway leading to her lodge. Once she's out of sight, the room explodes into action, like we've all been holding a collective breath.

Estelle nudges Zyra, taking her aside, while Magnus commandeers Kali as the other member of the cohort most inclined to reason their way out of this, and they rapidly assemble arguments with emphatic gestures and thunderous expressions.

'Does anyone have the means to call anyone? Since Olga seized our phones?' Magnus demands.

'Yeah, I need to reach my team right away,' Kali says. 'You won't believe what it took to get off-grid for four days. And my people have had instructions not to interrupt this summit. So I need to get hold of someone right *now*.'

As I think about my iPad and firing off some messages, Asha shakes her head. 'Olga's shut down all comms because she's made the island's Wi-Fi password-protected—'

'But . . . *you* must have the password. Tell us what it is!' Uri says, looking astounded. 'Once we have that, we can use an iPad to send a message. You *must* know it, Asha, if you're putting out the comms for the sign-or-decline event.'

Asha gives a short laugh. 'Olga doesn't trust anyone with it. She changes the password daily. She'll type it directly into my laptop tomorrow morning, once she's set up the sign-or-decline live stream on her own device.'

'You're *kidding* me?' Kali looks outraged. 'We can't reach *any*one? This is . . . *crazy*.'

'Then get her people to help,' Hugh barks. 'There must be a phone or a pager or something.'

'The staff are *away*.' Asha emphasises. 'You *saw* them leave. Olga sent them off on the yacht.'

'Weren't they just going off for dinner, and then back to their quarters?' Zyra asks hopefully.

'Which are on the other side of the island, aren't they?' Kali asks. 'I think it's something like a three-mile trek through the jungle. Isn't there a quad bike?'

'Yes, there's quad bike – parked at those staff quarters,' Asha says. 'There's just no *staff*. Olga sent them away until she summons them again.'

I catch her eye, remembering her words on the plane. That Olga has carefully selected everyone here. Then isolated us. Olga isn't a woman to leave anything to chance, so what's her real aim?

'Jeez, what I wouldn't pay to get out of here right now.' Magnus paces like a caged lion, the only way he can vent his fury. Sweat sheens across his brow.

As Zyra and Estelle back away from everyone, deep in conversation, Hugh half-turns from the bar towards them, listening.

I strain my ears to do the same, as Estelle whispers to Zyra, 'Are you thinking of supporting Olga in this? Because I hope you're calculating the risks. Not just about what she's asking, but the risk of *Olga herself*.'

Casually stepping closer, I listen, intrigued.

'She'll try something, Zy, to make sure you're tied in. Could she buy your label and force you into it?'

'Nah, I own it. Any attempt to control me like that wouldn't work.'

For a nanosecond, Estelle's face flickers with admiration and envy. Her tone is icy. 'What a . . . *fortunate* position to be in.'

Huh. So if Estelle's envious of Zyra's agency, does that mean Olga has some kind of leverage over Estelle? Who else might that apply to . . .?

The way Asha, Uri and Kali are observing everyone also sends a shiver through me: they seem as detached as scientists watching lab rats navigate a maze. Are they really this unaffected? Or do they have a plan, some clever way to extricate themselves from Olga's trap?

The word *trap* echoes around my head as I look at the guests. Olga might have been counting on making some legal progression in her quest to go truly global, but given the international nature of supply chains, the UK-US bias here is ... odd. Yet this cohort all cleared their diaries, left their teams behind with instructions not to be disturbed, then handed over their phones. For such powerful people, Olga really has them backed into a corner – alone.

I think about my invitation, how it hinted at giving me something I wanted; was framed as something I couldn't refuse. And I recall the veiled comments in the boardroom.

These aren't random guests. They're selected because Olga can manipulate them. People like this must have plenty of dark deeds underneath their exalted successes, but what skeletons are hidden in their designer closets that give Olga such power?

As Zyra goes over to the cocktail bar to pour a drink, Hugh oozes up beside her. She moves away, and he trails her, pushing right into her personal space.

Ignoring him, she pours her drink, but her hand is shaking.

His smile at her discomfort is spiteful, and his erection is visible through his trousers.

'Looks like you need some ice,' Zyra says, reaching for the bucket. With a quick flick of her hand she tips it over, sending ice skittering across the bar, flooding the front of Hugh's chinos.

He leaps back, batting away the freezing liquid, his face purpling with rage as Zyra walks over to join Estelle.

The two women watch him, smirking, but I know that Hugh won't let that go. There will be consequences.

So I *cannot* believe it when Charles walks over, pours a brandy and passes it to Hugh with a thick napkin. *Appeasing* him. I feel ashamed to be married to him. At least it's not for much longer …

As Hugh dries himself, Charles murmurs, 'So, what are your thoughts, Hugh? Given that you cannot, of course, endorse Olga's venture. Not *yet*, anyway.'

'Whyever not? Seems like a win-win to me.'

'That's true, if you're only thinking about the international networking. And, while you excel at that, Hugh, these are serious commitments. This is a question of credibility. Of *gravity*.'

'And I have those in abundance, Charles. I can make those kind of decisions.'

'Indeed, Hugh. Quite right. But these are far-reaching decisions of state. Such decisions can't be made in a vacuum. This needs coordination, cooperation, collaboration. No matter how mighty the man, this isn't a one-person undertaking. The Firm will have a view, no doubt.'

'Olga's simply asking me to initiate communications. I'm happy to honour that.'

I roll my eyes. How surprising that our millionaire-on-benefits can't bear to pass up this gravy train.

'On the face of it, that's true. But what happens next?' Charles persists. 'Let's say you succeed – what costs will that impose, politically? What deals might that enmesh us in? There *will* be a price, and your name will be attached to it.'

Uncertainty creeps across Hugh's face, and he purses his lips, apparently considering the consequences. Sensing the imminent breakthrough, Charles steps closer, conspiratorially.

'We should also consider – what if this fails? You'll be the public face. The figurehead. Which is entirely right in a well-conceived plan. But this a complete misappropriation of your influence. Olga, I'm sorry to say, is overreaching here by asking you at this early stage.'

Hugh pouts in disappointment, displaying emotions that have never matured beyond schoolboy entitlement. 'But—'

'We can, of course, review this position once we have proof of concept. Once we can see the trajectory has been thought through. *Then* would be the time to invite you to be president of this initiative, to bestow your patronage. No risk, but the glory of successfully elevating the scheme. Which would then be *your* success.'

Downing his brandy and sighing, Hugh nods.

I check my new pocket watch. It took less than two minutes for Charles to talk Hugh – stubborn, immovable Hugh – into a total 180. That was a record, even for Charles.

It makes a streak of hatred burn in me, that he hadn't done that for Drew. He could have done, I can see that clear as day; but he chose not to.

He'll intervene only if it serves him. He must have sided with Olga until now, when he dissuaded Hugh who hadn't seen any risk in Olga's challenge – indeed, he'd actively welcomed it. So is Charles following the mood of the room? Or has he been thinking about how impossible his own part would be? Or if he'd end up scapegoated for Hugh's involvement? He doesn't look happy. Neither does Hugh; his glower could rival Magnus's.

And Magnus is fully fuming at this entrapment as he strides over to Zyra. 'Hey. I gotta question for ya. How did your stage get set up, with the bay enclosure closed?'

'What?' Zyra asks, confused by the unexpected inquiry.

'The harbour enclosure was shut *after* Zyra's show, and my entrance,' Estelle says. 'It stays closed all night. It's part of Olga's island security.'

I glance at her. *So Asha isn't the only one who's been here before.*

'Someone tell her to open it, then,' Magnus snaps. 'Or *we* will.'

'Won't happen,' Estelle asserts. 'It's absolutely sacrosanct.'

'There has to be a way outta this hellhole.' Magnus is pacing again.

'I think the point is that there *isn't,*' Estelle says. 'Olga, for all her faults, is at least thorough.'

Faults? Estelle really isn't impressed with Olga, is she? But of course, if Olga *is* exploiting her leverage, then those being manipulated would despise her for it.

A chill shivers over me. There's an obvious answer to that, isn't there? One sure way to ensure secrets stay secret, while removing the person trying to control you.

As I gaze around the group, I can easily imagine them accepting Olga's invitation as a way to wreak revenge. My heartbeat speeds up, and I catch my breath.

This isn't just a gathering. This is a reckoning.

I feel like an island, adrift at this uneasy prospect, that no one else seems to realise. Everyone else is focusing on Estelle's confirmation that there's no way out.

Collective cries break through my thoughts – '*There must be a way!*' and '*What can we do?*' – until they're silenced by the sight of a TV rising from a sideboard, blinking into life to show various social media accounts.

Estelle's face, all glowing skin and towering cheekbones, is flawless in high-res close-up as it fills the screen.

'That's my *Insta*!' Estelle peers at it, and I see a curated list of messages and stories that are clearly posted by an expert team. She's probably never read any of them.

A message loads, as if from Estelle:

Can't wait to share a new venture with you. You'll find it at this link, 10 a.m. AST tomorrow. Brave new world for me – and for us all!

'She's hijacking your *socials*?' Zyra gasps on Estelle's behalf. 'She . . . she *can't*.' Zyra's gaze swings wildly before latching on to me. '*Can* she? Isn't it . . . illegal?'

'Olga's under the assumption we'll all agree to her plan,' I say. 'She said you'd be the part of the team to evangelize, and this is what she means. Using your social media, your reach, to spread her message as far as possible, as quickly as possible.'

'But Estelle *hasn't* signed up yet,' Zyra protests. 'And the deal *wasn't* Olga faking it.'

'You've told me your team send your messages, Zyra. Estelle's team, I'm sure, do the same. Olga's acting in the same way.'

'But . . . but . . . what if I disagree tomorrow? She's only asking the money-makers to sign-or-decline. What about *us*?' Zyra stands up beside Estelle. 'She can't make public announcements on my behalf to my fans! If she wants our *publicity* instead of money, she has to understand its value. It's our brand, our reputation. She's treating it like it's nothing!'

Estelle nods, but her silken tone is far more measured than Zyra's. 'It's quite the presumption. She hasn't considered if we have any competing issues. Other contractual things to consider.'

'Like what?' I ask.

'That's not the point.' Estelle folds her arms. 'Those Olga's asking to invest their money have a choice. Not a great one, but still – a choice. Us non-investors don't. We're second-class allies.'

'Quite.' Zyra looks mutinous. 'But the answer's simple.' Her jaw sets. 'We can't let her get away with it.'

Zyra's found a comrade in arms: Estelle's gaze meets Zyra's, and she gives a grim nod.

Chapter 6

Saturday 5ᵗʰ April – 11.30 p.m.

THE TV FLICKERS OFF AND sinks into the console again, but not before we all saw the comments under Estelle's Insta blowing up, while she and Zyra unite in growing fury.

Uri searches for a remote, or a button on the console to work the TV. When he can't find one, he says, 'I guess the TV was set to a timer, to show us that. Just in case any of us were thinking of disagreeing.'

The thought of being made public puppets of while we can't flee – from Olga, her island or this irrational challenge – sends a flare of contagious urgency around the group.

Magnus paces, snarling like a caged lion. 'How can this be happening?' He kicks the sofa, making Asha jump, before he moans, 'This is . . . this is *imprisonment*.'

Then Uri starts to chuckle. Everyone turns to him, outraged at the situation – and at him for not taking it seriously.

'What?' Uri laughs. 'I like a person who thinks through all the permutations. She knew *you*,' he points at Magnus and Hugh like a headmaster scolding naughty schoolchildren, 'would want out, yet wouldn't have the balls to face her.' His laugh is gleeful. 'She sees right through you, doesn't she? She's got both of you by the short and curlies!'

'God, if this wasn't bad enough, I have to be incarcerated with an *idiot* like you,' Magnus growls as he paces back to the cocktail bar, sloshing whisky into a glass.

I like that Uri – self-made billionaire and genius, if a bit of an oddball – couldn't care less about nepo-waster Magnus calling him an idiot. There's no pettiness to Uri; he's secure enough in himself not to even raise an eyebrow.

He's still laughing as he gestures at Magnus. 'The only way you could get out of this now would be by growing wings and flying.'

Magnus freezes and stares at Uri. He sets his glass down but still grips it, his knuckles paling.

Whatever's dawning on Magnus crackles across to Hugh.

With a stab of icy shock, I recall the lone helicopter on the roof. *Can Magnus pilot one? It wouldn't be a surprise . . .*

Then Hugh – with his specially fast-tracked Royal Navy flight training – scrambles up, looking momentarily confused at where to go, before darting towards the wide marble stairs.

With a roar, Magnus flings his glass tumbler at Hugh, missing him, but making him stagger sideways as shards explode from the wall. Cowering, covering his face, Hugh whimpers, and Magnus uses the advantage to catch him up.

He bellows as he throws himself at Hugh, flattening him against the marble stairs. They wrestle, grunting, both fumbling to land a solid right hook.

Hugh twists in Magnus's grip, which just makes his chinos edge lower down his blotchy buttocks. Kicking out, Hugh fends Magnus off, squealing, 'It's my *right* to commandeer it.'

Staggering to his feet, Magnus snarls. 'This ain't your quaint little kingdom—' He hauls Hugh up. 'You . . . pompous . . . little . . . prick!' He swings a clumsy, gorilla-like punch.

Hugh flinches away, and Magnus overbalances, falling heavily to the floor with a winded *oomph*.

Seizing the advantage, Hugh kicks Magnus in the gut, making the financier foetus-up, whimpering, hands over his face.

A cruel smile flickers on Hugh's face as he steps back, then does a prissy little jump into a goal-scoring kick, right into Magnus's covered face. Blood sprays as Magnus's head snaps back, making him squeal.

Around us, the room is in chaos from the bumbling fight. Cushions strewn, glasses broken in puddles of whisky. Estelle and Zyra are pressed into the corner of the sofa, looking on in scandalised, delicious disbelief. Zyra's covered her mouth and I suspect she's trying not to laugh at the ridiculous sight.

But I'm terrified. These men are more vicious than I think she realises.

Charles steps forward, and my heart pounds at what he might say – or do. 'Enough, Hugh.' His tone is low, commanding, and at the sound of it dread slithers inside me. My eyes dart around the room as I wonder if everyone sees what I see: this worrying dynamic between the two of them. The clear history, the exclusive trust. 'This is . . . *unseemly*. Surely, you – *we* – could share the helicopter?'

Hugh turns to Charles, his face twisted with disgust. '*Judas*.' Saliva catches on his lips as he spits the word with more venom than a viper.

Charles recoils, holding his hands up in defeat – and demonstrably washing them of Hugh.

I expect to feel relief as Hugh turns his back on him – but it feels like something else has just shifted, something dangerous and deep.

Hugh has his eyes on the prize now, Magnus is just an obstacle. Tugging up his trousers, he hurries up the stairs, just as Magnus puts his hands out for support. Hugh stamps on his rival's knuckles, making Magnus howl, yet spurring him on. With a growl, he throws himself at Hugh, and it looks like the debacle is about to repeat.

But Hugh has a taste for blood now. His elbow flashes out, catching Magnus in the cheek, sending him staggering back.

Arms windmilling, Magnus grabs the banister just in time to stop himself plummeting backwards. He hauls himself up, grabs a small marble statue from the column in a staircase alcove, and hurls it at Hugh. It drops, whacking the back of Hugh's legs as it smashes to the ground.

Hugh plunges forward, stumbling. This time, Magnus gains on him, and lands a vicious kick to Hugh's kidneys. The scream Hugh emits is full of desperate, outraged fury. But Magnus pushes his lead and scrabbles up the stairs.

I can't help following. It's not out of concern; if they were more competent, this might be a fight to the death, and I honestly wouldn't mourn either of them. But the fighting is too schoolboy, too petty, for that. I'm more worried that one of them will succeed with their plan – because *that* will change the situation entirely.

I'm also afraid that they're too drunk to fly, and too stubborn for that to stop them. So I rush to keep up, as they waddle, stumble, slip up the stairs. I sidestep shards of marble and spatters of blood, trying not to skid.

I can hear someone following me, but I don't look back. My heart is pounding now, the fear, the unpredictability of it all, fizzing in my veins.

Panting and groaning, the two overweight men ahead of me are heaving their way to the top of the stairs, towards the mezzanine. In daylight, the view from the top of the house must be astonishing. In the dark, just the lights of the bay's enclosure glint at us as the waves in the bay swell with the rising wind. A few hours ago, this looked like the ultimate in luxurious, protected privilege. *Now, it's a prison.*

Hugh is trailing. As Magnus reaches the top step, Hugh stretches out, grabs Magnus's back leg, and yanks him down.

Falling smack on his face, Magnus groans, and spits out a tooth. As Hugh leaps over him, Magnus grabs Hugh's leg, slamming him to the ground.

They teeter on the edge of the top stair, and I crush myself against the banister, certain that they're going to topple towards me – and make me plunge to my death, too.

My heart thunders in my ears, my grip on the rail slippery with sweat.

They're both pressing forward too hard to fall, as they pummel one another and strain to pull ahead. Magnus is less bothered about fighting, more about getting free, and he manages it, dragging himself towards the far door, out onto the roof – and over to the single helicopter.

Hugh takes a massive glass ornament and launches it at Magnus. The American leaps aside just as it explodes into glittering shards on the door in front of him. He brushes wicked glinting splinters from his face.

I jump, jittery as a cricket, but desperate to keep up. I'm not sure if I want to try to stop them, or if I want to observe how this will unfold.

From the mezzanine, I look down at the array of upturned, staring faces.

Uri looks like he's finding this better than Netflix, amusement softening his spiky features.

Kali looks aghast at the turn of events, but Estelle looks … numb.

Asha has followed me up. 'You OK?' she whispers. As I nod, she asks, 'They're not really going to try and get away with this, are they?'

I shrug. I can't really blame them for giving it a shot; yet they're both so odious that I can't bear either of them to get off the hook so easily.

They wrestle their way through the door now, and the wind is strong enough to whip it open, leaving them half-strangling each other in the staggering gusts.

Asha darts past me, sprints across the mezzanine, and pushes past the brawling men. She's knocked back as Magnus stumbles, but as he lunges for Hugh again, she crawls beyond them, towards the gleaming black helicopter. I wonder if *she* has a pilot's licence, and if she'll be the one to get away, while Hugh and Magnus are still fighting it out.

Or is she planning to stow away, so that whoever gets there first will fly her out of here with them?

I'm struck that no one else is pitching for a ride, bargaining with favours to get away. Or that Magnus and Hugh didn't agree to share the transport, or cut deals to take others.

But this is a group so used to getting whatever they want, and getting it *now*, that they're no longer used to having to play nice. They'll literally entrap themselves while blaming Olga for it. No wonder she resorted to such strong-arm tactics.

I see now that taking our phones and making the internet signal for the island password-protected – then not giving anyone that password – was a masterstroke. And sending the staff away, too, meant that only those who could fly would have a hope of commandeering the chopper. And that's only Magnus or Hugh – as far as I know.

They don't notice Asha duck under the body of the helicopter and climb up to the door, sneaking it open.

Floundering, Magnus attempts a punch. Hugh dodges, and throws a left hook like he thinks he's a boxing hero. With a visceral snarl, Magnus rallies, putting all his might into one last attack. Pulling his shoulder back, then lunging forward, he lands a hefty blow to Hugh's cheek, splitting skin, sending Hugh staggering.

The two men stare at each other, the wind buffeting them, tearing at their clothes, as Asha ducks back under the helicopter. Raising her voice above the wind, she calls, 'No keys!'

As the men turn to her, baffled, she clarifies, 'There are no keys. So no one can fly it.'

I'm so deflated that I nearly double over, and the men stumble, leaning against the railings.

I trudge back downstairs to the great room, feeling like I've run a marathon, wheezing and drained – yet I sense that another fight is simmering up to a boil.

The imposing room is in even worse disarray now, with artwork lying smashed around my feet. The violence of it, the disrespect it exhibits, somehow makes the reckless abandon displayed by Hugh and Magnus feel contagious. Desperation is sharp in the air, like sweat rancid with fear.

Only Uri seems unaffected, like his mind is somewhere else, and he approaches Kali. 'Surely our master negotiator has a winning line of argument to get us all out of this? Use your Jedi mind tricks, like when you got the FDA to drop their more onerous restrictions!'

Kali's withering look tells him she doesn't appreciate his request. 'If I do, I'll speak for myself. I'm not your mouthpiece. *You* get *yourself* out of this, if that's what you want.'

Uri shrugs, grinning. 'I'm quite happy for my business to be under the public spotlight.' He leans in, affecting the air of a concerned friend although his tone is sinister. 'But are *you*?'

'Olga may have raised concerns about my companies.' Kali's voice is low with threat. 'My legal team will address that. And they'll deal with *you*, too, if you repeat her baseless accusations.' She tilts her head. 'Clear?'

'Hey, no accusations here!' Uri holds his hands up. 'I'm just underlining the point that, if Olga goes ahead with this, she'll be influencing, maybe changing, laws. I don't know many companies our size,' his circling finger takes in himself, Kali and Magnus, 'that could evolve fast enough, even if we're in this as partners. You heard how irrational her plan is. She doesn't even know if she wants to effect real change or not. She's just disrupting for disruption's sake. Using *us* as part of her reputational renaissance.'

Kali looks unmoved, but Uri's on a roll. '*We* have strength in numbers. We can walk away from this together. And if I was as persuasive as you, I'd use my superpower for good.'

'Really?' Kali folds her arms, making herself comfortable as she settles into the argument. 'And what superpower are *you* using for good? Your Neptune project?'

'Yeah, maybe. The ocean's taking over. Sea level's rising at an accelerating rate. High tide flood risk is three- to nine-hundred per cent *more* than fifty years ago. No fighting it. Adapt or die, right? How about I express my thanks by reserving you your own private Sea Estate on Neptune II? Luxury home, offices, coral reef view? In a few decades, when the earth is scorched, you'll be glad.'

Kali groans. 'I'm not buying underwater real estate based on your scare tactics.'

'Not mine.' Uri shrugs. 'The offer's there. I'll even throw in a kelp martini.'

'Well, as generous as your offer is, I won't be taking you up on it,' Kali says. 'And I'm intrigued that it suggests that you need someone to bail you out. Why *is* that, Uri? You don't think you can reason with her? You don't think she'll listen? Or is there something else that puts you under as much fire as you seem to think *I* am?'

Uri forces a smile. 'Hey—!'

'Let me be clear, Uri. You're not hiding *your* failings behind *my* capabilities.'

'Not failings, but *risks*. And not mine, but *ours*,' Uri insists.

Kali frowns at him. 'I expected more from you, Uri. You can't be unused to risks like this. Why are you so rattled? Why are you trying to get me to have the showdown that you clearly need to have with Olga?'

'I'm just seeing if you're a team player, Kali. Nice to know you're out for yourself.'

'Oh, Uri!' She gives a short laugh. 'We're *all* out for ourselves. I'm sure it's easy for you, to bamboozle everyone in tech with shiny new things that no one else understands. I'd like to see you last two seconds in my world. You've no idea what it takes.'

'I'm glad you're so sanguine. Given the inevitable lawsuits. Once Olga's spotlight is on us, people will dig for every scandal they can find.'

'Lawsuits are part of the cost of business. I leave that to Legal.' But Kali's quick glance in my direction is uneasy, and my radar twitches.

Is there more to this? Does Kali have something to hide?

I wonder if Uri noticed, because he rounds on her like a shark detecting blood. 'If you're saying you're not bothered by this, I don't believe you.'

Kali shrugs off his attack. 'Despite Olga's slurs, we have a robust environmental policy. And, *unlike* Olga's, our supply chain has no forced labour—'

Uri's eyes narrow in disbelief. 'If you claim a hundred per cent traceability of your supply chain, you're lying. Especially with the deals you drive.'

'That's *enough*.' Kali leaps to her feet. I half expect her to fling her drink in his face, like we're in a bad soap opera, but she holds herself in check. 'I've told you again and again not to bad-mouth my companies—'

'See?' Uri almost looks gleeful. '*This* is how you're reacting to *one person*, a peer, asking you – *in private* – if you're likely to have any legal challenges. How do you think it's gonna feel when it's *anyone* and *every*one in the *entire world*? In *public*? Your employees. Your customers. Your *shareholders*. Not just hypothesising, but actually digging things up? Real accusations and global scandal.'

The slap Kali unleashes on Uri *zings* across the room. He recoils, horrified, placing his hand over the reddening mark on his cheek.

'I warned you, Uri. I won't have *anyone* attack my business. If you don't back off, I'll hit you where it really hurts.'

As Uri eyes her warily, Kali downs her drink, turns on her heel and strides off, heading upstairs.

Saving face, Uri turns to the others in the room. 'Well, if she hit *me*, then *I* must have hit a nerve.' He stalks to the bar but doesn't pour a drink, just rearranges glasses and garnishes, looking agitated.

Magnus and Hugh stumble back downstairs, their egos as battered as their faces.

'Come on, Hugh.' Charles offers an arm, and a face-saving out, to retire to his room.

I feel sick at my husband demonstrating his loyalty like this – especially after Hugh denounced him earlier – as the prince staggers to him. 'No keys, Charles. Bloody ridc'lous. I blame you for this. Stupid bastard. Why couldn't you keep me out of this mess?'

'Maybe things will seem different in the morning.' Charles steers Hugh away, not upstairs to the bedrooms but towards Olga's walkway and what looks like a large lodge.

'Why? You going to buy her off or something?' Hugh demands as they disappear from view.

I only just catch Charles's reply. 'Something like that.'

My blood runs cold. But no one else heard. Uri and Asha are eyeing the state of Magnus as the financier collapses into a seat and snores. Zyra and Estelle collude in the corner.

I take the opportunity to slip away, following Charles. I'm burning to tell him that I'm divorcing him, even though I know I should hold my cards close to my chest. And I have a sick fascination with how he always clears up for Hugh. Seeing him in action is reinforcing that I have no other reasonable choice but to separate from him.

Creeping along the path, my heartbeat races. I feel horrified and betrayed as I watch Charles assisting Hugh into his suite. I stand outside the room, in the dark hallway of Olga's lodge, in silent judgement.

I can't decide if I want Charles to find me here, to see my anger, to catch him in the moment. But something makes me squash myself out of sight, in one of the hallway's decorative alcoves, shielded by a lush shrub on a planter.

Two such alcoves flank Olga's door – which is opposite the walkway to the main house. As I face the house, Hugh's ocean-fronted suite is to my right, and Charles's forest-view suite is to my left; suites for favoured guests, with double storeys of plush facilities.

Now that I've hidden myself, I suppose I'm technically spying, rather than watching: not very dignified, it must be admitted. It takes Charles ages to settle Hugh into his suite. My discomfort grows and I shift, irritated, as I imagine him tending to the prince's every comfort, rather than dumping him fully clothed on the bed and leaving him.

Eventually, Charles emerges and darts across to his room, opposite. And somehow I know – I just *know* – he isn't going to be there very long.

But when I hear someone else approaching from the main house, I hold my breath, praying that I'm adequately hidden, hoping the dim lights help ...

Estelle's model stride is unmistakable, and her rap on Olga's door determined.

Is Estelle making a case on her own behalf? Or for both her and Zyra?

Olga flings the door open wide with a seductive smile, wearing slinky night attire – then does a double take at the sight of Estelle. Something in my gut squirms at that.

But Estelle doesn't wait for an invitation. She pushes past Olga and stalks inside.

My mind doesn't have to wander too far to work out whom Olga expected to see. So I have to wait, to see if I'm right – if Charles *is* going to visit our host tonight.

Shadows play across the walls as I wait, half holding my breath in case Estelle comes out, or Charles does.

Then I hear the argument. I'm not ashamed to admit that my ears prick up. Anyone's would, wouldn't they? And I *am* a lawyer; I can easily justify my interest as being entirely professional.

Estelle's impassioned voice rises – then a few quiet seconds pass before she cries out more anguished words. For me to be able to catch even some of what she's saying through the muffling of the door means that Estelle must be fully *yelling* at Olga.

I'm astounded at Estelle's volte-face, from her earlier display of composure – critical of Olga though she was, she had kept a tight lid on her emotions in the woman's presence – to this full on argument. Maybe Olga's veiled hints had hit home more than I'd realised.

I'm half terrified that Charles or someone else will walk into the hall and catch me; but my more daring half persuades me to come out of hiding, to sneak across the hall, heart pounding in my throat, to listen at Olga's door.

'How can you *pretend* like this? When the reality is, you don't care about *anything*!'

'[something . . .] so melodramatic!'

'*Melo*dram*atic?* How *dare* you! You saw what happened. *You* were *directly* responsible! Because of you . . .' Her voice cracks and I don't catch the next few emotional words until: 'How can you possibly not care? You're . . . you're *callous*!'

For the first time, Olga's voice grows loud enough to hear. 'You've got *no* idea what I was dealing with at the time. No idea at all. And if you want to know what callous *really* is, you should watch out for Kali.'

'But even afterwards, you didn't reach out, you didn't help.' Her voice wobbles.

There's a long pause, and I hold my breath, my legs shaking as I hover on the balls of my feet, ready to dash back to my hiding place if Estelle walks out.

'The least you can do is make a toast to what he did for you. Have you ever done that, Olga? Because I know you never even bothered to say thank you.'

Estelle's voice fades, like she's moved farther into the room. I have to press my ear to the door to catch the next words. 'Here. To Tony.'

My self-preservation kicks in enough to recognise that this would be Estelle's parting gesture. I shoot back to the alcove, sucking myself in to squeeze behind the plant, its fronds still swaying when Estelle slams the door behind her.

Out here, though, her brittle bravado drains away. She slumps against the door like her trembling legs can't hold her upright.

Dashing her hand over her cheeks, she draws two shuddering breaths, then nods. 'Done. It's over.'

Chapter 7

Sunday 6th April – the next morning –
6.00 a.m.

JERK AWAKE WITH THE COLD-SWEAT sensation of being torn from disturbed, fractured dreams by the sound of my own scream, dragging me into the stark Caribbean sunlight, which is already too bright at 6 a.m.

Ugh. I wish I'd closed my blinds last night. If it wasn't for the icily effective air con – useful for tropical *and* peri-meno climates – that I turned to morgue-mode last night, I'd be clammy, even in this flimsy camisole and men's pyjama shorts (better, like all men's clothes, with softer material and *pockets*).

My mouth tastes stale because I haven't brushed my teeth. By the time I got to my room last night – after Olga's crazy Pledge and all of the fallout and *fighting* that followed, not to mention Charles putting on his moral blinkers – I was seething.

He did go to Olga's room. Of course he did. And the sheer disrespect of him sleeping with her when I'm practically in the same building, *and* when he doesn't even know I'm planning to leave him, ignited my temper.

Once I was alone in my suite, there were so many fantasies of revenge and retribution worming around in my brain that I just couldn't bring myself to care about routine ablutions.

The scream shrieks again. *It wasn't a dream?* Confused panic catapults me to my feet, and I grab the silk robe at the end of my bed as I run to the bifolding doors that lead out to the veranda. Yanking open the door, heat engulfs me, sending sweat sliding over my skin like a fever. My eyes dart around my private garden below, as I home in on the sound of terror.

The sound is coming from the separate lodge to the left of the main house, across the walkway. I know – only too well, now, after last night – that Charles's suite is there.

Has something happened to him? Huh … Do I care if it has?

Caring isn't the same as knowing, so I bolt across my veranda, down the steps and across my garden, wrapping my robe around me as I run, then scramble through the verdant hedge – not even *thinking* about the lurking snakes and spiders. I dash across the next garden and scrabble through more bushes, reaching Charles's garden by the largest lodge.

I stop dead.

There's … nothing here.

I turn, gazing all around Charles's private garden. There's no chaos or calamity: this is a perfect, calm oasis. Not a cushion out of place from the reclining sunbeds by the pool. Nothing awry, not even a snapped branch in sight.

Grass tickles my bare feet and the already sweltering heat, as well as the unexpected cardio, sends sweat slithering down my back. My heart is pounding in my ears – but the morning is eerily still.

The screaming has stopped. Did … did I imagine it? Was it a weird remnant of a nightmare? I feel like an idiot and I'm desperate not to be caught apparently stalking my husband. Especially as I'm not – *well, not now.*

Creeping back, my tiptoed steps seem to thud in the silence, every brush of a plant frond crackling like thunder. Wincing, holding my breath, I catch another sound: sobbing. It's soft, and I have to strain my ears to hear it, but then it grows louder. It's coming from the suite beyond Charles's.

Turning, I race across Charles's garden, and push through the neat hedge towards the sound. I'm wary of what I'll see – of what's been found – so I peer out from behind the cover of the palms. The garden fans out before me in a slash of green, spiky with flame-coloured flowers and heady with scent, leading down to this suite's private pool. Someone is crumpled beside the azure water, rocking and crying, a shrill, strangled note of fear under the despair. As the person shakily stands, I see that it's Asha, shivering with shock. Overwhelming dread crawls over me, and I rush to her.

'Asha? What's happened?' I slow my approach, so I don't scare her.

She jumps anyway, twisting round to face me, her face trembling. 'Thea! Oh God!' Her voice is shrill with panic. '*What should we do, Thea?*' She points into the water, her horrified eyes fixed on what she sees there. My clammy skin is prickling with foreboding: I know what I'm about to see.

Creeping closer to the pool, I see it. A body, floating face down, contorted as if in pain, and naked. *Olga . . . dead?*

Asha's face trembles. 'I just came here to finalise the announcements with Olga for the sign-or-decline event. She insisted I meet her here . . . in private. So, when she didn't answer, I came round the side, through the hedge, to . . . check the garden. And now . . .'

Hot nausea burns through my chest and throat as I stare at Olga. Last night, she gave every impression of being immortal, invincible. The world's wealthiest individual. Successful business guru with everything imaginable – including, apparently, eternal youth. But even she wasn't immune to death.

Covering my face, I turn away; Asha might think it's because I'm distressed by the sight, but I'm distressed by the *reality*. The law of nature, that nothing can protect you in the end – no matter who you are, or what you have. It's that kaleidoscopic shift again – but somehow this is even worse. *Everything* isn't enough.

The ludicrous futility of Olga's weird youth transfusion ritual, mere hours before her death, ping-pongs me between pity and wanting to laugh. What a waste of actual life. And it didn't make her any happier, did it? Her last few hours, as it turned out, were full of dissent and, ultimately, vicious retribution against her.

I try to evaluate our situation. 'Right. So. There's no staff to help. We have no phones. And no way of sending emails without Wi-Fi.' I rub my head, pacing. 'So how do we get hold of the authorities?'

Asha frowns. 'I can go to the office and search. There's a satphone—'

My heart lifts at that – right until she says, 'But that's in a safe.'

'Do you know the code? Or how we can break in?'

'No.' She chews her lip. 'I don't even know where it is.'

I feel my legs buckle at the lack of options, the shrinking possibility of outside contact. 'Surely Olga's staff will come, if they don't hear anything from her?'

'They won't. They wouldn't dare,' Asha asserts. 'Olga instructed them to stay away until her summons, after the sign-or-decline event. But now, of course, she can't summon them, and we can't tell them why.'

'*Why* didn't Olga think that sending the staff away might be a problem?'

'She wanted everyone to make up their own minds whether to sign or not. She didn't want people to access outside help or opinions. So, she limited all communication channels, sequestered phones, locked down the Wi-Fi, made sure there was no way to reach the outside world. She wanted everyone to feel *pressure* . . .' She swallows. 'I guess someone *did*.'

We both go silent at that.

After a long silence, she glances at me. 'You must know what we should do? With your legal training? In these situations?'

Yes, I do, and I'll seize that opportunity . . . 'Since we can't notify anyone, we'll have to safeguard the scene.' My eyes narrow at Asha, who's been so quick to arrive, then so quick to flatter me into taking control, and I harden my voice. 'Then, we'll need to assemble the suspects, so I can take statements.'

She looks like she's in shock as she stares at me. 'B-b-but . . . but this *must* be an accident! A morning swim gone wrong? Maybe combined with an early mimosa . . .?'

'Do you know what Olga ate or drank this morning?' I ask her.

'N-no, I don't. I think her habit is to have breakfast on the deck.' She points to the platform to the east of the house, where the sea breeze cools the heat of the morning sun.

So Asha knows her habits. 'Does she usually swim first?' I ask.

'Sometimes.'

'Naked?' I recall Olga's Gucci swimsuit, her body confidence, and wonder if the comings and goings of staff would make a difference.

'No. Never.'

'So this is odd, then.' I take a long breath, thinking. 'We must leave everything in her room exactly as it is: any carafes of water she might have drunk from during the night, any glasses or cups she may have used. The police will want to test them—'

'Thea, surely, this *has* to be an accident?' Asha looks desperate for it to be true.

'Really?' I look at her, making her keep eye contact. 'You saw everyone's reactions last night. You saw the crazy maelstrom Olga stirred up. Deliberately. She was *delighted* at the state she left everyone in when she headed to bed.'

Asha's breathing becomes rapid, laboured, and I wonder if there's a hint of guilt.

I can understand why; after all, she knew what was happening here. So I push the point. 'You saw the effect Olga's outrageous request had on everyone, Asha. *You're* the only one who could have anticipated it. You organised this *with* her.' A memory of our chat on the plane sparks. 'When you said we were all carefully selected, for a specific reason, did you mean for the Pledge? Or something else?'

Fear creeps as I remember Olga's veiled barbs. I wonder, not for the first time, why these billionaires had dropped everything to come here – disrupting their life, their business, to comply with someone else's whim ...

Asha heaves, dropping to her knees like she's reaching for Olga, like she's going to haul her out of the depths. She retches, then vomits, aiming at the tiles instead of the water. At least she's trying to preserve the scene now ...

Wiping her mouth, she looks up at me, shaking. 'Oh, God, Thea. What have we done?'

Awful possibilities flash through my mind. If Olga doesn't swim naked, I wonder if she sleeps naked. There's one thing you *definitely* do naked, and I know – from spying last night – that Olga had been doing exactly that with my husband. I might *know* that, but what if someone else *guesses* that?

The logical conclusion fireworks in my brain: what if these lovers argued? What if . . .?

Oh, God. Has Charles . . . Could he . . .?

I need an excuse to check the room. Because if Charles *did* do anything awful, I don't trust him to clear up after himself. It might be poetic justice for him to be accused of this, but what if that finger of suspicion swings to me? The wronged spouse?

I feel my core turn to steel. I'm not going to be publicly cheated on *and* framed.

I'm galvanised into action, trying to take command as I veer wildly between possibilities, picturing spelling out 'SOS' in the sand or setting a fire on the vast beach. 'How can we signal for help?'

'Let me see if I can find the safe with the satphone. There may be a radio to reach emergency services on the nearest main island.'

'Perfect. Where would the safe be?'

'I don't know . . . Maybe the office?'

'Great. Start there. If you find it, bring it back here and we can call together. Meanwhile, I'll . . . make sure Olga's door is locked, so we can preserve the scene, and think of a way to get Olga out of the water.'

We nod, then Asha squeezes out through the garden hedge while I check the bifolding door from the garden. Finding it locked, I guess that Olga must have come down the steps from the balcony. I dash up them, scanning hungrily for clues.

No footprints, in either direction. The door from the balcony to the bedroom is wide open. Inside, at the bottom of the bed, a sofa and coffee table overlook the view – but the wall beside her bed is a view in itself, covered in framed photos of Olga with various celebrities, presidents, titans of industry. A pair of frames hold a *Forbes* article about Olga, the magazine's cover dominated by her picture.

It's like a shrine. I can imagine her whispering her desires, willing them to come true, *manifesting* here, and I shiver.

The sheets are twisted across the bed, a slip and dressing gown strewn across them, and a used condom lies on the floor, mere metres from the bathroom where it could have been disposed of. The sight of it makes me heave.

At least now I know why Olga had put Charles and me in separate rooms. A detail that cannot have been missed by our astute company. Fear grips me. I can't afford for this evidence to be found.

Before I have time to think, I've run to the bathroom, wadded some luxury, quilted, aloe vera-infused, gold-leaf-flecked toilet roll, picked up the condom with it, and used another handful of tissue to press the flush before dropping the lot down the loo.

I'm shaking, sweating, yet my brain is still gathering facts.

I notice the bathroom is damp, rivulets trailing down the glass. There's a smear of ... something clay-like and greenish-grey on the shower lever. I smell it, but all I detect is the warm scent of spa-treated mud. It's a rasul treatment, like the one left in my own room. Alarm bells ring. I experience a wave of fresh worry about Charles, about what he might have done ... then I realise why.

If you're going for a swim in your own private pool, you don't take a shower first, do you? You certainly don't use a treatment right beforehand only for it to all be stripped away in the pool; even if the expense was meaningless to you, it would be a waste of time. And time is precious to anyone, no matter how wealthy.

Back in the bedroom, I search – in desperate hope – for something, anything, to show that Charles wasn't Olga's only visitor last night.

Because I know, from skulking in the shadows, that someone else *did* visit her – and I need to make sure those tracks are very much *not* hidden.

The empty champagne bottle and champagne flutes by the bed make my heart thump, though. These must have Charles's DNA all over them. I can tell Olga's glass from the peachy impression of lip gloss, but Charles could have poured the glass, handed it to her . . .

I'd need to wash the lot – properly – to get rid of any finger-prints, and I grab the bottle, champagne bucket and flutes, and dash downstairs.

Olga's sitting room is orderly, and it seems eerily normal. I rush to the door, turn the key that's in the lock and ease it open, checking the hallway of the lodge like a panicking criminal – because that's what I am now.

If Asha is in the office, which is in the main house, just along from here beyond the covered walkway, then at any point she could return – and see me.

With no time to waste, I drop the napkin from the neck of the bottle to plug the door jamb and stop the door from closing, then dart to Charles's room. I knock, anxious, insistent.

Eons seem to pass, and my eyes flick up and down the hall as I wonder whether to just leave all this outside his door, hoping no one but him will notice it and that he'll somehow understand and dispose of them. But that's a risk . . . Especially if Asha sees it . . .

Then the door is flung open and Charles is standing there, a towel round his waist, hair slicked back. His questioning face becomes baffled, but I just thrust the items at him.

He takes them as I blurt out, 'Wash these, and get rid of them.' I don't wait for a response, just dash back the way I came, feeling him watching me, and hoping he will understand the urgency.

Softly, I close and lock Olga's door, pocketing the key. I fold the napkin carefully at the bottom of a drawer in the kitchenette, adding it to a pile of others, hidden in plain sight. Then I hurry past the downstairs bathroom, towards the locked glazed door to the garden. Asha isn't back yet, so I quickly scan the sitting room.

Two brandy glasses! The sight stops me in my tracks. *Of course.* One bears the ghost of Estelle's deep burgundy lipstick. Olga didn't partake much: a full measure of liquor remains, but a kiss of gloss on the glass shows she at least took a sip. It's confirmation they were together.

But ... what if Estelle loitered after she'd been here? Might she have seen Charles visit Olga? What if she poisoned Olga, then spied from the garden to make sure it had worked – then saw Charles, and an opportunity ...?

The poison hadn't taken effect until morning – was that because only a small amount was given? Or did someone else visit in the morning and poison her then? Could Olga have been poisoned at night with something slow-acting, to give the poisoner time to get away ...?

Is Charles ... Oh, God ... is Charles brutal enough to have poisoned Olga and then have sex with her while she was actually dying ...?

My stomach knots. Yes ... yes, I think he is.

I shut the thoughts down and keep moving. I head back upstairs to the bedroom and balcony to retrace my route back outside. I pause only to make sure there's no rogue baggy Y-fronts under the bed, then rush outside.

Scanning the garden, I sag in relief to see that Asha still isn't back. Then, as I stare down at Olga, floating nearly directly below the balcony, I swallow hard: I have to deal with her next.

As I hurry over, I know I must account for the time I've taken. I'll have to make it look like I've tried to get Olga out of the pool. Despite my urgency, I seize this opportunity to examine her. She's not the first dead body I've seen; my early foray into criminal law – before moving into more lucrative corporate then environmental law – meant I've watched pathologists carefully, methodically assess victims for signs of their demise. It's different, though, when it's someone you know, however slightly – who you've seen in vibrant life. And it's different again when you've keenly, *viscerally* wished them dead. My conscience bites.

Olga *could* have drowned while swimming; or, she might not have intended to swim at all, but rather fallen in and drowned. I squint up towards the balcony. She could even have fallen from there. There are no splashes on the textured marble around the pool, but they'd have dried quickly in this unreasonably bright sun. This *could* be accidental . . .

Yet something nags at me. A background murmur of that awful warning clamour that tells me something here is . . . dangerous.

There's no indication of a head wound, or any other wound for that matter; no traces of blood in the water. There's no sign on her golden skin of foul play – no bruising, no red marks, no signs that she'd been gripped or pushed under.

If she'd drowned, there would be tell-tale frothing at the mouth and nose, yet there's nothing. She was dead before she was in the water.

Right after an assignation with Charles. Fear spurs me on.

Olga is fully submerged, her limbs trailing downwards, her hands and feet already purpling with pooling blood. I can't reach her. There's no avoiding it: I have to get in. I have to get in the icky *corpse water*, then touch her, and move her. I would be grossly sick, but I don't have the luxury of agonising over it, or the delay will suggest to Asha that I've been busy elsewhere, interfering with the crime scene. And anyone else could turn up at any time, intending to talk to Olga before the sign-or-decline event.

I grimace, whimpering at the thought of inching in, so I take a deep breath, clamp my mouth shut and wade with purpose down the steps. The water chills me. I'll need to swim to reach Olga but I am absolutely *not* putting my face in the same water as a dead body. I kick out my leg – hoping to somehow hook her with my foot – but instead I push her further away, towards the deep end.

I nearly gag as I realise I'll have no choice. Once I've reached her, I'll need to get a good grip on her and pull her in, like the world's most pointless rescue. Holding my breath, and keeping my eyes tight shut, I launch myself off the side, kick towards her, and stretch out.

My silk robe pulls me down, under the water. I submerge as panic rockets and collides with my revulsion. Flailing desperately, I propel myself to the surface, breaching like a whale as I splutter and gasp and frantically kick back, away, *away*.

The death-water is up my nostrils, in my mouth, in my eyes. It feels as if it's burning me from the inside, polluting me with putrefaction. I flounder wildly, doggy-paddling desperately to the shallows, skidding and slipping on the steps, as I clamber to the safety of the terrace. I sink to my knees, gasping, wheezing, nearly sobbing.

I don't care what Asha wants to do with Olga; I've done enough.

As my breathing calms, I spot the pool net lying in a discreet inset. Asha won't believe I haven't had the initiative to use it, so I stagger to my feet and steer Olga's body with it to the shallows. Even that takes effort as I prod Olga's torso and try to nudge her along.

I won't be able to lift her to the surface and out of the pool, so I haul over a sunbed, collapse the front legs and slope it, like a ramp, down the pool steps. I have to wade in to move Olga to the makeshift gurney. It's worse now that she's closer, now that I can reach her. Now that I can't put off the *actual contact*.

I reach for her, shuddering, half turning away. She's heavy, her limbs growing rigid.

Even when you know a body won't move, there's something about that deadweight unresponsiveness that spikes alarm. My hardcore gym avoidance habit is coming back to bite me; I don't have the muscles for this. I have to grapple more . . . *thoroughly* . . . with Olga's naked body. I cringe as my manoeuvring pulls her close, and I bat away the flies that have detected death. Her face lolls against mine, squishing my cheek, nearly making me heave.

As I pull her over the sunbed, I nearly weep with gratitude when Asha's hand darts out to help. Together, we haul Olga out, dragging her onto the sunbed then hefting it out of the water. I'm panting, sweating, by the time we've staggered up the shallow steps.

I hold the end while Asha snaps the legs back down – and now we can wheel her wherever we decide to take her. But where, though? Where's cold enough to store a body? To preserve evidence?

I'm panting as I sit back and wipe my dripping forehead. I peel off my robe, wishing I'd taken it off *before* I'd gone swimming so I could wrap it around myself now instead of feeling so exposed in my soaking top and shorts. My skin prickles as I air-dry in the heat.

'When are the police coming?' I ask.

'They're not.' Asha's voice is flat. There's something . . . sinister about it.

'What do you mean? Of course they'd come!' I stare at her.

'No. I told you. No one's coming.' She looks so defeated that I wonder if it's calculated. I want to provoke her, to wake her up to the severity of the situation.

'Asha, we have to get them here. We're trapped with a killer, and no phone, with no access to any other help.' My eyes narrow. 'Or is there a reason you haven't called the police? Because any of us could have attacked her opportunistically. But only one person could have planned her murder – and that's *you*.'

'You think I'd plan *this*?' Asha gapes at me. 'I'll show you why I can't call anyone.'

My heart sinks like an anchor as Asha herds me through the hedge, to the main house, and into Olga's office. I notice I'm dry enough by now to not even leave ghosts of footprints. Despite expecting something awful, I'm still shocked at what she shows me. The office is in total disarray: the desk commanding the ocean view has been ransacked, its drawers wrenched open, and wooden filing cabinets have been torn into, paper and stationery scattered across the cool porcelain floor.

A bookcase has been pulled forward and sideways, out of line with the rest of the fitted shelves, and it's the doorway to a comms room. My heart lifts – until I see the state of it. Peering around the edge of the hidden door, I see stacks of electronic equipment – all smashed to smithereens.

I turn to her, suspicious. 'Did you do this?' *Is this why she'd been gone so long?*

'No! Of *course* not! When I saw this, I checked the radio. Well, what's left of it. In case there was any hope of it working. No luck. Then I searched amongst all this … *mess* to see if I could find where she put our phones, or maybe a safe or a code written down. Nothing.'

The worst thing is that this comms room was here last night. Within reach of all of us, if we'd had the initiative to look, instead of making utterly *disastrous* use of our time.

Rising panic whips up bile, fogging out the dangerous truth that I daren't admit yet.

My brain fights to catch up with my instinct, to understand why things in this … this paradise-turned-prison somehow just got worse.

Even though Olga's death looks accidental, it can't have been. Not if the comms have been destroyed like this.

If someone wanted to make sure we couldn't get help for Olga, then that means someone killed her.

More than that – it's a message. The murderer didn't need to destroy the radio. They wanted us to know that Olga was killed.

And I have to wonder: *why*.

Chapter 8

Sunday 6th April – 7.30 a.m.

I KNOW FROM HER FROZEN FACE and wide eyes that Asha shares my terror – but whether that's because she realises we're trapped with a murderer, or because I've emphasised that she's the only one who could have planned this, I'm not sure. Keeping her on the hook as the prime suspect is helpful, though; she's highly motivated to follow my suggestions, to prove her innocence.

After returning from the trashed office, we'd wheeled Olga into her suite on the sunbed. I'd dashed up the stairs to the balcony, into the bedroom, and down to the sitting room to unlock the immense bifolding door, so Asha could push her inside. I hadn't wanted Asha to know I had Olga's room key in my pocket.

We'd agreed we couldn't leave Olga out in the open, so we steered her into her downstairs bathroom. I draped a sheet over her, more for my benefit than out of any feelings of tenderness towards her, as Asha whacked up the air con. We left, wincing, but short of alternative options.

I've tampered too much now with the scene of the crime to be able to claim any moral high ground, but all this still goes against years of training. In one morning, I've moved the murder victim, destroyed evidence and perverted the course of justice ...

I can't worry about that; I'm more concerned that Olga's self-created privacy fortress prevents us from getting help. And the undercurrent of desperation – my terror that Charles may have implicated me, the wronged wife – vents itself as fury; fury that I can't make myself safe, or escape. Having my impotence so starkly emphasised, being *this* vulnerable, makes my breath catch.

I might kid myself that I'm angry, but really, I'm frightened.

Even if we *could* call the authorities, they couldn't actually reach us: the helipad – the only safe landing spot on this godforsaken volcanic island – is occupied by a grounded helicopter that no one can move, as was made all too clear by the ridiculous fight last night; and the island's harbour gate is locked shut, so no boats or vessels can gain access, either.

If it didn't make me sick with fear, I might see something poetic in how Olga's trap for us is now blocking justice for her.

But then, the fogging clouds of terror lift a little, and an idea glimmers ... If the police can't get here, then *I'll* be the sole representative of the law. I can take charge, take refuge in my professional objectivity. I can gather facts. I like facts. Facts are power. Facts unlock secrets – such as, maybe, who did this.

When I'd found her by the pool this morning, Asha had seemed to think I would naturally take the lead, so I use this to my advantage. 'Since the authorities can't help, I'll do what you suggest, and oversee the situation.' Before she can object, I continue, my tone authoritative. 'You've seen Olga at least once prior to this. Have you been *here* before?'

She nods. 'Olga flew me in for a chat a few months ago, to decide how to handle the reporting for this event.'

'How did she know you?'

'She'd seen my articles, some business analysis pieces, tagging her company and her directly, amongst others. I didn't expect anything from it; I'd added them to boost exposure.'

I weigh her word choice. 'Exposure? Of *your* work? Or of her?'

'Of what her company was doing. Greenwashing is rife. She wasn't the only CEO to do it, but she *was* the only one I wrote about who contacted me. I was surprised by her intentions to do something so bold about it.'

'When was this?'

'About three months ago. It was the only time I've been here.'

'Did you see much of the island?'

'I got the full tour. There weren't many guests then. And because I helped identify who should come to this—'

'Hold on – *what*? *You* helped decide this guest list? *You* helped determine who should be in this firing line?'

'No!' She swallows. 'Not *people* – *roles*. The functions needed to accelerate things.'

'Did Olga confer with you on the guest list, once she'd given it some thought?' It made sense that she would, so I'm not convinced when Asha shakes her head. 'Did you know any other details? What suites we were all assigned?'

'Yes, I know who's where.' At my raised eyebrows, she continues. 'Well, you already know there are huge guest suites on the upper level of the main house. The two on the south side, facing the ocean from east to west, host Magnus and Kali. Opposite, with the forest view, it's you, then me.'

I nod, picturing the rooms.

'All the suites have bifolding doors to a private balcony, and most have steps leading to private gardens, which sit beyond the communal garden that's accessed from the great room, and which the balconies provide shade for. I don't have a garden because my balcony doesn't have steps, it has a tree-top walk that stretches out to the jungle instead.'

I shudder at that, glad I don't have Asha's suite. I wouldn't want an easy route for those creepy critters to find their way into my bedroom.

I'd loved the discovery of a private garden last night; but now I'm worried about the free access they'd allow a killer, slipping through hedgerows from garden to garden, with only a small risk of being seen. I wonder if anyone could access Asha's suite from the jungle.

'To the west of the main house are three cabins, connected by walkways. Estelle's spans views of both ocean and forest; whereas Uri's and Zyra's cabins are side by side, between Estelle's and the main house. Uri's cabin has the ocean view, and Zyra's overlooks the jungle.'

I've seen the cabins, from a distance, but haven't had the opportunity – or excuse – to explore them yet. *I'll work on that.*

'Olga's lodge, as you saw, is to the east of the main house, linked with a walkway. It has three plush two-storey suites, each with a private garden and pool outside, and a bedroom upstairs. Two guest suites are on the west side – Hugh's has the ocean view, Charles's has the forest view. Olga's massive suite spans both outlooks.'

I saw for myself how jaw-dropping it was, but Asha is side-eyeing me now and I'm keen to move the conversation along from the conclusion she's about to reach. 'Those suites are for favoured guests,' I say. 'I wonder why she'd show Hugh preferential treatment . . .'

'His royal ego, I suppose?' Asha says.

'No one here is short on ego. And I don't see Olga being especially deferential to anyone. So why did she want Hugh so close at hand? Out here?'

'My money's still on sycophancy.' She continues eyeing me thoughtfully. 'The more interesting question is why Olga did the same for Charles: giving him the suite right next to hers, while putting you, his wife, not only in a different room, but a different *building*.'

I shrug, but feel heat crawl up my neck and cheeks. 'They know each other from previous conferences. I know only too well how political work can strike at antisocial hours, why Olga may have needed to be able to readily consult someone on policy.' I smile, like the weak argument is a winning one, like the arrangement has never bothered me. It never has, really, as long as it remains private.

'It does mean that, of everyone here, it would have been easiest for Charles to access Olga's room.' Asha echoes my own worries, making sweat prickle down my back. 'As you say, any one of us could have *opportunistically* killed her. But only *one* of us could have slipped in, unnoticed, from the room next door: your husband.'

I swallow, then manage a conspiratorial smile. 'Touché. But we can surely see any movements, can't we? Olga must have security cameras—?'

'No,' Asha asserts. 'There are no cameras, it's very private.'

I dredge my mind for anything else. Any other options. I feel the primeval urge of fight or flight kick in, and the instinct is like a sharp, fizzing awakening. It's unsettling, but everything is unsettling today, and it pales beside the stark horror of being trapped on an island with a killer.

I can't help aiming my ire at Asha. 'Interesting that *you* knew about the lack of security, the absence of staff, the opportunity that this situation would allow . . .'

When Asha's hot gaze flashes at me, I relent – but only a little. 'So tell me, Asha. Where were you last night and this morning?'

'I waited until everyone had scattered last night, and then I went to my room, to bed. I was up early, had a shower, went straight to Olga's room – and you know the rest. I couldn't get her to answer the door, so I forced my way into the garden – and that's … that's when …'

'Did you see anyone? Anything? Spot anything out of place? Hear anything? In the morning or last night?'

She shakes her head. 'Nothing. Even though I can't honestly say I slept well. But I *was* in my bed all night, Thea. You have to believe me. I was either trying to sleep or going through in my mind what would happen this morning …'

My frown catches her eye and stops her in her tracks.

'Not about *this*. Not about the *murder*. About the sign-or-decline event. About how everyone would be feeling.'

I can certainly hazard a guess at that. But whose discontent mutated into something darker? I fix Asha with a stern look. 'I'll have to question everyone here to find out who did this, Asha. So I hope you'll support me taking a legal standpoint. Especially as the authorities will need statements in due course. I propose to gather those while everyone's movements are still fresh in their minds.'

Her lips part with a sharp inhale at the reality check. I tilt my head – both an answer and a question – and she replies with a nod, and a hint of a relieved smile. 'I'll feel better – safer – if someone's taking charge. Thanks, Thea. I trust you.'

'Right. First I need a shower and clothes, then we'll tell the others.'

We walk through the gardens to avoid meeting anyone else. Asha follows me up my balcony steps, into my room.

'Can I … can I stay with you? In here, while you dress in there?'

I frown at her intrusion, but she disarms me.

'I'm . . . I'm scared, Thea. I don't want to be on my own. Not until we've told them and watched their reactions.'

'You think the killer will give themselves away? Just like that?'

'I think I'd be able to tell.'

'Oh! Wow. Get over to the CPS immediately. Save us from our lengthy trials and cumbersome evidence.' I grab fresh underwear, a shirt and palazzo pants. 'See you in a few.'

I don't trust her for a moment, so I leave the door ajar and watch her in the mirror as I rapidly wash, dry, dress and clean my teeth.

Together, we walk downstairs, where someone has tidied up the mess. My newly suspicious mind makes me wonder if anything there might have been evidence.

I'm still amazed at the sweeping views, but now, the vast, empty ocean just charts our distance from the rest of the world: how utterly alone we are.

This sobering reminder is the only motivation I need as I adopt the assertive persona that I use in courtrooms and pressrooms, and I speak clearly to command the attention of the company, who are all variously making or drinking coffee, eating breakfast and conferring among themselves.

Everyone pauses – and I realise how many are here early, perhaps to dissuade Olga, or perhaps to ensure that everyone sees their 'concern', while knowing they'd actually eliminated the threat.

'I'm sorry to share the awful news that Olga has been found dead this morning.'

I scan everyone, watching for tells. But it's like an adult game of musical statues. Frozen horror, then cautious side-eyes, then ripples of fear, guilt – *relief.*

'*What?*' '*How?*' '*When?*' The questions shoot at me, and I hold up a hand.

'We've got a few additional complications. We don't know where our phones are, and we can't get any messages out.'

'Yeah, we know. So, what does that mean? No one's coming?' Zyra sounds alarmed.

'Surely we can contact the authorities somehow?' Kali asks, eyes wide.

Uri frowns. 'There's gotta be a "break glass in the event of an emergency" piece of kit. A radio, or a satphone, or something?'

Asha glances at me, and everyone shifts, staring.

'What?' The collective questions rise again.

'Yes, there *was* a radio. But it's . . . it's been smashed.' Asha winces.

Straightaway, Kali gapes. 'So Olga was *murdered*?'

Estelle and Zyra grip each other's hands and sink onto the sofa, looking shellshocked. Magnus and Charles look from Kali to me, then exchange grim expressions with each other.

Hugo looks completely unaffected, so assured is he of his immortality. But Uri's demeanour changes. His restless energy drains away as he folds his arms; his grave stillness the most significant marker I've had of the danger we're in.

'Thea?' he calls softly, and I turn to him. 'Show me the radio.'

I'm so grateful that someone here wants to try to find a solution, to fix something, that I feel pulled towards him.

'I'll take you,' Asha jumps in before I can nod. 'Because Thea has something else to do.' She shoots me a meaningful glance, and I take the cue.

'Given it's clearly a . . . suspicious death, we'll need to take statements while events from last night and this morning are still fresh in everyone's mind. Since I know the drill, I'm volunteering to take them.'

I pause, scanning them, adding the challenge, 'I trust only *one* person here would object to that and, since that person would be the killer, then they probably don't want to admit that.' I arch an eyebrow. 'Unless anyone here wants to confess and put themselves under civil arrest?'

Despite my argument, I prepare for immediate refusals. But there are no groans, tuts, head shakes or cursing. There *are* shifty, appraising sidelong glances, but I'm watching for worry. For whoever really has a reason to say no.

'I'll decline, thanks.' Magnus looks at me from under his heavy grey brows, his voice whistling slightly through the new gap in his teeth. 'You're treating ush like we're all shuspects. What if shomeone elshe got onto the island and ish hiding out here?'

'No way.' Asha shakes her head. 'I *wish* it wasn't one of us, but you've seen her security. It's *beyond* extreme. She can lock the bloody *bay*!' Glances dart between us at that unhappy confirmation.

'Even sho. I know my rightsh. I'm not shayin' anything, to *anyone*, without my brief.'

'Of course. That's your right.' I smile. 'It does mean that all I can record now is your insistence on having legal counsel, rather than a simple statement.'

Ooh, that feels weird. To push for the opposite of what I'd usually advise. I almost shudder, but I channel the energy into goading Magnus. I make a show of typing something into my iPad. At least I don't need Wi-Fi to capture notes and make voice memos. I exaggerate my wince for Magnus's benefit, and he glowers.

'Noted, Magnus. And I'm sure the authorities won't take that as an admission of guilt.' I grimace. 'Especially after ...', I mouth the rest, '*what happened last night.*'

I turn away from him, so that he'll see his chance to defend himself is slipping away. 'Uri? Before you look at the radio, would you give a statement?'

'Sure, I've nothing to hide.' Uri's grinning, like he knows he has a part to play and is happy to turn the screws on Magnus.

'Wait. What?' Magnus interrupts. 'Don't you *dare* shuggest I've got shomething to hide! And don't you *dare* make a statement that might incriminate me.'

'I'm just giving a statement about what I saw, and when.' Uri shrugs in faux innocence. 'My *words* won't be the things doing the incriminating.'

'How dare you!' Magnus lumbers up from his seat to loom over Uri. 'This is my good character you're defaming.'

'Then make a statement, man.' Uri turns his hands up. 'Either accept the implication of guilt and own it, or give a statement and defend yourself. It's only to Thea, and she saw you at your worst last night, anyway.' Uri winks at me behind Magnus's back as the aged financier grunts and sinks into the sofa. 'Unless you *did* sneak out and kill Olga. I mean, in *that* case, definitely don't make a statement. That would be stupid.'

Everyone freezes at that. The air crackles – and now I know they'll all comply.

Chapter 9

Sunday 6th April – 8.15 a.m.

URI SHOOTS ME A GRIN that makes me smile in return as he says, 'Shall we?'

I nod. 'I'll set up a private space.'

Asha holds up a hand. 'Actually, Uri, could I show you the comms situation first? Maybe get you thinking about if it's possible to fix, at least?'

'Sure.' He shrugs at her and turns to wink at me. 'I'll take my turn with Detective Harrington in a few minutes, then?'

As he follows Asha, I look around for who else might be an easy first interviewee.

'OK, Thea, I'll go first,' Charles volunteers.

I smile, like I believe it's him showing solidarity. It isn't, of course. It's self-preservation. As always.

Off the main room is the hall to the walkway that leads to the lodge. Off that hallway is a huge kitchen, the bathrooms, Olga's (now trashed) office, and a peaceful library. I lead Charles there, but barely notice the forest view, or the languid trickling waterfall.

Charles sits across the desk from me, the wall behind him lined with harmoniously arranged leather-bound first editions. He slumps in his seat. 'Let's get this over with.'

I eye him, relishing his irritation that I already know more than he wants me to.

'I'm aware of the affair. That's not really the issue here.' I don't care about the affair at all. I hate that he dissuaded Hugh from being part of Olga's plan, yet didn't talk him down from that revolting assault on Drew. He proved he *could* have, and so he proved that he *chose* not to. It also proves that, even though he was sleeping with Olga, he didn't support her. Everything about that makes hatred slither all over me.

'Can't blame me.' He gives a half-smile like a kid caught stealing sweets. I can't believe I once thought he had a charming devilishness. He sickens me. I feel my upper lip curling. The grubby lechery of him suffocates me. I can't wait to be free of him.

But I have to protect him, in order to protect myself. And if I play the divorce card now, he won't cooperate. I haul my emotions back into check and force myself to rally. 'So, let's cover the critical points. Was Olga alive when you left her?'

He gapes, glances over his shoulder, then hisses at me, 'What kind of fucking question is *that*?'

'The obvious one. You know I'll protect you. Us. So, you know you can be honest. You *need* to be, for both our sakes. I can't help you if you're not.'

His gaze at me is appraising, doubtful.

With a grimace, I realise how I can convince him. 'I disposed of your used condom.'

'Oh. Shit.' His shuddering sigh tells me he hadn't been mentally retracing his steps since hearing about Olga. Maybe he wasn't guilty – of murder, at least.

'How did she die?'

'She was found in the pool.' I avoid stating any details. 'So I'm asking about what you did after you left her room.'

'Aren't you getting a little carried away?' He settles back, steepling his fingers. 'With your taste of power.'

'Oh, yeah, flushing my husband's condom has me high on hubris.' I enjoy the instant contrition across his arrogant features. 'And *for* the record, I'm taking the opportunity to find out who may know what, who may have done what, to get *you* out of the frame.'

'*Me?*'

'Olga was naked. If someone was with her when she was killed, then it was someone she was comfortable with *au naturel*.'

He nods slowly. 'Well, then, it might be in my best interests if I can share some … information. Of what others were up to with Olga …?' I wait and he adds, 'You'll want to speak to Estelle.'

I shift, knowing she was there, wondering what he knows.

'After that godawful fight last night, when Olga had left us all to debate between ourselves, I deposited Hugh in his room. I thought about heading over to Olga's then, but Estelle beat me to it. I saw her in the hallway, when I'd opened my door a crack to check the way was clear before going to Olga's room.'

I shiver, wondering if he'd spotted me. I weigh the odds. If he had seen me, he'd want to hold it over me, as leverage. And the more on the back foot I could make him feel, the sooner he'd be inclined to play that perceived advantage.

'Do you think Estelle could have seen *you?*'

He hesitates, and I cheer on the inside.

'No, I don't think she saw me.'

'You don't sound very certain. If you went to Olga's room after Estelle had left, how do you know she didn't hang around? Or think of something else she wanted to say, and came back and saw you?'

'No … I … no …'

'Could anyone else have seen you, or her? Who might be able to confirm that Olga was alive when you left her?'

'No, darling.' His voice drips with sarcasm. 'When one's creeping the corridors to find their mistress, one's *avoiding* witnesses.'

'You'd know.'

'Anyway, I didn't linger to watch for Estelle. I had a quick shower, picked up the tray of champagne and glasses, and came out to the hall to try again.'

I try not to roll my eyes at my husband's persistence.

'*But* I opened my door to see Zyra creeping away from Olga's room, towards the main house. I waited until I was sure she'd gone, then I knocked on Olga's door.'

I raise my eyebrows at the apparent revelation, but I'm really reflecting on the fact that there had been no evidence of her visit in Olga's room. I can't dwell on that now, I have to brace myself for the next bit. I may not have any fond feelings left for Charles, but I don't really want to hear the post-mortem — so to speak — of his sex life.

'Olga was in a silk slip and silk dressing gown. Very elegant. I asked if she was expecting any more guests, she said she hoped not.'

'Did she tell you what Estelle, or Zyra, had said to her?'

'I didn't ask, she didn't volunteer. We didn't really do much … talking.'

I feel my lip curl again and Charles laughs. It's a horrid, knowing, throaty laugh, like he thinks I'm repulsed because I'm a prude, rather than because he's … repul*sive*.

'So, you shared the champagne?'

'I poured her a glass, and one for myself.'

'Did you …?' I ask the rest of my question with my eyes.

'Yes. I washed the glasses and the bottle. I put them in the kitchen.' He sounds tired at the thought of it, rather than appreciative. I note he hasn't thanked me for covering for him. *What an ungrateful, vile prick.* 'I toasted to her vision, and then we imbibed.'

Ugh. I can picture his sycophancy all too well.

'And *then* we went to bed.' He purses his lips. 'I'll draw a veil over that, *dearest.*'

I hold his eye contact levelly. I'm not about to dignify this with a response, or give him the satisfaction of looking ruffled. I wait until I've eroded his bravado and he's forced to look away. The victory gives me a sense of my inner steel, and I cling to it.

'I left around five. As I got back to my room, I heard someone coming in from the main house, so I waited and watched through the peephole of my door.'

'And?'

'It was Kali.' He gives a significant nod. 'Looking furtive, in contrast to her bullish position last night. She was heading to Olga's – who was alive and well when I left her. I went to bed then, and slept like the righteous. I think I must have had some kind of nightmare, maybe a premonition, because I dreamed I heard some bloody awful scream.'

'Did it wake you?' I don't tell him it was Asha, finding Olga.

'I was . . . groggy. Between the whisky and the champers and barely any sleep. So I dozed, I think. Horrible dreams. Eventually I got up and needed a shower. Then you knocked on my door, shoving a load of washing-up at me.'

'Keeping you out of the frame,' I remind him, firmly.

'I can't still be in it,' he protests. 'Not with all these other people coming and going.' He has an irritating hint of a swagger now, like he's extricated himself from any suspicion.

'An affair could give you a motive for all manner of reasons,' I press.

'Ah.' He gazes at me, and his lip twitches. '*Now* I get it. Yes, my affair could give *me* a motive. But it's much more likely to give *you* one.'

* * *

I can see Zyra adopting her interview persona as she walks in. Like Estelle, she's had training in hiding her true feelings while talking convincingly about something. I'll have my work cut out to spot their lies. But I do have the advantage: they're both likely to deny going to Olga's room, and then I'll see their body language tells.

I give a warm, disarming smile of comfort, acknowledging the awful circumstances as Zyra sits opposite. Before I can ask anything, she reaches out and clasps her hand over mine. 'May I just share my condolences. We're all guests – no, *friends* – of Olga's, so her loss will be keenly felt. I'm here for you.'

I stare at her, holding back the awful laughter that's bubbling in my throat at her earnestness. Her audacity in trying to gloss over the feelings she made so clear last night is ludicrous.

My laugher wins. 'Wow! Zyra! I can see why you're such a terrific performer! That's . . . that's quite the reversal from what you said last night, about – what was it – needing to stop Olga.'

Zyra shifts on her seat, flicks her hair. 'Sure. Yeah. I wanted to stop her actions, stop her making a mistake that would reflect unfortunately on all of us if she made public statements that had to be retracted.' She grimaces. 'No one wants that.' Then she gives me a perfectly innocent head tilt, just slightly widened eyes. 'Why? What did you *think* I meant?'

'It could easily be taken as a threat against her life, Zyra. By any one of the witnesses you said it in front of.'

'Oh!' Another picture-perfect impression of astonishment. 'And are the people you're referring to as *witnesses* also people you're treating as suspects in your little,' she draws rapid circles with her finger, 'murder mystery game?'

'Yes.' I smile, enjoying her reaction as her argument deflates with my simple agreement.

She sits back, crosses her legs and regards me. 'Is that all?'

'No. The statement I'm gathering must record exactly what you did last night. So,' I tap my iPad, holding it at an angle so the screen isn't visible, as my tone grows brisk and business-like. 'What did you do after, let's say, Kali retired for the evening?'

'Absolutely nothing. And you can check with Estelle. We were together, chatting in my room. The whole time.'

'It's a bad idea to start your statement off on a lie, Zyra. Why don't you try again?'

'I ... *what?*'

'Tell me where you went, Zyra, because I *know* you didn't go straight to your room.'

I see her biting back the question, *How?* as she frowns, her brow creased and heavy.

Then the confusion veiling her face lifts, and she must have realised Charles was the source of that information.

'Ohhh. I see how it is. OK. Yes, I went to see Olga. It was super brief, hardly worth mentioning. I simply asked to be exempted from the Pledge.'

'Good. Tell me how that conversation went.'

'I explained I was concerned she might put out an announcement on my behalf, and recommended that she didn't.' She holds my stare, then leans back. 'That's *all*.'

'If that was all you said, then you wouldn't have needed to lie initially about not seeing her.'

She gapes at me, clearly used to a more sycophantic kind of interview.

'I can easily picture a very different kind of discussion between you and Olga. Given how upset – no, angry – you were with her last night. *Mutinous*, even. So much so, you were inciting others, like Estelle, into a plan to stop her.'

As I watch the blood drain from Zyra's face, I push the point.

'Is that why you two are each other's alibis?'

She rolls her eyes. 'Let's not be melodramatic. It *seemed* like a much bigger deal last night. This morning, I have some perspective.'

I note that she doesn't answer my question, but she's opened a more interesting door.

'Indeed. Is that because this morning, the person threatening you is dead? After *you* spoke to them.' My smile is the sugar cube delivery for the stinger: 'That would make you a prime suspect, wouldn't it?'

*　*　*

As Zyra leaves, Estelle slinks in and gracefully takes her seat. I can't drag my eyes from her.

She's so spectacularly beautiful that she's ... *other-worldly*. Elegant, effortless. Immaculate to a degree I've never encountered in real life. Her skin is bare of makeup, and smooth, flawless as glass. Her features are so symmetrical, so gorgeously shaped, it's like she's an idealised version of a human. And she's haughty with it: she knows she's in a different league, and that all her value lies in maintaining that charismatic mystique. She's

112

trained herself to keep that up – at all costs. Even in the face of murder.

'Thanks for this, Estelle,' I say, trying to break the ice-queen silence. 'I just need to record your whereabouts between midnight and 7 a.m.'

She examines her nails and elegantly splays her fingers. 'Asleep. I have a regime.' Even her voice is poised. She speaks with the modulated tone of someone who's had a lot of media training: neutral accent, well-spoken, deliberate, slow. Like the world will wait for her.

'And what's that? Your regime?'

Her stare conveys that I've just asked for the secret formula of life; something mere mortals like me must never be privy to. Grudgingly, judgingly, she lists: 'Face yoga, gua sha massage, double cleanse and mask. Hair treatment. Full-body exfoliation and rasul treatment. Meditative yoga, including inversions for blood stimulation, and gong bath. Rosehip oil nourishment. Then I hydrate with my nighttime water, vitamins and supplements. I sleep in an eye mask, listening to a rainfall recording on my phone – not that I could last night, since I'd handed it over to Olga – to ensure I get my full eight hours.'

God, I'd need a good night's sleep after faffing about like that. How bloody draining. 'You wouldn't have got your full eight hours last night, though,' I point out.

'No. Well. Close enough.' She looks pained at that. It's the first time a hint of any lines crease her perfect face.

'I'll still ask if you saw or heard anything.'

'Nothing.' Every head tilt could be a *Vogue* front cover; her composure is unbelievable. I can imagine her modelling through some extreme situations, keeping her face serene or enigmatic or alluring as required, no matter what's going on just out of shot. I realise how hard it will be to detect her tells that reveal if she's lying.

'Did you go straight to your room last night?' I invite her to lie, so I can see what she does. 'You didn't go anywhere else first? Speak to anyone on the way?'

Ah, a slow blink, a slightly deeper inhale, before she meets my eyes with a smile.

'I don't enjoy small talk. And my wellness time was already compressed. I had no reason to add further delay.' There's defiance in her voice now, despite her graceful shrug.

'How did you feel about Olga's plan?' Her dark eyes widen so I let the question hang.

Her tight smile prepares me for the rehearsed soundbite, and I catch another extended blink and inhale, like she's trying to make herself steady enough to fool a lie detector. 'Olga's vision for a better world means that she pushes boundaries. While that can be a challenge, I admire how she learns from the past to make a real difference. I'm excited ...' Her voice trails off and she glances at her lap. '*Was*. I *was* excited about what we could achieve together.'

'I'm not buying your official version.' I soften my words with a smile that I hope suggests empathy and confidence. 'Last night, you were so incensed with Olga that you openly agreed when Zyra suggested you all stop her.' I hold eye contact, sensing that she wants to look away, but she holds my gaze, defiant as a warrior. I press her. 'Is that what you did, Estelle?'

'*No!* No, of course not.' She gapes at me, wide-eyed, fear cracking her composure. 'Last night, I ... I got caught up in the emotions of everyone else. I had no idea something ... something as awful as this would happen.'

The corners of her mouth tug, like she wants to say more, before clamping shut. Instead of speaking, she swallows and stares at her lap.

As a lawyer, I've watched a lot of people lie. There's the twitchy, looking-over-their-shoulder types; then those with bravado who brazen it out and dare you to prove otherwise; and the clinically cold arrogance of the psychopathic. Later, I expect to see bored superiority from Hugh; a display of the rare levels of entitlement afforded by a life of doing whatever he wants, with full protection from the consequences. But Estelle's reaction is all too familiar: the rising fear of being involved in something that's gone too far; that's morphed into something they can't control.

I regard her, weighing her reaction. 'Why are you afraid, Estelle? If you're innocent?'

'Because we're trapped here, aren't we? With a m-murderer.' She shivers. 'And what if my stupid words riled them up? Made them more angry? Instead of calming things down.'

'So you feel guilty.'

'No! Not in the way you're trying to suggest.'

'And what way is that?'

'Like I actually . . . *did* it. I didn't. You *know* I didn't.'

'I don't know that, actually, Estelle. I *do* know that your anger with Olga last night was valid. Your point was fair, and you didn't incite anyone – because they all felt the same. Things wouldn't have . . . *exploded* in the way they did, otherwise. With that awful fight.'

She grimaces at the reminder. That single, unphotogenic response makes me believe she could be genuine. I press her. 'You saw how Olga baited everyone. You're not the only one who felt forced into this. She delighted in putting all of us under pressure.'

Her clasped hands twist as they rest on the desk, and it makes me adopt a more conciliatory tone. 'I'm not the police, Estelle. I'm in the same boat as you. Did you have any contractual conflicts that would have prevented you from doing this for Olga? Or any other reasons to deny the request?'

Her gaze meets mine, sharp with questions and uncertainty. There's something here. I pause, letting her take the time to tell me.

The silence stretches, burgeoning with … whatever that something is. But Estelle's guard comes up again, and doesn't crack.

'If you need anything …' I hold her gaze, not sure what I'm offering, but wanting to say enough to insinuate myself into her confidence.

Her tone hardens. 'Too kind.'

Estelle, it seems, isn't the type to trust easily. It's not hard to speculate why a woman who started out young on the international modelling circuit would have issues in that department, but it does make me curious about her background.

I lean in. 'I know you don't know me. I can see that it's hard to share anything. But … I do know about your … conflict. With Olga. Last night. In her room. Which means you lied when you told me you went straight to bed without speaking to anyone.'

'How—?' Her already taut body stiffens, her eyes sliding to the door and I sense her wondering if Charles saw her and told me. And I'm quite happy to let her believe that that's the only way I know about it.

I continue, carefully, 'So if you *can* add any details, it will help me sift out those interactions that are important from those that are … less so.'

Her face becomes a mask, betraying no further vulnerability. This woman has more control than a drawer full of Spanx as she gives her measured reply. 'I *did* go to speak to Olga, yes, but our . . . *conversation* was brief. Barely worth mentioning.'

'Any interaction with a murder victim immediately before their death is critical. As the police will confirm. It's best to be completely clear about what happened.'

Her eyes narrow, but she does tell me more. 'I had a nightcap with Olga. She only had a sip. I asked if I could be released from her plan. I was worried that our . . . history would undermine it.'

'What history is that?' I ask. Her account doesn't match what I overheard last night.

She frowns. 'Are you joking?' Disbelief ripples across her perfect features. 'I mentioned it in the boardroom. Olga tried to do this to me before. As the face of her brand. She exploited me to add credibility to her supposedly ethical production methods, only for journalists to report far and wide that her brand was built on sweatshops. It was *awful*. I couldn't believe the conditions of those poor women, or Olga's blatant deception while she cashed in on having a responsible reputation. The *scandal* of it . . .'

She chews her lip, shaking her head, and I see angry tears glisten. 'She did exactly the same to the COO of the line of smartwatches. Left him to take the fall while she weathered the storm.'

She clamps her mouth shut, but I spot the slightest hint of a tremble.

'Wasn't that . . .' I pretend to search for the name, 'Tony . . .? Tony somebody . . .?'

'Tony Franklin.' She whispers the name and stares at her lap. With a deep breath, she meets my eyes. 'You asked me if there was a *contractual* conflict stopping me from putting my name to this? No. It was an *integrity* conflict. *My* idea of what that means versus *hers*. She leaves others to deal with all the fallout. Yet now she's here trying to play the *saviour*? Are you *kidding* me?' Her chest heaves, like she's fighting for breath.

'How did Tony cope?'

Estelle's dark, deep eyes fix on mine, and waves of sorrow hit me. Her pain is so tangible, so piercing, that I catch my breath. 'Not well, I take it?'

'Correct.'

'Did Olga make amends? For him? Or improve conditions for those women?'

'No and no.' She sits up even straighter. 'Why would you care? Did you accidentally find your conscience while you were looking for legal loopholes?'

'I …' I stop trying to excuse the inexcusable and look her in the eye. 'Yes, I think I did.' My admission isn't enough to erase Estelle's suspicion. '*You* obviously care—'

'Of *course* I do! In another life, that could have been me, my mother, my sisters, my daughters.' Her lip trembles and she bites down on it, hard. 'Who *wouldn't* care?'

I feel instant shame at her words. It's dangerously easy to keep out-of-sight problems firmly out of mind, to not think of the far-flung fates that have been shaped, however indirectly, by my own actions over the years.

'I'm sorry for what you've gone through, Estelle.' I reach across the table and place my hand on hers. She wears a huge, glittering ring on her right hand, and the brilliant yellow stone – which has to be some kind of rare diamond – presses into my palm.

She stares at the table, but she doesn't flinch away.

'And I'm sorry that I didn't know the history, despite the fact that it was clearly very public and very painful. May I ask … how is Tony now?'

I might have a horrible suspicion, but I need to know for sure.

Estelle takes a sharp intake of breath, and pauses. She meets my eyes with that controlled dignity. 'He killed himself. Olga let him take all the heat, all the blame, while she used me as the face for non-existent improvements. Instead of supporting the workers, Olga stopped the works entirely, ending Tony's career under the blackest cloud imaginable. It was awful, for both of us. And . . .' she swallows, takes another breath, 'ultimately, it was . . . too much for him to bear.'

This glimpse of the wound festering under Estelle's polish – together with the toast she shared with Olga last night in memory of the unfortunate Tony – gives me the certainty I needed that Estelle came here with an agenda.

Was she the only one, though? Or does everyone here have a score to settle?

As I watch her, she drops her gaze to her lap, where her elegant fingers are twisting the eye-catching ring. I wonder if those same fingers might have dropped something into Olga's drink, something so strong that just one sip would be enough . . .

Chapter 10

Sunday 6ᵗʰ April – 9.45 a.m.

KALI ENTERS THE LIBRARY AS soon as Estelle has left. She has a determined set to her jaw. Resilience and stamina seem to be in her DNA, along with fierce intelligence and ruthless ambition. You don't get into the top five of the Forbes Rich List by accident. Kali probably hasn't slept but she looks fresh, determined, full of fire as she sits opposite me.

'Kali, I wondered if I could ask for your help?'

She regards me with interest, but not concern. I'm guessing she's not into the sisterhood. There are women like that, who smash the glass ceiling, then pull the ladder up behind them. She's not the type to follow the mantra, *Never look down on anyone unless you're helping them up.* My conscience prickles. I have no right to feel so needled by it; I'm just the same.

I try again. 'I need your *professional* opinion. Your medical training.'

'Oh?' She doesn't stand; she looks wary.

'Would you examine Olga? You're the only person who might be able to determine cause of death.' I make sure I give no hint of my past experience alongside forensic investigators. I don't want her to realise this is a test.

'I'm not a pathologist, Thea. If I mistake something critical, and you record what I say and it influences any . . . investigation, it would be worse than me doing nothing.'

'You didn't get to where you are without relying on your capabilities and taking a few risks. Please. Come with me.' I walk away, praying that she'll follow and I won't have to crawl back to the table and beg for her statement instead, like a prize fool.

Maybe it's curiosity, or maybe it's self-interest and the chance to cover her tracks if she's the guilty party – but she follows, and I turn my surge of relief into a smile of thanks.

The rest of our company don't see us as we walk along the hall and out onto the walkway leading to the lodge. I continue my questions, maintaining the businesslike tone that seems to get results. 'So what did you do last night, when you retired for the evening?'

'After Uri and I argued?' She side-eyes me. 'We were all agitated by Olga's orders. Uri and I weren't the only ones. And at least *we* didn't resort to a fistfight.'

'Are you thanking Uri for not retaliating? Or isn't a slap serious enough in your book?'

Kali groans, reminding me she's doing this under sufferance. 'It's not like a slap would really hurt him, is it? And he *was* doing his best to goad me, in that moment. Anyway, it's old news now. When I retired for the night, Uri caught up with me and apologised. I can respect someone making a good case.' She smiles. 'And I know which fights are worth pursuing, and which to concede.'

I wonder if Uri really did apologise, or if Kali's preserving her image. Her magnanimous half-shrug only adds to my suspicion, but I manage not to purse my lips; I can't blame her for trying to present herself and her reputation in the best light.

Everyone likes telling people that others have acknowledged how right, how clever, they are.

So, I smile my agreement as I direct Kali around to the garden, and she smiles back. I'm not sure if it's in intellectual kinship or satisfaction that she thinks I believe her.

Either way, it gives me another glimpse of the real Kali. I sense she is a born fighter, so fiercely reserved that she's quite the lone wolf, holding her own counsel. Despite the nature of her company, with its focus on saving lives, it doesn't seem as if Kali actually even *likes* people.

Once we've squeezed through the hedge, I question her, in order to watch her body language. 'What did Uri say, when he apologised to you?'

'I let him grovel a bit, and retract the accusations he'd made.' She scratches her nose. *Classic.* 'But I'd reflected on what he said, about us having strength in numbers. It was interesting that, when we all felt under threat by Olga, our prevailing instinct was self-preservation, in the individualistic sense, rather than working together.'

I eye her, managing not to laugh at her moral backtracking. She was the one who said they were all out for themselves!

'Uri also made the point that Olga is proposing this just to deflect from her own damaged reputation. Rehabilitating *her* image at the expense of all of ours: we'd be the patsies, thrown to the wolves, while her sins are forgotten under the glitter of her visionary leadership.' She shoots me a look. 'I didn't like that idea very much. I've built something too important for someone else to treat it like a pawn in their game.'

I nod, seeing her point. 'So what did you do?' We're loitering in Olga's garden now, both of us delaying confronting Olga's corpse.

She looks at me levelly. 'I *intended* to negotiate.'

'To stop her?' I pause for a beat, looking her dead in the eye. 'One way or another?'

Kali shakes her head. 'You quite fancy yourself as our interrogator, don't you? No. To negotiate my way around it. I'd gamed out every option that Olga could throw back at me, and put a solid case together. But it took all night. I hadn't realised how fast time was passing, and at dawn I headed over to speak to her.'

'So what was your case? Your solid, un-rebuttable case?'

'Oh . . .' Kali sighs. 'Something like, while I'd love to be a part of this, I don't want to overshadow the ambitious goals by drawing attention away from them. There are some unwarranted concerns over my companies that could lead to scrutiny.'

She rubs her nose again; the gesture of concealing her mouth betrays her need to hide the lie. 'Then, something like . . . you've inspired me to consider my challenges and improve things – but those challenges count me out from being included at this stage. If Olga released me on that premise, without the public "sign-or-decline" dilemma, then I'd be in a stronger position and would commit to joining the Pledge in two years. *But* if she put me in the position of having to decline, I'd not join down the line. I'd have no incentive, if I'd been publicly embarrassed.'

I stare at her. 'That's a decent argument. But it can't have taken you five hours to assemble it. So what else were you doing during that time?'

'Oh.' She waves a casual hand, but she looks rattled. 'Late-night thinking isn't my forte. I'm a morning person. After being up all night, I'm *buzzing* with caffeine now.'

'And how did Olga respond?'

'What do you mean?' Kali glances at me, wary.

'When you went to see her.'

'Oh. Well. I didn't, as it turns out.'

I frown. 'Yet you said that at dawn you decided to speak to her.'

'Oh. Yes. I'd intended to see her. But it didn't happen.' Another nose scratch.

'No?' I hold her gaze until she drags her eyes from mine to stare at the pool, and I wonder if that's significant, given it's where Olga was found.

I wait while she rallies, then looks at me. 'I came down to the main room, to see the lie of the land, if Olga was here already – and then … I heard the news. So I stayed there.'

'Except that isn't true, is it?' I challenge in a light tone. 'What happened when you went to Olga's room, right at the time of her murder?'

Kali's head snaps round to stare at me. *How gratifying.* 'Nothing.'

'If that were true, you'd have given me that account to begin with.' My stare is hard. 'But you chose not to. So what are you hiding?'

'Thea, you need to understand that you're not the police. I'm doing you a courtesy by speaking to you, but I don't need to.' She starts to walk away.

'True.' I reach out and pull her arm gently. 'Though you *will* need to answer to the police, of course. Not many people have the chance of a dry run with a legal expert first. So. Convince me.'

She stiffens but pauses, then turns to face me. '*I* don't need to convince *you* of anything. I might have knocked on Olga's door to speak to her, but she didn't answer. She wasn't there. It's a non-event.'

'So there's no harm in being honest about that, then, is there?' I smile.

When Kali narrows her eyes in return, I push a little more. 'Olga had strong opinions about the ethics – or lack of them – in the pharmaceutical industry, didn't she? What was she referring to when she accused your company of making profits while depleting the resources of the origin countries?'

Kali's chin lifts and she regards me for a moment. 'It's a fair criticism of the wider industry, but she wasn't accusing my company of anything along those lines.'

'Wasn't she?'

Kali shakes her head.

'Well, she was certainly making an accusation about unethical drug trials.'

'Again, some companies can be ruthless.'

'That's *your* reputation, isn't it?'

Her lips twitch. 'How kind of you to notice.'

'Olga got quite emotional when she referred to drugs that don't live up to their claims. She specifically said that you – *personally* – have deeper responsibilities than anyone else here because, and I quote her, "you're not selling a product, you're selling *hope*."'

'Yes, I saw how emotional she was. Maybe she'd had a bad experience with healthcare. That doesn't mean that me or my company were responsible. It can be quite usual for people to fixate on a representative to vent their anguish on. And if Olga did go through something like that, I wouldn't hold an emotional outburst against her.'

I find myself being swayed – and sense how easy it is to succumb to Kali's talent for persuasion. I can't help feeling that empathy is a disguise she's willing to adopt when it suits her, then shed like a snake so she can push ahead unburdened.

'So let's put your healthcare credentials to good use, then.' I unlock and open the bifolding door, cross the suite and approach the bathroom – then recoil at the flurry of flies.

Kali gags. 'Oh, fucking hell, Thea. I'm not going in there.'

'Oh, you must have seen worse, Kali. In your professional capacity. And . . . I *thought* we'd put the air con on.' I stab the button, and the air con starts up. *Ohhh.* It's on a motion-sensor time delay, so it only stayed on a few minutes after Asha and I left Olga here.

'You realise that isn't a long-term corpse storage solution,' Kali observes. The sheet covering Olga is fuzzing with insects, and more flies circle low, crawling to the edges of the sheet, seeking a way in.

'Well, there may be a handy morgue somewhere on this idyllic island, but if there is, I don't know where.' I sigh – in frustration at the situation and at Kali's sarcasm.

Pointedly pulling her T-shirt up over her mouth and nose, Kali lifts the sheet covering Olga, ducking from the squadron of flies she releases. 'How was she found?'

'In the pool.'

'Drowned?'

'I don't know.' I hold my breath, waiting to see what Kali will say, and if her descriptions are accurate.

She squats, squinting at Olga's limbs. 'I can't see any . . . injuries . . .' She leans back, surveying the body, swatting away clusters of insects. 'No external signs. No head wounds, bite marks or punctures, or signs of strangulation.'

She sounds like she's in *ER* or *Grey's Anatomy*, and I almost feel removed from the horror, except for the fat, persistent flies buzzing around us, crawling across Olga's skin.

Kali's assessing gaze travels all over Olga's body. 'This livor mortis, the purpling here, shows she died on her front, with her arms and hands lower than her body.'

Flies pause as they scuttle across Olga's face, their legs twitching. I scratch my own creeping flesh. But Kali is leaning in, studying Olga, not deterred.

'There's no signs of foaming around the mouth that you'd see with drowning,' she murmurs. 'Could she have been dead already and fallen in?'

I nod, remembering how well her balcony lines up with the pool's deep end, and am relieved to see Kali straighten up and move towards the door. We close it behind us, then stride out of Olga's suite. Emerging into the garden, we gulp lungfuls of fresh, uncontaminated air.

'It could be an internal injury, like a haemorrhage,' Kali assesses. 'But that would need to be caused by either an untimely health incident – which may not show external signs – or an external injury, which would be self-evident.'

'Or?'

'Or, it's something that you can't see from the outside. Something like poison.' Kali confirms my own assessment. She's been honest. But partial truths are the best way to hide lies . . .

'So we'd need to know who could have tampered with her food or drink.'

As I nod agreeably, I'm thinking, *or her blood plasma.*

*　*　*

Back in the library, I'm studying Magnus across the desk. His bruised eye is puffy and bloodshot, his lip is split, and he has a tooth missing.

'I'm relieved you agreed to give a statement, Magnus.' I pause a beat, toying with him, before tightening my control of the conversation. 'For *your* sake.'

'I'll hire you. As legal counsshel. I just don't want a breath of this getting out.' I notice that his whistle is fading as he adjusts to the new gap in his gums.

'I'm flattered, but of course I can't—'

'Half a million change your mind?'

'It's not that—'

'One million? Five?'

I stare at him – and confess I'm momentarily tempted. *What would I do, with five million dollars?* But as I look at him, I see how meaningless the numbers are to him. It's disconcerting … and it feels … hollow. Adopting the moral high ground, I remind him, 'I can't represent *anyone*, Magnus. But as you're so certain of your innocence, it shouldn't be necessary.' I smile, softening him up. 'Do you regret the fight?'

He sneers. 'That snivelling little prick owes me more than a damn helicopter ride. If he'd had any sense, he'd've stood aside. But he's thick as pigshit. I got more secrets on him than a fucking sorority. And he can't see I owe him nothin' now.' He shakes his head like he's spoiling for another fight.

I hold my breath, in case he's angry enough to run on, to spill those secrets. It tugs on my hazy recollection of those scandals. But how many are there?

'I don't regret hitting him.' He flexes his fingers, with their scabbed knuckles. 'I *do* regret trashing Olga's art. Chucking it at Hugh. And *missing*.' He shakes his head. 'The rest of the night is a bit of a blur. Charles took Hugh away. I had a drink. I think it was Uri who pushed me towards my room, telling me to sleep it off.'

'What happened after Uri helped you to your room?' I ask.

If Uri *did* help Magnus to his room, then it's unlikely he'd had the chance to apologise to Kali. I wonder if her little face-saving lie means that larger lies might come easier to her …?

'Fell asleep in the armchair, in my clothes.' He tugs at his trousers, like I hadn't noticed they were the same, creased and rumpled.

He doesn't say more than he needs to; he's guarded, like he's withholding something.

'And . . .?' I invite more details.

'And what?' He shrugs. 'Then I woke up in the morning.'

'You slept straight through?'

'Like the innocent.' The split in his lip makes his attempt to smile extra sinister.

I ignore his provocation. 'What woke you in the morning, then?'

'Couldn't say. It seemed like I heard somethin'. A scream, maybe. I had a thick head, I didn't want to move, but I took a leak, drank some water, then heard more noise. I came out to see what was going on. But there was nothing to see. So I headed downstairs.'

'How did you feel?'

'Hungover.'

'Not worried?'

'What about?'

'The upcoming sign-or-decline ceremony. The one you were so desperate to escape.' I glare at his bloodied knuckles and mouth. 'You should find a first aid kit for your injuries.'

'Sure.' He looks unbothered by the battle scars.

'So you'd have me believe you *weren't* worried about Olga's meeting?' I laugh. 'Then I'd have to wonder why that was, Magnus. *Why*, right before the signing, were you suddenly so unaffected by Olga's threat?'

He doesn't answer, so I press him. 'Is it because you *knew* it wasn't going to happen?'

His silence borders on belligerent, so I continue, like the multitude of sergeants I've seen dealing with intractable 'no comment' interviewees.

'Is that why you didn't want to give a statement, Magnus? Is that why your first ask of me was to pay me off?'

* * *

Since Magnus left, I've been trying to compose myself. I'm more used to people confiding than holding out, and I wonder if I need to adapt my strategy.

Uri darts in through the doorway, interrupting my thoughts. 'Is now a good time?'

'Perfect.' I smile at him, hoping he'll be more forthcoming.

He doesn't let me down; as I tap my iPad to make notes, he doesn't even wait for the first question.

'You want to know what I was doing all night?' He adopts a jokingly official tone as he paces, pulling books from the shelves then pushing them back in. 'I don't think any of us could have had a restful night after that brawl and all the chaos.'

Olga wanted to shake everyone up. I can't help but wonder if she'd known the peril she was putting herself in, or if she felt as untouchable as everyone else here seems to think they are.

I rally, focusing on Uri. 'If you weren't sleeping, what were you doing?'

'I helped Magnus to his room and then . . .' He beckons me to the door. 'I'll show you.'

I wait for him to come back, then realise I'm expected to follow. I grab my iPad and rush across the great room, past the surprised faces, down the stairs to the conference room.

The chill of it hits me again. There are no creepy IVs now, and the room is blindingly bright as Uri flicks on every light. The whiteboards lining the walls are crammed with equations, graphs, abbreviated notes that make no sense.

'See?' Uri gazes around, and a smile floods his face as his shoulders drop. 'This is it.'

'What?' I frown at him. 'What am I looking at?'

Uri holds his hands up, gesturing in impatience. 'Isn't it obvious?'

I stare at spidering structural formulae of chemical compounds and complex maths.

'This is what I was doing. All night.' Uri points at a lengthy equation. 'Olga wasn't really *solving* anything. We need truly radical thinking for that. But she raised an important point: our dependency on rare earth minerals for *everything*. I've been looking at how to manufacture some, rather than mining depleting resources. They're the ultimate in appreciating assets; having a never-ending supply is *better* than creating your own gold mine.'

He points at a diagram. 'I *think* I've had a breakthrough. The key piece that *might* make it possible. And *if* I could just get a signal, and call my lab, I could get them working on it *today*.' He paces again, giving a very convincing impression of being agitated at the delay.

He seems immune to my scepticism as he follows the coded notes spidering around the room. I *could* believe this is genuine excitement, and it's as contagious as the fear that gripped us all last night. But this is my best chance to validate that it's real.

'So you've solved this critical global problem. Alone. In one night.'

'Yep. That's what I do.' He's gazing at the wall, eyes flicking along the formulae, with quiet satisfaction. His understated certainty is like electricity. 'It's just … giving yourself the gift of time to think about it, isn't it? I didn't know what to do last night. I usually only sleep for four hours, and I catch up with my teams across the world late at night and early in the morning. But I couldn't do that last night, so I was … restless. My brain just never stops. I need to feed it. Keep it busy. And I kept thinking back to what Olga and I had discussed.'

His critique of her approach wasn't a discussion, but he clearly sees it differently.

'I have no way of telling if this really took you all night – or if you were … otherwise engaged, then scrawled this out in twenty minutes. I can't decipher it.'

'You can decipher it if you want.' He shrugs again. 'You're choosing not to, because you think you can't. You're capable, you just have to mentally apply yourself to it.'

'Fine.' I reach for my phone to take pictures, then realise I don't have it. My heart sinks. Pulling out my iPad to take notes instead, I remember it has a camera, and start snapping photos of every inch of the whiteboards. 'I'll give myself the gift of time to think about it.'

'Smart.' He points at me, grinning. 'I *knew* you'd be smart. I *knew* you'd get it. I better get you to sign an NDA. You can't appropriate my IP.'

His concern over intellectual property rights and his apparent keenness for me to scrutinise his work makes me re-evaluate him. Maybe this is all gobbledegook and he's trying to make it sound realistic.

I must remain objective. 'Uri, when Olga pitched us the Pledge, she said you use AI software for military defence, so your specialist tech would be Fort-Knox secure, unhackable. You both exchanged a significant look. Was she making a point? *Is* there an issue?'

He folds his arms. 'Who knows, with Olga? She had a rich imagination. She had plenty of theories, and she likes to think she can manipulate you, doesn't she? Even *you* weren't immune. You said what she wanted to hear, against your better judgement.'

As I feel my face flame, he nods. 'If you're playing sleuth, be careful what you read in people.' He reaches out, touches my arm. 'I'd hate for you to accuse the wrong person.'

His tone is so kind, so full of genuine concern, that I have to force myself to remember how impervious he seemed to Olga's threat: that he either felt certain he could think his way out of it … or he knew he wouldn't have to.

*   *   *

Returning to the great room, I find Hugh looking irritated. He follows me, making clear it's under sufferance, as he yanks out a chair to sit across the desk from me.

'How are the injuries, Hugh?' I feign a sympathetic smile, looking at his split cheek.

He waves away the concern. 'Barely a scratch. It's not like it was a war zone.'

'Hmmm.' He has no knowledge of war zones, despite the medals on the dress uniform he parades in every Remembrance Day, alongside those who do. 'Of course, Magnus—'

'… Has come off worse, and it's no more than he deserves,' Hugh instructs me, as if all he has to do is make a statement firmly enough and it will magically become true.

'No,' I disagree on principle. 'No, I'm not sure that anyone deserved that. And what an embarrassment; two grown men fighting like that. It was a disgrace.'

I enjoy the fact that he's turning purple, gaping like a fish, so I press him: 'Why were you so driven to that?'

'I … he … I needed … *Well*.' He huffs.

'I don't think that's an explanation, Hugh. Why the need to debase yourself like that? Why were you so desperate to leave?'

'You heard what Charles said,' he blusters. 'You heard his warning. I *had* to leave.'

'So you thought Charles was right?'

'I … he … I …'

133

'Or not?'

Hugh frowns and I wonder if this man has ever had an independent thought. If he even knows how to critically evaluate anything at all. 'What were you afraid of?'

'Afraid? Don't be bloody daft—'

'You were fighting like your life depended on it. You certainly looked afraid.'

'I didn't want the shame of it,' he hisses. 'For the *Family's* sake. Can you *imagine*?'

I nod. 'Yes, I can, and I rather think that was Olga's gambit.'

'If Magnus hadn't been an arse, I could have got away. The man's a festering turd.'

'Nice way to talk about someone who's rescued you many times.' I prod, hoping he'll reveal more than Magnus. 'Did it ever occur to you to *stop getting into* compromising situations?'

'Those things are private.' He clamps his lips shut but it looks like it takes effort.

'Maybe Magnus thought it was your turn to repay the favour?'

'What do you mean, *repay*?'

'Ah.' I laugh out loud. 'I forget, Hugh. Whyever would you need to?'

'If he had a shred of decency, he'd have realised I took priority.' Hugh nods, believing my tight smile is sincere. I'll leverage his imagined rapport.

'Last night, after Charles escorted you to your room, what did you do?'

'Well … I … I … *Slept*. Obviously.'

Hugh isn't in last night's clothes, so he did at least shower and change. I'm surprised at the evidence of competent, independent life. If ever a royal needed a groom of the stool, it's this one. But I have to *try* to wonder if I could have underestimated him.

'I always wake at oh-six-hundred hours.' He alludes to his brief tenure in the Navy. 'A few exercises, quick shower, dress.' It's only then that I notice another cut on his cheek, from shaving. I wonder if he was shaken, or rushing.

'Were you in a hurry?' I tap my own cheek to indicate the nick. 'Maybe you wanted to see Olga? Try another way to extricate yourself?'

'No. I . . . I needed to find Charles. I was relying on him to get me out of the frame.'

I raise my eyebrows. 'Out of the frame, Hugh?'

'Ah. Well. Out of the meeting.'

'And what did you expect Charles to do, exactly?' I ask. 'To get you out of it?'

'Well . . . I . . . I couldn't say. But Charles always has a plan.'

Does he, indeed? My stomach drops at that. Swallowing back the roiling nausea, I manage to ask, 'You think you can call someone Judas – and still rely on them?'

Was that accusation the final straw for Charles? After all the things he's done for Hugh – most of which I'm sure I'll never want to know about – was that a push too far?

Is Charles capable of this?

A new horror rises. What if there was more to trashing the comms than preventing us from raising the alarm about Olga? What if it's to stop us getting any help *now* – because the killer is going to strike again?

My mind races over the facts of the remote, isolated setting, and the impossibility of separating Hugh from his equerry. Is this why the comms are trashed? Is having Hugh in this vulnerable state an opportunity too good – and too rare – to pass up?

Is Hugh the next target?

Chapter 11

Sunday 6th April – 11 a.m.

As I join the rest of the company, I'm aware of the abrupt silence, the shifty looks the air that's pulsing with expectation – and resentment.

Always one for addressing the elephant in the room, I brace myself to acknowledge it. 'Thanks for your statements.' I give a businesslike nod – like that's all this has been, just an act of lawyerly due diligence, not a valuable fact-gathering expedition – and head to the coffee machine in the corner, in desperate need of caffeine and something to do.

'Happy now you've played detective?' Magnus drawls from across the room.

Glancing up, I notice someone has cleared up from last night. As I select a coffee blend to brew, I wonder who it was. Then I notice that everyone is glaring at me, while shooting each other sidelong, pointed looks. I take my time slotting the coffee pod into the machine and choosing a delicate artisan mug, while trying not to seem unnerved.

Uneasy whispers flutter just beyond my grasp. I don't mean to glance up, to scan the group, but I can't help it.

They seem to have moved closer. Kali is now standing, and Zyra's edging forward. Magnus has swivelled his plush chair to face me. This is how lions move in for the kill.

The sea of faces share the same expressions: accusation, outrage, revolt.

'Happy now, Thea? Now you've lorded it over all of us?' Hugh's voice is iced with threat as he paces towards me. 'You've always seen yourself as the one with the brains, though, haven't you. Think you're cleverer than the rest of us. Such a party killer.' His lips twitch. 'But is that the *only* thing you've killed?'

'*Wh*-at?' I hate the tremor in my voice. I try to pass it off as a laugh, as disbelief.

'Well, that's what we're all asking ourselves.' Hugh nods at Magnus, who stands, drags his chair to the middle of the room, then pushes me into it, making me spill coffee onto the porcelain floor.

Fear floods my stomach: only a common enemy unites two warring parties like Hugh and Magnus as fast as this, and I can see, plain as day, that *I'm* that enemy . . .

My heart's *thumping* but I cannot afford to look weak. I know – right in the depths of my gut – that any hint of weakness now will be deadly.

'Why else would you be so keen to take our statements?' Estelle asks as she glides over, like a beautiful serpent. 'To question *us* and our actions? It's classic deflection.'

'Yeah, you're trying to make it look like we have something to hide,' Magnus asserts.

'Who have you decided to point the finger of suspicion at?' Kali demands, hands on her hips.

I try to downplay it. 'Look, I'm just getting ahead of the admin. We'll all have to give a statement – me included – once the authorities can get here. I'm just making sure we gave them while everything was easy to recall. To make this easier for all of us.' I fall back on the original logic that had won them over. 'After all, the murderer is the only person here who *won't* want to follow the standard protocol.'

I've gathered myself now. I should have expected this. They've all had time to collude, to share their fears and their opposition to what I'm doing.

At least Asha will be an ally. But, as I let my gaze travel steadily around the room, Asha won't meet my eyes.

Dread thuds in my gut like an executioner's drum.

'So where's *your* statement, then?' Hugh asks. He circles behind me, to unnerve me – and it's working. My skin shivers at the sense of a net closing in on me, a trap that I can't escape. But I refuse to twist around, to look rattled, to expose my fear.

'Yeah, we've all been wondering what *you* might be coverin'' up,' Magnus adds. He and Kali prowl around me, like predators waiting for the moment I'm worn down enough for them to strike.

'No one's questioned *you*, have they?' Magnus snarls, pushing his face near mine. I'd laugh – if it wasn't so petrifying. His features are twisted with frustrated rage and displaced fear: offence as the best defence is being put into action, right in front of me.

Asha sits on the periphery, unable to mark herself out as a non-colluder, while Charles looks like a reluctant participant who can't quite bring himself to defend me.

Only Uri stands apart, still studying us like he's the lab professor, taking notes on our behaviour under these testing circumstances. All the others circle me, challenging me, like a pack. Their avid faces are lighting up with the awakening arousal of the scent of blood.

'*We* should question *you*,' Kali says. '*Now*. Just to make sure the record is complete. I'd hate for us to miss something.'

'Go ahead.' I sit back and sip the remnants of my mostly spilled coffee, trying to show how relaxed I am while fighting to steady my shaking hand. 'I'll answer any questions you have.'

'OK then. Where were *you* all night and this morning?' Zyra asks, and I sense her enjoyment at a revenge interrogation.

'After the arguments in here, like most of you, I left for bed. I felt exhausted from the travel, and the unexpected ask from Olga, and ... everyone *else's* ... *response* to it.' I pause, letting them all be reminded that my own reaction wasn't so extreme – because it didn't need to be. 'I was so tired I didn't even brush my teeth.' I pull a face. 'How's that for honest?'

Estelle and Zyra grimace.

'And this morning?' Magnus asks.

'I woke up to the sound of a scream. I headed towards it – I didn't know at that time it was coming from Olga's private garden. I found Asha there, with Olga. Who was dead by then.' I take a long breath, and hope that they'll all think it's prompted by the memory of finding her, rather than my fear of how this interrogation will go.

'She was already dead when *I* found her,' Asha adds, her eyes darting around the room as suspicious gazes swing towards her.

I press sweaty palms onto the seat fabric and take another long breath.

I'm amazed that no one challenges my account. No one has noticed that my stated route would take me through Charles's garden – making the link that Olga had put my husband and I in separate suites. And they all believe I went straight to bed;

no one knows that I spent the night in the shadows, watching my husband betray me.

'Tell them, Thea,' Asha prompts.

I refocus. We'd got up to Olga being found . . . murdered . . .

'Tell them Olga must have been dead a while by the time we got there . . .?' Asha pleads.

'I don't know when you got there, Asha,' I remind her. At her widening eyes, I relish a spiteful gleam of satisfaction that she, like anyone else, could replace me in this particular hot seat at any time.

Her defiant glare shows me how little she likes it – but also how much I could use an ally. So I soften the blow, a reminder of our alliance. 'Though, based on my professional experience, rigor mortis had already set in. Meaning Olga had been there a while.'

Asha, visibly grateful, nods at me. As if trying to prove her loyalty, she deflects the interrogation. 'Charles, I've been wondering how you scored one of the preferential rooms, right next to Olga. Were you having an affair?' Her tone is innocent, light, like an illicit relationship with our recently murdered host isn't a big deal.

All eyes skewer him now, avid for gossip.

'How bloody parochial of you.' Charles scoffs. 'Whether I was or wasn't, it's no one's business. Least of all petty moralisers.'

'So that's a yes, then,' Asha says. 'And it was a useful arrangement, wasn't it? Being neighbours. You got to spy on everyone's comings and goings, didn't you?'

Collective jaws – and pennies – drop at that, in light of my own revelations when taking statements. I can feel the mob mentality rising again.

Zyra, Estelle and Kali all flick guilty glances at Charles, then me, and I nearly chuckle at the brief slips of their masks.

Kali is first to rally. 'What's your story, Charles? Were you with Olga?'

Charles shrugs, as if inviting further interrogation so he can refuse to answer. Like this is sport.

'Why, exactly, are we treating Charles like a witness when we should be treating him as a suspect?' Hugh asks, a leer on his face.

I stare at him, my theory about their fracturing relationship confirmed, and the clamouring in my head rises again. The loyal bond between him and Charles has worried me for years. In any other circumstances, I'd rejoice at Hugh breaking off that attachment. *But now . . .?* Fear churns. *Why is Hugh turning traitor* now?

And what might Charles be driven to do about it?

As Hugh throws my husband to the wolves, I feel my breath catch, and scan the company for their reactions.

The hot attention that had burned in my direction moments ago is blazing towards Charles now. I see him shift as he tries, like I did, not to look ruffled. His neck is turning puce.

I can't help wondering if he *does* have something more than his affair to hide. Unease squirms. Why else wouldn't he explain himself?

One thing I do know: he's not holding back to spare my feelings . . .

'Why? What motive could Charles have?' Magnus asks. I can't help noticing the hopeful, predatory note in his voice.

'Oh, I don't know.' Hugh shrugs, a swagger in his step as he begins to circle Charles. 'Petty jealousy. Spite. Envy. Classic user, aren't you, Charles? Befriending people for what they can do for you and treading on them once you've used them.'

Hugh voices his own fear: that people like him for his position, not for who he is. He'd be right about that, though I'd substitute 'like' with 'tolerate'.

'You didn't want to be part of Olga's plan, either, did you, Charles?' Magnus says. 'Look how fast he talked *you* out of it, Hugh. I know you always need someone to think on your behalf – but once Charles had joined the dots *for* you, your motive was bigger than all of ours, now I think about it.'

'But *I* wasn't sleeping with the enemy, was I?' Hugh's tone is vicious. 'Collecting all your secrets. Using them against you. Did she spurn your charms, Charles? Turn you away? Laugh at your inability to satisfy her? Is that why you killed her? Were you saving your ego, or saving your career? Or did you have another motive for murder?'

'Oh, for God's sake.' Charles stands, pushing against Hugh's body, which is looming over him. Then he pauses, his face close to Hugh as he chokes out the words, 'I thought *you*, of all people …' He can't finish the sentence. He stares into the eyes of his once-trusted – what, friend? Associate? Loose cannon? Liability?

I still can't fathom the nature of their relationship, or what is passing between them now, but as Charles shoves past Hugh and storms out, in the direction of his room, I feel unsettled.

The same panic that's fluttering in my throat is flickering around the room, in the form of sidelong glances, frowns, winces and shaking of heads.

'What was that about?' Kali demands of Hugh.

He gapes at her, and I watch, intrigued at how he'll respond to being asked to explain himself – and by a woman, at that.

'What did he mean by "you of all people"?' Kali presses him, undaunted by his reaction. 'Were you in on it together? Did you both plot to kill Olga?'

'I … *No!* How bloody preposterous!' He's blustering, backing away. His eyes dart around the room, looking for someone to dive in and rescue him, to mop up the mess. Like usual.

But Kali steps forward, not letting him distance himself from her barrage of questions. 'You certain about that? You seem to think people are pretty disposable. You sure you weren't making us question Charles to hide your own guilt?'

'*Guilt?* Me?' He stops in his tracks, gawping at the alien concept. 'I think you're forgetting who you're talking to.'

'I know a little light murder probably doesn't seem like a crime to you. Considering mass murder was required to put your family in their position. So thank you for the reminder that your moral compass is more than a little . . . *off* . . . compared to the rest of ours.'

'Hardly.' Hugh scoffs. 'But if you're accusing me of having dubious morals,' he sneers, 'then it looks like I'm in good company.'

If nothing else, Hugh has learned to quit while he's ahead, beating a retreat under the force of Kali's indignant glare. I notice he heads off in the same direction as Charles, and the back of my neck tingles.

Kali turns to the rest of us, and I see the strain on her face. 'Well, *one* of us here is a killer.' She scans the company and we all shift, as if she can see our secrets. 'And while Hugh might be a cesspool of immorality, I don't know for certain he's done anything. Whereas I *do* know, Thea, that you and Charles have both leveraged your positions to gain knowledge on the rest of us.' She glares at me. 'And I don't like that.'

Magnus shakes his head. 'I don't either. I don't like this at all.' He stares at me and fear swells again.

'Oh, come on, Kali. I just tried to get some statements together. If I had anything to hide, I'd have kept a low profile.'

Her head tilts as she regards me. 'No. No, somehow, I don't think you would. I think you're too clever – or at least you *think* you're too clever – for that. You'd lean into the part of the system that you know. And you'd try to find out where you can point the blame.'

'OK. So follow that theory through to its conclusion,' I challenge.

At her frown, I shrug. 'See? I haven't blamed anyone.'

'You haven't. But you've made sure to steer the rest of us towards blaming Charles, given he's the only one who could have given you the information you used against us.'

'Firstly – how can I use anything against you if you haven't done anything? And secondly, why would I accuse my own husband?' I affect a laugh, but I can see the obvious riposte coming.

'Because that's the neatest outcome, surely. Killing his mistress and framing him; you get rid of them both without the inconvenience of a divorce and settlement negotiations. Win, win, *win*.'

'I wish I could negotiate life as well as you, Kali. But I'm just a lawyer, used to finding a path through the chaos. Not creating it.'

Her eyes narrow at that, but her body relaxes a little.

'And I will just say this. Charles and I haven't had a monogamous relationship for many years. So he may have had a dalliance, but he hasn't been unfaithful, in the fullest sense of the word. And even if he *had*, it doesn't mean that I'm the guilty party. And it bloody well wouldn't make him the innocent one.'

I see Kali's eyebrow twitch and I wonder if I've found common ground here. Maybe we've both been wronged by an unworthy partner.

'It's lovely that we've fixated on who's sleeping with who.' Estelle tries to disguise her fear with a bored drawl. 'But I'd really rather focus on who's been doing the killing. So that I can actually sleep tonight.'

'Me too.' Zyra stands with her. 'I don't feel safe here. We must be able to do *something*?' She turns to Uri. 'Did you get the radio working?'

'Not yet.'

I shoot him a sidelong smile, appreciating the fact that he didn't say 'no.'

'I'll try again after lunch,' he reassures her.

'And what happens if it's too broken to repair?' Estelle asks.

'Exactly.' Zyra sticks close to Estelle. 'What's the plan? If we can't get away, or call the authorities, then don't we have the right to make ourselves safe?'

Ohh. As she voices what everyone's thinking, I glance around, wondering what we *will* do.

'Because I feel like we're trapped.' Zyra swallows. 'Like we're . . . just target practice.'

Uri shakes his head. 'A random attack is unlikely. Though I do agree that the killer will strike again. Even if they didn't *originally* plan to, you only have to watch a coupla episodes of *Columbo* to know that when someone's killed once, they have to keep going to cover their tracks. That's pure logic in action.' He nods gravely at all the faces turned towards him, then – when they all turn back to barrage me with questions – grins with glee.

He turns his hands up, raising his eyebrows at me, when Estelle winces and asks, 'Oh no. What if some of us heard, or saw, something that incriminates the killer? Without us knowing it was significant?'

'So what are we doing, then?'

'Are we just gonna wait? For someone else to be killed?'

'Oh God!' Zyra covers her ears, shaking her head.

I can't answer. I'm wondering what the killer *did* originally plan; if trashing the radio comms was less a message, and more a device to make sure the next victim can't be rescued before they're killed.

Uri's still grinning, like this is a game. 'Yeah, Thea. We need to *do* something.'

'What do you suggest, Uri?' Kali snaps. 'That we work out who it is? Lock them up?'

'Yes!' He pauses to think about it, and I see the idea take hold as everyone leans forward, eyes bright for battle. 'Yes. That could work.'

Kali pauses, assesses him, then nods. 'We'd only have to secure the person for a night ... maybe two, while we figure out how to make contact with our people. Even if we can't, by then our teams will be in touch, and they'll alert the authorities, who can make an arrest.'

I try to quell the contagious rise of vigilante fervour. 'You can't forcibly – *realistically* – lock someone up, though—'

'Yes, we can.' Estelle's disagreement is polite but firm. 'There are enough of us.'

'Citizen's arrest, Thea. You legal eagles gotta know all about that, right?' Uri is enjoying this too much.

'Yeah. Point me at 'em.' Magnus cracks his knuckles. Previously I'd have laughed at this lazy, overweight bloke casting himself as the muscle of the group, but after seeing him land a few punishing punches on Hugh, I'm more wary.

As the group all turns to me, accusation in their eyes and hungry for blood, I find myself shrinking back into the chair again, clammy-palmed.

Oh God ... they're going to accuse me? They're going to try to lock me up ...

Chapter 12

Sunday 6th April – 11.30 a.m.

I FACE THEIR STARES, BRACING MYSELF for the onslaught. My swallow is dry. I just about manage to shrug as fear lumps in my throat.

'We'll need the room key,' Magnus says.

My heart is hammering at the thought of being accused; of being incarcerated. 'Surely this is all a bit much—'

'Yes, and once we've locked them in their room, we can keep the key,' Zyra says.

'W-what if you've got the wrong p-person?' I stammer. 'And then the real killer uses the key to get *into* the room?'

'Jam something under the door handle.' Estelle is so matter of fact about it that my blood runs cold. I suspect that's also part of her nightly routine when she's away on shoots.

'Besides, if we've made a mistake, and leave the real killer to roam free, they're not likely to go after the patsy, are they?' Kali's cold logic snatches away any hope of reasoning my way out of this.

I lean into my desperation. 'How are you going to persuade this person to meekly stay in their room so they can be locked up?' I inject as much defiance into my words as I can, but

I really, *really* don't want them to demonstrate how they'll do that.

'Easy.' Magnus's smile is sinister. 'We'll ask him nicely.'

Him?

I nearly fall off my chair with relief.

Who, though? Hugh? ... Or Charles ...?

'He won't go quietly,' Kali warns.

'Then let things escalate.' Magnus shrugs, clearly still battle-ready after last night. 'Does anyone know where the staff security passes are?' He looks around, and I glance at Asha. She's kept out of most of this, looking uncomfortable with the conflict. I wonder if she knows where the keys are, or at least where to look. And I wonder if she'll volunteer the information if she does.

I see her squirm with the dilemma.

Something in me urges her to speak up – even though my husband could well be the person they imprison.

Because if the focus is on him, at least it isn't on me.

The guilty heat of disloyalty flashes over my body, and then I nearly laugh at myself. Charles has never lost any sleep over betraying me, has he? He's made up his own rules, and I can be damned.

'Asha?' I hear the words coming from my mouth. 'Don't you know where the room keys might be kept?'

Twisting her hands in her lap, she avoids looking at us. 'I . . . I don't know, really.'

'But you've been working with Olga, haven't you?' Uri asks.

'And you've been here before.' I get to my feet, challenging her. It feels better to be on this side of the interrogation, but the urgency is still real.

She winces. 'I . . . maybe . . . I could suggest where to look. But it'll be a guess.'

'A guess is better than nothing,' Magnus says.

'Great, let's go!' Uri leaps to his feet like he's on a 'choose your own adventure' quest. He pauses only to ask, '*Where* are we going, then, Asha?'

'The office.' She stands, hesitant. 'Near the kitchen.'

We barrel, *en masse*, through the great room, to the hall with the kitchen off to the left. Beyond the Martha Stewart-esque dream kitchen, whose decor is all gleaming tropical hardwood cabinetry and thick gold-threaded marble, I catch a glimpse of the professional half, where the chef works, which is ironically clad with more stainless steel than a mortuary. Then, we reach the office.

The room has been tidied a little since I last saw it in its trashed, chaotic state, and I detect the work of Uri here in restoring order. As we all rip open the drawers and doors of the hand-built cabinets, finding only stationery and folders full of paperwork, I catch sight of our wild desperation reflected in the black screen of the computer monitor.

It's Zyra who spots the locked box on the wall and points it out to Uri; he searches the drawers for the small key and opens the box. Inside are rows of fobbed guest room keys. Copies of each one are already in our possession.

I lean across and snatch the one on the hook labelled *Hibiscus*. My room.

Suddenly, there's a scrabble as everyone else does the same. Zyra leaps back, cradling her hand, crushed in the melee. 'Jesus. Bit of patience wouldn't hurt.'

'Hey, hey, *hey!*' Uri yells, pushing everyone back.

There's no disagreement – everyone's already grabbed their key. Only three remain: Olga's, Hugh's, and Charles's. Without shame, I grab them.

'Well, then, Thea,' Magnus drawls. 'You got the keys. What you gonna do with them?'

I grip the keys tightly. The thud in my stomach thumps like a drum again, but this time I feel like the executioner.

'Jesus, Thea. I didn't think you had it in you to lock up your own *husband*.' Zyra's eyes are wide as she stares at me. It doesn't even occur to her I might not do that. It hasn't occurred to *anyone* that by taking the keys, I'm trying to *stop* that from happening.

As I look around the group, though, I see I wouldn't stand a chance. Even if I wanted to. A feral light gleams in every gaze, the scent of the hunt high on the air, thick and tangible all around us. If I don't direct this rising wrath towards Charles, it will strike at me from all directions, like a hydra.

I pray my voice won't crack. 'Let's find him, then.'

The company is almost whooping as we hunt for him, starting with his room. The sense of taking action changes the tone. Now we have to psych ourselves up for confrontation, and very possibly conflict. The spike of energy is dizzying, but I'm too anchored with guilt to be buoyed by it.

As we stride along the outside walkway, the air on my face is humid, oppressive. It slows my steps, but I'm jostled along, engulfed in the sharp scent of anxious sweat.

Charles doesn't answer his door.

'We need to go back outside,' Asha says. 'To his garden.'

I side-eye her, remembering this was how she found Olga. For all Asha's reticence, she isn't a woman who takes no for an answer.

She leads us around the lodge, to a small gap in the foliage, and pushes through. On the other side, she stops abruptly.

Oh, God ... he's not ... he's not already ... dead?

I shove through the branches, panicking as my gaze swings to search for him. I see a body in the pool. Just like Olga ...

Then a lazy arm moves.

'*Oh, God.*' I heave a sigh, then glance at Asha. 'I thought we had another body on our hands for a second.'

'So did I.' Her face is trembling, and I regret my lack of sympathy. Being the one to find Olga must have been awful.

I wait for the others to clamber through the hedge and we stand there, waiting for someone to take charge.

We all instinctively know Kali will lead the arbitration.

She's already pursing her lips, weighing Charles up as he splashes towards us. As he reaches the end of the pool, he reaches up for the whisky he's left on the side.

He starts as he catches sight of us. For a minute, he flobbles around in the water trying to find his footing. I nearly burst out laughing at how ridiculous he looks.

I realise I don't have any sympathy for him. Indifference has grown – no, *festered* – into distance, distaste and disgust.

So I don't care at all when Kali says, 'Charles, there are two ways to do this, and we'd like to do it reasonably. With dignity for all concerned.'

Worry flickers across his face.

'We're going to need to detain you until we can reach the authorities.'

'What? How?' He laughs. 'Don't be bloody ridiculous.' He searches for me. 'Tell them, Thea.'

'We're all agreed on this course of action,' Kali says.

'Oh, *thank* you, darling wife.'

'What would you have me do, Charles? Make both of us the enemy? I haven't done anything to make me a suspect.'

'Neither have I!' Charles protests.

'Except sleeping with the victim,' I can't help snapping.

'Well, at least you're getting your revenge now. Is it making you feel better?'

It isn't, but this isn't why we're here. I shrug, trying to disengage.

'We're putting you under room arrest,' Magnus confirms. 'Will you cooperate? Or will we need to make you?'

Charles groans. 'Get real. You're *not* going to do this. You don't *need* to do this. I'm not the killer.'

'What if you are, though?' Zyra insists. 'We can't have you wandering around. We need to feel safe.' She wraps her arms around herself as she glares at him.

'And you think the killer would let you incarcerate them meekly and willingly, do you?'

'Well . . .' Zyra flounders with the logic.

'And what if I'm innocent? One of you – at least – is lucking out that the attention's on me, because it's giving you – the real killer – free rein!' He glances at Zyra. 'So would you prefer I protest my innocence or not, then?'

Zyra looks confused, but Uri is grinning his annoying grin at the sight of us tying ourselves in knots.

'I have the advantage of knowing if your accusation is true or not,' Charles continues. 'And that I'll be separated from the killer by a locked door. Because the murderer will be on the other side of it. On the loose – amongst all of you.'

Zyra shudders. 'B-but . . . it *has* to be you.'

'Righto.' Charles sounds cheery. 'So you want me to cooperate with your theory: to lock me up in my suite and garden . . .' He gestures around him, about to continue pontificating, but Kali interrupts.

'No, Charles, you have to be inside your suite. Actually locked in. So that you're unable to go anywhere else.'

Charles looks to each of us in turn, as though for confirmation that she's serious. Seeing Magnus forming fists, spoiling for another fight, he laughs.

'Oh, good grief, I don't want a boxing match. I saw your form last night, Magnus, and I already know you're no challenge.

So let's keep this civilised. You want me to cooperate. So, persuade me.'

Kali's lips twitch, and I see her silently berating herself for not anticipating this.

'What have you got to offer?' Charles leans back, arms outstretched along the sides of the pool. At the dumbfounded silence, he makes suggestions. 'Kali, Uri, you both have challenges in your operations. How about moving your manufacturing and assembly lines to the UK, Kali? Or benefitting from the billion-pound investments the UK's made in AI talent, Uri? It'll be a win-win.'

Uri shakes his head. 'I've got established research labs and engineering teams. I'm not looking to change those for the sake of it.'

'Think about it. What about your data centres?' Charles persists. 'All of those could be running on clean, renewable energy. That's good business for the UK and a great benefit for you.'

'That's an *expensive* way to do business,' Magnus cautions. 'And think about the greenwashing criticism you'll get for the carbon footprint of moving those to the UK in the first place.'

'Yeah. *Exactly*,' Uri agrees. 'This is what happens when you tinker, rather than solve. You swap one problem for another.'

'We'll agree to your terms, Charles.' Kali raises her voice above the hubbub. We all stop dead, staring at her in shock. She gives Uri a hard stare. 'I'm sure I can *persuade* my colleague here.'

Charles nearly chokes on the whisky he's been swigging while we've been arguing amongst ourselves.

'So, Charles,' Kali presses, 'will you go inside so we can secure the doors and windows, please?'

Charles downs the last of his whisky, puts the glass on the side of the pool and pushes himself out of the water. He turns to Uri with a serpentine smile and a handshake. 'I look forward to doing business with you.'

He leads us all inside, but Uri nudges Kali to hang back. I dawdle, enough for them to think I'm out of earshot. 'Why did you do that?' I hear Uri whisper. 'You can't make decisions on my behalf!'

'Because it doesn't matter. It's not going to happen.' Kali turns to him with a hard stare. '*Is* it.'

The crowd hustle me along to Charles's double-storey, ultra-luxe suite. He looks amused as we all studiously make sure the room is secure. Magnus locks the bifolding doors to the garden, then Estelle checks them, and hands me the key.

'Windows are all locked, and the keys are all removed.' Uri holds them out to me as he returns from his circuit. I take them.

Charles has negotiated a safety plan: he'll barricade his doors against any potential threat, while Kali has agreed to two people preparing and bringing him his food, who will taste it in front of him like he's a bloody medieval king.

'You're the keeper of the keys, then, Thea?' Charles murmurs, his breath hot against my cheek.

'Would you rather someone else was?'

'No. I trust you. Even if you do have wicked designs on me.' His grin is as louche as it was when we were students, and I hate him for a second, for reminding me of how we once flirted.

'I've no doubt you trust me.' I arch an eyebrow. As everyone starts to leave, locking him in and giving me the remaining key, I take spiteful pleasure in whispering, 'The question is, *should* you?'

Chapter 13

Sunday 6th April – 12.30 p.m.

FOLLOWING CHARLES'S SUCCESSFUL INCARCERATION, ZYRA high-fives everyone. Even me. And she *beams*.

'We *did* it! I knew we would figure this out. We are awesome! We worked together and we're all safer now. We are stronger together.' I can tell she's used to psyching up a troupe of dancers before a stadium show.

Her optimism is heady, fizzing between us, and she slings a lean arm around Estelle's shoulders.

Their heads meet and Zyra starts singing *Walking on Sunshine*. Estelle joins in, and they dance back towards the house.

Their singing stops dead as they halt just inside the doorway, looking at the kitchen.

When we all catch them up, I see why: Hugh is miserably mooching around the larder. 'Who's making us lunch?' he barks.

The realisation of actually fending for ourselves hits me. I hide my smirk: *Hugh won't cope with this at all!*

I may hate cooking, but I'm not about to let anyone else prepare my food for me.

But, as I should have anticipated, Olga had prepared for four days with no staff. In this kitchen idyll, the walk-in larder, integrated refrigerated drawers, and massive, sub-zero fridge all have sections labelled with our names. Some provisions won't even need cooking, like kale and spirulina for Zyra's and Estelle's smoothies, the freshest oysters for Uri, and picnic fare of cured meats, pies, quiches, fruit, and crudities.

In the butler's pantry, a barbeque is set for Magnus's spare ribs, and inside a pizza oven are fresh bases awaiting toppings. A barista's fantasy of a coffee-making wall dominates one side, with pressurised and aerated wine dispensers on the other.

Olga's staff will return on Wednesday . . . I hope. So all we have to do now is wait this out. Unless Charles isn't *the killer . . .* I seem to be the only one with doubts.

'I actually think I could eat something, now he's locked up.' Zyra pokes around in the section of the walk-in fridge labelled with her name, and returns with a selection of salad leaves and vegetables that don't look enough to keep a small rabbit alive.

'What?' Hugh glares at her, then scans the company. 'Charles?' He starts to laugh, a cruel lift to his lips, and my hatred for him burns white hot. 'What have you done?'

'We locked him in his room.' Kali's voice is flat as she plates pie and salad from Charles's section of the larder. 'Who'll join me when I take Charles's lunch to his room?'

'He gets sodding *room* service?' Hugh splutters. 'If you're making something for him, make it for me.'

'He can't get his own food, because – and I appreciate you're hard of understanding, so I'll say it again – he's *locked in his room.*' Kali doesn't address his demand, and I love her for ignoring it.

'Magnus, will you join me while I take this to him?'

Hefting his shoulders like a bodyguard, Magnus nods.

Zyra and Estelle make green soupy things in the blender from Zyra's leaves and spices. As I shudder at the composty smell, Estelle proclaims, 'Mmm, delicious,' through puckered lips.

As LA-positive as ever, Zyra says, 'Well, we've handled the threat, so all we have to do is wait this out for two or three days, for either Olga's staff or our teams to reach us.'

Estelle nods, glancing at the tycoons. 'We might not have liked Charles very much, no offence, Thea, but he's saved all of you lot from giving up a fortune, and your reputations.'

There's an awkward silence at this public reminder of our individual motives.

Zyra recaptures the positive vibe. 'Yeah! He did. And now the *awfulness* is handled, we should declare today a spa day.'

'Sure.' Estelle refills her glass and the two women head across to the infinity pool with its hot tubs, ice room and rosemary-scented steam room with hammam slabs.

Asha tucks into her pre-made picnic of delicious-looking morsels, and I'm pleased to find I have the same. I load my plate with generous servings from a wide selection, featuring more cheese than a French market.

I hear Magnus's booming voice as he and Kali return. 'You know as well as I do, we already got the solutions for clean energy. Truth is, people ain't got the *appetite* for 'em.'

'What do you mean?' Zyra asks as he and Kali reach the kitchen.

'The answer's nuclear fusion. If governments invest enough, then – bang.' He brings his hands together in an unfortunate thunderclap. 'Clean fuel. But folks are wedded to oil and their profits. They don't know fission from fusion, so they get scared.'

I groan. 'Then you must know that fusion *seems* perfect, because it doesn't generate greenhouse gases, but it *does* generate radioactive waste, and – for now, at least – only yields a little more energy than it needs to start the reaction in the first place. It may be our commercial saviour, but the development will take years – and even more billions – yet.'

'It's never tech.' Uri takes his fresh seafood from the fridge. 'It's always adoption.'

'I agree with you there. But there's a solution for that too.' Magnus raises his eyebrows as he and Hugh covet the oysters. 'Start a war. That's the only thing that makes people take on new technology fast enough.'

'Oh, nice.' Kali stares at him. 'Why don't you and your Republican pals just hand out guns at school gates,' she snaps.

'This illustrates the whole situation, Kali.' Magnus opens his arms, palms up. 'Solutions may exist, but that doesn't make them possible. That's what Olga failed to understand. She had theories, but none were gonna work.' He glances towards her suite. 'At least she's been saved the embarrassment of announcing her Pledge to the world.'

Kali plates up her own food and heads to the great room, muttering, 'If a solution isn't feasible, then it isn't a solution.'

But Magnus is more concerned with seafood than semantics as he watches Uri shuck the oysters. With a wink at me, Uri loads two platters generously, leaving one in the kitchen as Hugh and Magnus practically salivate – then takes the other to the great room.

I don't stick around to see whether Hugh or Magnus win this fight for the second plate. I walk with Uri to join the others in the great room, make a G&T at the bar, then sit in the plush chair tucked away in the corner.

As Magnus and Hugh wander in, I do a double take. They both have damp shirts, as if iced oysters have been flung, and neither have anything to eat. In silence, they both raid the bar snacks. The crisps, nuts, fruits, sweets and popcorn are plentiful, but not satisfying.

They compensate for their small plates with large whiskies – and I see a powder keg being created.

One more whisky sees Hugh snoring, his chin lolling on his chest. I wander over to Magnus, offering to top up his drink. I'm buttering him up for information.

He nods so I pour, whispering to him, 'You'd think Hugh could spare you a meal.'

He gives a short laugh. 'Stupid bastard doesn't know how to make an ally.'

'Especially after you've bailed him out so many times.' I'm fishing; so far I only have rumours of the scandals from which Hugh has been rescued by someone else's payouts, but getting anything *substantiated* is another matter. The prince is basically untouchable. Since Magnus hasn't been subtle about helping him, though, I'm hoping for the murky details.

'More times than I could count. But it's a useful score to keep.' He grabs a handful of nuts and chews them. 'Even if Hugh doesn't redress the balance, the secrets are still currency.'

'Ah, always. In which case, I couldn't possibly ask you to divulge.' But I give him my best inviting smile, and nudge the rest of the plate towards him.

'Shouldn't come as a surprise to you. You and Charles were college chums with him, weren't you?' His eyes narrow at me.

I give a hesitant nod. 'We were at uni at the same time, but I wouldn't describe us as chums.'

'Your *husband* might disagree. He goes to his parties.'

'My *husband's* a politician. Leveraging Hugh's association in much the same way as you, I suspect.'

Magnus chuckles, spearing an olive. 'That's fair.' He chews thoughtfully. 'But I don't think Charles has had the same epiphany that I have.'

'Go on,' I murmur, holding onto this conspiratorial spell.

Magnus sighs. 'The guy's an idiot. He lands himself in hot water easy as breathing, hocked up to the eyeballs for a lifestyle he's jealous as all hell of, but can't afford. You Brits, you go in for the pomp and circumstance, you like appearances even more than the billionaires livin' the American dream, showing off what they've earned. But there are levels, and he didn't have enough to play at the level he wanted.'

Never enough flashes through my mind. *It's true. There's always someone with more.*

'Along the way, he got involved with some sketchy people, and I had to cover his ass too many times. And that always means trouble.' He glances at me. 'But they weren't the only type of bailouts.'

Reaching for his glass, Magnus shakes his head, then takes a long swig. 'More often, it was girls. Or boys, for that matter. The usual: sex, inappropriate behaviour.'

His lip is curling and I wonder why. 'Is this what you had the epiphany over?'

He nods. 'I got a daughter. She was a teenager when he was going to the same parties. Him and his rovin' eye and his wandering hands. Made me feel sick that he might treat *her* like that. Made me see the whole scene differently. Made me see *men* like that differently. Too many men think with the wrong organ; but it's the women they land in trouble, who pay the price.' He knocks back the rest of his drink and leans over to pour another. His hand is shaking. *Is he a functioning alcoholic?*

I'm surprised at how sincere he sounds, so I lean into the stereotype to see how he responds. 'This epiphany makes you a bit of an outlier, as a Republican, doesn't it? Women's emancipation isn't exactly a priority. Look at the horrific abortion laws the party's pushing.'

His head snaps round, his glare so searing hot that I lean back, away from him.

He's too politic to speak until he can give me the rehearsed line. 'Thea, you've been around the block enough to know no party's perfect.'

'Didn't have you down as pro-choice, Magnus. You better not let your party hear you suggesting that.'

'I didn't suggest anything, as you well know.'

'I know you can shape the policies you want with business backhanders.'

He raises his glass to me, deflecting like a pro. 'Similar to your royal family. Or at least, the ones that need a pet billionaire to bail them out.'

I don't mind being led back to Hugh, so I give him the line he's teed up for me. 'I don't see you as anyone's pet.'

That wins a chuckle, and a shared confidence. 'I didn't either, but I sure have been a schmuck. I *thought* I'd get something out of it. Some grace and favour. But, nah.'

He gives me a rueful, live-and-learn smile, and I nod. 'I think expecting manners or sense or reciprocation from Hugh is like expecting a toddler to be able to get a degree. The world serves him.'

'Yeah, I can see why. It's quite the wheeze your royals have got for themselves.' He takes another sip of whisky. 'Never seen a business plan like it, and I've seen some *slippery* ones. Kickbacks from taxpayers, charging rents above market value because *they* can monopolise in a way other businesses can't, tax law exploited in ways that would be illegal for any corporation. Offshoring profits – sending their money *out* of the country they supposedly 'rule,' whatever that means, to prevent that *same* country reaping tax benefits! Further reducing the already minimal taxes they volunteer on undisclosed accounts, while they hike up their charges for charities and your military to the *max*. It's a disgrace. And it doesn't matter what party you're in, at least back in the States, we'd go after them and get back what they owe.'

This is the same man, I remind myself, proposing *war* as the only way to get people behind technological advances. Yet he's so disgusted with how our royal family make money from us that they're less palatable to him than the ripely impeachable presidents who have headed his party.

'No offence, Magnus, but I can't say I really expected you to be the moral compass in matters of business. Not after Olga's comment about capitalism undermining your values. Why did she call you a hypocrite?'

He frowns. 'I guess she's making the point that I don't always personally agree with every value of my party. But she ain't in politics. A party has to respond to public opinion, to a point. And everyone in a party has an opinion. We can agree on a basic tenet, even if we disagree on certain points. Folk like Olga might think that disagreement is a bad thing. But in my opinion, respectful disagreement and robust debate is a surefire way to shape stronger policy. I don't see it as a disadvantage at all.'

'Oh, I couldn't agree more.' I nod, but I'm not convinced. Magnus is too smooth, too politic, for that. 'So what did Olga think you should be making a stand over, then?'

'Is that what she said?' He shrugs. 'That's got me beat. Guess we'll never know.'

I smile agreeably, even though his reply has just made me all the more determined to find out.

'So, how much did you pay, then?' I push, gently. 'To bail Hugh out?'

'Oh, a million or so.' He shrugs, like it was nothing more than buying him a pint. 'It wasn't the money that bothered me. It was whose pocket I was lining with those payouts. What that kinda person would *do* with that money. That, and Hugh was too dumb to take notice of my warnings.' He shakes his head. 'A guy like that will never learn. Doesn't *need* to learn.' He thumbs his chest. 'But *I* can. I'm not the schmuck cleaning up his mess anymore.'

He leans in, his tone low. 'And your Charles would do well to mind my advice. *He's* cleaned up plenty. Some might say he knows too much.'

Sunday 6th April – 1.30 p.m.

The afternoon takes on that weird quality of days when you lose track of time.

We've locked Charles up – but there's an unspoken risk, rumbling in the background like a distant storm, that we might have got the wrong man.

The only way we'd know for sure is if the killer has the chance to strike again ... and does.

Everyone's itchy. It's like the days between Christmas and New Year, when you're flung together with distant relatives: you have time on your hands yet nothing to do with it, and you're trying to ignore the family argument that's tainted the atmosphere for fear of things degenerating even further.

Only here, the unspoken threat isn't a disagreement; it's being cooped up with a killer. We may do our best to paper over our fight or flight instincts, but the urge to escape is overpowering.

It's simmering, making me jagged-nerved – and afraid.

After lunch, Zyra and Estelle swim in the bay. I notice their singular purpose as they swim out to the gate, bobbing under-water as they investigate it.

Over my book, I see Magnus and Hugh head towards the movie theatre, where they squabble over what to watch from the library of downloaded films, which is all we can access without internet. Meanwhile, Kali and Uri are deep in conversation about something.

My attention's drawn back to the swimmers. *Are they actually going to escape?* If they tooled up properly – and we have wetsuits, snorkels, supplies – there's a slim chance they're fit enough to reach another island. I shudder at the gauntlet of sharks and exposure.

There's no way I could do that. And after getting in the pool with Olga's body, I never want to go swimming again.

When Asha comes into the room, wiping her hands like she's been clearing up the kitchen, Uri nods at her and heads to the office.

Kali stretches and stands. 'I think I'll check out the spa.'

Asha tilts her head, angling for the invitation, and Kali obliges. 'Anyone else?'

Surprising myself, I nod and stand. Wandering out under the covered walkway, we're still sheltered from the sweltering heat; and then we don't just enter a spa, we enter a cool oasis.

Soft music complements the burbling of the full-height waterfall, cascading over fern-fringed rocks into a river that weaves across the polished floor. The landscaping is something else. The waterfall rock garden graduates into an actual cottage garden.

'Wow. You don't expect to see that inside a tropical spa,' Asha says. 'Those delphiniums are amazing.' She gestures at the spears of sapphire, hood-shaped flowers.

'Those aren't delphiniums, they're herbal species,' Kali corrects her. 'Maybe used for treatments, so they're as fresh as you can get. Or for remedies. That one treats snakebite.'

I shiver at a sudden spike of memory, of another conversation about delphiniums: my gardener insisting a plant that resembles it be removed from the garden. *What did he say it was? Something 'hood'?* I do recall agreeing, but I rarely contradicted him …

But Kali doesn't look concerned. 'Olga's quite the specimen collector.' She continues walking towards the pools and indulgent treatment rooms. Amazing scents roll towards me: herby, cleansing lungfuls of rosemary and salt, a heady hit of jasmine, and rich notes of osmanthus.

Tempting as it is, I hesitate. No amount of spa time will make me feel relaxed today. The act of trying to unwind will just make me even more fraught. 'I might go back and read.'

'Me too,' Asha says. She tries to loosen her shoulders. 'I can't really get into the spa vibe today.'

'Well, I'll do my best to enjoy having this place to myself.' Kali smiles. 'See you later.'

As we leave, Asha nudges me. 'How do you feel about Charles being locked up?'

I think carefully about my reply. I daren't disagree with Charles being scapegoated. I'm afraid that if he's freed, the next person to be locked in their room will be me. And if someone *has* to be in the firing line, then frankly, I'd rather it was him.

Asha presses for an answer. 'Do you really believe he's *guilty*? What if it's someone *else*?' She tilts her head towards the main house as we dawdle along the walkway. 'What if we locked up the wrong person, and the real murderer is still among us? And, like Uri said, might kill someone else?'

Chapter 14

Sunday 6th April – 2.30 p.m.

I F WE BELIEVE THAT THE real killer is still on the loose, returning to the main house is unthinkable.

'Do you want to check on Charles?' Asha asks. 'Don't you think he's *innocent*?'

My mouth is too dry to answer. I realise Asha is steering me towards the lodge. As much as I'm trying to avoid the main house, there's no way I want to see Charles.

'I think we should check on Olga,' I suggest, striding towards her room. 'I keep thinking about her decomposing in her bathroom. Is there anywhere else we can move her to?'

Asha shoots me a sidelong glance, but soon we're staring at the covered corpse, which gives off a scent that's quite distinct to Olga's luxe oud and ambergris.

'There's a massive walk-in refrigerator and another walk-in freezer. But that would mean moving, or using, or dumping that food.'

I can see those options starting a mutiny. No one would live with a corpse in the kitchen. I certainly don't want to. Not now that Olga's thin arm, dangling below the crisp white luxe-thread-count sheet, is already turning green, her hand livid.

In desperation, I suggest, 'What about the staff quarters? Won't that also have a kitchen with a freezer and a fridge?'

Asha's eyes widen. 'Brilliant! Yes! And if we empty them to put Olga in there, we can bring the food back with us. Earn some brownie points by increasing supplies.' She eyes me. 'Just in case Magnus and Hugh raid everyone else's again.'

My nod is grim. I know Kali and the others are confident that their teams will insist on getting hold of them – and I'm not disagreeing that those moguls will be in high demand. But that's quite different from being able to make contact, deploy transport and breach the harbour gate. All those things could take painful extra hours, or even days.

I can hear time ticking by, like there's an ever-present clock hanging over us – or a bomb.

'So if we bring food back on the quad bike,' I say, appraising Olga's form, 'How do we get her over there? A three-mile hike, you said? Through jungle?'

'Well, there's a track. You don't need to hack a path.' She frowns for a moment, then nods. 'There's a gardening hut. It might have a wheelbarrow?'

As Asha dashes off to see, I reflect on how keenly she's taken up this idea. I'm horribly aware that she knows this place better than I do. She clearly isn't going to volunteer to go alone, though.

She returns, looking pleased with herself. 'Found one!' She wheels it right into Olga's suite, through the bifolding doors, parallel parking barrow alongside body.

'Ash, only one of us can wheel her. And only one of us need ride the quad bike on the way back.'

'Safer as a pair, aren't we? And then we can share pushing her. It'll be really hard going. I couldn't do it alone.'

We haven't told anyone what we're doing, or where we're going. But, now that I'm looking at Asha, I don't want to go with her, either.

I gaze beyond Olga's garden, to the jungle. It's a terrifying prospect. But I'd rather go by myself, than go with someone who could be a killer, into a hostile environment where a fatal accident will be all too easy to fake.

There's something else, too, and the thought is making my pulse fizz. This is maybe my only chance – a rare, dazzling chance – to scour the staff building for any other means of contact. A radio, a satphone, *anything*. If there's something to be found, I don't want anyone else getting to it first. I can't risk another person obstructing my only means to make contact with the world beyond this island.

The effort of heaving Olga's body into the barrow is a harsh reality check. Slim though she is, she's still so heavy and unwieldy, it almost makes me think twice … *But … what if I find something?*

'I'll take her, on my own.'

Asha stares at me. 'Really? But … do you know where you're going?'

'Yes. Roughly. I'll work it out.'

'It's a long way there, on your own. Nearly three miles.'

Ugh. That'll be tough, especially in this heat. This is the worst time of day to do it, of course, but hopefully I'll be shaded from the blazing sun. I can't let her see a flicker of regret – or I'll be heading off into the jungle with her. And I'd rather risk it alone …

'I'll be fine.' I smile with bravado I don't feel. 'And I'll bring back supplies.'

Trying not to shudder, I focus on the benefit of the trip as I steer Olga's sheet-covered body out of her lodge and around the building. I find the trail to the staff quarters. It's just two tyre tracks heading straight into the jungle, with vegetation sprouting between them. I pick one track to aim my wheel along, and the barrow bumps and judders over the rutted earth.

The blaze of the sun makes it feel like I've walked into an oven. Sweat slicks over my body in an instant, my top lip tanging with my own salt.

Glancing around, I flinch at a bird chirruping in song as it flits between branches. But I'm sure no one has seen me. No one except Asha – who waves, then turns to the house.

The weight of what I'm doing grows heavier as I plunge into the dark depths of dense vegetation. Just a few metres in, my shoulder is brushing leaves.

I'm terrified of walking on. I'm scared of what might be creeping and crawling around in there, and I'm scared that someone will follow me, and *attack* me, while I'm alone.

Things ... *creatures* scuttle and slide and I shudder. Sticky cobwebs cling to my cheek. I take a trembling step forward. *Just keep going.* The line I need to follow is literally marked on the ground, I just need to walk. It's three miles, so I have water and I'm wearing boots from the sets provided for guests who want to enjoy a nature hike.

I cannot believe anyone would be crazy enough to enjoy *this ...*

The track narrows as trees close in on each side, vines dangling overhead, swaying like snakes. Shuddering, I try to balance keeping my wits about me while not freaking out, imagining what's there. I scan the ground, the branches around and above me, petrified of something dropping from the canopy right onto me. The jungle fills my nostrils with the earthy, humid, dark scents of a dangerous, alien world. I might be an environmental lawyer, but I never really wanted to get this intimate with any actual ... *environments ...*

A lime-green, arrow-headed snake slithers, fast as lightning, across the ground, ahead of the wheel. I jump back, squealing in horror, and another immediately flashes right in front of my booted toe. I'm nearly sick with fright.

Sweat slicks as my heart *pounds*. I'm sure animals can smell fear and, if they can, I have to be ripe with terror. I'm fighting the overwhelming urge for *flight*, to dash in any direction, but I know that won't help; I'll just have less control over legs that are rapidly turning to jelly. I can't do anything other than walk on steadily.

Somehow, I manage it, despite several more snakes criss-crossing the path, millimetres from the wheel – *and my feet*. I shudder, heaving, shaking, but I'm committed.

I have to continue.

It's not just snakes that fill me with dread: despite the sun, the jungle is so dense that the filtered light is gloomy, and it heightens my fear that someone could have followed me. I'm alert to every insect chirp, which are nearly constant, every rustle of the lush vegetation. I'd be checking continually over my shoulder, if I weren't so fixated on what's under my feet and over my head. I'm as twitchy as a deer in the open, exposed for attack.

An incline builds and it tests my stamina as I realise how unsuited a wheelbarrow is for moving a dead body. The wheel looks nearly flat, and every stone or rock needs extra oomph – that I do not have – to manoeuvre over it. With my hands occupied, I can't swat away the million mosquitoes that besiege my sweaty skin. I can't even scratch the infernal burning bites that balloon immediately in their wake.

Away from the chill of the air con, slowly baking in the heat, Olga's aroma is becoming … more pronounced. Flies and midges are buzzing above her, and I'm scared the smell will attract gruesome carrion feeders.

As badly as I want to make progress, I'm forced to pause, to catch my breath. Panting, I flex hands that are sore from the pressure of the handles. Tracing the initial tender patches of blisters, I wonder how I can protect my skin. I didn't think to bring gloves. I stretch my aching back, and know that I've barely dented the journey across this treacherous terrain. It isn't restful to dawdle under a living canopy. I'm terrified of something sliding down the back of my neck, and my hackles are prickling so much that it feels like a hundred creatures are already doing exactly that.

I need to get on with this – urgently. Heading onwards, as briskly as I can manage with the load, I try to keep my mind occupied. Asha pressing me on whether I really believe Charles to be guilty weighs as heavy as this wheelbarrow.

Is he innocent? I can imagine him doing plenty of unsavoury things – but not killing. *Surely* … So … does that mean we wasted the chance to imprison the real killer?

I shiver, glancing around me, my sense of impending doom building.

With a swallow, I try to focus, running through everyone's motives and behaviour.

Uri and Asha seem to be the least affected by Olga's proposal, but impressions can be deceptive. Asha may have an organisational role here, but that's given her useful knowledge to make planning a murder easier.

Uri is so self-sufficient that he seems unassailable. But that could equally be hubris – and the knowledge that he's dealt with the threat.

Dear God, this hill and Olga's weight will surely kill me.

Zyra might be upset enough about Olga's attempt to control her. Magnus and Hugh were so desperate to not be embroiled in a scheme destined to fail that they literally fought for the chance to escape.

I'm ... not ... pausing again ... keep going ... keep going ... Sweat trickles from my forehead and slicks down my back, my hands stinging.

Kali and Estelle had grievances enough to send them marching off to Olga. But did they just try and dissuade her – or did they act?

Ah! The top of the hill! I gasp in hot, earthy air – and with it, a pungent hit of Olga's ripening aroma.

At least I can hurry along the next section, which pitches slightly downhill. Cresting the embarrassingly shallow summit, I nearly have to trot as the wheelbarrow picks up momentum. I peer along the narrow track, hoping to catch sight of the staff quarters in the distance – no such luck – so I don't notice the rock. The wheel bounces, juddering the barrow off course, then I trip on the same rock – and the wheelbarrow lurches, tipping sideways.

Olga rolls, then thuds to the rocky earth with a sickening wet slap. A high, hot stench of putrefaction shoots into the air and I realise something must have ruptured.

Sure enough, as I force myself to look, catching the reek – *ugh* – and half turning away, I see something dark and oozing around her abdomen, blurring into the sheet tangled around her corpse.

I hunker down, studying her. Her body is so slight that she looks deceptively easy to lift and slip back into the wheelbarrow, but I know it's a lost cause. *What the hell can I do now?*

From here, I'm disturbed to see how alive the ground is. Tides of insects – the most horrific things I've ever seen, with peculiar head-claws and unreasonable amounts of scuttley legs – march across the terrain with more purpose than an invading army. If I linger too long, I can all too easily imagine being sliced and diced a trillion ways and carried away to alien compound nests, to feed the incubating eggs of some horrific over-organised creature that communicates through waggling antennae.

But before I can jump up, I hear something slithering in the wheelbarrow. I hold my breath. Did something terrible sneak in and hitch a lift under the cover of the cadaver?

One of those godawful lime-green arrow-headed snakes pushes its way up the barrow's steep side – then halts on the edge, eyeball to eyeball with me.

I squirm away from it, only too aware that the undergrowth is heaving with them, that I could be encroaching on *hundreds* if I back away from this *one*.

As I scramble to my feet, the snake I'm fixated on recoils, poised to strike. Its body ridges with muscles, all taut control, its plan of attack clear. *Great.* In my corner, I have panic that I'm struggling to contain.

It takes all my self-control to force a step backwards. I'm itching to look where I'm treading, what I'm backing into, but I daren't take my eyes off the one serpent I can see.

Its long pinky-black tongue flickers – *ugh*. I shudder, nearly gagging, and take an involuntary stride back. The snake twines around the barrow's handle, hanging from its tail to lower itself gracefully to the ground – exactly as I've been imagining them in their hundreds doing from trees: dangling down to land on my head or slide down the back of my shirt.

I shiver so hard all over that I wish I could rip my skin off.

The alarmingly green snake ribbons into the undergrowth, and I take a breath, then stride past at a brisk march.

I leave Olga, I leave the barrow, and I press on towards the staff quarters. *What else can I do?* At least there I'll find those little trailers that attach to the quad bike, the ones I saw them jenga-ing our luggage into when they unloaded the yacht.

More snakes criss-cross my feet, and I dread taking a step in case I tread on one of the muscular, undulating bodies, sending it squirming around me to strike at my ankles.

But still I push on, nearly sobbing with the fear that holds me brittle and upright – until at last I see the buildings.

I want to weep in relief.

These are more basic offerings. I can hear the hum of a large generator – about half the size of a shipping container – which must be keeping our main house and lodgings going. There is a block of apartments, and a main building which looks to contain a common room and offices. I head there.

The building is locked, of course. I'm not a 'nip through the smallest window' kind of woman, so I find a rock. Dusting off the rich soil, I decide to make my life easy, lobbing it through the huge pane of the nearest bifolding doors.

The glass crazes, but doesn't break, so I hurl a second rock, and the glass shatters and splinters to the ground. Poking out the remaining shards, I walk inside, so glad to be out of the heat, out of the clutches of the jungle's wildness.

Beyond the common room is a dining hall, and then a kitchen – all stainless-steel efficiency. I lean on the sink and run the tap, washing my hands – blistered for nothing – and then fill a cup. I down the water like I'm a dying woman. On impulse, I plunge my head under the tap, letting the cool water wash over me. I grope around for a tea towel and rub myself dry vigorously as I wander into the freezer.

Ahhh . . . the chill breezing over my skin is heaven . . .

The space is vast, and well-stocked. If I can find a quad bike, I might be able to man-handle Olga here, and claim these supplies. With my hands on my hips, I consider the work ahead of me – and grow heavy with regret that I didn't let Asha join me.

Maybe I could move in here. Just me. Asha might believe something happened to me on the way. Snakebite, perhaps.

Would she try to find me? Or would she be relieved to have one more suspect out of the picture: one less reason to watch her back …?

It makes me wonder about communications, and with hope lifting my heart and speeding my tired legs, I search for an office, for any devices.

Off the dining hall are two small offices, both neat and orderly. One has a wall of folders and a pristine desk, the next has maps of the island, information on tides and lists of adventure experiences and event leaders.

On the underside of the desk is a panel of buttons. I crouch then lie down, staring at them. Would one of these open a comms room, like the one in the main house?

One of them is red. I press it – and hold my breath. Nothing.

I press them all, then scurry out from under the desk and stare around me, as if I'm expecting the space to transform with hidden sliding doors.

Still nothing. What do they all do?

Continuing the search, I press the walls, check behind pictures, scrutinise everything. But it's in vain.

The common room is clearly the gathering place at nighttime, or when it rains. There's a ping-pong table and bar at one end, coffee machines and games at the other. Another movie projector with a library of films – and the shattered glass of the bifold door glinting across the teak floor. I wish I hadn't broken it, then holing up here really would be an option.

But my hope is rapidly draining away in any case. There's no obvious safe here. Or devices. Or radios. Everything must either be securely locked away, in a well-disguised location, or in Olga's safe – wherever *that's* hidden – at the main house.

Or . . . *oh no* . . . it's with the absent staff. I kick a table in frustration, invincible in my boots, and head back to the office for one more look around.

I catch sight of a key chain on the wall, a room key with a neat fob embossed with 'Pass Key All Rooms'. I stare at it for a nanosecond, then I grab it and shove it deep in my pocket.

Returning to the kitchen, I see my short search is complete. I realise there's no point delaying the inevitable. I should get back to the house. And you know the rule: if you're not there, you're the one being gossiped about. I can't risk them turning against me, having only just got their collective deadly focus to swing towards Charles. I unlock the door, and wander outside in search of a quad bike.

Three are parked in a neat line at the back of the building, in front of a massive iron gate on motorised sliders that seems to have been left open.

I'm not here to explore the gardens, so I start the nearest quad bike and drive it haltingly, getting used to the controls. As I loop around, the trailer on the back bounces and judders over the uneven ground.

It wouldn't take much to throw a few supplies onboard and gain some kudos. Gaining some goodwill amongst the company would be invaluable right now. I contemplate moving Olga, wondering if I could use anything to make that easier. Then I remember how much effort it took for two of us to get her out of the pool. I'm not sure I can manage alone, especially not with something ruptured spilling all over me while I grapple with her.

Bleugh. Better not to move her again. Nothing can really be gained from it, can it? If more body parts split or tear, it will limit any meaningful post-mortem anyway.

So I haul a few crates of food onto the quad bike, trying to ignore my protesting blistered hands, my tired limbs. I'm not built for days like this. I think of Magnus and Hugh, slumped in front of the cinema-sized projector screen and the others, lounging on the beach, and resentment seeps in.

With an eye for cake, crackers, biscuits, crisps and other snacks, I make a little bonus box just for me. My reward for all this. I've earned it. I tuck it in the footwell, in case anyone thinks of helping when I'm back, so they'll be unlikely to grab it.

I have room for just a couple more boxes, so I do one final sweep of the larder. Some large pieces of meat are curing, and I scoop them up and head outside.

Before I can add them to the trailer, I freeze in shock as I see something moving near the open gate.

A powerful black panther paces by the opening, then gives a bone-rumbling, thundering *roar*. It's guttural, like it comes from the bowels of the earth. And it's *terrifying*.

Oh God, oh God . . . If only I could see how to close the gate, I could put a barrier between me and *it*. As I scan the gatepost for the mechanism, the reason becomes clear.

My blood ices at the realisation: the gate was opened by one of those buttons on the control panel, wasn't it? By me.

This is my fault . . .

The panther prowling towards me pauses as I face it. It hunkers low, taut muscles wrapped in midnight velvet. Its growl is deep, and as menacing as the snarl that reveals long, glinting canines, roped with glistening drool.

I'm frozen to the spot. I'm *burning* to dash to the quad bike, but if *I* move, *it* will move. I attempt one step . . .

It *roars*, head lifted in aggression; I almost feel myself being blasted back with the force of it, and by my sheer terror.

I feel hot liquid gush down my thighs as the beast stealths slowly towards me.

Its head is low, and, I can't help noticing, mainly made of skull-crunching jaws. The powerful shoulders are hackled, back legs haunched: it's poised to pounce.

Its muzzle contorts in a ferocious snarl.

I can't think. I can't run. I just react.

I heft the curing meat in my arms, and I *hurl* it as hard as I can, beyond the predator, towards the wide-open gate, praying that my aim – just for bloody once – will be somewhere in the area I'd like it to be. Then I can dash into the house and punch those buttons.

The hunk of meat flies towards the yawning goal. And then, of course, it bounces off the gatepost, propelling back towards me, landing by a quad bike.

The panther flinches, the roar taken up a notch to compensate, but its head swings towards the meat, nostrils flaring.

It's then that I see the panther's collar. The jewels encrusting it dazzle in the sun, a reminder that Olga owned everything. Placing a broad, heavy paw on the meat, the panther ploomfs down on the ground, tearing into the sinews with its massive jaws, tail swishing, head high as it gulps mouthfuls of flesh, alert for scavengers.

I'm not going to wait for it to eat this, then hope that my next carcass-lobbing effort lands beyond the gate. I need to get away, to put distance between me and this beast.

I scrabble onto the quad bike and slam my foot on the accelerator. Labouring with the weight of the trailer, the speed I manage is pathetic if the massive cat decides to race me.

I recall when I first arrived at the island, I saw it lying beside Olga, thinking that it had looked like it was sedated. If it was *then*, it isn't now.

I just pray it was fed recently. Big cats are feast and famine animals, aren't they? Quite adaptable. But is that still the case with pampered pets? How often is this one *used* to being fed? And how much of an issue is it that now the staff have been away for longer than expected . . .?

Regardless of its routine, a serious predator is now on the loose, on this island, because of me. Near us – and accustomed to humans being its source of food.

A panther, plus a whole host of other deadly species.

Oh God. How soon can I get out of this bloody awful place?

Even if I'd wanted to move Olga and collect the wheelbarrow, there's no way I'm stopping now, in case the beast is on my tail.

Sure enough, I *think* I glimpse the panther in the rear-view mirror, and I press the gas as hard as I can to cover the rocky ground, jolting my body and the trailer.

I steer past Olga's body, muttering an apology to her, but not even slowing down.

The canopy branches overhead screech against the metal roof, reminding me that I could be joined at any moment by another hitchhiking snake, or maybe a spider this time. Like I'm nature's bloody Uber driver.

The panther is still tracking me, but then it veers off. I stare in the mirror, wondering what has caught its attention.

My question is answered when I hear a distant, but unmistakeable sound: the sickening crunch of jaws snapping bone.

Chapter 15

Sunday 6ᵗʰ April – 5.30 p.m.

I PULL UP TO THE HOUSE, shaking.

I leap off the quad bike, rubbing my arms, checking nothing has landed on me, looking anxiously around for any sign of the panther – who's now added 'human' to its menu. Doesn't that make a species more dangerous?

Waving wildly at the windows, I pray some people will see and help. I daren't yell. Even though the panther probably knows exactly where I am.

Reason tells me that the panther will be sated . . . for now. But I imagine its natural prey on the island will be limited . . . and now possibly include us.

'Hey! Hey!' Zyra sprints over from the spa, flagging me down. 'Oh? Thea?' Her pace slows as she approaches. 'God, I thought you were some angel member of staff come to save us.' She sighs heavily, exhaling her disappointment. 'What's all this?'

'I went to the staff quarters. To check for any means to make contact. I brought back some supplies.'

'You . . . you hiked there?' She gapes, stepping closer, her hand tugging my arm with the same urgency that floods her voice. 'Did you? Find a phone? Or a radio?'

When I shake my head, the bright hope on her face crumples. 'Oh . . . Jeez . . .' She paces away from me, processing the bad news. 'I never even thought there might be something out there. And now I'm mourning the loss of hope I didn't know I had.' She rubs her face. 'We're really out of options, aren't we?'

I realise I'm glimpsing rare vulnerability. Her real fear, underneath the positive gloss. I should mention the additional threat of the panther, but I just haven't got the heart to give her something else to be upset about. And I really don't want anyone asking how it got out of its very safe, secure, unbreakable enclosure.

Then, in a flash, Zyra's photo-ready smile is back. 'But we only have to wait it out. It'll be fine. We *are* in paradise, after all.'

'Uh-huh.' I grab a crate and add my own box of hard-earned treats, hoping Zyra will take the hint and help me unload – and get inside.

She does. Hauling one of the plastic crates alongside me, she says, 'Bit hypocritical of Olga to use so much plastic when she wants to ban it. My tours never have any single-use plastic, and I set up recycling centres for anything else.'

'Only some plastic can be recycled, though, and then only to a certain degree.' I walk briskly to the house. 'Plastic breaks down to microparticles that can't rot away, so, via our water and our food, those particles get into our bodies. Every man now has plastic in his testes, and we all have plastic in our brains – already at some horrific percentage, and it's infiltrating us at an accelerating rate. So—'

'*Ugh!* It's a poison.' Zyra looks disgusted yet fascinated. 'So Olga's right, then. Why *haven't* we banned plastics?' She shifts her crate to open the door and holds it for me.

'We're still actively inventing them. It's profitable for the petrochem industry for us to be reliant on the thousands of new variants they create every year.'

She gapes. 'But . . . how can that be allowed?'

'Because it's convenient for us, and profitable for business. A deadly combination.' I heave the crate onto the counter, beside the one that Zyra lugged in, but hang onto my box of treats. 'I need to shower. Maybe you could ask the others to help bring the food in?'

I trudge up to my room and dump my sweaty, stained clothes in the corner, first turning them inside out and checking obsessively for unwelcome hitchhikers. Then I let the heavenly water ripple over me, relishing the reassuring fragrance of bergamot and jasmine after the stench of decay, and the earthy, *biological* smell of the jungle.

My skin is blotched with rashes, bumpy with bites. I'm itching like I'm on *fire*.

I ache everywhere. I'm exhausted, and my blistered palms sting.

Rinsing gingerly, I turn off the shower and wrap myself in my robe, flumping on my sofa with a vast slice of pilfered passion fruit cake. I gaze out at the jungle, which just yesterday had looked so lush, so idyllic . . . I stab the button on the remote to fire up the TV, only to find that this won't offer me any solace, either. *No internet, no access.* At least I have a book . . . I can lose myself in a nice bit of . . . *ugh*, murder mystery.

Sunday 6*th* April – 6.30 p.m.

Dressed, but still stiff from the kind of exertion my body is very unused to, I head down to see what everyone's doing for dinner, and how the extra food has been received.

'Great thinking.' Uri grins at me. He has a kind smile, I notice. It creases his whole face, like a pickled walnut. 'This is good. It feels like we're becoming a team. I've spent all my time working on that damn radio. Whoever broke it really went to town.'

His words are a stark reminder of the danger we're all in; that there's still someone in our midst with deadly intent. I glance around, wondering whether to share the news of the panther, but I still can't bring myself to explain why it's loose. A bit of extra food definitely *won't* make up for that. I stare at my plate.

'Yes, thanks for the supplies.' Kali nudges me, and I manage a smile, despite my secretive thoughts. 'But … I wish you'd found *some*thing … anything … to use to reach someone.'

'Sorry.'

Nice. I'm glad my ordeal has been so bloody disappointing. I give a helpless shrug. 'I looked everywhere. I guess everything is kept centrally here.'

Kali sighs. 'So, we haven't found our phones, and we haven't fixed the radio – though I appreciate Uri's working on it – so we *still* don't have any way of getting hold of anyone.' She side-eyes Magnus. 'And today's venture, to see if there are any other hidden comms rooms, wasn't exactly successful.'

Magnus – and Asha – look sheepish, and I wonder what ransacking has gone on.

'We *could* swim over the harbour gate,' Zyra offers. 'But even if we do, Estelle doesn't think we'll get to another island. And we haven't found anything, like a dinghy, that we might be able to use. Well,' she shoots a half-smile of forced hope at Estelle, 'Not yet.'

I move towards the fresh bread and cheese I brought back, cutting generous slices. Alongside my own plate of bread, cheese, pickles and fruit, I make a sandwich for Charles, served with a glass of fruit juice and a whisky.

Kali joins me. 'The extra food really is a bonus. I didn't mean to sound ungrateful earlier. I just … I'm *itching* to get out of here. And I'm not alone.' She tugs me into the library. '*Look at this.*'

I stare around the room. It's a wreck: the place has been torn apart. Books have been ripped from the bookcases and strewn around the room, in a fruitless search for levers or secret buttons. 'Asha has been hunting for the safe where Olga stored our phones, and Magnus has been searching for the helicopter keys. With no luck.' The desk's drawers and cupboards have been thrown open, stationery dumped on the floor.

'And what's Hugh been doing?' I ask, noting he hasn't been mentioned, and I haven't seen him, either.

'Watching movies. Today is movie day at his house and he doesn't see a reason not to uphold the tradition. That, and demanding to be waited on.'

I arch an eyebrow at her, and she smiles back, confirming our aligned thinking. 'Yes, you assume correctly that those demands have been completely ignored.' She shrugs. 'I don't think he ate any lunch. Which is fine by me.'

'He hasn't looked for anything? Had any ideas?'

'What do you think?'

We stop outside Charles's suite, and Kali knocks. I juggle the tray to unlock the door.

'Hi, Charles. I've unlocked the door. It's me and Kali.'

I hear furniture scraping on the floor, then the door is ripped open. 'Bloody hell, I thought I'd have to start eating my own arm.'

'We usually eat dinner much later at home—'

'We usually *eat* decent portions for lunch! What's with all this "just a sandwich" crap?'

'Well, you've got another one for dinner, plus juice and a whisky.'

'Hoo-fucking-ray.'

'We're doing what we can to get help,' Kali says. 'This could all be over sooner if you, with your intimate relationship with Olga, were to know of any way to make contact – with the authorities, or anyone …?'

I wince at 'intimate relationship' and pretend that my dignity isn't being trampled on.

But Charles's face changes. 'What if I do? What's it worth?'

'Typical.' I shake my head. 'Here's an opportunity to help, but instead you're turning it to personal gain.'

'Help? Help the people who have locked me up? Because they think I'm a *killer*?' He gives a hollow laugh. 'You know what, for the first time, I've had a chance to be alone with my own thoughts. And it's not very fucking pretty. And, since you ask, *no*,' he holds up his hands, 'as it happens, Olga didn't trust me with any useful information, because you women don't, do you? You're all snakes. Out for what you can get. You make quite a pair, don't you? I've seen you, Kali, happy to grind anyone else into the dust to drive the best bargain for yourself—'

'That's *exactly* the kind of thing you respect in someone like Magnus!' The protest rips from my lips instinctively. 'Because he's a *man*. Or in Olga – because she was sleeping with you. That says everything about your baseline opinion of women, doesn't it?'

I don't need the answer. I didn't really need to ask the question. But it makes him round on me next.

'*You*, Thea, you're the worst of the lot. You used me and literally spat me out, didn't you? The least I could expect is a wife who'd defend me against an accusation of murder. But where's your loyalty? Where's your devotion now? Oh, have you used it all up, draining me dry? Using my connections to get where you need? Where's your support when *I* need it?'

There's spittle on his lips, and, as he thrusts his face near mine, I can smell alcohol on his breath, from where he's clearly spent all day raiding the bar in his suite.

'So I don't care what happens next, but I promise you: whatever you want, you're not going to get it. Divorce? I'll refuse, and if you force it, I'll make sure you're left with *nothing*. Separation? I'll track you down and *show* you that you can't treat your husband like this. And if you cut your losses and decide to play happy marriage?' His gives an ugly laugh, and his next words chill me.

'I'll make your life a living hell.'

Chapter 16

Monday 7ᵗʰ April – 9 a.m.

I'M STILL FUMING ABOUT CHARLES'S venomous barbs this morning as I go through the motions of making The Prick his breakfast, which Kali and I will then have to take to his room.

Since you can tell when food has been cooked with love, I'm pouring all my bitter resentment into this meal, slicing fruit haphazardly and flinging bread and cheese, juice and coffee onto the tray, not caring if I spill things.

Kali appraises me with puffed-out cheeks and raised eyebrows, then nods. 'Yep, I share your unbridled enthusiasm.' She leans in to whisper, 'I'd let the bastard starve, personally.' She grins before tucking into her bowl of granola, Greek yoghurt and berries.

I've warmed to her; she was a rock last night. Her small gestures of support, and lack of surprise at what she witnessed, tell me she may have experienced a similar relationship.

'I'm more disgusted with myself. I thought I was intelligent. How can it have taken me so long to see him for the arsehole he is?'

'There always has to be a trigger,' Kali says between mouthfuls. 'You put up with so much, drip by drip. But then something happens and boom!' She snaps her fingers. 'Don't question it. Just be grateful you've had the revelation. Don't waste another second of your precious life on him. What are you waiting for?'

I glance at her. 'It's not so easy, when your lives are tied together. And you heard him last night. He plans to prevent whatever I want.'

She laughs, staring at me. 'I know you're not a family lawyer, but what would you or a colleague say, to someone in that position? You'd point out your leverage; how you can protect yourself, how you can break free. The same applies to you, you know? You just need to believe it.'

I'm shocked at that pure, simple fact I've been unable to acknowledge. I'm lost in reflection as we take the tray to Charles's room. It's a potent cocktail – inertia mixed with fear of the unknown. One that can petrify you into an arrested state, a prison of your own creation.

I realise how much I've lost confidence in my own judgement. Not professionally, of course, but personally. Something in my soul slides sideways at the realisation. I've always thought of myself as confident, assured. I want to weep, to mourn the loss of a part of myself I always considered strong, dependable, *there*.

So what does that make me now? I'm a living paradox: I can't trust my decision to leave because if I made good decisions, I wouldn't be in this predicament in the first place. And the tyranny of not wanting to *admit* a mistake forces me to *live* that mistake – every single day.

Kali's cool logic and her unshakeable self-belief are the right challengers; but it takes time – too much time – to let yourself trust them. And in the meantime, Kali's right, you're just wasting your life. Even Olga, with her extreme wealth, couldn't buy enough youth blood plasma to halt time altogether.

I wonder what my life would be like – how my achievements would feel – if I had a greater sense of agency, more self-reliance.

'What would *you* do, then, Kali?' There's no challenge in my voice. It's a plea for help, for inspiration from a woman who still believes in her own strength.

She looks me dead in the eye. 'Leave, and not look back. Get your legal affairs in order, if not already – that shouldn't be a problem for you. Protect what's fairly yours, and file for divorce.' She shrugs, like she could tick that off her 'Thirty things successful billionaires do before breakfast' list, along with meditation and a four-hour gym session.

Then she side-eyes me. 'Although, if you want to avoid the paperwork and stick something in his food now, I promise I wouldn't blame you, and I *couldn't* give you away because I wouldn't see a thing.' She lets her gaze travel to the ceiling, then grins, and I'm grateful for her attempt to lighten my heavy mood.

I smile back. It's nice to catch a glimpse of the woman beneath Kali's armour. And I'm grateful for her compassion, for not using what she's seen of me and Charles against me, only to hint at common ground between us.

So she's kinder than she appears … Does that make her more vulnerable?

But her suggestion is taking root in my mind – *freedom* – and it's making my heart beat so hard that, when we reach Charles's door, it takes concentration to knock at a different speed. When he doesn't answer, I groan and knock again.

Even if we unlock the door, we couldn't open it until he removes the barricade on his side, so I listen, trying to hear if his shower's running, knowing it's futile in a suite that large. With a sigh, I jerk my head at Kali, and we walk out and around the lodge to the garden. The gap in the hedge is more pronounced after everyone bursting through it yesterday.

Even so, it isn't easy squeezing through with the tray. 'Bloody Charles. *All* he has to do is answer the bloody door.'

Kali eyes me, but doesn't say anything. Something about her seems . . . wary.

Her concern is contagious. My skin prickles as I approach the bifolding doors. Peering through the glass, I hold my breath so I don't fog the pane.

My instincts kick in before my brain can make sense of the strange scene.

I scream and I *scream*, dropping the tray with a ringing clatter as my fists hammer the glass, the scene clouding over with my hot, ragged breath. I blink, but I'm not imagining it.

My shrieks bubble into hysterical, disbelieving sobs as I stare at my husband in his blood-soaked bed.

Syrupy, ruby-red puddles congeal on the floor, from where the luxury cotton sheets blooming with his blood have dripped rivulets of gore. His head is flung back, his throat slashed, his body gouged and pierced a thousand times, darkening with claret clots.

The elaborate Murano glass chandelier is pinning him to the bed.

Those decorative shards have impaled him, slashed his skin, ruptured his organs.

Jagged, smashed glass glints wickedly across his rumpled sheets, and the long steel rod that held up the chandelier is lodged in his chest, like a jousting lance.

Kali pulls me away. 'You're OK, Thea. I promise, you're OK.' Her arms are strong around me, her chin pressed on my head, a reassuring presence that I'm struggling to sense through the fog.

But she keeps talking, low and steady, and she pulls me out of my shock. 'You're going to be OK. We'll work out what happened here. We'll work out who did this.'

I take a gasping, shuddering breath, like I've just come up for air from a murky pool, and look her in the eye. As I steady my ragged breath, I stutter, 'B-but t-they'll think it was m-me.'

'Maybe. But none of us would blame you. Well, none of the women.'

'Oh, God!' I sink onto the floor, my body turning to jelly at the thought of the next level of horror I have to deal with. 'I didn't do this!'

Kali gives me a 'who else, then?' look. *I imagine that accusation spreading … the mob locking me up …* I shake my head, trembling, and she kneels beside me, reaching for my hands, holding them in hers. 'You're freezing. You'll need something for the shock.'

As I haul myself to my feet, I manage to look again at my butchered husband.

I can't help the churn of my analytical mind.

Who would use a chandelier as a murder weapon?

* * *

Kali has somehow scooped me towards the kitchen, where she sloshes rum into a glass and wraps my shaking fingers around it.

'Sip,' she orders, glancing towards the door. 'I think we'll be left in peace. It looks like most people have had breakfast.'

Through my clouded thoughts, I can see the evidence strewn across the kitchen: boards with sticky remnants of fruit, crumbs from toasted bread and trails of cereals. I grope for a chair, trying to bring order to my mind.

'What … time did we give him his food last night? Half-s-six-ish?'

'Yeah, it would have been about six thirty when we left him. Maybe a bit after.'

'So he was in bed. He must have been asleep when … when …'

'Yes, he must. So that would make it nighttime. He'd eaten his food; his plate was by the bed. Looked like he was wearing just his pyjama bottoms.'

'Yes.' I swallow. He must have been, for me to spot the slashes across his upper body.

Crouching beside me, Kali looks into my eyes, and lowers her voice. 'I meant it when I said I wouldn't blame you. But I *am* asking you for the truth. There's a *massive* difference between you taking righteous revenge on your bastard husband, and a crazed killer being on the loose. So I'd kinda like to know what we're dealing with here.'

I take a breath and meet her eyes. Her brows are raised in the hope of hearing a confession. In the hope of being told that the danger closing in on us isn't real.

When I shake my head, Kali stares at me, like she can't bear to believe me. Then her shoulders slump. 'Fucking hell, Thea. What are we looking at here, then? Do you think Olga and Charles will be the end of it?'

'Only the murderer knows that.' An awful thought sends a tide of nausea flashing through me. 'Assuming there's just one.'

Monday 7ᵗʰ April – 11 a.m.

Before I face the others to tell them what's happened – unleashing the obvious barrage of questions about who was where, and when – Kali agrees to revisit Charles's room with me. Looking for evidence.

I'm bracing myself not to vomit, knowing what's beyond the glass door, but I swallow down the acid rising in my throat and ignore my churning stomach.

Part of me desperately needs to make sure I didn't imagine it … because … because …

Grabbing two rocks, I hurl one – splintering the glass – then the other, bringing the shards crashing down. Kali nods, pulling a face that's half approving, half mock-astonished, then follows me in.

The piercing, metallic tang of blood makes my head ache. Covering my nose, I tiptoe past Charles's bed. Kali's observations were correct.

I stare at him. He is very, very dead.

So I am free …

My heart lifts, soars like a songbird, and somehow I'm looking down on this mess from a different vantage point, from somewhere where the danger can't touch me and the possibilities of a new life stretch out … And then the fear swoops back in, and I heave burning bile.

Swallowing hard, I look at the mess Charles has made of the room: empty bottles from the bar standing or lying on the sideboard, snack wrappers by the sofa and the bed, clothes dumped on the floor, his tray left on the table near the door – everything consumed.

I stare up at the vaulted ceiling. A small hole, not much wider than the supporting rod's diameter, with no apparent damage around it, seems a poor explanation for the devastation in front of me.

Surely, if the chandelier fell somehow, the ceiling would have been damaged?

Even though the electrical cables are strong, the immense light fitting would have been far too heavy to stay held up by the wires if the fixings failed.

Something like this would need a back plate, at least, to keep it secure. So what happened to that?

Avoiding the puddles of gore, I lean over Charles's bloodied body and examine the chandelier's fitting. Its supporting rod spears out of the mess of Charles's clotting chest, which is covered in smashed glass. The rod must be about an inch in diameter, and roughly six feet long. About two feet from the end, there's a hole that goes right through it, which you could probably push a marker pen through. I imagine the end of the rod threading through the ceiling for about two feet, and then a metal pin sliding in, across the rod, to fix it to the back plate. I crawl on the floor, searching everywhere, but there's no sign of the pin.

The chandelier's wires snake out, dangling over the end of the rod, ripped from their circuitry.

Up close, I'm horribly aware of how vast the light fixture is, how *massive*. There's no moving Charles to try to give him any dignity in death. At least any forensics will be preserved, though I'm sure they'll be scarce. Someone this calculated would have covered their tracks well.

Kali unbarricades and unlocks the door, peering out into the hall.

I don't need to remind myself of the layout. Olga's suite is next door — and so is Hugh. The one person, other than me, who may have wanted to kill Charles.

And who just might have had something to gain from it.

* * *

Kali gathers everyone to the great room and shares the news. 'There's been another death.'

Immediately, eyes dart around, taking stock, checking who's absent. We've all got used to gathering without Charles now, and no one would expect to see him while he's under room arrest, so it takes a moment before realisation hits and jaws drop.

I stare at Hugh, watching for his reaction. He frowns. '*Charles?*'

My suspicious mind imagines him pantomiming shock, as he stares at Kali, then at me, brow furrowed. 'How?'

My chest heaves. I can't say it. I look down and Kali comes to my rescue, saying, 'Charles has one of those massive glass sculpture chandeliers over his bed.' She nods at the dramatic one hanging above us, its fine fronds glinting with jagged edges. 'It fell on him and lacerated his throat and chest while he was in bed. The rod that held it up has driven right through him.'

Everyone raises their gaze to the ceiling, eyeing the massive, elaborate chandelier, then shuffling away, out of range.

'So it was an accident, then,' Hugh asserts.

Kali and I exchange a glance.

'No,' Uri says. '*Look* at that thing. Think how much it weighs. It'll need some serious support. That's not gonna fall by accident. So,' he grins – actually *grins* – at me, 'who's glad he's dead?'

I see the shift in mood flash around the assembled company. Zyra's face encapsulates it best – a gasp of pure horror, her hands over her mouth, worried looks at me from under a brow furrowed with sympathy, then eyes widening with the fear of what will happen next – before finally hardening into an expression of self-preservation.

I see it; I know it: things are going to change.

We'd thought we were safe, with the killer locked up, yet the primal urge to *escape* was still strong. Now, though, this is survival. And the call of the wild is keening to us.

I absolutely cannot question them this time. They'll lock together like they did when I took their statement about Olga's death, and turn on me. And now, they'll give no quarter.

Last time I questioned everyone, it was common knowledge that Charles was a key informant. If Charles has been killed because he saw or heard something – and if the murderer thinks Charles shared whatever incriminating intel he had with me – then I could be next.

With a glance at Estelle, Zyra is first to slip away, heading for the kitchen. Estelle follows, and I realise they're plundering like doomsday preppers, so they can set themselves safely apart from the rest of the group.

Kali dashes through to the kitchen. 'Hey! If this turns into a free for all, it will be carnage.'

'It is already, don't you think?' Zyra retorts.

As we follow, Kali stares at the meagre supplies they've collected to stash in their rooms, and laughs. 'You girls and your regimes. If that's all you want, take it.'

When the two of them leave, I realise we have a bigger problem as Hugh and Magnus start their own ram-raid. They snatch at everything within reach – bread, cheese, meat, fruit, fish – with no thought to how they'll store it or consume it.

Their frenzied smash and grab looks desperate, and Kali and I gape at them.

'What are you doing?' Kali asks.

'There's plenty of food, Hugh,' I point out. 'You're taking things you're not even going to be able to eat.'

'You don't need to *do* that!' Kali tries again. 'This is completely unnecessary—'

She jolts as Hugh shoves past her, arms full of produce, and glares at him. 'I hope you die of food poisoning, then!' she says cheerfully to his back.

Magnus glowers, muttering, 'Unless you starve first,' as he leaves with his spoils.

I raise shocked eyebrows at Kali. The greed is something to behold, and we're not even starving yet!

The contagious panic ignites, flickering around the group.

And then I spot movement beyond the window and I freeze. Estelle and Zyra have raided the huts of sports equipment, and they're running back to the house holding up *harpoons*.

Fuck.

Kali's eyes widen at the sight. 'Jesus. It's all a bit *Lord of the Flies*, isn't it?'

I realise Estelle and Zyra are hunkering down together, making one of their cabins into a secure, shared haven.

Envy at their confidence in each other, at their mutual security, flashes through me – but then I wonder if one of them is a traitor using the other for cover.

I realise how rabid my suspicion is becoming.

And it does nothing to allay my mushrooming fears: that whoever killed Olga and now my husband – for whatever reason – might have been framing me.

Unless they plan to kill me next.

Chapter 17

Monday 7th April – 1 p.m.

I'VE RATTLED BETWEEN THE GREAT room and the kitchen like an addict counting seconds before their next fix.

I'm waiting, waiting, *waiting* for everyone to decide to eat, hoping it will keep them all occupied – because I have a plan.

Finally, Kali heads to the kitchen with Uri, and they begin making lunch. But I have something else to do.

I wait until I see Magnus and Hugh panting like lazy labradors waiting to be fed.

I hear Kali ask, 'What are you both doing here? I thought you'd got your own supplies now.'

A mumbled reply from Hugh makes Kali respond with a short laugh and 'Good luck with that!'

I close my book, pretending to have finished it as I stand – then slip up the stairs as if just heading to my room to get another.

As I walk up the stairs, I spot Estelle and Zyra walking along the beach, heads together, and I make a snap decision to start with them.

My hand is clammy on the banister as I brace myself for someone to ask me where I'm going. But no one does.

Olga's veiled remarks, the memory of the pointed looks exchanged during that godforsaken blood ritual in the boardroom, has made me think that there are scores to settle here. I haven't found out what they are yet, so I'll have to be more devious.

My heart is thumping so hard that it feels like it must be audible. I try to control my breathing, but I can feel sweat collecting on my brow.

I rush to my room and lock the door behind me, then dash to my bifolding doors, again locking these behind me, and hurry down the steps. I skirt through my garden, pausing to scan for the panther, then head round to the cabins, reaching Estelle's first.

Shooting furtive glances over my shoulder, expecting to be spotted at any moment, I'm almost amazed to see the coast is clear.

Using the staff key to let myself in, I step swiftly inside, closing the door behind me.

Now, though, I won't know if anyone's approaching, or walking past a window, or if Estelle herself is returning, and my coordination crumbles. I knock into things, brushing a glass off the sideboard, thanking the deep rug for preventing both damage and noise.

As I hastily replace the glass with shaking hands, I force myself to pause and take stock, ignoring my rapid breaths, my galloping heartbeat. Drawing a steadying inhale, I scan for ... something. *Anything*.

I don't know what I hope to find. But something tells me that I have to try.

'Cabin' makes it sound small and basic. It's neither. This is a vast, plush suite. The sumptuously draped bed is piled high with fabrics so fine they actually gleam. The closet is magazine-shoot ready, filled with exquisite, colour-zoned designer pieces. The immaculate bathroom is stocked with ordered rows of high-end cosmetics and supplements in jewel-like vials.

I poke around everywhere: in all the cupboards, under the cushions on the sofa, in every drawer, between garments, in shoe boxes ...

Moving on to check the 'bar', I note how it's been curated to Estelle's preferences – with pots of fresh, sprouting wheat grass, jars of collagen powder, and an irrigated fridge containing fresh green vegetables and ampoules of oils and aminos – so that she can shake up a vitamin cocktail in the rose-gold NutriBullet in an instant.

But there are no ... clues.

I had hoped to find a gift from Olga, similar to the barbed one she gave to me. But I can't find one. There's not even an empty gift box in the bin.

On the coffee table, though, is an envelope, almost hidden behind a copy of *Vogue*. I open it with trembling fingers, glancing at the door, twitching at every imagined sound.

It's a letter of resignation.

I re-read it, heart thumping. So Estelle was serious about extricating herself from Olga's contractual tyranny.

But she didn't need to hand it in in person, did she? Why would she go to the inconvenience of coming all the way out here? Or make that flashy entrance that she'd obviously made at Olga's bidding?

Had it all been a test? To find out what Olga's proposal was? To see if her talk of reparation was genuine?

The only reason I can think of to deliver a letter like this by hand is because it's personal. Because you want to make a point. You want to see the other person's face when you take back control.

Is this because of the wound she carries from being the face of broken promises? And for Tony, who lost his career, then his life?

As I return the letter to the envelope and the table, I consider the fact that Estelle had visited Olga, but not given her the letter. Was this a fallback position? Or had she been driven to take another course of action – one that would have made resigning unnecessary?

I glance around. There's a framed photo on the bedside table.

It's of Estelle and a man, in extreme close-up, laughing. Her hand caresses his cheek. An engagement ring glitters on her left hand's fourth finger.

An engagement ring that she now wears on the other hand.

*   *   *

My legs are still shaking when I let myself out. I feel too exposed searching the cabins, and I don't want to push my luck. But I still want to search. So, before I can overthink things and talk myself out of it, I'm dashing back to my room via the garden, eyes darting everywhere for signs of anyone and any*thing* that might be watching, then hurrying up the steps to my balcony, through my suite, and out to the hall.

I heave a deep breath, trying to look casual, checking no one's around – and then I let myself into Kali's suite.

I *pray* she doesn't have a sudden reason to pop up to her room. I make a note of where I can hide if I have to: either under the bed, or in the closet. Slim pickings.

Her room is organised, her clothes hung up, her case locked. Her large handbag contains only an iPad, makeup, and vitamins and suncream by her company's medical-grade brand.

Her bathroom is a study in self-care: her toiletries are all elite. I notice that the luxury rasul treatment and body oil Olga provided are left untouched.

The glasses from the bar have been rinsed and left beside the bathroom sink, and I spot snack wrappers in the bin. And something else below them.

I crouch, poking a wrapper aside to see what it is . . .

It's the corner of Olga's signature luxe navy gift box. Reaching in, I lift it out. It rattles. With a frown, I ease it open.

Inside, the necklace glints.

She's thrown away the gift, too?

Then I remember how barbed my gift was, and my pulse quickens. So this was a message – and one Kali didn't appreciate.

I study it. It looks like a vial of something, hanging on a fine chain.

Turning the vial sideways, I make out a word written in delicate script. The word *Profairin*.

Shit. I drop the necklace as if it's burned me.

I know about this absolute travesty. Everyone must. But I didn't realise it was Kali's company. Of course I wouldn't; Estelle has shown me how easily the founders can stay in the shadows while others take the heat.

But the trials for this cancer-treating 'miracle drug' had sent shockwaves through millions of families . . . So many lives had been lost by trusting in it instead of in more proven, but more gruelling, treatments.

I pick up the necklace again, double-checking the name in case I misread or misunderstood. But it's there, engraved in the gold. As I turn it over in my hands, I spot the special extra detail Olga added: a skull and crossbones, inlaid in the base of the vial.

Something about this feels like more than just professional criticism. It's personal.

As fear prickles across my neck, I suddenly remember that I shouldn't be here, shouldn't be seeing this. I scrabble to replace the necklace in the box, shove it in the bin, put the wrapper back on top, grab my book and dash to the door.

I can only listen at the door and try to hear if anyone is in the hall. The plushness of the rooms deadens sounds, so I can't rely on *not* hearing anything outside.

Each second I'm here is another second I risk being caught. So I slip the key safely into my pocket and open the door a crack. Still nothing. I slip out, quick as a cat, and pull it closed behind me.

I peer over the edge of the landing and see that the group are gathered downstairs.

Everyone but Uri. Scanning wildly, I see him heading up the stairs – but I don't think he's seen me.

I dart across the hall to the side where my room is, as if that's where I'm coming from – just as Uri reaches the landing. 'Thea? We all wondered where you'd got to.'

I search his face for signs that he spotted me near Kali's room. He gives me a knowing smile – but that's how he always looks at me.

So I play it cool as we walk downstairs. 'Thanks for coming to get me.'

'Didn't want you to miss lunch. Not after we've been plundered and the gluttons are back for more. Only fair you get your share.' His smile is warm, approving. Then he glances at the book in my hand. I squirm, wondering if I'm projecting or if he spotted me pretending to finish it, even though I thought he was in the kitchen at the time. The guy's too damn sharp.

But all he says is, 'You'll want something else to read soon.'

I pray my cheeks don't flame and give me away. I try to style it out. 'Got anything I could borrow?'

'I might. Do you like quantum physics?'

'Will it help me make sense of those equations you say you were coming up with when Olga was killed?'

'Nope. Totally different field. But you might still enjoy it.'

'You don't seem very anxious to convince me of your alibi for Olga's murder.'

'You don't need to be anxious if you're not guilty. Do you, Thea?' His amused expression makes me wonder again if he's making a point, or if I'm projecting.

So I smile, but my heart pounds. If he, like Kali, was beholden in some way to Olga, then he's guilty of something, too. I just need to find out what …

Only now, if I want to keep digging, I'll have to be even more careful – since I know he is at least keeping tabs on my whereabouts.

The lunch Kali and Uri have made is delicious. Herby, fragrant couscous with red mullet, which I think I brought back from the staff quarters.

It makes me think of my failed mission with Olga, and about what we should do now, with Charles.

I'm absolutely not going back through that bloody jungle. Not for anyone. Even with the quad bike.

When we've eaten, I clear the plates, keen to move away from the company and hide the layers of guilt I'm carrying. Leaving the kitchen door wide open as I stack the dishwasher and run it, I keep watch for anyone going past – to Olga's lodge or to her office.

I pour myself a long glass of water from the filter tap. I'm parched from creeping around; from the fear, the tension and all the endless *sweating*.

And then I hear a creak. The door to the office opposite opens, and I spy Asha sidling into the room. If I don't move from this spot, I can see her through the crack in the door as she moves around, checking drawers, taking down folders from shelves.

I smile at her need for information. If she's trying to solve this too, maybe we could help each other. I need an ally here.

Checking the hall, I dash across to her and close the door behind me. 'Looking for clues?'

She freezes, staring at me. 'Yeah. You too?'

'Of course. No one's saying it, but I'm the prime suspect, aren't I?'

'I'd feel safer if I was certain of that,' Asha says. 'But it feels like we're a hair trigger away from going full feral. I don't really want this to turn into the Wild West. So I'm looking to see if anyone has any motives. Or secrets that they'll kill to keep.'

She pulls down a folder bursting with papers, and frowns as she glances through them. 'Looks like … medical records.' With a shrug she starts to put the folder back, but I hold out my hand and take it from her, trying to look casual as I flick through it.

This can't be a coincidence. Not after the discovery in Kali's room.

These are medical records. Mammograms. Positive test results. I swallow.

So Olga did have a personal complaint. But if she fell foul of Kali's fake wonder drug, at least she lived to tell the tale, which is more than can be said for most participants in the trial.

Then I see the name at the top of the records. Freya Helgesdotter.

'Who's this?' I ask Asha, turning to show her the page.

'Freya?' Asha's face scrunches in thought. 'I think that's Olga's sister.' She searches on the desk amongst the photos, and pulls one from its frame. It shows two young women in evening dress at a casino. One is clearly Olga, the other a younger, smilier version of her. On the back, in tiny lettering, is written: *Me and Freya, Monte Carlo, 1999.*

I know what I'll find at the back of the medical records. Sure enough, there's a coroner's report, citing Freya's cause of death as breast cancer.

With shaking hands, I put the papers back in the folder and return it to the shelf.

So Olga did have something to settle with Kali.

And Kali needed Olga to stay silent as the grave.

Chapter 18

Monday 7ᵗʰ April – 2.30 p.m.

I'M NOT SURE WHETHER ASHA, who's now searching Olga's desk, realises that Kali is implicated in Freya's death. I guard the information I've found like treasure. It's currency, one way or another.

Finding nothing of note in the pages she's removed from one of the drawers, Asha feels around inside it instead, and catches onto something. A small compartment pops out from the side of the desk, and Asha gasps.

'Oh my God! Look!'

She takes out two blank envelopes, a couple of newspaper cuttings and what looks like printed emails.

As Kali wanders in, Asha casually drops a folder of maps on top of the paperwork we've found. 'Still searching for the safe,' she says, like the excuse was prepared. I feel a flush of delight that she trusts me with the truth, and that she has the sense to hide our findings.

'No luck yet, I take it?' Kali raises her eyebrows in sympathy and wanders over to the desk, where Uri has been working on rebuilding the radio. He's made some progress, but it's a complex jigsaw puzzle of components.

At the sight of the debris, Kali groans. 'God, you'd think between all of us we could find a way out of this, wouldn't you? I'll carry on the search. There's plenty of places to check throughout the house.' She manages a hopeful smile. 'Do you think Olga went for the traditional, behind-a-portrait option?'

'Anything's worth a try,' I say, trying to sound encouraging.

'I guess it's no hardship to get a closer look at all the gorgeous artwork.' She hesitates, eyes us both carefully, then leaves with reluctance.

I've always been able to mask when I know I'm talking to someone on the wrong side of the law, like the violent offenders I encountered during my early years of criminal law, or, more recently, corporate felons. To get the inside story and construct a case, I have to make them trust me. I might look at Kali differently now, but she'll never know it.

I'm reminded of Estelle's argument with Olga, and Olga's retort that Kali was the callous one.

I watch Kali return to the great room, and I have to wonder – did she know the extent of the hatred Olga felt for her? And, if Olga was dropping hints about Kali's buried scandal to Estelle, then who else's sensitive secrets had she divulged?

'I don't think there's anything else to find in here.' Asha is looking around, then pauses as she looks out of the window. 'Estelle and Zyra are at the beach again. They might confide in you, Thea, if you felt like talking to them?'

I wonder if she's re-directing me away from the pages hidden on the desk – that I'm burning to read – so that she can take them herself.

'They're more likely to talk to you, Ash. You're a good listener.'

'Why don't we go together, then?'

I wonder if I misjudged her. We *are* the only two showing any curiosity about motives. Maybe lawyers and journalists are used to raking over the secrets and lies that people hide. Maybe the others are in denial. Maybe they don't want to draw attention to any of those secrets.

But Asha doesn't move – not until Uri wanders in, and waits for her to move aside so he can take the seat at the desk. She loiters as he leans over the tiny, shattered radio parts in silence, and I gesture to Asha to go ahead. The second she turns to leave, I pick up the documents that came out of the secret drawer and shove them inside my wrap top.

She turns back, as if hearing the rustling paper, and I smile. 'Let's leave Uri to it.'

Now I know that Uri's absorbed for a while, I seize the opportunity to investigate Uri's cabin.

'I think you'll get further with Zyra and Estelle on your own, Ash. I've got a headache. I'm going to have a rest in my room.'

I head to my suite. As I cross the great room, I see Kali teetering on a chair. She's trying to tilt the huge impressionist painting that dominates the wall while feeling around behind it, presumably for any indents that suggest a hidden safe. Magnus and Hugh aren't helping; they're absorbed in barbed debate. I skirt around them and climb the stairs.

In my room, I hastily hide the documents Asha found. Unzipping a cushion, I push them inside, re-zipping and placing the cushion right-side up on the sofa. I chuck my robe over it, for extra casualness.

Then I slip out of my balcony door, down the steps and through the garden, and dash towards the cabins.

Fumbling at Uri's door, I unlock it, slide inside and look around.

His vast suite is clean and highly orderly. There are rinsed used glasses beside the sink and the bin is full of wrappers, but nothing is strewn around. It's not just organised, it's all neatly lined up, like room tidying is a military operation for him.

His clothes are hanging in the closet, evenly spaced, and there's no sign of a gift in there. When I search the cupboards, I find one full of random items that Uri has seemingly deemed extraneous: the fiction books from the bookcase, the body treatments from the en suite, the nuts from the snack bar. I've seen him refuse nuts, and I wonder if he has an allergy or just a dislike. Either way, this seems to be the reject cupboard. Everything that doesn't fit, hidden away.

Hope rises and I stand on tiptoe reaching far into the back, until my fingertips find a familiar object. I know, from the luxurious, substantial feel of it, that it's Olga's quilted navy gift box. I pull it out, gratified to be right. This would hold something about the size of a deck of cards.

I wonder what Uri's message from Olga is . . .

Inside the package is a box, made of polished onyx. It looks solid, yet each side is lined with a row of tiny, delicate padlocks. I'd guess they're made of platinum and rose gold – but, as I peer at them, I realise that none of them have an actual lock.

Is this a nod to the security work Uri's doing, which Olga acknowledged when she described the Pledge to us?

I lift the box out of its case to study it – and the base falls away, scattering the ineffective padlocks, tipping glitter over me.

I panic at the state of the floor and my hands.

Scooping up what glitter I can, I tip handfuls of it back into the box, replace the top, fumble to fit the padlocks, then push it all into the gift box and back inside the cupboard.

Running to the en suite, I wash my hands, which only makes the glitter stickier. I scrub frantically at them with tissue, with slightly better results.

Grabbing a wad of tissue paper, I dash back to the mess I've made and try to wipe up the telltale sparkles.

It works to a reasonable degree, and I run back with more damp tissue to get the remnants, then flush the lot down the loo.

It turns out glitter doesn't really flush. I might admire how decorative it's made the toilet bowl, if my heart wasn't fluttering in my throat with the hot panic of being discovered.

It's agony to wait for the cistern to fill again. Even worse is how exposed this bathroom is, specifically the rainfall shower with its glass wall. It's been designed as a tropical haven, with privacy provided only by the banana plants and bird of paradise flowers growing outside. The presence of a few leaves, though just enough to protect the occupant's modesty, are *not* reassuring when you're up to no good and desperate not to get caught.

Thankfully, the cistern has refilled and I flush again, adding tissue as a topper to help sweep the sparkly specks away.

It's better, but I'll have to do it a final time.

I peer out of the window, praying that Uri isn't in view. He isn't – but *Magnus* is. He's walking up to *this cabin*, and knocking on the door.

Oh no …

I freeze, hold my breath and cower down beside the curving bath.

'Hey, Uri? You gotta minute? We should talk.'

The cistern is still whooshing and I squeeze my eyes shut at the damning sound.

'I can hear you in there, Uri,' Magnus calls.

Oh, God, oh, God! My stomach drops and I press myself against the bathroom's cool marble floor, trying to stay out of view of the massive window.

I pray that Magnus isn't the type to peer through the glass.

And I wonder what he needs to discuss with Uri.

'You can't avoid it forever, Uri.' He hesitates, like he thinks Uri will still answer.

I jump out of my skin at the angry *thump* of Magnus's fist on the door. It makes me cower, whimpering, hoping this isn't the start of him breaking in. There's no handy cupboard or shower curtain to help hide me. This bathroom's design is very much *au naturel.*

He pounds on the door again, then yells, 'I didn't think you'd be such a goddamn coward about it.'

I cringe, praying that this isn't exactly the sort of erratic noise that would alert a hunting cat . . .

Cursing, Magnus storms off. He's muttering, glancing over his shoulder, heading to the main house. I hold my breath and watch him – as much to confirm he's actually *gone* as to make sure he gets back unscathed. With a squirm of guilt, I realise that's less for his benefit than mine.

I wait a few agonising seconds, then shakily get to my feet.

With a long exhale, I add more tissue and flush a third time, and this time, it's good enough.

Checking that the room is as I found it – almost – I dart out of the cabin, closing the door carefully behind me and skirting the side of the building, heading in the opposite direc-tion from Magnus, whose pace is slow and ponderous as he trudges back, so that I can return to the main house unseen.

I hope.

Monday 7th April – 3.30 p.m.

The bar in the great room is a popular destination at this time, for drinks or a nibble of something, so I saunter there as if I have nothing on my mind.

But my nerves are jangling. What if Magnus and Uri come over? What if Magnus asks why he didn't answer the door when he heard him in his cabin?

What did he want? What's Uri trying to avoid?

The sound of approaching footsteps from the hall makes me hold my breath – and I'm weak with relief to see that it's Asha.

'Asha!' I practically have to hold myself back from hugging her. 'Find out anything from Zyra and Estelle?' I ask in a conspiratorial whisper.

'Not really. They're too wary. It's them against the world now. How's your head?'

There's a beat before I remember my excuse earlier. 'Much better, thanks.'

She reaches for a couple of glasses. 'Smoothie?' When I nod, she adds, 'I've been thinking. Do you recall Olga telling Zyra that she'd invited them to be part of the Pledge because she was making amends?'

'Of course.'

'Do you have any theories about what Olga meant? Amends for what?'

I puff out a breath and shake my head. 'I don't know. But Zyra seemed worried that Olga might force her hand with a public announcement, like she'd done with Estelle. If that's what Olga was planning, it's not the *ideal* way to go about making amends.'

'Yeah. Provocative.' She reaches into the bar fridge for a selection of fruit, slicing it into the blender. 'That was Olga all over, though. Everything for leverage.'

We wait while she blitzes the fruit with ice from the dispenser, so our words don't compete with the blender's screech. Then Asha pours the fruity concoction into two glasses, offering me one.

It's sensational, and I down half the glass. She grins at me as she finishes hers. 'Hard to make a bad combo with all this fruit.'

The camaraderie feels genuine, and I risk an unguarded question. 'I've been wondering about that. Olga's leverage. You've had a hand in helping her decide what kind of people she'd need for this enterprise. And she must have needed leverage to invite this group. The four tycoons here are all in the top five of the Forbes Rich List. But there's someone missing. The current second wealthiest individual: Noelle Ascari. Why wasn't she invited?'

I don't ask 'why didn't she attend' because Olga's proved one thing: if she summoned you here, it was because she used more than a mere invitation.

I recall Noelle's mini-bio, which I read along with the others' when I first looked up Olga. Noelle's billions have been made in tech, no surprises there, but she's notable for pioneering different approaches to the standard model. Most recently, she made her AI software freely available to conservation groups to map habitats and species for preservation projects.

It would have made her a perfect candidate for Olga's mission. Yet she's missing.

Asha's eyes meet mine, and there's recognition – and a flash of respect. So I know.

It's because Olga didn't have any leverage over Noelle.

Someone in such an elevated position of wealth is unlikely to be squeaky clean. But perhaps she and Olga have just never crossed paths? Or perhaps Noelle's reputation is too sound for Olga to find that chink in her armour, the weak point she can exploit to manipulate her into doing her bidding.

'So Olga had nothing over Noelle. And that's why she's been excluded from this.'

Asha arches an eyebrow. 'I'd say that's a reasonable assumption.'

We clam up as Uri and Kali wander in and pilfer the snacks. Next, Estelle and Zyra arrive, standing back on the fringes, wary but wanting to hear any news. That human need to be part of the group, even though they've broken away from it.

'Still no luck trying to find a way out across the bay,' Zyra volunteers, like she's trying to atone for her plundering, and justify her rejoining of the group. 'Man, I need a soda after all that swimming.' Side-eyeing us, she opens the fridge, relief rolling off her when Kali smiles and hands her a glass.

As Estelle grazes on olives, I see Hugh then Magnus stumble in, clearly already tipsy, to pillage any provisions the bar might have.

I pour myself some iced water, because I'm hot with panic that Magnus might mention to Uri that he heard him in his cabin, when Uri would have known he wasn't there. In the silence, I'm fighting to compose myself.

I am desperate to ask questions and dig for the truth. But I'm afraid that, if I do, the urgent need to blame someone will shift straight to me: the only one with an obvious reason to want both Charles and Olga – my husband and his mistress – dead.

But questions are my weapons: I can read so much in someone's answer. With my heart thumping, as people gravitate to seats, I take the gamble.

'Can I ask you all a personal question? You don't need to answer. But I need to ask.'

Collective shrugs and a 'Sure,' from Kali spur me on. Their interest crackles palpably beneath a layer of caution and effected casualness.

'Did anyone else get a gift from Olga? A rather … pointed one?'

The group stiffens with silent tension. People stop chewing, and stare, then side-eye an ally: Estelle and Zyra exchange glances. Kali and Uri raise eyebrows at each other. Magnus and Hugh look at no one – but Asha catches my eye, frowning.

I wait, knowing for sure that Kali and Uri have both received a gift – and both rejected it, so they understood its message.

I don't look at them, but I watch them in my peripheral vision. They give absolutely nothing away as they continue eating, and shrug.

'Just me, then?' I try to look like I'm laughing it off.

'What did you get?' Asha asks.

'A bracelet designed to look like an endless ladder. To reveal my habit of climbing every ladder going – social, political, career, power – when the reality is that it doesn't actually get me anywhere. Least of all where I want to be.'

'Deep.' Uri's comment is sarcastic, and I give a self-deprecating laugh.

'Annoyingly true, as it happens.' I shrug. I search for an elegant way to avoid looking like I've been singled out by the murdered woman – and Magnus saves me.

'Yeah, I got a gift. And it sure was a message.'

He finishes a handful of nuts and reaches inside his jacket's breast pocket. 'Here.'

He tosses the luxe navy gift box to me, and I catch it. 'May I look inside?'

'Sure.'

Nestled in the satin lining is a shining rose-gold coin, intricately etched with an elephant. A miniature representation of a giant beast.

'Symbol of the Republican party?' At his nod, I say, 'That's not a secret, though. We all know you're a generous donor.' I hold his eye contact. 'Enough to sway opinion, as you've stated.'

I gaze at Magnus, sensing I'm missing something. He rotates a finger. 'Turn it over.'

On the other side is an exquisite engraving of a beautiful young woman. I don't recognise her, so I glance at Magnus again.

He takes a massive breath and his gaze sweeps over each of us. 'I'm gonna share something now that's real private. And this is not my tale to tell, so I can say that I'm deeply aggrieved at Olga pulling a stunt like this. That there is my daughter. And she was put in a position where she had to take an action that the party *I* support would not condone.' Another deep breath, this one shuddering with emotion. 'Would vilify her for, in truth. And worse.'

The penny drops. 'You don't need to spell it out, Magnus.' I pass it back to him and pat his arm in a gesture of support. 'I'm sorry she had to face a decision like that.'

His nod is full of gratitude for the understanding, and he adds, 'She didn't make it lightly. I guess no woman does. But it made me see that particular part of our policy in a whole different light. She even reported the man who attacked her. She's been strong and brave ...'

His voice falters and he squeezes the bridge of his nose as he shuts his eyes, before trying to continue.

'Truth be told, she's put me to shame.' He takes a deep, shuddering breath, and his gaze scans all of us. 'She's shown me how weak, how cowardly, men can really be.'

He flicks a thunderous glance at Hugh and, for a split second, I see real hatred for the prince and his lecherous behaviour. Now I know why Magnus has such a changed view of that behaviour, and the consequences of it – and why his epiphany was so painful. I guess that's why his hand shook when he spoke to me about it. I note that he's only been inclined to think critically about this issue once someone he cares about was directly affected. It's that problem proximity paradox again. I'm guilty of the same thing; I don't protest about things that affect others, only those that impact my own quality of life.

I squeeze his arm – but my sympathy is tempered as I realise that Magnus hasn't shunned Hugh's company when their interests have aligned. I realise this group has a next-level ability to sideline personal feelings if there's something to be gained, but if Magnus hasn't changed his own behaviour, then he can't really claim he's had an epiphany at all.

'So, Olga was trying to imply she'd make your daughter's predicament known? To your party?' Kali demands. Her tone conveys her outrage.

'Exactly. And she knew that I'd do anything to prevent that.' Anything, eh?

'But . . . how could she have known about it?' Kali asks.

'People with enough power, influence, money can find out pretty much anything they want.' Magnus purses his lips. 'Haven't we all used that fact to our advantage at one time or another?'

Awkward acknowledgement ripples around the room, and Magnus adds, with a note of defensiveness, 'And I'll say this, if she could find that out about me, she could unearth any of *your* dark secrets, too.'

I note how everyone looks down or away, fidgeting.

Kali's the first to deflect the focus back to Magnus. 'But why would your party care? Even if it created a stir, one thing you can count on in politics is that there's always another scandal brewing.'

'It's true,' Uri agrees. 'You'd just need to ride it out. Why the big threat?'

I side-eye Magnus. I know: the tiniest taste of being doxxed drove me here.

Magnus fixes Uri with a hard stare. 'I realise you're not the best equipped to weigh up *risks* and *tackle* them. But surely you can figure this one out?'

His emphasis grabs my attention. Magnus wanted to discuss some risk or other with Uri. Relating to his tech? I stare at Uri. In his line of work any unaddressed risk would be a major issue.

But Magnus is replying to the question anyway. 'Because Olga wouldn't just tell my *party*. It would become public knowledge. Have you got any idea of the bile people spout from behind their computers? The hate they whip up? The threats she'd get? The threats that might be *acted* on?' He's panting now, as he imagines the devastation that Olga could have caused to his family.

I recall the threats spewing from my own phone. That would have been a fraction of what Magnus's daughter would likely go through. What a world, that something so deeply private could be so publicly judged.

'I'd have done anything to protect my daughter from that.' Magnus shakes his head. 'Olga knew she had me on this one. I'd have to sign up to her precious Pledge.'

'This is what Olga was saying you should make a stand about? So she wasn't just threatening to expose your daughter's secret, she was pressuring you to speak up to your party?'

'Yeah. She thought the second point was the problem. It wasn't; it was the first.'

I look at him with more sympathy than I ever expected to feel for him. No wonder he literally fist-fought Hugh in a desperate bid to escape on that helicopter. Getting away would have meant avoiding the sign-or-decline event, and prevented Olga from using the leverage of his own daughter against him.

I also can't help wondering if Magnus welcomed the excuse to land a punch on Hugh. I can imagine the resentment that's been boiling under the surface for a while now. And this gift would have triggered all of that.

Yet ... Magnus hadn't escaped, had he?

Maybe instead he'd silenced Olga, to save his daughter from being hurt again ...

Chapter 19

Monday 7th April – 5.30 p.m.

AHEAD OF A DINNER THAT Kali and Uri are cooking, I wait until Hugh is settled by the bar and deep into a bottle of premium frozen vodka before peeling away from the great room and heading up to my suite.

I use my balcony to access the garden again, so I can get to Olga's lodge without being seen from the kitchen.

Instantly, I'm sweating – with fear rather than exertion. I've been having nightmares about that panther, roaming the grounds of the lodge with a newly acquired taste for human blood. It's eclipsing even my fear of snakes and spiders, despite those featuring highly on my panic-meter, so sheer terror is tremoring through me with every step.

Inside the lodge, I see Olga's double-fronted suite before me, and Charles's to the right. By now the panther surely must have caught the scent of his ripening corpse – *ugh!* – through the broken door, or it will very soon. Hugh's suite is to my left, and I know he isn't in there – for the moment. With a quick glance around me, I pull the staff key from my pocket, then let myself into Olga's suite.

I can't shake the feeling that there could be a clue in here, something that might tell me how she persuaded everyone to come. Some insight into her strategy.

There's an impressive bureau on this floor, which looks like it's brimming with secret compartments. As I methodically wrench each firmly locked drawer as hard as I can, I realise they'll stay secret.

I crawl underneath, trace my fingers over joins, but nothing yields. I check the ornate back of the desk, too, but there's no way in. There's not even a keyhole, just her company's emblem, miniaturised and engraved in the wood.

I have to admit defeat, for now. I wander around, ignoring the clues I've scouted before, trying to spot something different.

Upstairs, I'm drawn to those photos on the wall. I scan them, in case anyone here is pictured. But they could easily have crossed paths at COP symposiums, like Olga and Charles, or at charity events and fashion shows, which is how I imagine she met Zyra and Estelle.

The framed *Forbes* article draws me to it.

Olga Helgesdotter has risen like a phoenix from the ashes of her reputation, having come under fire for greenwashing.

We live in an age in which ESG commitments and progress are critical to – and critiqued by – increasingly conscious consumers.

No one knows this better than Olga, whose reports charting the supposed progress of ethical practices in her supply chains were overturned by an extensive investigation into exploitation of her workers.

These serious allegations ignite fury, inflame loyal customers and scorch share prices. Yet Olga isn't burned.

> Having tried to turn around the issues within the manufac-
> turing process, she's taken the lesson to heart and has
> now closed those lines.

Oh, nice. It's too hard to solve, so she's stopped that income for those communities. Her quick-fix gain is their long-term pain.

I scan the rest of the article and spot the quote from Olga.

> 'I was recently asked, *what do I want my legacy to be?*
> And this valuable life lesson has opened my eyes, not only
> to the challenges *we* endure as humans, but to the oppor-
> tunities *I* have as a visionary leader. My legacy, my gift to
> the world, will be to spearhead the change needed to
> address the gravest threats our planet, and humanity, will
> ever face.'

A footnote adds, 'Olga's autobiography, *Vision and Courage*, is out next summer, and available for pre-order now.'

This articles blurs over the gritty details, but it essentially outlines the story Estelle told me. There's nothing else here that's leaping out at me, and I have more searching to do.

So I dash downstairs, slip out of Olga's room and across the hall – where I let myself into Hugh's room.

My chest is thumping like a hare's foot beating a warning, and my hands are slick on the handle.

Hugh's downstairs sitting room is a mess. He is evidently a man used to someone else clearing up after him – in every sense. Empty bottles and snack wrappers are scattered across the bar top, the coffee table, the floor.

Upstairs, his bed is unmade, clothes strewn across chairs, and in the en suite, his half-squeezed toiletries pebble-dash the sink. If I didn't know a royal was in residence, I'd assume a stoner student was staying here.

But here, *somewhere*, will be Olga's gift. And if I can decipher whatever point Olga was making with it, then at last I'll have *something*: some valuable leverage or vital knowledge to work with. And I would *love* having something over Hugh.

Yet it feels icky, sifting through his bedroom detritus. The bedding and clothes are greasy with his sweat. The room is as fuggy as a teenage boy's. It makes my flesh crawl to touch anything. Visually sweeping the room, I check the bin. It's the only thing in here that's clean. I open cupboards, hunting for that telltale luxury gift box.

There's nothing on the shelves in the bathroom, or the bookcase. I unlock the bifolding doors and check the balcony. I don't even glance at the view, let alone take a moment to wonder at it. A towel has been dropped out here, and I prod it with my toe to check it's not covering something. *Nothing.* I pull the doors shut with frustration, but my eye is suddenly caught by a cupboard that's open a crack, and I dart over.

Opening the door fully, I see it's another drinks cabinet. Olga obviously knew how to personalise a room. There's only glasses and whisky – good whisky, and quite the collection – in here.

Moving downstairs again, I glance over more shelves and sideboards. I'm starting to feel like this is a fruitless exercise, and I'm only too aware that I've been here for several minutes already. I can't afford to be much longer.

Hurriedly, I glance around the room one more time – and notice the TV remote threatening to disappear down the side of the sofa. Dashing over, I check down the back of each cushion. Nothing … nothing … and then – just as I'm about to give up hope – my fingers catch on something.

I grapple with the edges of what feels like a box, my hopes rising, and pull it out . . .

Yes! That navy quilting! My mouth is dry as a desert as I open the gift box, sitting in the centre of the room. I'm totally exposed here, so I'll have to be quick . . .

Inside is a medal. It looks like an OBE: the stylised cross topped with a crown – in this case, studded with jewels – hanging from a wide navy ribbon. Why would Olga give Hugh this?

The royal honour is a sharp reminder of what Hugh did to Drew on the yacht. Had Olga witnessed something similar? Was that her warning to him?

On the other side of the mock OBE, some words are engraved: *Our Benefactor . . . Eventually.*

As I stare at it, some of those nagging memories about Hugh's scandals crystallise. Cash for honours. Of course. The accusations had been rampant, flying across the royal households, and coming to land on Hugh. And he wasn't averse to the cash, that much was certain.

I'm shaken out of the recollection by a sound at the door. That quiet *click* of the key in the lock.

God! He's here!

Jumping up, I fumble with the box, trying to slide the medal back in.

The handle's turning . . .

I can't get the damn medal into its inset position, so the lid won't close.

The door's opening . . .

Panicking, I shove the half-closed box down the side of the sofa and try to throw myself under it.

I'm scrabbling on the floor as Hugh walks in. He sways towards the bar, turning his back to me, and I think for a split second that I've got away with it.

Then I hear him chuckle at my undignified – vulnerable – state. When I peer up, he's looking at me in the mirror, his cruel mouth lifted into a sneer.

'Thea. Presenting yourself for the pleasures of the prince? I never knew you cared.'

I'm already panting before I even leap to my feet. Well, I would have *liked* to have leaped, but I stumble in my desperation to get up off the floor, putting myself at even more of a disadvantage.

My head is shrieking with that warning clamour. My own stupid ambition has put me thoroughly in harm's way. No one knows where I am; no one would hear me if I screamed the place down.

Like a clumsy bear, Hugh turns to block the door, and stares at me. His eyes travel slowly up and down my body, his expression lewd. 'Take off your clothes.'

I don't answer that. I'm not giving it oxygen, nor him the satisfaction.

He moves towards me, still blocking my exit, but closing the gap between us.

Just his presence makes me feel violated.

I step back, my gaze darting around the room like I'm a hunted gazelle.

Fight or flight is zinging in my veins and the answer comes: *The bifolding doors to the balcony are unlocked . . . if I can just get upstairs . . .*

So I edge towards the staircase, hating how it makes him leer in anticipation.

'*Now* you're thinking, Thea.'

I shudder, but I reach the stairs and scramble up them. I can feel him near my feet, literally hot on my heels.

At the top of the stairs, he shoves me. I'm just far away enough that I don't take the full force of it, but it sends me staggering towards the bed.

I'm flailing out of control, and he's closing in on me.

In another stride, he's closed the gap between us, and he pushes me again.

Desperately, I try to dodge him, but I don't recover my balance in time, and he sends me falling onto the bed.

My face is pressed into his sweat-soaked, BO-drenched sheets and I gag, fighting to sit up.

Horror spikes as he grabs an ankle and drags me towards him, parting my legs. His whole body weight seems to be bearing down on me, making sure I can't struggle free.

I use his pressure to lever myself up, groaning at the sit-up manoeuvre and using all my force to shove him away.

But I just bounce off his bulk like a rubber ball – and then he grips my wrist, pinning me down as he climbs, grunting, on top of me.

'No. Get off me, Hugh. This is assault—'

He moves to cover my mouth, releasing the pressure on my wrist, but his heavy hand is over my nose, too. I fight for air, thumping him, grappling with the hand he's encased my face with. The struggle is making me run out of breath faster.

My hands wander wildly anywhere and everywhere, casting around for something to use, and I feel the cord of the bedside lamp. I tug it, and the heavy lamp falls over. I haul the cord towards me until the base is within reach.

I know from those pathologists I've worked with that the side of the head is the tender part, the softest part of the skull. Right by the temple.

My fingers spider around the lamp base, trying to find purchase.

If . . . I . . . can . . . just . . . grip the base enough to . . . lift . . . it . . .

I brace my stomach muscles, take a gasping breath through Hugh's fingers, and grit my teeth.

If . . . I . . . can . . . just . . . swing . . . it . . . upwards . . .

With all my might, I heft the lamp up . . .

Then I *smash* the solid glass and gold base against Hugh's soft parietal bone.

He slumps on top of me.

It's shockingly immediate – and he's shockingly still.

He's crushing me, and I *push* desperately, tipping him off me just enough to slide out from under him.

I'm shaking so much I can't stand. My legs buckle under me and I collapse in a heap on the floor, staring at Hugh's unresponsive body, his head bleeding, blood and hair sticking to the lamp which – amazingly – isn't broken.

Horrified, I realise that Hugh could very possibly be dead. I can't see signs of breathing, and I'm not about to touch him to check for a pulse.

Somehow, this possibility makes an otherworldly calm settle over me, like a mantle of protection. I've saved myself once, and now I have to do it again. As if I'm being directed, I take the lamp to the foot of the bed and smear the blood and hair that's on the base carefully onto the flat edge of the ottoman. It's a better fit for the shape of the lamp base than the corner.

I run to the en suite and wipe the lamp base with soapy tissue until it's clean and dry, then carefully replace it, with its shade, on the bedside table, in its correct position.

Bracing myself, I grab Hugh's sheet and heave it, so that I haul Hugh off the bed along with it – but, crucially, *without* the accompanying drag marks that might abrade his skin.

I tip him into the position that matches up mark on the ottoman, and put the rumpled sheet back on the bed.

Taking a wad of tissues, I wipe down everything I've touched, including the medal, which I put back properly.

Then I leave by the balcony, taking care to wipe down the door of any fingerprints.

Certain that I've covered my tracks, I leave the door to the garden closed – but unlocked.

So that any of us could have got in and killed him.

Chapter 20

Monday 7ᵗʰ April – 6 p.m.

Away from Hugh's room, my head is spinning. I feel sick and dizzy, and yet also weirdly calm.

That clamour of danger that I've associated with Hugh for so long has stopped. *Finally.*

I can't look like I've had any kind of … incident. I have to find a way to explain my absence – and quickly.

Then I notice the blood spattered up my arms.

It's not mine.

With a surge of panic, and yet knowing exactly what to do, I skirt round Olga's lodge and into her garden, then cut through the hedge to Charles's garden and into my own. I jog up the steps to the balcony and use the key to let myself into my room.

There, I strip my clothes off and run the shower.

I scrub and scrub and *scrub* my skin until it is red raw. I think about using that rasul treatment, wondering if it will make me smell, or feel, anything other than Hugh's over-powering stench, the shuddery sense of his meaty hands. I swallow back the rising bile at the thought. But the thought of caking myself in mud is nauseating, like it could lock Hugh's DNA into my own skin.

The heady fragrances from every single glass vial eventually make me feel human again – but the fear is more real.

Of what could have happened – and what did happen.

My hands are shaking too much now to wash myself. Then I realise my whole body is shaking.

I sink to the ground, warm water streaming over me, and I sob my heart out.

*　*　*

At dinner, I smile, make conversation, try to distract everyone from Hugh's unusual absence at the arrival of food.

But Kali is too sharp. 'Where's Pavlov and his dog?'

As Magnus joins us, as if summoned, Kali grins at me, but no one seems inclined to chase up Hugh.

And Magnus, naturally, is happy to see the upside. 'All the more for us, if Hugh's sleeping off a hangover.'

Maybe someone here would have bothered to check on him if he'd been more of a team player. Or less of a sleaze.

I force myself not to shudder.

'We can always leave him a plate,' I suggest.

Was that too much? My guilty gaze darts around the table, but everyone is shrugging and tucking into the katsu curry.

'Who made this?' I ask.

'Uri's the chef.' Kali points at him. 'But this is my recipe.'

'Quite sweet that we're pooling provisions. This is lovely.' I feel like a traitor, praising teamwork and collaboration, when I'm a killer.

'Made a little progress with the radio today,' Uri says. 'There's a tiny chip that I cannot find anywhere but I can't give up hope on it.'

'Need a hand looking?' I ask, too keen to make up ground. 'I'll join you.'

'Thanks. But I thought it might be worth asking you to check the treads of your shoes. Anyone who's been in the office. Just in case.'

'Sure.' I smile. Then I grimace. 'Oh. That will include Charles.' I wince, then hear myself volunteering, I suppose to prevent anyone else from suggesting it: 'I'll check his.'

'We've searched behind every painting and piece of art in this place,' Kali says, 'But still no sign of that damn safe that has all our phones in it.'

'Never known a place more secure.' Magnus sounds disgruntled. 'It's making me fantasise about hot-wiring that helicopter.'

I gape at him. Why hasn't anyone tried that yet? 'Is that possible?'

'Not easily,' Uri answers, chewing. 'I had a look at it already.'

'Of course you did,' Magnus says. Now that I know he and Uri have a strained relationship for some reason or other, I pick up on the challenge in his tone. But Magnus's smile is cordial, and makes the barb sound like a compliment.

'We still can't find any suitable vessels to get us to another island or any boats that might be nearby,' Zyra says.

'Not that they'd be any use, since we also can't figure out how to open the harbour gate,' Estelle adds, more practically.

'So essentially we're no further forward?' Kali sums up.

We finish our food in tense silence. There's an unspoken expectation that people's entourage and teams will start to make contact soon. But the uncertainty in the meantime is ... *unbearable*.

And I'm bracing myself to fulfil my offer to Uri. After dinner, I decide to just get it over with. I take a deep inhale outside Charles's door, unlock it, and slip in.

Even through my held breath, the smell is putrid. Hot, sickly-sweet decay rolls over me like storm waves.

As I approach the stairs, the stench only grows stronger, and I cover my mouth and nose with my top.

Even so, as I approach the bed, I gag. I can hear the buzz of flies.

I won't look at him. I'll just check his shoes, then I'll get the hell out of here . . .

But I can't help it.

His skin is greenish except for his buttocks and legs, which are lividly purple, and his chest that's clotted with dark blood. I know that the adrenaline from the past few days combined with the heat would have accelerated his decomposition. He looks like a prop from a horror film. It's so surreal I almost wouldn't believe it, if it weren't for that punch-in-the-stomach stench.

His chest is alive with flies, fuzzing over him. As I lean over him, in sick fascination, I spot what's nestling in the cuts slashing his body: clutches of eggs, like miniscule grains of rice. They are everywhere; he is riddled, and when the maggots hatch in a few weeks, they'll feast on his flesh.

Jostling for position on his soft, exposed tissues, some flies shoot up and hit me in the face. I recoil in disgust at the thought of the bacteria they're brimming with, having crept all over his decaying wounds.

Hot bile burns in my throat. I swallow it back, and turn away from the natural desecration of his tender tissues.

I can't prevent the onslaught of nature. So I focus on what I came here to do. Searching, I see three pairs of shoes lined up against the wall near his bed. Very bloody boarding school. I check the soles carefully but quickly, running a fingertip over the treads in case I can feel something that I don't see.

Nothing. This has all been for nothing.

Unless … Might Olga have given Charles a gift? What would her message have been to him?

I rummage through Charles's clothes and trinkets. All of them are so achingly familiar.

The issues I had a few days ago seem pathetic next to the present danger.

Why didn't I just get a divorce? Yes, it would have been messy, maybe acrimonious, probably bitter. But it would have meant freedom.

It would have meant I'd be living my life now, instead of vying for survival.

Without thinking about what I'm looking for, I spot the gift box.

Like Kali's, it's half-covered with wrappers, in the bin.

So he didn't like his message either, then.

I open the box, and stare at the gorgeous, old-fashioned compass, exquisitely etched with triangular compass points.

But something about it is off. Squinting at it, I study the finely engraved letters, and realise there are five main compass points, not four. The needle is fixed to the top one, which looked like *N*, but is actually an *M*. The other points are *O*, *R*, *A* and *L*.

Next to the *M* something is etched in even finer writing, and I have to move towards the window to read it.

Misdirection.

That thud of danger begins to beat, faint but steady, building and building, until the awful shriek in my head, that terrible warning clamour, starts up again.

* * *

I'm trying not to shake as I head into the office to see Uri. Then I remind myself that I've just visited my dead, decaying husband. I would be shaken.

And it's obvious he can see it as soon as he looks up from the desk.

'Oh, man. I knew I shoulda gone. I'm sorry.'

'No, no. It's fine. It had to be me. But it was . . . vile.' I sink onto a seat and let out the long sigh I've been holding in. 'And I wish it had been worthwhile, but there was nothing on his shoes. Or mine.'

'Yeah, I know it was a long shot. But still.' His shrug is friendly. 'When long shots are all you got, you gotta take 'em.'

I nod. 'Quite. But we're rather running out of any shots at all, aren't we. Long or otherwise.'

'That's the spirit.' Uri winks at me. 'This is when the best innovations happen. Comfort zones are the killer of invention. When you're *really* uncomfortable, you're probably on the brink of genius.'

'Oh, great. Will that stop the murderer we're trapped with going on another killing spree? Or the panther from eating us? Or the mosquitoes from completing their life's work of draining me sodding well dry?'

Desperate fear and panic sweep over me, engulfing me, and I sink into the desk chair, leaning my head into my hands, sobbing.

'Hey, hey . . .' Uri takes my hands gently, crouching opposite me. 'There haven't been any more deaths, have there? We're working together—'

'For now.'

'Yes, for now. That's better than nothing, though.' Seeing me nod and try to rally, he tilts his head. 'Did you just say something about a *panther*?'

Oh ... great.

'Yes.' I gulp. 'Olga's pet has got loose ... somehow. It might come near the house, if Olga used to feed it.'

'What the actual *fuck*, Thea?' He paces to the window, peering out. 'Those are serious predators. If they associate us with food, that's dangerous.'

'Yes.' I should tell him that it's even more dangerous now that it has eaten human flesh, but his face is blotched with anger and fear.

'It might be fine for you, staying in the main house, not having to set foot outside unless you choose to! But *others*,' he thumps his own chest, 'have to run the panther-stalked gauntlet to and from those cabins.'

'Yes, I should have—'

'Too right you should have! Who *have* you told?'

'Um. No one.'

'*Jesus*, Thea. We better have a house meeting. Share the good news.'

'Sure.' I throw my hands up. 'Go ahead. Share that information with our company when at least one of them is trying to kill us. I don't want to give that person any advantage, or a new opportunity.'

'I think it's reasonable to hypothesise that the murderer had issues only with Olga and Charles—'

'How nice of you to believe that your flawed *assumption* gives you the right to dictate what *I* share to a group that includes a killer. *My* take is quite different. The victims are my husband and his mistress, and *that* brings the whole thing rather too close to me for comfort. I might be *framed*, or I might be *next*.'

'Well, there *is* good logic to you being the prime suspect.' Uri nods like this is an interesting theoretical chat, not him accusing me of a killing spree.

'You can't be serious?' I gape at him.

He just shrugs. 'I like data. Empirical evidence. You can't deny facts, or where they lead you.'

'What *I* can't deny is that I've no intention of giving up every bit of intel I find, because, somewhere amongst that information, there might be things I need to protect *myself*.'

I'm panting, and I know I must look insane. I know that my face is taut with intense fear, that the emphasis in my voice has tipped towards desperate . . . *mad*.

I take a deep breath, reach for the rebuttal argument. 'Besides, Uri, you were the one who said the killer would need to keep killing, to cover their tracks. Any one of us might know something incriminating. How easy would it be for them to "accidentally" lock someone outside?'

Uri assesses me in that irreverent way of his.

'You do have a point. We can't afford to get complacent.' He looks at me uneasily, as if weighing something up. 'We might want to be . . . prudent with our data. So I could get on board with not broadcasting the fact that we have a panther for company.'

I frown, letting the silence hang to give him a chance to elaborate. He does.

'Look, let me share something with you in strictest confidence.' At my nod, he continues. 'Someone broke into my room today. So you may want to barricade your door.'

'What?' I gasp: my shock and horror at his realisation of *that* is real, at least.

He leans forward, and I mirror him as his tone grows conspiratorial. 'I leave a hair trap on my door, and today it showed that someone went in there. I don't know what they were doing, or why. But it's a bad sign. I can't help wondering if the murderer is doing a reccy. If I'm *next*.'

He looks so worried that I reach out and awkwardly pat his arm.

With a smile, he catches my hand, squeezes it fondly, then releases it. His eye is caught by something, and he stares at my hand … frowning …

'What the *fuck*, Thea?'

He grips my hand, pulling it towards him to examine my cuticles. 'Jesus fucking Christ!'

And then I see what he sees.

Two treacherous, bastard flakes of black glitter stuck down the side of my nail.

'So it was *you*.' He leaps up, explosive in his outrage. 'Of *all* the people here, Thea. Of *every*one, you're the *last* person I would have thought would go behind my back.' He paces, shaking his head, then he laughs. 'Of *course*! *That's* why you were fishing for information about Olga's gifts.'

His stare is devastating. I want to turn inside out with guilt, at regret for ruining a useful alliance.

'What has it told you, then? All this sneaking around?'

'Nothing.' I grasp at the only opportunity I'll have to convince him. 'I didn't understand it. And all it's proved is that everyone here – me included – is in the same boat. Olga invited *each* of us because she believed she had some leverage that would work on us.'

I stand and look him level in the eyes. 'Even if I knew your secret, Uri, it would just show me that you're the same as everyone else here. With no more or less motive than any of us.'

'Oh, very fucking reassuring.' His eyes are wide with indignation, with fury at me for not understanding. 'That isn't the fucking point! I thought you were someone – maybe the *only* person here – who I might be able to trust. And it turns out you're an utter fucking liar.'

He storms off.

I know that when he calms down, he'll realise that I must have got hold of a staff key somehow. And then he'll realise that when he saw me on the landing, he'd caught me creeping in and out of other rooms.

And then he may want to know what I know.

But until then, I have another concern. If I haven't washed off all the sodding glitter, then I won't have washed off all Hugh's DNA.

Chapter 21

Monday 7ᵗʰ April – 8 p.m.

I CAN'T FACE ANYONE ELSE TODAY. I'm walking to my room on shaking legs, hoping that no one will intercept me and sense the quivering panic that must be pulsing off me.

Beyond the great room, I spy the company assembled in the movie theatre, where Uri's searching through the downloaded films. He must have seen me walk past the door, as he glances up and glowers before continuing his search.

Magnus, mellowing in a chair, replete from dinner, is ready for whatever entertainment Uri finds; while Kali looks restless, shifting in her seat, her mind clearly elsewhere.

Estelle and Zyra are scooping popcorn from a machine styled like a vintage popcorn cart, their friendship clearly strengthening.

I'm dreading the moment Hugh is found. With a flash of clarity, I realise this is how the murderer must have felt as they waited, with burgeoning expectation and the fear, for their victims to be discovered: for the world to slide around and everything to change.

The anxiety gnaws at me, and I'm questioning my reactions to everyone and everything, wondering if my expressions are normal, or if every gesture is revealing my guilt. I keep going, heading upstairs, having to grip the banister to steady myself.

'Hey!' Asha looms out of the shadows on the landing and breaks into my thoughts. 'Have you got a minute?'

'Not really.' I keep walking. 'I don't feel great. I just want to have a shower and an early night.'

My hands are clamped at my sides. I feel like Lady Macbeth, like they're giving me away.

'OK, I'll walk with you.'

I force a smile, trying to hide my annoyance. As we continue along the hall, Asha whispers, 'Did you take a look at those papers that we found in that secret drawer?'

I blink. That seems like a lifetime ago. 'Not yet.'

'So you've got them?' Asha confirms.

Damn. I try to rally. I can't let a second's weakness make me even more vulnerable. 'No?' I hope my voice is convincing, but the note is too uncertain. 'I thought you had them?'

'No, I went back to get them but they weren't there. I'd hoped you'd put them somewhere safe.' Her glance at me is not convinced. 'I wonder where they are, then?'

I glance over my shoulder. Then I realise I can't possibly be paranoid – about anything – since I am actually sharing accommodation with a killer.

Asha does the same, then nods at my door. 'Can we . . . speak in private? It's just . . .' now she mouths the words, 'I've found something *else*.'

My skin prickles, and I somehow know that I'm not going to like this. I fumble with my key. 'Once a journo, always a journo,' I try to tease, to hide my discomfort.

But she grimaces at me, and my unease builds. I swing the door open, and as she darts in before me and I check the empty hallway, I wonder if this is a ruse, and my heart thumps, nausea churning through my stomach.

Closing the door, I swallow.

'You're not going to like this,' Asha warns. 'But I hope you'll see that I . . . well . . . that I had to show you.'

I turn, appreciating her cutting to the chase. I lift my chin, feigning readiness for whatever this could be.

With a deep breath, Asha pulls a folded piece of paper from the pocket of her denim shorts. She unfolds it, and I see it's a copy of a tabloid's front page, the photo blurred but damning. Immediately, that clamouring shrieks in my head again.

I know what it is, and I don't want her to show me. If my legs weren't trembling, I'd step back, create distance. I hold out my hand, fending it off, pushing it away.

But she mistakes the gesture and offers it to me, like I'm trying to take it from her.

And now somehow I'm holding it, *looking* at it, with almost academic detachment, and somehow my hand isn't shaking.

'Hugh?' I say what I see. 'A little worse for wear? Looks like he's leaving a party?'

'Yes. This is the only copy. It was in Olga's locked drawer, right at the back. I think the palace must have clamped down on circulation.'

I nod, unable to speak or swallow.

'I wonder who that is?' Asha points at the large hand filling the foreground, pushing the camera away. 'Hugh's companion? Security?'

All you can see of the man is his chin. The cleft and that freckle are distinctive . . . *familiar.*

I shrug. But I know. It's Charles. Nearly thirty years ago. The millennium party. When we were at uni.

Asha is staring at me so ... searchingly. I meet her gaze and have to fight the urge to shudder, sick with fear. *Does she know?*

Her eyebrows flicker, almost hopefully, and I'm suddenly certain that she *does* know, and she's testing me: seeing if I'll admit it, seeing if she can trust me.

Charles is dead, and so, now, is Hugh. I'll have nothing to lose ...

Even so, I can't bear to face it. To revisit that ... that *time*.

'It looks like it could be Charles. Also at the party. Probably while they were at uni. There were sometimes photographers sniffing around.'

I stop talking. I could give too much away ...

'Yes, I can imagine why he ... *they* ... wouldn't like that much.' Asha's gaze is as fixed on me as a cobra's on a mongoose.

The shrieking in my head rises ... I fight to block it out, like I have done all these years.

And yet I'm transported right back to that night. In my memory, it's tinged with red, like a sepia photo that's soaked in blood. I see it differently now from how I did then, of course. A few decades of life experience stripped away the naive gloss, exposing the sordid and ugly reality for what it was. One of the reasons I've buried it all so deeply is my shame: at my judgements at the time, at how I giggled along, at how I didn't find the courage to speak up – and at how that traps me more tightly as time goes on.

Already, my treacherous mind is flooding with the sights, smells, sounds. I can hear the crunch of gravel under my pinching high heels as Charles and I walk to the door of the manor house. These are Hugh's uni digs, located out of town and easy to make secure and discreet – a secretive lair for his notorious house parties. I shiver as the wind picks up, making the fiery torches lining the driveway gutter; like we're entering the gates of hell.

Passing through the security detail, we enter the dimly lit hall, with doors leading off it cracked open, inviting yet mysterious.

When I hesitate, Charles tugs me close, looks deep into my eyes and strokes my cheek. His whisper is warm on my skin. 'You. Look. Gorgeous.' His kiss is slow and sensual, and the gleam in his eye is teasing. 'You make me the envy of every man here.' He steers me gently ahead of him, through the door, and murmurs against the back of my neck, 'And I *love* it.'

Pounding music reverberates through my chest. My coat is whisked away, a drink is pressed into my hand and, as we move through to the banqueting hall, we're drawn to the heaving mass of bodies, dancing to the DJ in the silver bikini who's playing in the minstrel's gallery.

The party's theme has lent itself to women wearing sexy, skimpy outfits while the men are fully clothed. Funny how that's absolutely always the way, isn't it? The music's addictive and I'm swept up along with the sweating bodies seething around us. Charles pulls me into his arms and we dance, swaying together, pressing close. With a devilish grin, he beckons, and we move on towards the next room, which seems to be some kind of antechamber.

There's a seedier feeling here, and my hackles go up, my eyes darting as unease rises.

Tapestries have been hung over the windows, like this is the recovery room, shielding dark deeds and hangovers from unwelcome, probing sunlight.

Low sofas are arranged around the central table, which is covered in bongs and caskets. Scattered pills spill out from the cartoon heads of PEZ dispensers. The table's glass is fogged with imprints of genitalia, suggesting games played under the influence.

'Want some?' Charles reaches across to one of the caskets, flipping it open and dabbing his finger in the powder, rubbing it on his gums. When I shake my head, he doesn't push me.

'Charles!' A boarding school-accented blonde in a gold sequined minidress, a golden halo askew over tousled hair, air-kisses him, then leans across him to take a pill. 'Hoped you'd be here.' Her smile is sly. 'Finty will be pleased to see you.' She places the pill on the end of her tongue and curls it into her mouth.

'How kind. I'll be able to introduce you both to Thea.' He takes my hand, lacing his fingers between mine, and his smile is wicked.

The blonde eyes me like we're about to spar. I expect a scathing veiled insult, but she's too clever, too calculating, for that. 'You've hooked up! *Amaz*ing. You better both come to my "Fuck the New Year's Resolutions" party. I won't take no for an answer.'

I give her a warm fake smile, registering that her method will be the takedown from within. Friendly concern and confidences, then flirtatious commiserations with Charles.

'No promises. We might be busy.' Charles winks at me, and his secret, sidelong glance is irresistibly magnetic. The blonde pouts and retreats, and Charles pulls me onwards, exploring the rooms, skirting the knots of people drinking or kissing. We gather speed as we roam through the dining hall and library, then he leads me up the wide staircase. His hands trail over me, our pace quickening.

As we burst into a bedroom, we find him: Hugh, outside on the balcony, lounging on a Regency sofa that's been pulled out to enjoy the moon-drenched view. Three naked women are draped over him. Well, girls. Younger teenagers, probably. They look awkward, uncomfortable, their rictus smiles assuring – who? Him, or themselves? – that this is worth it.

'What's this? Charles and Thea!' Hugh pushes the girls away as he stares at me. 'Welcome to my millennium "Kinks 'n' Drinks" party. So … what have you come as, Thea, with a costume like that?'

I wish I could say that I bit back a grimace. But I *giggled*. I've squeezed myself into a black leather catsuit, a chunky gold chain wrapped artistically around one arm, one leg, then padlocked at my hip.

With a smile, I say, 'I'm all those deepest, darkest secrets. Safely locked away.'

'You'll go far in law, Thea, dearest.' Hugh's hand is on my back, straying low … lower … and I know he's searching for the zip.

I realise now that was the only smart decision I made that night: wearing an outfit with hidden fastenings. Useful for evading wandering hands, like Hugh's, who'd unzipped me in public at a gathering before; not so good when you need to go to the loo. But then again, a reason to spend a little longer in the sanctuary of women-only places can sometimes be a blessing.

Charles's eyebrows knit together and his gaze on me is heated with concern. I force a smile, turning towards Hugh as an excuse to twist out of his grasp. 'Amazing place. Thanks for inviting us.' I include Charles in my smile, letting him know I can handle this.

Hugh's draping teenagers pout at being displaced, and my sympathy for them evaporates. Now I realise their show of reluctance was just to appease the men, while probably disguising relief. No different to me giggling at Hugh instead of kneeing him in the balls. Back then, with a spike of spite, and pompous ignorance, I'd assumed they were there by choice.

'I hope you'll make yourself very . . . comfortable, Thea.' Hugh is still leering at me. 'We might get you to loosen up a little tonight.' He draws a slim gold monogrammed box from his pocket, taking out a tablet stamped with a heart. He holds it up, just above my nose like I'm a puppy doing tricks for treats. 'For me, Thea dearest. Go on.'

The idea of being drunk or high around Hugh scares me. My instincts are firing, telling me in no uncertain terms that I need my wits about me, at all times. 'No, I'm fine, thanks, Hugh.'

Hugh's scoffing snort makes the girls laugh.

'Don't hold out on me now, Thea. Not now you've gone all Catwoman on me. Now I *know* you're not the straight-laced student you make out.' He strokes one finger down my throat, down my chest, straight over my nipple, down my stomach, and cups my crotch. 'Take it for me. Like a good girl.'

I cringe to think that I giggled again. *Giggled.* Even though I know now that *friend, freeze* and *fawn* are the other aspects of the fight or flight response. I was trying to play along just enough to get myself out of what I could see this situation becoming. Worse than a grope; worse than playing along: the risk of saying no. Because 'no' to men like Hugh was not an option. The danger of saying it was far too great. And *that*, right there, was the whole problem, the entire issue I was too weak to speak out against.

So I giggle, and gently push his hand away. 'Another night, maybe. Not tonight.'

But Charles is looking at me, and that's when that warning note, that's haunted me for so many years, first begins to keen in my head. High pitched, like an alarm; the shrill alert of danger.

When Charles suggests refreshing our drinks, Hugh joins us downstairs. And I don't know if I'm imagining it, expecting something to be wrong, but my champagne tastes bitter. I linger over it, tipping it into plant pots, or slopping it onto the antique rugs when I think I can get away with it.

I fake growing drunk. But I *don't* imagine Hugh's fevered interest, his hot rancid breath, him pressing close when we join the dancing, the room a human tide ebbing and swelling, arms raised, eyes closed, as the DJ's tracks wash over us.

But I *do* have to try to convince Hugh that his attempts to spike my drink have worked, so that he doesn't try something else, something worse. So I let myself go with the music. On one level it feels great to just dance without inhibitions, for once – but I'm edgy with the ever-present threat. Suddenly, I realise Charles has disappeared and Hugh is nudging me out to the antechamber.

In the corner, a man with his trousers down is thrusting at a barely conscious woman, and I want to speak out, yell at him to stop. But then I remember that I'm also supposed to be barely conscious, so I can't. I mustn't. I'm more scared of what will happen if I give myself away, even though I don't know, *daren't* know, what that might be.

Hugh steers me towards the sofa, pushing me down, fumbling around for the invisible zip. I let my body flop, making sure I'm lying firmly against the fastening, blocking the access sought by his questing fingers.

His frustration grows evident as he manhandles me more roughly, and I let myself become an unresponsive deadweight. It doesn't deter him. If anything, he's more excited, more urgent.

The clamouring shrieks louder and louder. I have to do something to put him off.

'Mmmf? Charles?' I wonder if my boyfriend's name might bring him to his senses.

I'm not sure if that did the trick, or if my leather encasement has protected me, but that's when Hugh gives up, pushing me away and charging off, growling. He spies one of the teenagers from earlier, and grabs her hand, pulling her along with him. She stares at me over her shoulder, her eyes dead. And I feel sick.

One of the catering staff walks past with more champagne and I shake my head at him. I've had enough for tonight. In every way. The young man hesitates, then whispers, 'Do you need help, miss? Can I call you a taxi?'

Over his shoulder, I see Charles approaching, and I make the shake of my head slight but firm. It can't look like I'm conscious enough to have a conversation.

Charles sits beside me. 'Thea, are you OK?' He turns to call to the waiter. 'Can we get some water over here?'

'Umhumm.' I keep up the impression that I'm rousing, but that makes the clamouring in my head even worse. So when I wince, it's genuine.

He helps me sit up. 'Welcome back. Here. Drink this.' He presses the glass into my hand and I sip the water. 'Good. Keep drinking.'

I manage half the glass while he watches. 'So, Hugh likes you, then.' His head tilts as he appraises me. 'I'm not the jealous type, Thea. I know you're a free spirit. And I know we both want to enjoy all the ... *opportunities* life sends our way.'

My pulse speeds up as I wonder what he's suggesting. A provocative twitch plays across his lips, and he has the gleam in his eye that I love, when I know he's going to say something outrageous.

He smooths my hair back from my face, his fingers lingering, his gaze approving, like we're in a romantic film. 'We're a strong enough couple to handle it, if you want to . . . shake things up a bit.' He gives a half-smile. 'I think we both enjoy disrupting the status quo.'

My younger self is too credulous, too innocent, to understand his self-serving transaction. Now, I realise it's where my hatred of Charles subconsciously took root; that something was already rotten in the kernel of our relationship before it could even bloom. Now, I wonder if he *knew* I'd been spiked, and had cleared the way for Hugh. My body bartered for our gain. For *his*.

Yet Charles's charm offensive continues. 'I'm realistic enough to know that Hugh's type gets what they want. I can't be surprised that he wants you. This is your opportunity, Thea. You can play your trump card here: encourage him, charm him, delight him – and just *imagine* what his loyal friendship, his connections, can bring us.'

Charles knows this is my Achille's heel. I don't have his privileged upbringing, or the network it affords; I don't automatically know the rules of the game. I *do* know I'm not the kind of girl his family would approve of, and I wonder if our relationship is some small rebellion on his part – if that's even part of his attraction to me. But there's a background fear that any short-term spark will burn out in favour of something more *suitable* in the long term. And yet, I know that if I really want to play at this level, if I want to access a network like this, then Charles is my key.

'Just think about securing those connections, the secrets you can be trusted with.' He tugs the padlock on my hip. 'That's *true* power, Thea.' He leans in, whispering in my ear, his words hot and resonant against my sensitive flesh. 'And you can play that game, if you want.'

Somehow, he makes it sound almost logical, easy. And he makes me feel naive for not understanding how the world really works.

I weigh Charles's words. I manage to massage his advice into some romanticised version, imagining myself like a modern Anne Boleyn keeping Henry at arm's length while getting what she wanted. I overlook the fact it cost her her head. I'm smarter than Hugh. And, probably, Charles. I can dodge Hugh's overtures while Charles hangs onto his coattails.

Because I want the power. I *really* want the power.

Looking back now, with the benefit – or curse – of more worldly wisdom, I see that Charles was wrong. The price isn't just an unpalatable fumble at a party; it's knowing what really happens behind these closed, gilded doors. It's being unable to deny how poorer mortals are commodified – and then disposed of.

I was at a crossroads that night: I could have spoken out about what I'd seen, but I'd have been one lone voice against the establishment, up against all that unassailable, impenetrable power. And that's exactly the point, isn't it? That protective wall of influence is what I'm so desperate for.

So, that night, in that moment, I decide to keep the secrets, to turn a blind eye to the more … unsavoury things. I'll walk the perilous tightrope of trying to protect myself while gaining favour.

I raise my eyes to meet his gaze, and give him a hint of a smile.

As Charles squeezes my hand, I feel something deep and important inside me erode – and I know that I've sold my soul to the devil.

How is it that the shortcut to climbing those social and career ladders begins with throwing yourself down this treacherous, slippery slope?

The night draws on. Charles and Hugh slope off, to drink or get high, and I'm glad to be alone in the crowd, dancing.

Eventually I find a spare bed, though I daren't sleep. I hear the slam of car doors and engines as guests leave – except for the sound of one car returning, maybe for something someone forgot.

I doze lightly and keep my eyes shut when Charles finally crawls in beside me, cold but clammy. He's snoring in seconds.

But when we leave in the morning, Charles is quiet and Hugh is edgy. I avoid him, not even grabbing a glass of water, let alone the coffee I'm gasping for. I spot the orderly activity of the agency staff clearing up, stacking empty crates in the branded catering van, murmuring together uneasily.

As I start to leave, Charles mutters something to Hugh, and the two of them head out to the frosted garden. I assume foggy heads need the bracing fresh air. I'm glad to hang back, out of the way.

I watch them walk past the clipped-back formal gardens towards the denuded winter branches of the wood – and that's when I see Charles lunge towards the trees with his arm outstretched. As the photographer staggers out from the cover of the undergrowth, I realise that Charles has been blocking Hugh with his body, protecting him.

For the first time, I wonder what price Charles is paying for his piece of power.

'Thea?' Asha touches my arm, interrupting my thoughts with a jolt. 'Sorry, I was just trying to place it.'

I sit there, still weighed down by memories. Asha is staring at me, and it feels invasive.

I grapple to remember what she'd said. That Charles and Hugh didn't like having the photo taken.

'Do you know what the photographer was trying to record?' Asha asks.

I shrug and shake my head. 'Nothing. It was just a general . . . intrusion.'

For a moment, I'm relieved Asha hasn't seen the headline. Then I remember, with a nauseating punch, that she's a journalist.

'You . . . you must know how the press try to get stories on people like Hugh. Did you see the story that went with this photo?'

'No. Not this one.' She tilts her head at me, eyes flicking over my face. 'But I can guess. I'm sure you can, too.'

I nod, swallowing hard. 'Yeah.'

Fighting back the clamouring is taking all my strength, and I feel drained.

But Asha's investigative instincts are fired up, and she leans forward. 'So? *Is* it significant, do you think? Could this be why Charles was killed? Do you think Hugh . . .?'

As I stare at her, the clamouring stops. My head clears. 'What? You mean . . .?'

'I mean, was Charles carrying a few too many secrets for Hugh? They fell out, and it looked pretty terminal. I'm guessing someone with an ego the size of Hugh's doesn't forgive easily. If you're in, I'm sure you're in *tight*. But if you're out, well . . . you're really *out* . . ."

She raises her eyebrows. 'But what happens if you're out – and you know where all the skeletons are . . .?' Asha draws her finger across her throat. I wince.

And I wonder if Asha knows how ruthless Hugh could be.

Chapter 22

Monday 7th April – 8 p.m.

M Y MIND IS RACING, BUT Asha is still talking to me. I drag my thoughts back to focus on her.

'Look, Thea, I hope I'm not being . . . insensitive. But, well, since I thought that Hugh might have killed Charles, I . . . well . . . I wondered if *you* might be in danger.'

Her eyes are wide; her concern looks genuine. She reaches out to touch my arm. 'It could be nothing. I can well imagine that Charles was taken into Hugh's confidence in ways that you might not have been.'

She tilts her head, emphasising the point. 'But I can *also* imagine that if Charles knew something that Hugh wouldn't want to become public knowledge, then *you* might, too . . .'

I swallow, struggling to moderate my reaction. *I* might know that the threat of Hugh is neutralised – but Asha doesn't.

'I'm sure this is a shock.' She's rubbing my arm now. 'I'll get you a drink.' Turning, she searches my minibar, and sloshes some rum into a crystal tumbler, pressing it into my hand.

Obligingly, I sip, and she smiles. The fiery liquid burns my throat and I cough, then sip again, letting the warmth infuse me.

'You're right that I've always been … wary of Hugh. I've always tried to keep him at arm's length.' I sip again, and my hand steadies. 'I don't think I've ever been taken into his confidence, though.'

'Good.' Asha nods. 'That's good. Hopefully that means you're not in danger.' She side-eyes me. 'Do you think I could be on to something, though? With Charles? Do you think Hugh killed him to keep his secrets safe?'

I shrug. 'The honest answer is that I just don't know. It's not …' My voice drops to a whisper. 'It's not impossible.'

I can't meet her eyes, and a silence stretches between us. I sense it's vital to distance myself from my husband.

'I wouldn't necessarily know. Charles and I have lived very separate lives, really.'

'Uh huh.' Asha's eyebrow arches. 'Just sharing the name, the house, the privileges …'

I wince at that. But, as I meet Asha's eyes, it somehow feels important to acknowledge the truth of it, even though the words stick in my throat. 'Yes. I know. You're right.'

Something in Asha's face softens at that. 'At least you're gracious enough to admit it.'

She heaves a sigh, helps herself to a drink and sits opposite me, nursing it as she muses, 'I was hoping you and I could put our heads together. I feel like we're both trying to make sense of what's going on. And if *I* have theories, you *must* have.'

She shoots me a hopeful, encouraging glance. 'Maybe we could partner up?' Her shrug is self-deprecating. 'I could be Watson to your Sherlock?'

I splutter through a mouthful of rum. 'Uh-huh. Wheeling out the flattery now. *You're* the investigative journo. I'd be the one trying to keep up.' I sense it's important to make her feel intelligent. Like she's a step ahead.

Her laugh doesn't hide her gratified expression. 'Since *that's* decided,' she drains her drink, 'I've … got something else I'd like you to take a look at. Shall we …?' She stands, tilting her head towards the door.

'Now?'

'Yes! Why wait?'

But as I stand, I'm crushed with exhaustion. Today has been a rollercoaster, and Asha might be playing BFFs, but there's something here keeping me on my guard. I can't afford to let something slip because I'm so fatigued … So *drained* …

'Could we meet up in the morning?' I look accusingly at my glass. 'When we've got clear heads and had some rest?'

'Sure.' But she frowns, obviously dismayed. 'Early though? How's six-thirty? Before most people start coming in for breakfast?'

I nod. 'I'll knock on your door, and then we can find somewhere quiet.'

'Sounds good.' As she sets her glass down, she spots the navy box on the console table. 'Ah, the famous gift from Olga?' She holds it up. 'May I?' At my nod, she opens it, confiding, 'I *did* get one, but I didn't want to say. Oh! Wow! Gorgeous, isn't it? That's the worst thing about them, they're exquisite works of art yet a total insult.' She glances at me. 'Would you wear it?'

'No, I think that's the point. Olga seemed to know what we'd all choose for ourselves, though. She was quite the taste sommelier, given her accuracy with the watches. So choosing something I wouldn't wear seems deliberate.'

Asha snorts. 'True. But *I'd* wear this. I love it.'

'What was your gift?'

'Oh.' Asha stops smiling. 'A beautiful solid-gold book. It was closed, with "Your Story" etched on the cover. About paperweight size.'

'A commentary on your career as a journalist, telling other people's stories? Or being glued to a desk? Always working?'

'Any and all of the above, I guess. Maybe she was making the "all work and no play" point. Like I've never heard that before.'

I can't see the insult in the gift, so I wonder why Asha didn't volunteer the information when I asked everyone if they'd got anything from Olga.

A thought strikes: Asha's been careful to not give anything away, about herself or about why she's here. And Olga clearly liked squirreling away incriminating morsels of information, to use against people when it suited her. Was she showing her irritation at Asha being a closed book?

I wish I could see it, examine it, and maybe work out what Olga was saying. I need to understand more about Asha.

I don't expect the words that suddenly spill from my mouth, my tone warm. 'Well, why don't we swap gifts? You said it yourself, they're beautiful. *You'd* wear my bracelet, but I couldn't. Even if I loved it, I'd hate the reminder. But there's no barb in it for you.'

'Oh! What a great idea! I bet mine would look *great* on your desk, securing massive files of legal papers. If we meet at my room in the morning, you can collect it then.'

She smiles, then hesitates. 'I hope you sleep well, and I hope I haven't worried you. Even more than you probably already were.' She leans in. 'I don't know about you, but I've been barricading my door.'

'Very wise. I'm going to take a bath and try to relax. As much as one can ...'

'Good. Oh, I can recommend the rasul treatment Olga left. Have you tried it?' When I shake my head, and shudder at the idea of smearing myself in mud, Asha laughs. 'Oh, you're missing out. It's yummy.'

'Well, I'm not into those kind of . . . unguents.' As I turn to gesture bathroom-wards, I spot the jar sitting on the shelf of the en suite. 'But if you like it so much, have mine.' I retrieve it, and hand it to her. 'I won't use it.'

'Really? *Thank* you!'

Taking her spoils of bracelet and mud, she grins and heads to her room. With a sigh of relief and exhaustion, I lock my door, then barricade it with a chair under the handle, lugging over the heavy coffee table as ballast.

Then I check the balcony door, and jam a chair under that handle, too.

I can't be bothered with a bath, but I take another long, soapy, scrubby, scalding shower.

Then I cry myself into an exhausted sleep.

Tuesday 31st March – 1 a.m.

I jolt awake, disorientated, disturbed. The darkness around me is so total it's like a weighted blanket, smothering and pinning me down.

Half asleep, half primevally alert, I grope for the sense of what woke me.

Time drags by, and my fitful exhaustion pulls me back towards the surrender of sleep. My head is heavy, my thoughts blurring . . .

Then, a faint *click-click*.

My eyes widen in the dark, ears alert as a bat's, skin prickling. *Did I imagine it?*

My heart is thumping louder than the sound I thought I caught, right at the edge of my hearing.

My eyes are adjusting, though, to the darkness. I make out the shapes around me. There's nothing at the balcony door. Exhaling, I turn to stare at the bedroom door, seeing the chair and table are still in place as fortifications.

Now that I can discern shapes in the gloom, I watch the door handle. My heart is pounding, picking up speed like the galloping hooves of a racehorse.

I hear the sound again. *Click-click click.*

It's a key! Unlocking my door!

Then, slowly, silently, I see the door handle move.

I sit up, throwing off my bedclothes, heart hammering, holding in my gasping breaths.

Grabbing my bedside table lamp – God bless Olga and her heavyweight decor – I rip off the shade, yank the plug from the socket and creep to the door, holding the lamp base high with shaking hands.

The handle turns again, and this time I hear a soft but forceful *thud* against the door, chinking light around the edges, and my fear spikes.

My arms shake, but I brace myself, ready to attack whoever has the nerve to break in.

I try to sense who's there, to catch a scent or a sound that will help me work out who this is.

I'm half dreading, half dying for them to get in, so I can see them. I need to know *who* I should fear – specifically, instead of generally.

My heart hammers faster than the forceful thuds against my door – and nearly as fast as the questions bombarding my brain.

Is it the murderer? Come to kill me?

Or is it someone I've pissed off? Like Uri? Looking for his own version of leverage? Or driven to silence me, so I don't reveal whatever he thinks I have on him – or what I thought *Olga* had on him?

Or is it someone who heard Asha mention the papers we'd found, that I'd tried to deny hiding in my room – someone who just wants to get to them before I can read them?

The secrets scatter in so many different directions.

For now, I can only focus on defending myself: on anticipating the next move.

But I'm ready: if they get in, I'm ready to hurt them. To incapacitate them before I can even find out what they're doing.

I acknowledge that change in myself with a sense of wonder, and horror.

My breathing deepens, and something in me shifts. A steely determination settles over me, and I feel something in my muscles tense, drawing on a deadly inner fire I didn't know I had.

Fuck it.

I'm ready to kill.

Again.

Chapter 23

Tuesday 8ᵗʰ April – 5.30 a.m.

I JERK AWAKE TO SUNLIGHT STREAMING into the room, the rays reaching me now. I seem to have fallen asleep crumpled against the wall, and remember sinking to the floor last night while I waited, making sure that the silence on the other side of the door meant my would-be intruder had actually gone.

I'd been poised and ready to attack, and I wasn't about to stand down.

But they hadn't got in, and they'd obviously given up.

Now, though, everything is different. Now I *know* I'm being hunted. By whom, and what for, I've yet to work out. And *that's* the danger.

By comparison, the staff quarters in the snake-filled jungle with a death panther still at large is starting to look like a sodding idyll.

As I creak to my feet, joints and muscles protesting, I feel like death: hot gritty eyeballs that feel like they've been rolled across the scorching, sandy beach; aching neck; fuzzy head.

But there's no point going to bed now; I'm due to meet Asha in an hour.

I run yet another shower, hoping it will wake me up, then brew a coffee with the artisan machine that every room is equipped with. I down it and pour another.

I'm a bit early, but I'm guessing that won't faze Asha. She's keen, so I dismantle my barricade and head out.

I wonder about leaving my room secure, and I'm reminded of Uri mentioning a hair trap. It won't stop someone, but it will tell me if anyone's broken in.

I rip a hair from my scalp, and lick a finger to stick it across the door and frame.

It holds, and I walk next door to Asha's suite and knock. After a few seconds, frowning at the lack of response, I knock again. Still no answer.

The third time, I thump on the door, then press my ear to it, listening.

A muffled sound shoots alarm though me. I think I can hear grunting – then anguished screaming.

Shit. Did my intruder get into Asha's room?

Even with the staff key, I won't be able to open Asha's door: she told me it's barricaded.

In panic, I dash back to my room. Fumbling with my key, I stumble inside, letting the door slam behind me, and grapple to unlock the balcony door.

But there, I stop short. Even if I run down my steps and push through the hedge, Asha's balcony doesn't have steps, at least not ones down to the garden. Her balcony leads far off into the jungle for that crazy treetop walk.

With some kind of superhuman effort, I haul aside the planter and the trellis that stand between my balcony and Asha's – and realise that her balcony is about six feet away from mine.

The garden – and the solid, neck-breakingly hard ground – is only one floor below, but the high ceilings here make that a significant drop. And I'm not comfortable with heights at the best of times.

If I ... *s-t-r-e-t-c-h* my hand out as far as it can go – I lean and make myself sick with fear of falling – I can barely reach halfway across.

There's a small ledge between the two balconies, for drainage. It's not a great option, but there's no other way.

With a gulp, I blot my clammy hands on my top and clamber up on the balcony rail. Then, I move a shaking foot to the building. I wobble as I transfer my weight, a considerable challenge for my weak grip and clumsy feet.

My foot slips – and I lurch wildly.

Grappling to find something secure to hang onto, my puny biceps twang deep within my bingo wings.

Wings would be useful right now ...

I grit my teeth, growling through them with the effort of hauling myself up, then ... I ... reach ... out ... a ... trembling ... hand ...

I catch the edge! My heart leaps! But the ledge is terrifyingly narrow, and I can barely get purchase on it with my fingertips. But it's all I have, as I haul my body across.

I try not to think about what I'm doing; I can barely believe the idiocy of it. I definitely can't believe that somehow ... it's happening.

Yet I swing my other arm, then foot, across; and now I've put my bloody life on the line for a woman I daren't trust, with muscles I trust even less.

My arms jangle with the strain, but I simply move my hand across, then my foot, then the other hand, then the other foot.

Repeat, repeat, repeat.

Shit. I'm halfway.

I open one eye and glance down. *Mistake.*

Fear flashes through me like fever, and I slip. A scream rips from my throat and I pant as I scramble for a better grip. My heart is thundering as I try to reach Asha's balcony – but I can't.

This is the worst place to be: exhausted, slippery with sweat, equally far from both balconies and horribly aware of how hard it will be to reach either one . . .

I glimpse the ground again – and heave. My legs tremor.

Come on. It's the same height as it's been all along. If I got this far, I can do the same again.

My jangling muscles disagree, but I force my hand to move along and re-grip, then my foot, hand, and foot. *Again, again, again.*

Just one more manoeuvre, and I'll be within reach of the balcony rail. With a final effort, I *grab* it.

My legs are shaking so much that I tumble to the balcony floor. Air judders from my lungs and I'm shocked – but, *oh, God! I made it!*

The bifolding door is locked, and I can't see anything inside.

But now I can hear the *screams* . . . they send a shockwave of terror through me. I pick up the planter. *God, it's heavier than I expected.* With a grunt, I launch it through the window, then shelter my face with my hand as I duck inside, avoiding the splinters of glass. I realise I've become quite adept at breaking and entering.

But the deafening screams focus me. They're coming from the en suite. I hurtle towards them . . . and find Asha on the floor, writhing in agony.

Her face is slathered in rasul mud, dry and cracking like a parched riverbed. Her fingers are clawing at it, gouging streaks down her cheeks as she sobs. 'I can't see! I can't see!'

'I'm here, I'll help,' I yell over her wails. 'The face mask? I'll get it off you . . . hang on.'

I throw a hand towel into the sink, drench it, then use it to soak the mud on Asha's face. The hardened clay softens and smears over the fluffy, blindingly white waffle weave.

I rub a clean section over her forehead, cheeks and chin, and around her eyes and nose.

Already, the towel's becoming caked with mud, so I chuck it into the rose-gold roll top bath, and repeat with a clean one.

Asha's eyelids flutter as she senses her face is almost clean, and she draws a breath – then gags, pushing herself up. Her eyes are puffy and so bloodshot they're completely red.

'Oh, God, I think I'm going to be sick.' Leaning over the wide sink, she retches but brings nothing up, then blasts the cold tap and sluices water over her face.

Her face is inflamed, and not all of it can be down to my scrubbing.

'Allergic reaction?' I ask, as I hand her the bathrobe on the back of the door. I hadn't registered she was naked until then; in all the panic and confusion, the focus had been on her pain and trying to help.

She shrugs into the robe, wrapping it firmly around herself. 'Bloody extreme reaction if it *was*. And I didn't react that way the other day when I used the whole lot … *every*where.' She nods towards the jar, and I can see hardly any has been used. 'It felt like my face was *molten*.' She touches her skin gingerly, like she expects it to be burning.

Taking another deep, shuddering sigh, she glances at me, half-embarrassed. 'Thanks for helping.' She frowns and glances around. 'How did … Did you … *break in*? Like Wonder Woman?'

'Um. Yes. I'm afraid I trashed your door.' I grimace, realising it's becoming a bit of a habit.

'Oh, fucking *hell*, Thea!' Her conspiratorial smile darkens into a scowl. 'How can I safely lock up at night now? With a murderer on the prowl?'

'You were screaming, Ash. I thought you *were* being murdered!' I glare at her. 'I climbed across the bloody balcony to try to save you. You're bloody *welcome*.'

'What?' She gapes, then laughs. 'You scaled the building? At this height? Oh, God!'

She peers round the bathroom door, wincing at the sight of the planter on its side, its lush ferns broken, earth scattered lumpenly across the luxurious rug – and the smashed door beyond, jagged glass glinting in the sunlight.

As I watch her, I realise my hands are tingling. I stare at them, turning them over. Am I imagining it?

'I need to wash my hands.' I move to the sink. 'Maybe I'm having a similar reaction?' I rinse them like I'm treating a burn, letting the cool water glide over my skin. Eventually they're soothed enough to turn off the tap.

As I rinse the smears of mud off the sink, I recall seeing the same smudge on Olga's shower.

Is this what killed her? She used it, had this reaction, rinsed it off, rushed for help, and fell over the balcony? Or maybe she didn't have a chance to rinse it – the pool could have washed it off, and the filter cleaned any traces of it from the water.

But Asha's frowning. 'Have you had that reaction to the rasul treatment before?'

'Well, no, I haven't used it before. You took mine, remember? This *is* mine . . .'

I feel the blood draining from my face as Asha and I have the same thought at the same time.

I scan the bathroom for the treatment and pick it up from the shelf, pinching the sides of the open jar, wary of touching any smeared mud on the outside. Tentative as a cat approaching a scorpion, I sniff the clay. The clean-earth scent of spa-selected herbs fills my lungs. An innocent, cleansing kind of scent.

As I examine the contents, Asha asks, 'What do you see?'

'Just ... *mud*?' But it can't be, can it. I'll need to work out what might have been added, by who, and how. And when. And why. Why does someone here want to harm me?

'We'll need to warn everyone that they shouldn't use their treatments, just in case any others have been doctored. Because *my* treatment *didn't* burn like an inferno on my skin. Something's been added to yours.'

I swallow, then meet her eyes and nod. 'Yes. Someone's added contact poison, haven't they.' Saying it aloud is awful. I screw the lid on the jar, and wipe the sides carefully, then tuck it into my deep pockets. 'I'm going to compare it to the treatment in the spa. Want to join me?'

Asha nods. 'I'll get dressed.'

As I loiter awkwardly in Asha's suite while she dresses in the bathroom, I spot a wrench leaning against the wall, beside the door. I stare at the tool. 'What are you doing with this wrench, Ash? Starting a sideline in plumbing?'

'Oh.' Beyond the closed door, Asha gives an embarrassed laugh. 'I found it in the hall. Yesterday, I think, but all the days seem to be a blur. I ... I thought I could use it if someone tried to break into my room. At least I'd have something to whack them with.'

She hesitates. 'I ... I know it sounds pathetic. Especially now it's obvious how under threat *you* are. But I've been so afraid since finding Olga. And I might be barricading my door, but I still don't feel safe. If I'd left that wrench where it was, someone else might have found it and hit someone with it. And I didn't want to end up being that victim.'

I frown. 'Where was it? Olga wasn't the type to allow tools to be left lying about.'

'It was tucked away behind a planter in the hallway, outside Olga's room.'

There were two planters, and I'd hidden behind one of them the night Olga was killed. I suppose this wrench could have been obscured behind the other one, meaning I hadn't noticed it.

While I'm still mulling this over, Asha, as though suddenly remembering, exclaims, 'Oh, while you're out there, you'll see my gift from Olga on the sideboard. You should take it, since we decided to swap.'

I spot the small gold book, exactly as she'd described. I reach out to pick it up and my hand gives a little at the sheer heft of it. It must weigh about the same as half a bag of sugar. It's like holding a chunky gold bar. The metal alone must be worth a few tens of thousands.

'Thanks,' I call out. 'It's amazing. You sure you don't want to keep it? Re-gift it? Or sell it?' I pray she says no.

'No thank you. I never want to see it again. Not after this weekend.'

I sigh in relief. Much more important than its monetary value is the insights it'll give me if it holds a secret message from Olga. I must keep my head clear and look for facts, for clues. Or I'll end up rotting here like Charles and Olga.

That thought sends hot nausea flaming through me, but I fight it back.

'Thanks, Asha.' I smile at her as she emerges from the bathroom. Suddenly, I'm overwhelmed with fear. It hits me like a tidal wave, stifling my insides and engulfing me from the outside, like I'm drowning. I can't breathe.

Her face crumples into concern and she hurries over to me. 'It'll be OK, Thea. Look at me. Look at me. I'm right here and we're going to be OK.'

'Oh, Ash, this is all so awful.' I cling to her like she's a life raft in a typhoon. 'Thank you. For being the only ally I have here.' A sob becomes a self-deprecating laugh, and then another sob.

'Friend.' Asha punches my arm, helping me see the lighter side. 'I think you just saved my life, so that's an instant promotion.'

My smile wobbles once more and she opens her arms, pulling me in, wrapping me in comfort. 'But that's the terrible thing, isn't it? Something that was meant to kill *me* has harmed *you*.'

I'm scared of all the implications of that. Not least that Asha will blame me, or see me as the weak link, better to make an enemy of than an ally.

'No.' Asha smiles. 'That makes me feel better, weirdly.' She holds my shoulders as she looks at me, her eyes wide, but calm and kind. 'Because if this was intended for you, then I know you can't be the killer. I know I can trust you.'

I know she's hoping for me to reciprocate the declaration. I open my mouth . . . but I can't say it.

We've all read the Marples and the Poirots, haven't we? We've all seen the murderers who administer a survivable dose of something deadly in order to appear innocent, to gain trust . . . right before they strike. And it's lucky, isn't it, that she only used the rasul treatment as a face mask instead of slathering her whole body in it . . .

But she's still looking at me, willing me to say it. And it wouldn't hurt for her to believe I trust her.

So I manage to swallow back a sob, appear like I'm rallying, smile at her with sincere warmth and say, 'Good point. You're right. I'm so glad there's finally someone I know I can trust here.'

I look her in the eye, I smile at her, and I lie.

Chapter 24

Tuesday 8th April – 8 a.m.

MINUTES LATER, WE'VE DROPPED OFF the gold book in my room but Asha's hung onto the wrench. She said she wants to show me something. I'm wary, wondering if she's going to whack me on the head somewhere when we're out of sight of the house. I'm itching to ask what she wants to show me, but I'm also making sure no one hears us as we creep down my balcony steps to the garden, and around to the ocean-fronted spa.

The spa music is still tinkling along with the waterfall that cascades into the rock garden and irrigates the lush cottage garden. We pass it, heading for the dimly lit pools and floatation tanks, with their view of endless sea through tinted glass, to the sauna and infra-red treatment suites. Here are the same jars, brimming with clay.

Taking a few, I return to the more brightly lit entrance, and sit in a deep wicker chair to compare these to the one Asha used.

The spa mud is pure, smooth clay. It's so even in texture and colour that it could be a paint sample from Farrow and Ball. I'm sure there must be a 'Spa Break Breath' on their colour chart.

The one Asha used is less uniform. I squint, lean closer – and realise there are tiny flecks in the mud. Small yet bright specks of verdant green mixed in with the olive clay. But this was a natural treatment, so I guess some … plant matter is to be expected …?

I check another sample from the spa – and it's the same as the first. No small fragments. The third is no different to the other two, which seems pretty conclusive.

'What do you see?' Asha demands.

'In the one you used, there are some tiny specks of what I think is vegetation.'

Asha leans in to look, then studies the treatment from the spa. She nods. 'I'm certain those plant specks were *not* in the first treatment I used. *My* treatment was like these, from the spa. And it *didn't* set my skin on fire.'

'I'm certain, too. I think those plant fragments are something deadly.'

'Do you think they were added by Olga? Who was just waiting for me to use it?'

'Not necessarily.'

'Someone else?' I ask. 'Maybe this was how they *did* kill Olga?' My mind is racing, and I glance around, my gaze resting on the plants. 'Kali? She knew these herbs were for remedies. Maybe something here kills instead of cures? A lot of things do.' I shudder, as a creeping sense of inevitability crawls over me.

'Maybe.' Asha shrugs. 'If so, anyone has access. To both the plants *and* the clay. They'd just need the opportunity to replace it and make sure it's swapped with the treatment in your room, like they must have done with Olga.'

My head whirls at being targeted. The room is spinning and I'm glad I'm sitting down. Even so, I lean back heavily.

The jolt through my body forces out the question. 'Who, then? Who would kill my husband, and his mistress, and then try to kill *me*? *Who*?'

The weirdly personal threat, in such an unfamiliar place, pitches me sideways. I can't make sense of it.

Asha starts firing off the questions *I* usually ask – and I don't like these turned tables; I flinch at her interrogation.

'Do you know of anyone who wanted to cause you harm? Have you done anything to anyone – well, anyone *here* – that might have provoked an attack like this?'

I stare at her. *Have I*?

I mean, who amongst us has lived a blameless life? But have I done anything to make someone want to *kill* me?

I swallow. 'Maybe ...' I gulp. And the clamouring in my head is louder than ever.

'Like what?' Asha demands, her eyes wide.

I can't answer her. I wouldn't want to give a roll call of my worst transgressions, because there *are* moments when I haven't been proud of my judgement.

'Well, I've been asking questions. Plenty of people think Charles has shared information with me, and while I can't think of anything incriminating, that won't stop a killer who's desperate to cover their tracks.'

I don't add that someone might have seen me breaking into rooms, or overheard Uri's accusation, instead attempting a shrug. 'Plus, I'm a *lawyer*, Ash. Making enemies is a professional hazard.' I'm trying to steady my breathing, to sound calm and in control.

Her gaze is hard, assessing, and I can't help the half-admission that spills from me. 'I know I'm not perfect. I will have done things that caused upset, or even distress. But I haven't ever knowingly *harmed* anyone.'

I meet her eyes just long enough. I know that holding her gaze for *too* long looks as guilty as someone unable to hold it at all; it gives away the body language-conscious liar.

Asha's face softens a little. 'OK, then. What do we do next?'

'We don't tell anyone,' I instruct. 'If someone has planted something intended to kill me at an indeterminate time in the future, then they won't know we *already* know, and that we're looking out for who it is.'

She nods. 'Agreed.' Then she shudders. 'It's creepy though, isn't it? Knowing that the murderer is still trying.' She hesitates. 'Do . . . do you think they're planning to kill anyone else?'

'Yes.' It's awful to say it aloud, and I shudder. 'Yes, I do. But . . . *somehow* . . . we're going to have to do our best to carry on as normal.'

Taking a long inhale, then letting out a longer sigh, Asha nods. 'Right. What do you want to do, then? Get breakfast?'

'Not really. But we should.' The thought of food makes me feel sick. I delay leaving, putting away the jars, pocketing the contaminated one, but as I trudge outside, it feels like a weight is crushing my shoulders.

I'm dreading facing everyone, knowing that someone has actually tried to kill me. Is it the same person who tried to break into my room last night? Or do two people have a vendetta against me?

I muster all my best barrister bravado in an effort to appear cool and in control.

'You have a good game face, I'll give you that,' Asha says. 'I wouldn't guess for a moment what kind of morning you've had.' She side-eyes me. 'But, since I know better, I'm guessing you're hungrier for information than muesli.' She hefts the wrench. 'So, could I show you something now?'

'Yes.' Despite my earlier misgivings, relief avalanches off me. 'Yes please. I can't bear to waste precious minutes when we could be sleuthing.'

'Good. Let's take a detour.' She turns towards Olga's suite, and I follow.

And then I see something that makes my blood run cold. On the trunk of a palm tree shading one of the walkways are two sets of vertical, parallel scratches. Three on the left and four on the right. About the height that, say, a panther might reach. Keeping its claws in good condition.

I gasp. That's far too close for comfort . . .

Shivering, I slow to a snail's pace, eyes darting around like a startled bird as I flinch at every sound. But Asha, who hasn't noticed the tree, just pushes me forward in blissful ignorance, putting my reluctance down to worries about our human predator. Over the whoosh of the tide, the high squawks of birdsong and the metallic chirps of God-knows-what insects crawling in the jungle, my ears are pricked for the roars, growls, or rumbles of a panther.

Dashing into the hallway of the lodge, I have to steady my hand to use Olga's key. Inside, Asha makes a beeline for the massive baroque bureau that I've already tried to open, pointing with the wrench to the tiny, engraved emblem.

'When I didn't find much more in Olga's office, even in that secret drawer, I remembered seeing this when we moved Olga into the bathroom. This is *literally* the only thing left that looks like it could hold something. And that emblem . . . Surely that's there for some reason?'

She starts tugging at the drawers. 'How can they have no locks, but *be* locked?'

She crawls underneath, like I already have. After an age of us both carefully pressing, pushing and feeling for levers, Asha hefts the wrench. 'Brute force it is.'

With no hesitation, she batters at the marquetry of the top middle drawer. The wood caves in, and the second bash sends inlay splintering.

Undeterred, she continues until the bureau is dented and scraped. Veneer cracks, revealing a metal frame, designed to defend against invasion like this.

Asha sits back, panting and red-faced. 'Any suggestions?' She thumps the desk. 'Our phones *have* to be in there – and if we can get them, we can get out of here.'

She shivers in anticipation of freedom from the threat that simmers around us all the time.

'At the very *least*, there must be information in there,' she urges, like she knows what drives me. '*Private*, *secure* information. We've both seen how she likes to demonstrate what she knows about us. She must have leverage over everyone here. Why else would a bunch of billionaires even *be* here? And she'd need evidence against them, wouldn't she? For the purposes of blackmail. So she must keep it safe *somewhere*. And *I* think it's in *here*.'

I examine the desk one last time, trying to pull open the drawers, straining to lever the mechanism between the split wood. I find myself contorting my hands and using all my strength, channelled through my fingers, as if sheer determination might be enough. It isn't. The strong, unyielding frame wins.

I'm sweating, annoyed, frustrated, and I sit back on my heels.

'Yep. I feel the same.' Asha's nod is one of conspiratorial sympathy.

I run my finger over the crest, feeling the indent. 'Since this is Olga's company logo, doesn't that just mean her company made this desk? Because if so, that's super discreet. Which might fit their brand. Unless … do you think it's here for another reason?'

'Why?' Asha sits forward. 'What are you thinking?'

'I thought it might be the kind of thing where you have the corresponding shape to insert into it, to release the mechanism? Like an elaborate key?'

I consider the tiny size of the symbol on the desk, and wonder what form a key with its likeness would take. 'Might we find its mirror image on the end of a pen? Or a USB?'

Asha scrunches her nose in disagreement. 'No. It wouldn't be on anything she'd have left lying around, would it?'

'You're right. A pendant, then? Something she never takes off?' I gasp as the answer fireworks in my brain. 'Her *ring*. Her signet ring's crest is her company symbol. I noticed it when I arrived.' It was almost lost amongst her jewelled knuckledusters.

'Yes!' Asha's face shines in delight, then falls. 'Oh . . . You put her in the staff quarters, didn't you?'

Not exactly . . . 'Oh, God . . .'

I recall that awful crunch as I left Olga to her fate.

So now it could be inside a panther. Or a pile of dung.

'Well . . . it should still be there, right? It's worth a look, isn't it?' Asha is energised with optimism, leaping up. 'Let's go!'

Chapter 25

Tuesday 8th April – 9 a.m.

I SHUDDER, TRYING TO BREAK THE news to Asha that this will not be a quick jungle trek.

'You don't know what you're asking . . .' I warn.

'How hard can it be? On that little quad bike, we can zip along in no time.'

'I didn't manage to get Olga all the way there.'

Asha frowns. 'What do you mean?'

'She fell off my wheelbarrow. About two-thirds of the way along the trail to the staff digs. I couldn't lift her back into the barrow on my own. I thought I could return with the quad bike, that maybe that would be easier to manoeuvre her onto, but—'

'*Ewww!*' Asha scrunches her nose. 'I see your point. So she's in the jungle, fast-tracking to decomposition in this humidity and heat?' She shudders.

'Yeah.' Asha's got enough of the picture. I don't need to add even grislier details. 'So we'd be scrabbling about in the jungle earth, with both the ground and Olga's corpse seething with creepy-crawlies.' My skin prickles and I have to shake myself bodily. '*Ugh.*'

'I get it.' Asha gives a firm nod. 'But it's still worth it.' She kicks the bureau. 'If this thing is *that* secure, then it *must* be worth getting into.' She raises her eyebrows at me, with the invincibility of the young. 'So? Are you in?'

Even though I can see there's no other way, I can't believe it when I hear myself saying, 'Ugh. Fine. But I'm driving, so you can fend off the snakes.'

'*What?*' Her confidence falters.

'And *you* can be the one hunting amongst the remains and the grubs.'

'Oh!'

'So let's get on with it before I think better of it.'

She's less keen now, but having made the decision, I don't want to hang around like panther prey.

We skirt around the lodge, kicking hot sand up the back of our legs as we run, and leap onto the quad bike.

It's then that I spot the massive paw prints in the sand – pads about two inches wide, four teardrop toes above – and above those, the tiny, precise indents of those honed and deadly claws.

The prints show that it loped towards the house, right past the window of Olga's suite.

I freeze. *Is it here? Now?*

Asha's gaze follows mine and her eyes widen at me. 'Shit,' she whispers. 'What the hell is that?'

'Olga's pet panther, which is on the loose.'

'You what?' She gapes at me. 'Will it … *hunt* us?'

'I hope not. But I'd rather not hang around here chatting about it.' I glare and jerk my head towards the quad bike.

'Right. Yes. OK. Let's hurry.'

'We can try to hurry, but you do realise that we can't outpace a panther?'

'Maybe this is the island version of "man or bear", then?' Asha tries to joke as I start driving. 'Murderer or panther?'

'Neither, thanks.' The quad bike has been built for grunt work; it's low speed with enough torque for towing, but not for acceleration too. So, no matter how much I stamp on the gas, the response is a pathetic dribble of speed.

'Lucky we're uncatchable in this, then.' Asha tries to joke, but her white-knuckled grip on the handles at my waist betrays her fear.

I press on, making reasonable progress. But almost immediately, Asha's flinching away from the vines and vegetation brushing over us, shrieking and squealing at every lime snake that flashes across the track.

'Are you *trying* to make us panther food?' I glare at her again.

But I'm dodging the sinister strokes of branches as well, hardly able to hold back my own shudders as they graze my exposed skin. It seems like an eternity – but finally, up ahead, I can see Olga . . . or what's left of her.

I pull up, concentrating on turning the quad bike so I don't have to face the corpse. I'm already heaving at the overwhelming, putrid stench, the remaining flesh falling away from crushed shards of bone, torn sinews straggling.

But a rustling noise makes me look over my shoulder. In horror, I see a large, dark brown bird tearing at Olga's flesh. On instinct, I clap my hands, the sound ringing through the trees. The bird hops away, its small suspicious eyes on me.

'Go on then,' I urge Asha. 'Get on with it.'

'Oh, God. I can't. I c-*can't*.'

'All you have to do is look for a finger, and see if it has her ring on it. Or see if the ring is there.'

Saying it out loud makes it sound ludicrous. Of course this is too long a shot. What the hell are we doing? You'd almost think living with the constant threat of being murdered was starting to affect our mental capabilities.

But Asha is frozen to the spot, so it's left to me – just as revolted as she is, but clearly more desperate – to scramble off the bike and take over. I pull my T-shirt over my nose to try to filter out the odour of rotting flesh, and swallow back the threat of nausea.

The heat of the jungle is close and humid, my skin sweaty and salty already. It makes the stink of decay pulse off Olga's devoured remains. The panther went for her stomach, hollowing out her organs where I guess the high-protein morsels were. But the bird has torn at her face. I'm repulsed by the savage rips and tears, the dribbles of entrails where other things have clearly gone for the rest of her. I can imagine rats and scavengers and birds pecking and pulling at her body. A whole community of insects and vile creatures are working away at what's left. Which already – terrifyingly – isn't much.

I'm scared to touch anything, or even to find a stick to prod her with in case I actually seize a very still snake. I don't want to interact with any part of this busy, efficient animal realm that can make a human feel all too mortal – and disposable. I'm ill-equipped for this world.

Trying to summon a sense of clinical detachment, I scan the remains. Limb bones straggled with flesh and tendons, naked ribs, a half-eaten face ... And only one hand is left. It's moving of its own accord, heaving with creatures under the green skin. But there's no ring.

The other hand is already stripped of flesh. Skeletonised, the pathologists I've worked with would call it. It happens quite quickly on thin corpses, even without all this assistance. Crunkley knuckle joints and spindly fingers splay from the rich earth, like a Halloween skeleton clawing its way out of a fresh grave.

It's horrifyingly intimate, and I can't help gagging and backing away, avoiding the lightning slither of an arrow-headed snake which comes streaking out from the rustling undergrowth, rippling over Olga's metacarpals. Under its belly scales, I see a sudden glint, and despite my terror of the snake, hope sparks. As its tail wriggles past, I wait a second to make sure the snake is gone, then lean forward.

It's Olga's signet ring! Circling what would have been her little finger. I unthread it from the fine bone, feeling like a grave robber, then check the pattern.

Yes! Her crest! A match to the bureau's mark!

In triumph, I leap onto the quad bike.

But Asha doesn't cheer. She's shaking. 'I don't know how you could leave me here like that.'

Every sound makes her jump and flinch round, her face stricken.

Then a low, resonant rumble makes her grab me, her teeth chattering. 'Sh-hit,' she stutters. 'That's *it*, isn't it? The b-bloody panther.'

Her eyes are wild, her head twisting in every direction.

All I can do is drive, or rather, dawdle, house-wards. But the rumbling seems to chase us. Desperate, I stamp on the accelerator, but it makes little difference. We crawl, bouncing and bumping over the ruts.

I focus hard on our destination, as if *willing* us there could get us there any faster. I daren't look back, but I can imagine the sinewy panther loping easily after us, like we're a slow-mo toy for it to catch at its leisure.

Asha's nervy shrieks at things falling from overhead branches don't help, and I flinch, sweat slithering down my back.

At the sound of another rumble she clutches me, practically sobbing, just as we're hit by a deluge of a downpour. Hot, fat raindrops power down from the sky, and now I realise that resonant growl around us is thunder. *Thunder!* I could sob with relief – until I realise how mired our wheels are in the dirt track, churning and bringing us to a near standstill.

'Oh God, this is all we need.' I can barely see my way. It's like peering through a waterfall.

'Faster! Please, *please* go faster!'

'I promise you, I'm trying.' My tone is tense through gritted teeth. I'm soaked to the skin, my clothes clinging. Even innocent raindrops are making me shiver – *what if it's not just water slithering down my back?*

But finally – *oh, thank you – finally* I see the distant glimpse of the house. I slam my foot on the accelerator and lean forward like a jockey on the home straight.

I don't attempt to park, I just haul on the brake as we reach Olga's lodge, pulling up as near to her garden as possible without crashing into the hedge. Asha and I leap out and dash into her suite, where we shudder and shiver, shaking off the rain and the *grue*someness.

The vivid memory of Olga sends revulsion pulsing over my skin. '*Ugh.*' I glance at Asha, still trembling too. 'Let's hope this was worth it.'

I walk to Olga's bureau and press the raised ring of the crest on the ring against the matching indent on the desk. I hold my breath, expecting a drawer to pop out, or a hidden compartment to spring open.

But . . .

Nothing . . .

I could weep. I adjust my position, trying to line the symbols up perfectly, pushing the ring against the desk. Still nothing happens.

'You can't be *serious*?' Asha gasps.

I want to kick the damn desk, imagining the secrets held within it; picturing our phones, our key to freedom, languishing behind a few millimetres of wood.

As I stare at it, I also imagine the power Olga might have felt while sitting at it: knowing the leverage it contained over such powerful people, knowing just what strings to pull to get them to do her bidding.

Putting myself in her shoes, I pull up the chair, sit at the desk and place the ring on my little finger. As I push its crest against the lock, I feel the ridges in the ring lock into place with the recesses in the desk, the angle just right, and I use my free hand to check the drawers.

And now, I can pull open each one.

Chapter 26

Tuesday 8th April – 11 a.m.

I HEAR ASHA GASP BEHIND ME at the opening drawers and feel her warm breath on my cheek as she leans in, eager to see what's inside.

My heart is pounding.

Three envelopes, labelled in tiny, neat writing, are stacked in the top drawer, and I wonder whose secrets these are as I draw them out and spread them on the desk.

'Any phones? Radios?' Asha asks, the urgency clear in her voice.

I scan the rest of the drawers but there's nothing else here.

'Oh God!' Asha turns away, her fists gripped at her sides. 'How – *how* – are we going to get away from here?' She turns back to me, I and see that tears are streaming down her cheeks. 'I can't take much more of this, Thea, I really can't. And there doesn't seem to be anywhere else to look. Me and Kali have scoured every nanometre of this damn place.'

I see the last of her hope drain away as she speaks the words, and her face crumples as desperate sobs shudder through her body.

She falls onto the sofa, holding her head in her hands, and her sobs grow into a wail.

I know I should comfort her, but the envelopes are a siren call. The lure of secrets, the lure of the knowledge Olga had; the tantalising closeness of clues to the killer's identity …

'I'm sure we'll find them. We just need to persevere,' I say. But I don't turn to her. I'm staring at the envelopes. 'At least we can see what there is in here?' I glance at her now, trying to cajole her. 'What happened to Sherlock and Watson?'

She shrugs, but her desolation lifts a little. I open the first one.

In surprise, I blink at the contents. This wasn't what I expected. A birth certificate. I pull out the page, squinting at the looping handwriting.

'Why does Olga have birth certificates?' Asha joins me. 'She doesn't have any children … Does she?'

'None that she's claimed,' I say, scanning it hungrily for details. 'And it must be pretty much impossible for someone in her position to keep a child a secret.' I stare at the date of birth. 'Especially if the child was in their mid-thirties.'

'So who is this?'

'The name's not much help: River Sullivan. Could be male or female.'

Asha squints. 'I don't recognise it. There's no one here by that surname. How is this leverage?'

I eye Asha. *She's* mid-thirties. 'Do you have some secret identity, Ash? Something you're hiding?'

She snorts. 'It'd be a bit rich, wouldn't it? Given I'm a journo. You can't really go around unearthing other people's secrets if you're hiding your own.'

'I'm not sure there's a moral code for journalists. Not the ones I know, anyway.' I regard her thoughtfully, letting her squirm under my gaze.

'I'm not pretending I'm perfect, am I? Who is? And no, I haven't changed my identity.' There's something about the way she says that, like it's a challenge, which makes me pause and really look at her.

If she senses me scrutinising her more intently, she doesn't show it. 'Is that what you think this is?' She picks up the certificate. 'Maybe Zyra? Or Estelle? Musicians and models change their names. It's not unusual, is it?'

'Depends if they're leaving behind more than a name, doesn't it?'

I replace the certificate in its envelope, and pick up the next one. Inside are just a couple of pages: scouring them, I see they're print-outs of emails, sent between Hugh and Charles. My heartbeat quickens as I wonder what else my husband was embroiled in. Somehow I know I won't like what I'm about to read.

The pages are thin in my fingers, revealing men who are as thick as thieves. Their exchanges are surprisingly brief, curt, even, amounting to only a few lines in total:

From: charrington@quickmail.com
Sent: 31 January 2020 09:44
To: Hugh@TheCrownFoundation.UK
Subject: Re: Magnus

Magnus has a strong case as Chairman of Yorke Investments, he does much to facilitate US/UK relations which more than meet criteria for an honorary KBE.

So Magnus was after a knighthood? Despite all his protests about the royal racket? This is what he meant by expecting some appreciation in return for his bail-outs.

From: Hugh@TheCrownFoundation.UK
Sent: 31 January 2020 09:55
To: charrington@quickmail.com
Subject: Re: Magnus

Sorry, Charles, been rapped on the knuckles on this one. Told I can't keep handing these out like sweets. No can do.

From: charrington@quickmail.com
Sent: 31 January 2020 10:10
To: Hugh@TheCrownFoundation.UK
Subject: Re: Magnus

Hugh, as you so often tell me, there's always a way. There must be something you can do, for an exceptional circumstance. You're the only man who could find a solution.

I'm a little bit sick in my mouth at the sycophancy, but I know Charles is just driving for what he wants. Seeing it in black and white, though, makes me wonder where his self-respect is.

From: Hugh@TheCrownFoundation.UK
Sent: 02 February 2020 17:20
To: charrington@quickmail.com
Subject: Re: Magnus

Not possible. Blocked by the top.

From: charrington@quickmail.com
Sent: 02 February 2020 17:56
To: Hugh@TheCrownFoundation.UK
Subject: Re: Magnus

Going to need you to do something about that. Quid pro quo, you see.

I feel my legs buckle. *A favour for a favour.* Hugh owed Charles, and I'm scared to think why.

Asha's face is hard as she stares at me. 'So what *is* the deal between those two?'

I try to shrug it off. 'Been friends a long time. There's all sorts of shared history.' But if Magnus didn't get his royal honour, then this *quid pro quo* didn't work. Which makes me more worried.

'Hmm.' Asha's nod seems so agreeable, it takes me a moment to register her sarcasm.

Not wanting to acknowledge it, anxious to avoid the questions she'll raise – and the answers I'll dread thinking about – I move hastily on to the next envelope.

More emails. This time to Uri. 'How did Olga get these? She wasn't copied in.'

Asha shrugs. 'Industrial espionage. Bribery. Easy when you've got money.'

These emails come from a sender whose name I don't recognise: Nigel Reni.

Despite a long list of attachments, they haven't been included in this envelope. They'd make heavy reading, judging by their foreboding names:

Memo: Code base concerns
Email threads: Raising unrealistic timeframes with Senior Management
Report: Algorithms are vulnerable to being hacked by bad actors
Formal alert: Systemic insecurity

Attorney-Client Privilege (ACP): Allegation: data used to train AI model was stolen / compromised

I scan the body of the long, technical email. Nigel Reni appears to be a whistleblower from inside Uri's company, stating that

Uri's rush to market with new, bleeding-edge tech is putting national security at risk.

The last line of the email couldn't be clearer: *The risks are globally significant; I won't rest until full responsibility for all transgressions is taken, and all issues are rectified.*

The ramifications of this are *huge*: Uri's company holds classified military data. Data which, because of his corner-cutting, is vulnerable to being both hacked, and altered, by systems that aren't reliable or secure.

If Uri has knowingly failed to make classified data sufficiently secure, then that's a federal offence, the highest sentence going. The US doesn't mess about with things like this.

I rock back, shocked at the revelation. Uri has seemed so sure of himself, like he was almost amused by Olga's machinations. Yet her knowing this about him and his business – and this *has* to be what she meant by that apparently locked box that spilled its secret contents, leaving an indelible mark everywhere – *had* to have felt like an existential threat.

In fact, I can only think of one reason why he would have been so laissez faire about it.

* * *

I'm striding towards the great room – the clip of my espadrilles is nearly as satisfying as the sound of my brogues echoing in the courthouse's marble halls – and I'm channelling that powerful feeling as I prepare myself to go into battle.

'Uri,' I bark, catching him out of the corner of my eye. He *was* lounging on the sofa, but snaps to attention like a naughty schoolboy. I know the reaction to my tone is instinctive; it lasts a nanosecond, until he remembers that we've argued, and slouches down, glowering like a teenager.

Kali and Magnus are sitting with him on the low sofas around the coffee table, while Estelle and Zyra are leaning on the bar, nibbling pistachios and chatting.

'I'd like to talk to you now, please, Uri. In private.'

He stands, but doesn't move. Instead, he folds his arms, eyes narrowing. 'Why?'

Oh, he should not go toe to toe with me. I can play to a crowd, if that's what he wants.

I sweep my hands out, an inclusive gesture. 'Because I've learned that each one of us here has a secret that Olga knew. *Dangerous* secrets, that Olga was leveraging to force us all to dance to her tune. And the financial expense would have been the least of the cost to us.'

I pace as I make my points. 'The thing is, someone here killed to keep their dangerous secret a secret. And now I've discovered just how dangerous *yours* is, Uri, I'm revising my view of you as being so very immune to Olga's threats. It turns out that you have *everything* to lose.'

A half-laugh erupts from him. 'You don't know anything!'

Here goes . . .

'I know a whistleblower at your company—'

'What? This is bullshit! There's no whistleblower!'

'. . . was raising issues around the cutbacks you'd made on your data security—'

'Yeah, right! As if!'

'. . . Alleging that you'd stolen your AI tech, and trained it on compromised data. And that the classified data wasn't *only* vulnerable to being hacked, but that someone could *alter* it—'

'This is *nuts!*'

'. . . And that matters for any data, of course. But when it's *classified military secrets?* We're talking a *lifetime's* incarceration.'

He's gaping at me now.

And so is everyone else.

'Fucking *hell*, Uri!' Kali's eyes boil into him. 'That's—'

'*Unforgivable.*' Magnus strides over, and I swear he's going to punch him, but he controls himself – barely. He spits the words at Uri, through gritted teeth. 'I knew it, you fucking bastard. You should get shot for that. That's brave men and women in our military whose lives you've just put on the line because *you*,' he shoves Uri's shoulder in punctuation, 'can't do your fucking *job*.'

So this is what he wanted to talk to Uri about. The risk he referred to. If rumours had reached Magnus, it gives some credence to the whistleblowing Olga uncovered.

Uri rounds on him. 'Firstly, Magnus, you don't have a clue about software development. Secondly, just because Olga makes an accusation doesn't mean it's true.'

'Bull-*shit*.' Magnus shakes his head. 'I heard rumours. I even tried to find you to talk in private about it, give you the chance to be honest and fix it. And look at you. Even now, you're more interested in saving your sorry ass than protecting the lives *you're* putting on the line. You lily-livered waste of space.'

'You want to know what's *unforgivable*, Magnus? It's Olga using these secrets for her own gain, instead of – oh, I don't know – actually doing her research. *You* know exactly how serious a crime this would be, yet Olga leaps straight to the worst conclusion without asking me herself – *despite* all the coalitions we're in – then uses her ill-gotten information for threats, leverage, extortion. *Just like Olga.* Information is a weapon to her.'

'Was,' I point out. 'Since someone here has killed her for exactly that reason.'

He backs away as I stare at him. I wonder who the whistleblower could have been; if *both* Magnus and Olga had heard from them.

Uri turns his attention to Magnus. 'You're not above criticism, yourself, Magnus. Something tells me you weren't coming to ask me about this out of goodwill towards me, or to warn me, either. You'll only keep a secret if it's worth your while.'

Magnus glowers. 'Goddamn you, boy. Don't you *dare* accuse me like that. I came to you once things had quietened down here to speak to you, man to man. To understand what was being leaked, what the risks were. Don't you go laying your guilt, your failings, at my door!'

'If you weren't being self-serving, Magnus, you would have reported it.'

'This is why you're makin' an enemy of me? Because *you* thought I was gonna do the same as *Olga*? When I know the consequences of an accusation like this?'

I hear the desperation as well as the fury in both men's voices, and I see the stakes were high enough to drive either of them to kill Olga.

There's no doubt Uri would have wanted to silence her.

And if Magnus had discovered the threat this would have posed to his nation's security and learned Olga was wielding it to her own nefarious ends, as a tool for blackmail, then that, together with the threat she'd been holding over his daughter's head, could have been enough to drive him to kill our host.

I keep wondering whether Charles might just have been collateral damage, killed in case Olga had said something casually to her lover; or in case he'd been made party to, or stumbled across, damning evidence while enjoying his intimate access to Olga's private suites.

'I can't believe this.' Kali stalks away, her upper lip raised in a sneer.

'I'm not sure why *you're* looking so disapproving, Kali,' I warn, making her stop in her tracks and turn to me. 'It looks like

Olga was poisoned, so you'd *have* to be the prime suspect. You'd know what would leave the fewest signs, and how to work within the right timeframe to ensure you'd have an alibi.'

'Ah, I can help you out there, Thea.' Kali glares at me. 'There's this new invention called Google. It's magic. Anyone anywhere can look up whatever they want.'

'Not here, they can't. No signal or Wi-Fi. So, yes, anyone could have come up with a plan in advance – but probably only you could have killed her opportunistically like that.'

'I'd still need a reason,' Kali shrugs.

'You have a few,' I counter. 'You've certainly done your share of hurting people, giving them drugs that promise cures they don't – *can't* – deliver. Olga said you sell *hope*. And you both knew it was *fake* hope. Even worse, people opt for your costly miracle cure over regular treatment; treatment which may have otherwise saved them.'

'Not true.' She shakes her head. 'Medical trials are exactly that. No guarantees.'

'This isn't about guarantees, Kali. This is about *life and death*.' I stare at her, unable to fathom how anyone could be so nonchalant about it. 'Did you know that one of the people your drugs killed was Olga's sister?'

Kali's eyes widen, but in an angry glare, rather than surprise. *So she* knew *that Olga knew*.

'Olga wouldn't have let that lie, would she? She'd wreak revenge. She'd need to make sure no one else suffered the same thing. She wouldn't stop until she'd *destroyed* you.'

Kali's face is trembling, but her eyes burn.

'It wasn't just that.' Estelle's voice is velvet, and my hackles rise in warning. 'Something else happened while Olga was trying to care for her sister, which might not have happened at all if Freya had got the treatment she'd needed.'

She turns to me, as elegant as if she's on a catwalk. 'That was when Olga made me deflect the issues at the sweatshops, while Tony took the heat. It was awful. She'd told me to go out there and make promises that *she* knew wouldn't be fulfilled, while Tony was thrown to the lions. The global press had a feeding frenzy. And we *all* know *exactly* what that's like, or we wouldn't care so much about our dirty secrets being dragged into the daylight.'

'That must have been awful, Estelle,' I murmur. 'Especially as Tony wasn't just a colleague, was he?'

She gasps, then swallows and nods. 'Tony was my fiancé. We'd kept that much a secret from the media. But he never recovered from the allegations, or from how *completely* Olga abandoned him. He ... he ...' she pauses sharply, bites her tremoring lip, '... killed himself.'

Her face shivers with unreleased sobs, and Zyra puts an arm around her, pulling her into a gentle hug. 'I'm sorry, I'm so sorry,' she murmurs into Estelle's shoulder. 'And you shouldn't be forced to speak about that awful situation.' She glares at me.

But Uri is raising his eyebrows. 'Exactly. You're digging into all our secrets. All our possible motives for murder. But you haven't shared your own, have you? Except that Olga thought you're a bit of a climber. Is that all? Big deal.'

'Or that's what Thea wants us to believe.' Magnus's tone is bitter. He glares at me. 'What are *you* hiding, Thea? Why are *you* here?'

'To tie up the legalities of the Pledge, I assume.' I shrug, but my heart pounds with foreboding. 'Olga knew how ambitious I was, and that it made me a little ... flexible with my morals.' Heat prickles my cheeks, so perhaps my confession will have a ring of truth. 'Given Olga's ego, it probably didn't hurt that she was shagging my husband right under my nose.'

'If Olga had wanted a slippery lawyer, there's a billion more cutthroat than you.' Magnus laughs. 'She didn't care that you wanted more. We all do. That's why we're here.'

'Like your honorary knighthood?' I ask.

'Oh ho, *now* she's sparrin'!' Magnus chuckles again. 'Yeah. And what of it? I bailed out His Right Royal Hot Mess a few times, so yeah, I wanted a share of that status. It matters in some circles, and I figured I'd earned it! It's not like it costs *him* anything, just a word in the right ear. Considering the other word he coulda said to me was *'thanks'* – yet he never, ever did – then I don't think my ask was unreasonable.'

'But you didn't get the honour, did you?' I frown, trying to recall the details. 'And then Hugh was involved in that cash-for-honours scandal—'

'Sure. Another month, another scandal. Hugh collects 'em like stamps. But if you think that was motive for me to murder Olga, you're wrong. Motive for Hugh, maybe. Given the reason he couldn't grant it, and what's on the line for him if he can't keep his rescuers sweet. But for me? Nah.'

'No. So you just had your daughter to protect,' I say meaningfully. 'I feel for you about that, Magnus, truly. But I can't deny it gives you a powerful motive.'

'I can't deny it either.' He looks me square in the eyes. 'I can't tell you the lengths I'd be willing to go to, to safeguard my family. I am *certainly* not above hurting someone who wants to hurt them. It's a natural thing, to protect your loved ones, your children.'

'Which is an important point.' Asha opens the envelope, and I know what's coming. 'Zyra, Estelle? You might be especially interested in this.'

They crane their necks. 'What is it?'

'A birth certificate,' Asha says. 'For someone in their mid-thirties. Like the two of you.'

I watch their faces. Estelle is unmoved, looking over in detached interest.

But *Zyra* . . . her eyebrows and forehead are doing a workout that Botox aficionados can only dream of.

'Zyra?' I step towards her. 'Do you think it could be you?'

Swallowing, she drags her gaze to me. 'Well . . . I . . . I . . .' Her voice brims with anticipation, then she sighs. 'I'm being stupid. I *was* adopted. But I've never known who my biological parents are. I've just . . . always *wondered*.'

She gives a dismissive wave of her hand, but everyone stays silent, waiting for her story. So she tells it. 'I was in a care home and got fostered, then adopted, by a family. A *wonderful* family. But my biological parents didn't leave me any information about them. No clue as to why they had to give me up.'

She stares at her feet, stubbing a toe into the floor. 'I never thought about it much as a young kid, but when I was twelve, a boy in my class shared his adoption story. For something like show and tell, I guess. He *knew* things about his biological family. He was given a *reason* for his adoption. An age-appropriate version, I guess, but it satisfied his curiosity, you know? It made me realise that was missing for me, and the question of "why" just kept growing.'

With a swallow, she strokes her left forearm, as if there's something there that we can't see. 'It made me feel like I wasn't . . . lovable.' She chokes on the word, and immediately shakes her head, qualifying it. 'I wasn't made to feel that way by my adoptive family, of course. They were amazing. Couldn't love me more. But that nameless rejection gnawed away. It made me wonder what I'd done. Because I just didn't know.'

Now she's rubbing her forearm firmly, taking a deep breath. 'I ... I used to cut myself. It wasn't an attempt at suicide, but it was ... a way to let out the pain, I guess. To show that I was hurting. I wanted someone to notice, to ask. To help, I think.'

'Did they?' Estelle asks, reaching for her, rubbing her arm.

She nods, her smile wobbly. 'Yeah. My parents were great. I was always singing. Mom got me into performing. It drew me out of myself. She used to take me all over for auditions. Cost a fortune. So did the laser treatment, to make the scars less visible.'

'Did Olga ever mention anything to you?' I ask. 'To make you think that she could be your biological mother?'

Is this what Olga meant by making amends to Zyra? Was she planning to tell her? Here? Or was it a secret Olga would keep forever, while she meddled in Zyra's business?

'Over the years, Olga had asked me to perform at her various events. I just thought she was a fan, or that my music fitted the company. She became something of a mentor. That ... that's why I thought she might ... she might ... it might be *her*.'

Asha hands her the birth certificate.

Zyra reads it, blinks, then whispers the date of birth, and the place. 'Oh ... oh, wow.'

I narrow my eyes at the poignant moment, remembering what an adept performer she is.

Had Zyra already known? And had the revelation originally spurred a very different reaction ...?

Chapter 27

Tuesday 8th April – 1 p.m.

WHILE ZYRA'S REACTION HAS THE attention of everyone in the room, I take the opportunity to observe what I hope are unguarded expressions. Magnus and Uri are glancing at her, and I can see their cogs turning as, like me, they weigh up if Zyra had already known; if perhaps she'd confronted Olga …

Kali looks on in sympathy, and Estelle hugs Zyra hard enough for her muscles to flex. I see how she feels for her friend; how her strengthening friendship with Zyra has made the ice-queen model thaw. Glancing at Asha, I see that she's also appraising the scene.

Our contemplation is disturbed by a distant thud.

I tense as fears splinter through my mind. We're all present and correct – so … it's someone else? Is the murderer someone on the outside all along, who's been roaming the island, taking their chance to strike, while we turned on each other …? Or has the panther got *inside*?

I follow the sound, finding myself staring past the curve of the staircase, and I blink.

Panic slides over me, makes me shrink back into my seat, as a silent scream fills my throat. I have to fight against it, I have to look calm.

Even if my mind is clamouring.

I realise my hands are gripping the arms of the seat so tightly that my knuckles are white, and I dry-swallow, forcing myself to sit up, trying to make my fear-frozen face cooperate with my attempt at a smile.

As Hugh – *Hugh,* for God's sake – shambles towards us, he barks, 'What's going on?'

I try not to gape as I stare at him. Is he risen from the dead? Is he some kind of zombie?

'Some truths are coming home to roost,' Asha tells him. I notice the challenge in her tone, the hint of threat, and the pounding of my heart gathers speed.

I can see the wound on Hugh's head where I hit him – when I thought I'd killed him. Syrupy clots are scabbing over, the wisping hair at his temple matted across them.

God, why didn't I bash him again?

Then the obvious terror hits me, constricting around my heart: does he remember? Does he know I tried to kill him?

'What happened?' Kali pats her own head to indicate his injury.

'Oh.' He taps it automatically, then winces, and I have to hide a flush of pleasure – which is immediately replaced by nightmarish nausea as I hold my breath and wait for his reply.

But he just shrugs. 'Don't know. Blinder of a headache, though. And I'm starving.' Sitting heavily, he scowls, waving a hand at Kali. 'Whip something up.'

'Oh yeah, because you're incapable, you pathetic, snivelling sack of skin.' Her voice is deliciously low, controlled, unemotional. She's just telling him – finally – what she really thinks of him; he's nothing to her, and neither is his opinion. 'Your royal entitlement isn't much use when it doesn't impress people, is it?'

The room crackles at the stand-off, and I want to cheer Kali as she casually ignores his belligerent glower.

Asha takes the opportunity to steer the conversation back to our motives. 'We've been getting into the possible reasons people may have had to commit these murders.'

Now, though, instead of welcoming the chance to rip open the group's dark secrets, I'm resisting, mentally backing away.

And then Hugh's eyes slide towards me, fixing me with his gaze, and I gulp. His expression is knowing, crafty, terrifying.

I see Zyra and Estelle pulling away from the group, Estelle's arm wrapped firmly around the popstar's shoulders in comfort. Asha ignores them as they walk outside; her focus is lasered on Hugh.

'Did you need to silence Olga because she knew about the cash for honours scandal?' Asha challenges him.

Hugh frowns, looking confused, then laughs. 'Hardly. Who'd give a toss about that?'

'The press. The people. The government. Your family. Surely it wasn't something you – or they – would want Olga confirming?'

He shrugs, swatting away her accusation like it's one of the buzzing mosquitoes that's so plagued me.

But what's that proverb: *If you don't think one person can make a difference, try spending the night with a mosquito.*

I know what it's like to be feasted on by a million of them. I scratch the lumpy bites I acquired in the jungle till they bleed, but still *frenzy* with an insatiable itch.

But I can see that Asha is going to be as devastatingly effective as that lone one, hungry for blood, her stinger at the ready.

'No. You *wouldn't* care about that, would you. So tell us, Hugh, since we know that Olga had leverage over everyone here: what did she have on you?'

He stares at her, and I hold my breath. His hot glare travels over her and he sits forward.

'You might be a pleb, Anna.'

'Asha,' she corrects him.

He ignores her. '. . . But I thought you were at least one of the brighter ones. I am not an ordinary person. Your silly little rules don't apply. Understand?'

She lifts her chin. 'Oh, yeah, Hugh. I understand.'

Sensing imminent danger, I push myself to my feet. Avoiding Hugh's and Asha's eyes, I head to the kitchen, just in time to see Zyra and Estelle hurrying outside, like they're gasping for air. Something about their urgency makes me follow them.

They skirt the walkway, doubling back through the garden to their cabins. I have to speed-walk, panting in the heat, to keep up. They're too engrossed in their conversation to notice me dodging through the bright-bloomed bushes, trying to stay out of their peripheral view.

Over my thundering heartbeat, I catch a few words.

'. . . Well, I think you deserve an Oscar,' Estelle hisses.

There's a pause, then spluttering laughter from them both.

'God only knows what DI Harrington would make of what really happened. Can you imagine?'

'I dread to think. Look at how she pounced on my history with Tony. Zero boundaries. None of it is her business.'

I stiffen, anticipating becoming the focus of another mutiny.

'Precisely. I'm so sorry you went through that, Estelle. Even sorrier that you had to talk about it, with no warning, in front of everyone. I decided then and there that if Thea somehow knew about my past, she'd get the revelation she was looking for. Instead of the truth.' Her tone hardens, and Estelle wraps an arm around her shoulders.

As they reach Estelle's cabin, I hang back, hidden by a frothy pergola of sweet-scented jasmine, while they open the door. Checking the way is clear, I crouch-run across the sand to the cabin, and skirt around it so I can listen at the window, unseen.

Unseen, as long as no one comes looking. My heart is galloping, and my hot flush in the tropical heat is like being in a sauna on the face of the sun.

'I hope you know that Olga's reaction reflects more on her than on you,' Estelle is saying. 'You don't deserve to carry it with you. Some yoga and mindfulness will help.'

I hear the clink of items being moved, liquid being poured. Whatever they're doing, they don't need to ask what the other wants. The Nutri-Bullet whirs. Smoothies?

'It's Olga's ego that I can't get over,' Zyra fumes, and I imagine her pacing. 'Absolute main-character syndrome. The sheer *nerve* of her. Telling me I was the biggest part of her legacy. That she wanted to hand over her company to me. Making this big gesture of it.'

'Anyone who's been part of it know that's a poisoned chalice,' Estelle warns.

'Yeah! Can you imagine? Thinking her bloody mess of a company is a prize? I mean, if I needed money, maybe it would look tempting. But it's just a bunch of problems, most of which she was about to thrust right back into the spotlight – and then not even solve!'

'Yeah, I hate … *hated* … her approach.' Estelle's voice is hard, the bitterness still raw. 'I'm glad you see things differently to her. Not that it should change your mind, but you'd probably make a decent CEO.'

'What gets me is that she was probably late twenties, maybe early thirties, when she gave me up. She was doing phenomenally well by then. She had every opportunity to keep me, if she'd wanted to. But she chose not to. And I'll never really know why. *Still.*'

They share a silence, until Zyra adds, 'And I asked her, outright, "If you want me to inherit, if you want to share what you have, why didn't you help when my – very ordinary – family were trying to get me to auditions and classes?"'

She gives another cynical laugh as she continues. 'You won't believe what she told me. She said she *had*! That all this time, she'd secretly supported me. Sponsored record deals. Made donations on the condition I'd be on gigs and tours. After everything – giving me up, letting me and my family struggle – *now* she's trying to take credit for my family's support, for my talent, for my hard work!'

'*What?*' Estelle actually *snorts* in indignation. 'That's . . . *beyond ridiculous*! The *ego* of her!'

'That's Olga, isn't it. That's who I get my DNA from.' Zyra's voice trembles with bitterness. 'And I fucking hate her.'

It takes some doing when you're having a hot flash in the tropics, but my blood ices at those words. I hold my breath, re-imagining Olga's reunion with Zyra in far more explosive terms.

Without warning, a figure looms from the shadows at the back of the cabin. 'Who are you double-crossing now, Thea?'

Hugh doesn't bother to speak quietly. He wants me to get caught.

'And if you thought you'd got away with what you did to me,' he growls, 'you're wrong.'

'What?' I gasp, hating how high and thin, how *vulnerable*, my voice sounds.

'I *know* what you did.'

I meet his eyes. 'Then you'll know what *you* did.' I turn, trying to get past him.

Faster than a striking snake, he grabs my wrist, his sharp tug whiplashing me back to face him. 'So? You've been a prick-tease since I met you.'

He leans in, his stinking breath hot on my neck. 'And you should know, Thea. No one gets to refuse me anything.'

Chapter 28

Tuesday 8ᵗʰ April – 3 p.m.

I TEAR MY ARM FROM HIS grip and stride away, my heart pounding.

Shit, shit, shit …

The warning clamour tells me, beyond doubt, that I'm now in a race. Hugh will attack me again, or kill me, unless I can get away.

But I can't, can I? None of us can.

In a fog of outrage and terror, I've marched towards the safety of the main house via the beach, and now I find myself staring out to sea. The vast, surging ocean stretches out uninterrupted towards the horizon. There are no other islands, no ships or vessels, no people to help.

I kick my foot into the sand in impotent desperation. Terror makes my whole body quake, but I have to fight that off; I have to *think*.

As I try to focus my thoughts, to push back the paralysing fear, a blessed idea strikes, and I stagger over to a sun lounger and wait for it to crystallise.

What if I can find out something about the murders; something that pins this on Hugh? Then everyone would put him under room arrest. Then I will be a little bit safer …

I can't imagine Hugh tampering with the rasul treatment – can't envisage something like that even occurring to him. But then, it's entirely possible that he's had every kind of treatment going. And I *can* see him detaching the fixings for the chandelier. So maybe there's something there.

And while I want to frame Hugh, I also want to uncover the truth.

Turning, I stare at the lodge where Charles was killed, looking for any way that someone might have accessed the roof void. There are no external steps at the front or indications of any way in. I can imagine a roof void accessed via a ladder, but somehow I expect Olga to have a more elegant solution. No dusty attic access through her sumptuous bedroom, workman boots on the antique silk rugs.

Sure enough, as I edge around the side of the lodge that's furthest from the main house, I spot an external wooden staircase, shielded by lush, leafy shrubs.

I check that no one is around to see me, even though I feel a hundred eyes on me, and I crouch-run, hunched but fast, up the stairs. I feel exposed as I reach the top, out of breath, and sweating more from the subterfuge than the exertion. There's a full-size door and I try the handle.

Locked.

Fumbling in my pocket, I find the staff key – and it *unlocks* the door!

I push inside, and I'm plunged into impenetrable darkness after the bright, clear sunshine that dazzles off the sea.

I'd prefer to close the door so I won't be spotted, but then I'll be in total darkness. Automatically, I reach for my phone to put on the torch, then remember *again* that I don't have it.

My frustration erupts in a sigh, and all I can do is blink and wait for my eyes to adjust.

Meanwhile, I try to work out the geography.

This side is Olga's suite, and spans from the ocean to the forest.

Across from me, Hugh has the ocean-fronted room. So I have to be careful that he doesn't hear me up here.

And Charles had the forest-view suite, with his bedroom on the top floor.

Shapes are forming in the gloom now. I can make out the boxes, pipes and ducts for services and air con. The air is musty, and the heat under this roof in the Caribbean sun is thick and sweltering.

I creep across to the section above Charles's room and try to imagine the layout below: the massive central bed below the chandelier.

There it is: the back plate that the light fitting's supporting rod would have been secured to. It's about a foot square, with strong bolts at each corner and a hole in the centre, just over an inch across, for the rod supporting the chandelier to slide up through. Once the hole for the fixing pin was above the back plate, the pin could be secured into position, and the chandelier wouldn't fall.

Charles's putrid stench wafts through the floor. I swallow hard, then hold my breath as I search. *Where is that damn pin?*

I kneel on the debris-strewn floorboards and peep down at the room – then gag and rock back from the smell of my decomposing husband.

Swallowing, I do my best to examine the back plate in the dim grey light.

The metal has certainly been tampered with: finger marks streak the dust and there's a clear *dash* along the plate that is shinier than the rest of the metal, like something has been scraped along it.

A few inches from the back plate is a junction box, and the plastic cover has been shattered. I crawl over, looking at it carefully.

The tiny screws that would have clamped the wires to the circuits are loose, and one has been jolted out of its insert completely.

Scanning the floor, I find it, nestled against a beam a few inches away: *the pin that would have secured the chandelier.*

It's been shot across the floor, dislodged from the opposite side of the plate that bears the shiny streak.

I imagine some kind of golf swing *thwacking* the pin out of its hole, the metal club *shinging* along the metal plate, leaving a bright scar.

Of course! That's what the wrench had been used for – and why it had been hidden.

Why not dust it off and return it to the staff shed, or wherever they found it? Were they hoping someone else would pick it up and put their fingerprints all over it?

Or had the killer run away in haste, under the cover of night; or got distracted and forgotten they were carrying it? Then they'd have to stash it somewhere where they hoped it wouldn't be found. Or perhaps they'd just had to leave it somewhere temporarily, intending to put it back the following day?

If it was Hugh, this was right by his room; it would have been a convenient place to leave it.

Oh ... oh ...! A terrible, brilliant thought occurs ...

Now I've seen all this, I could plant the wrench in Hugh's suite. And then I could insist on a search ...

Would the chandelier rod have a dent in it that matches the wrench? I frown, trying to recall if there was one, wondering if I could *make* one before planting the wrench on Hugh ...

But the pin would have taken the force, and the wrench could be held at various angles, so the shape of a dent, or lack of one altogether, wouldn't be that conclusive.

As I start to move towards the open door, I catch the sound of the stairs outside creaking, and I cower, holding my breath.

I creep back, towards the corner, into the shadows, watching the door.

I'm already sweating in this stuffy, muggy heat, but now it's pulsing round me, suffocating me.

The door creaks but doesn't open. Is someone there? Have I been spotted?

If I have, I need to know who it is. I've already got Hugh threatening me; and either him or someone *else* trying to break into my room, *plus*, possibly, the murderer still to worry about.

With careful steps, I tiptoe towards the door, terrified of an attack but more terrified of yet another unknown danger.

I wince at the creaking boards, instinctively hesitating, then press on.

A sudden draft shivers over my skin, as the door swings open and I freeze in the shadows. I hold my breath, heart pounding in my ears, as I wait for someone to appear . . .

Sweat slips down my spine, and I shiver with a new fear: of being shut in this hotbox. It's enough to make me rush to the door, shoving it open firmly in case someone's behind it, ready to ram them down the stairs if they attack.

But my force meets nothing – and I stagger out as I slam the door against the wall.

There's no one here. I wince at the retina-melting sunlight, squinting around like an unearthed mole as I blindly check for figures on the stairs, or in the garden below, or on the beach beyond.

With my bleached-out vision, I can't see anyone – or anything. Gradually, my eyes adjust, coming to focus on the shrubs that sway occasionally as the breeze picks up.

My legs buckle in relief that it was just the wind making the door creak. I reach for a nearby bough and snap off a twig, jamming it into the hinge so the door doesn't close, then hurry down the steps.

Inside the hallway of the lodge, my heart is pounding as I slip the key into Olga's lock.

Please, Hugh, don't come out now . . .

Letting myself into her suite, I wince as I take a couple of seconds to ease her door closed. Then I dash to Olga's desk, frantically looking for wherever we discarded the wrench.

Seizing it up off the floor, I hurry to her kitchenette. I grab a napkin from her drawer, wipe down the wrench, then use the cloth to turn the door handle without my fingers touching it.

Darting out to the hall, I close her door softly behind me, praying no one will appear.

A few paces across the hall and I'm standing outside Hugh's room. My mouth is dry.

What if he's in there?

I wish I could check, to see if he's still in the great room, or elsewhere. But if I go looking, he may see me. And for my plan to work, it has to look like I've come straight from the roof void.

So I compute the options. If Hugh's in there, he'll attack me, and I'll whack him again with this wrench. Then, I'll make sure his fingerprints are on the handle to incriminate him for Charles's death, at least – and then possibly, by implication, for Olga's.

I'll be able to say that I confronted him and he attacked me. With one head injury already sustained, another would certainly be fatal. And I thought I'd killed him once already. What difference will it really make if I try again . . .?

I brace myself to unlock his door. But my body is frozen. I just can't do it.

The terrifying memory of his attack, the strength he could use against me without even really trying, the repulsive heft of him; the fear of that horrific violation.

The stench of him is still in my nostrils, on my skin, polluting me.

I turn sharply, sure I'm going to be sick. Hot bile shoots into my throat. I fall beside the planter and retch into it.

As I cling to the plant pot, I'm reminded of that night, seeing the sparks of alarm that Olga had ignited, seeing how the flames took hold and engulfed everyone. And I'm reminded that the killer *also* paused – right here – to hide the weapon they'd used to kill Charles.

If I'm going to limit the dangers around me, I have to face Hugh.

So . . . OK . . . I'll open the door and I'll deal with whatever's on the other side of it, whether that's framing him . . . or killing him.

I let myself in, my eyes darting around like I'm a hunted rabbit, and leave the wrench against the bar. It's around the corner from the door, so it's not obvious, but not hidden, either. I dump the napkin on top of the bar, with others, and let myself out.

Then I hurry to the great room, as if I'd taken the direct route from the roof void, managing to make my stride commanding again. At least that comes easily, no matter how jangled my nerves are . . .

I command their attention. 'Good. You're all here.'

'Before you begin, Thea,' Hugh leers at me, 'We've all been having a little conversation. And what we've discovered is very . . . enlightening.'

I give a theatrical sigh. 'Hugh, you couldn't be enlightened if you were spotlit on the face of the sun.'

His cunning eyes narrow in his dissatisfied face, and he tilts his head at Kali.

She looks reluctant, glancing around the rest of the group.

Their faces are hostile. The same fear crawls over me that I felt when they all sat me down and grilled me before putting Charles under room arrest.

Then Kali shrugs. 'We can't deny that you, Thea, are the only person who would have wanted both Olga and Charles dead. No one else has a motive for them both.'

'That's not true. Every single one of you had a damning secret – and you'd reasonably have assumed that Olga shared those secrets with Charles. Olga might have extracted leverage over you, but Charles was never one to ignore an opportunity, either.'

I pause, giving extra oxygen to my point. 'Anyone desperate to prevent their secrets seeing the light of day would *have* to silence them both.'

There's an awkward silence at that. Oh, I know how to work the audience. I soften my voice, letting them play right into my hands . . .

'I *do* see why you'd think – at first glance – that I'd be the obvious link. But don't you think it's *too* obvious? The motives are far wider than they first appear. And we – *all* of us – must be on guard against the perils of an incorrect accusation. What if the killer expects me to be accused and uses that to their advantage? Maybe they only wanted one of the victims dead, but killed both so I'd be easier to frame? That might even be why I'm here.'

I pace over to Magnus. 'After all, *you* wondered why Olga appointed me when she could have hired any big-name shark in the business.' I shrug, turning to include the entire group. 'Everyone here has the capability to conduct a little light industrial espionage, so it's not impossible *someone* with an agenda *suggested* me to Olga.'

'Who, then?' Magnus asks. 'Who could have suggested you to Olga?'

Oh, the perfect segue for my plan ...

I frown, pretending to think, as my eyes scan them all. Then I nod. 'Hugh. It has to be Hugh. He knew me, Charles *and* Olga. He's embroiled in endless scandals because he's a morality-free zone. There are too many opportunities to count. We all saw him argue with Charles, saw their falling-out. He couldn't afford for Charles to have an axe to grind – *and* risk him living to see just how sharp it was.'

I sense the tide changing. Sidelong glances between the tycoons show my logic has hit home. Estelle and Zyra nod as they glance at each other, their instincts keen.

'And we do have an easy way to check,' I say. 'That's what I was going to suggest when I came in. I've worked out how Charles was killed—'

I pause at the collective intake of breath, then continue.

'Someone got into the roof void, which has been wedged open, and they used some kind of tool to release the fixing pin that secured the chandelier to its back plate. Now, I'm sure this person might have been sensible enough to hide the tool, or return it ...' I pause now. It's imperative the suggestion comes from someone else. So I give a leading shrug.

And all this talk of murder and motives has got everyone doing their best Marple impression, so I just need to wait a few seconds ...

'But ...!'

'What if ...?'

'Hang on ...'

I give them time to all arrive at the same idea. Finally, Kali's voice commands the room.

'It's possible the killer might have just dashed back to their room? They might not have wanted to risk returning the tool, or they might have forgotten, in the . . . I guess . . . panic of it?'

Asha is staring at me, wide-eyed, disbelieving.

I can't afford to smile at her, but I try to soften my expression, to show her she's not incriminated.

'Let's search Hugh's room!' Magnus bellows. He pushes Hugh ahead of us as he leads the way. In an instant we're all following him, along the walkway to the lodge.

Hugh protests at every step. 'You're being preposterous. This is ridiculous! I'm not letting any of you search my room!'

'What if we search everyone's room, then?' I offer. I have to get that in first, to look innocent. 'Then it's fair on all of us.'

I see Asha bite her lip and turn her face away as we walk, before rallying to keep up with the rest of us.

We all stare at Hugh's door. 'Unlock it, Hugh.' Kali says.

'*No.* You're idiots to think you can make me.'

'If you don't unlock it, we'll break the glass door to your balcony. Then your bedroom air con won't work,' Kali tells him, with the voice a patient parent might use to reason with a recalcitrant child.

'And then you could have a panther for company.' Uri grins.

'What?' Everyone turns to him.

He shrugs. 'You didn't know? Olga's starving pet panther is on the loose.' He waggles his eyebrows. 'And looking for *meat.*'

Kali's eyes widen. 'Oh, well, Hugh. There's a silver lining for *all* of us then, if you keep refusing to unlock your door.' She turns to me and Uri. 'Shall we go round and—?'

'Fine. *Fine.*' Hugh groans and unlocks his door. 'You are all despicable. Every last one of you.'

I hang back, so that someone else will make the discovery.

It's Estelle who notices. She doesn't point the wrench out, she waits.

Then Hugh notices, and grabs it. His astonished gape looks exactly like someone covering their guilt. My heart cartwheels at the sight of him, so pompous and untouchable, walking right into the trap.

'We'll need to bag that,' Estelle murmurs, her understatement powerful against Hugh's bluster. 'Fingerprints.'

Zyra darts to the kitchen, bringing back a small bin bag which she deposits the wrench in, sealing it with care. I sense everyone watching, holding their breath.

Everyone but Asha, who shoots me a blink-and-you'd-miss-it questioning glance, wondering how *her* wrench has been transferred to this locked room.

I try to keep my face neutral, but even this small triumph feels epic.

'And?' Hugh scoffs. 'What do you think you're going to do with any fingerprints?'

'Proof,' Zyra responds simply.

'Yeah, proof that Thea planted it. She broke into my room! She did this to me!' He points at his head.

'When?' Uri asks.

'Yesterday, around dinner time,' Hugh asserts.

'No,' Uri lies. 'Thea was helping me with the radio before I went to cook with Kali.'

'And then she came up to speak to me, in my room,' Asha invents.

My heart hammers at them covering for me.

Hugh glowers, shaking his head. 'You don't have any proof of anything. And, even if you did, what are you going to do with it?'

My stomach rollercoasters. Jeez. A few days on this island, in this hot, sinister climate, has melted my brain cells.

Because *of course* Hugh won't be charged with anything. He's never been held accountable for anything in his life. Even if we handed the police a smoking gun, with Hugh's DNA all over it, he'd still walk away. You can't stop people like him.

The realisation is like a slow-spreading poison. My plan is all for nothing. At least one person here is a killer – but no one will be brought to justice.

Chapter 29

Tuesday 8th April – 5 p.m.

DESPITE MY PESSIMISM, SOMETHING IS happening: brilliantly, unexpectedly, Magnus and Kali are securing Hugh's upstairs balcony door, shoving him towards the sofa, informing him in no uncertain terms that he won't be leaving his suite.

It takes quite an effort to make the prince do something he doesn't want to, but the company is determined. I'd have enjoyed watching him literally being put in his place but, while the room arrest is underway, Asha tugs me along the hall.

'What were you doing with the wrench?' she hisses at me, glancing over her shoulder to make sure we're not being overheard.

I whisper back, just as cautious. 'I just saw an opportunity. I went back to Olga's room to get it—'

'Oh.' She subsides. 'Yeah. I forgot I left it there. I thought you'd broken into my room. Sorry. Just that ... someone ... someone tried to get into my room last night, and it's made me a bit ... twitchy.'

'Understandable.' I rub her arm, but I don't tell her the same thing happened to me.

Was it the same person . . .?

She's looking at me oddly, and it occurs to me that she's wondering how I got into Hugh's room. So I add hastily, 'As luck would have it, Hugh had left his balcony door unlocked.' I don't think she saw me grab Hugh's spare key after Olga was killed, and I *definitely* don't want her knowing I have an access pass.

'What? *Really?*'

'Yes.' I shrug. 'I guess he doesn't feel as vulnerable as the rest of us. He's . . . used to being un*touch*able.' I can't hide the bitter edge to my voice, and her quick glance at me tells me she caught it.

She opens her mouth like she's going to say something, then closes it, then says, 'I told you the truth, Thea. I just found that wrench in the hall.'

'I believe you.' It's not true. I don't believe her, but it isn't personal. I hardly ever believe anyone. As a lawyer, that would be foolish. But people often want to hear that you believe them. And that lie can sometimes invite truths.

'I wiped it down,' I add, in case that's worrying her, and her smile reveals her relief.

'Maybe I've reunited the weapon with the guilty party?' I whisper.

She darts another quick, hot glance my way. 'Do . . . do you think so? Do you think he could kill someone?'

'I think a man like that could be guilty of *anything*.'

We've been swept into the great room, and I need to satisfy the question that's taken root in my brain. I need Asha to stay here.

I pull her back and whisper, 'I want to see if I can spy on Hugh from his garden. See if he's doing anything suspicious, now that he's been incarcerated in his room.'

'Good idea.' She begins to move towards the door.

'No, hold on.' I stand still, beckoning her back towards me. 'I was going to ask if you could stay here and keep an eye on everyone.'

She frowns.

'Because if it's not Hugh, and someone here is watching me, trying to kill me, then they might realise I've gone off on my own. They might ...' I grimace. I'm not faking that. I can't bring myself to say what they might do.

Nodding, Asha says, 'I'll keep everyone occupied somehow. I'll suggest we have dinner. Most people gather for that, to see who makes what.'

'Thanks.'

But I don't plan to watch Hugh. I have a different objective.

I slip through the walkway towards the lodge – then circle back via Olga's garden, through Charles's and Asha's, to mine. I dash up my balcony steps, hurry through my suite and out into the hall – and finally slip into Asha's room.

And then I begin the search.

I go through the drawers and cupboards in the bedroom area, then through the pillows and sheets, before checking under the bed and between the frame and mattress – oof, that's heavy.

I'm sweating and puffed. But I press on. I separate and look behind every garment in the closet. Nothing. Just neatly hung clothes, perfume and jewellery.

In the bathroom, there's nothing in the cupboards or the cistern of the loo. Returning to the main room, I check the bar, the console table, under trays, the drawers, down the back of the sofa; for anything folded into the ice bucket or hidden in the fridge. Under the coffee table, behind the TV ...

Nothing.

Huffing, I sink onto the sofa and look around.

Then I remember the papers I stashed away for my own safekeeping, and check the sofa cushions.

I find nothing, but it makes me wonder about the papers in my room: if perhaps I missed something. I hadn't had a chance to read them yet: what if a clue's been sitting right there, *in my own room*, all this time?

Trembling, I listen at the door, praying no one's out there. I have my key ready as I let myself out of Asha's room and dash back along to mine.

My fingers shake but I manage to slide the key into the lock and turn it, tumbling inside and closing the door softly behind me.

I head straight for the sofa, seize the cushion, rip open the zip and pull out the envelopes and pages that Asha retrieved from the secret drawer in the office, and which I'd retrieved after Asha had hidden them from Kali. I tear it open, hungry to read the contents.

But the contents are unsettling.

There are grainy images of naked limbs, tangled on a mattress, with unflattering facial expressions. Somehow orgies never look as glamorous as you'd think. It's the ultimate 'you had to be there' situation, I suppose. The pictures are at a weird angle, suggesting they've been snapped by a hidden camera. The voyeurism, the unsavoury feel of them, is disturbing, and I instinctively recoil.

I have to work out who this incriminated. But I'm kidding myself, aren't I? I already know. In the pit of my soul, I know who this is going to be.

I scan the pictures for Hugh's face – only to stop dead.

Not Hugh. But Charles.

Shit.

I drop the photos as if I've been burned, and my arms sag heavily at my sides. It feels like something is crushing my chest, and I wonder if I'm having a heart attack.

As I fall back against the sofa, the room swirls black around me, pressing in.

Dear God . . . Imagine if I'm found dead, at the sight of Charles's sex photos! The thought rises like hysteria, bubbling up through my body so forcefully I feel like I'm floating.

No . . . No . . . I'm not giving in this easily. They won't have the satisfaction.

I rally, breathing hard, sitting up, blinking the stars from my blurry vision.

I look through the photos again, and this time I see Hugh, in the corner but very clear, now that I'm examining them. So this was one of his notorious parties, of which the press had rumours – teasing the accusation with risqué nicknames – but never proof. So whoever had this didn't go to the press. They weren't after public humiliation; they wanted a private advantage.

That was Olga all over, wasn't it?

It puts her relationship with Charles, and Hugh, in a new light.

Did Hugh kill her? And then Charles? To silence them? I know he wouldn't usually get his hands dirty, but in extremis, he's certainly cruel enough, ruthless enough . . .

As I start to put the photos back, I find a single slip of paper still in the envelope. I draw it out, and my heart starts to pound as I recognise the format of a police Missing Persons notice.

The name is redacted, the photo covered.

██████ went missing from the Oxford area on New Years Eve, 1999, after working at a party as part of the Elite Caterers' team.
Last seen wearing black tie, ████████ is 5'9" with a slim build.
If you have any information, please contact Thames Valley Police.

I hold the page up to the light, squinting, to see if I can read the redacted bits, or see the image, but I can't. From the spacing, I think the first name is four or five letters long, and the surname four letters. It might end with an 'I'? Maybe 'MI' or 'NI'?

Then I re-read it, and the date sinks in. *Shit.*

And the location. *Oh, shit . . .*

And why this notice might be with these photos. *Oh, God . . . Oh, God . . .*

A memory floods back, unwelcome, sinister-edged. It feels dangerous to let it in, but I've resisted thinking about it all my life.

My head rings with that warning shriek.

But I can't block it out anymore. After everyone had left the party, *that party*, with Hugh and Charles, there was one car that came back.

And Charles had been cold as he crawled into bed, like he'd been outside – for some time – in the freezing mid-winter night air.

And why would he have been?

There's only one reason that makes sense of these clues.

I rush to my bathroom, and grip the sink as I heave up my fear, my panic, my loathing, and the fact I can't deny it any longer.

Chapter 30

Tuesday April 8ᵗʰ – 5.30 p.m.

GOD BLESS MY BRAIN; IT searches for clarity like torchlight in the dark. Through my fug of fear, a clear plan forms.

I carefully put the documents back in their envelopes and return them to their hiding place inside the sofa cushion. Then, I retrieve the rasul treatment from my pocket and, under the bright bathroom lights, use tweezers to remove some of the plant matter, dabbing the miniscule particles onto the underside of the lid until it's covered in green specks.

I might be hurrying to the kitchen to join the others but it's my mind that's *racing*, reinforcing that I'm taking the right course of action: Hugh *has* to be the guilty party. He's already attacked me, and now he's threatened me. Even if we happened to be magically rescued by a passing cruise ship right now, and taken back to real life, off this lawless island, he'll still come for me.

The danger won't die, unless he does.

As I speed-walk through the great room, I see that Zyra and Estelle are eating gigantic salads out of crystal bowls with more enthusiasm than any salad deserves.

Kali, Magnus and Uri are tucking into something that looks like linguine and smells as delicious as only carbs can.

'Thea?' Uri calls. 'We wondered where you'd got to. I made enough for everyone. Help yourself if you want some.'

I glance at Uri. We haven't spoken since he blew up at me for snooping, or since I found out how serious his secret is. But he lied for me when I most needed defending. I feel like I'm on a rollercoaster, never knowing who to trust. Was he helping me? Or storing up a favour for later?

A spike of memory jabs. A five-letter name with a four-letter surname. Nigel Reni. The whistleblower. I blink. Do the timelines match? The disappearance was twenty years ago. So surely it couldn't . . .

Hiding my shiver, I manage to say, 'Thank you,' to Uri as I head straight through to meet Asha, who's preparing a sandwich for Hugh.

I hesitate, not knowing how to play this. I hadn't imagined anyone else would bother to take him food; I'd *thought* I'd have a clear opportunity. I keep my hands below the island counter, so that Asha can't see what I'm holding.

'I can finish up, if you like?' I offer. 'So you can have your meal?'

'It's fine.' She slops mango juice into a glass and throws some cheese and salad between the slices of bread she's haphazardly buttered.

Seeing that she's doing this with as much care as I did for Charles, I bite back a grin. Maybe she's more of an ally than I thought.

'I wanted to add a special ingredient.' I nearly gasp at my own audacity, and Asha actually does.

She glances at the open door and widens her eyes at me. 'What are you saying, Thea?'

'I know he's a murderer, Ash. And none of us are safe while he's here.'

'Sure. Hence the room arrest.' Her tone, and expression, are cautious.

'But it's more than that, isn't it? He's above the law.'

She looks at me, her brow clearing of its deep furrow.

'What's our endgame?' I ask, as if any of this is logical. 'Report him for his crimes? And then what? There won't be any form of justice, will there?'

This isn't just personal for me. It's professional: it's about how the system I'm part of fails people every day. And I'm the worst kind of hypocrite because, *despite* being part of it, I want to be above it. I yearn to be that untouchable.

But Asha's face has a flicker of optimism. 'So . . .?' She leans towards me, urging me to say it.

'So sometimes justice needs a helping hand.'

'Thea? You're not . . .?'

'I'm not trying to involve you in anything, Ash. Go, have your dinner, and I'll take care of this.'

She looks at the sandwich for a second, then she looks at me. 'I think if anything is happening, Thea, then we're in it together.'

I didn't expect that. I expected her to take the out I offered, to be relieved at having plausible deniability. I'm not sure if she's daft or brave. But our eyes lock in some deep pact.

With a firm nod, I place the rasul treatment on the counter, open the lid, and scatter the extracted plant fragments between the salad leaves in Hugh's sandwich. I press the bread back together and look at Asha.

I feel calm. The sense of closure is tantalizingly close.

'Before we take this to Hugh, I think we should clear the air between us all. This really is a final reckoning, isn't it?'

Asha frowns. 'O . . . K?'

I take the tray, to make sure no one else accidentally eats the fatal sandwich.

I command everyone's attention as I enter the room. 'Before I take Hugh his meal, I'd like to take a moment to discuss something.'

The murmured conversations fall silent. Uri, Kali and Magnus set down their forks. Zyra and Estelle fold their arms and sit back.

'This has been an awful time. But now we think we've incarcerated the right person, can I ask – did anyone try to break into my room last night?'

Collective frowns all round.

'And mine!' Asha adds.

More frowns, but no admissions.

'Do we conclude it was Hugh, then?' Asha asks.

'Probably.' I outwardly agree, but it's more likely he was concussed. Though . . . it *is* just about feasible, and he is certainly guilty of dark crimes.

'And there's something else. I believe Hugh was guilty of killing someone, several years ago, that Charles helped him cover up. I think that Olga found out and used it as leverage. And *that's* why I think Hugh killed Olga. Then, after he and Charles argued, Hugh was afraid their broken bond would mean the secret still came out, so he had to kill him, too.'

Everyone gapes at the revelation.

'So it's imperative we keep Hugh detained. And I think it's also pretty likely he'll put up a fight. So if Asha and I are taking him his sandwich, would anyone be willing to join us? As backup?'

'I will.' Magnus stands, unconsciously rubbing the knuckles of his clenched fist. With his healing split lip, he looks like a bouncer fresh from dealing with trouble, who's ready for more.

'Thanks, Magnus.' Asha turns and we head over to the lodge. I take a deep breath and knock on the door.

'What?' Hugh barks from within.

'Room service,' Asha sings, with saccharine sarcasm.

There's a muffled shuffling while Hugh dissembles his barricade and then I use his confiscated key to unlock the door.

As Asha pushes it open, Hugh lunges forward with something glinting and dangerous held out ahead of him, the tang of single malt drenching the air.

Her scream *shrieks*, making me jump and drop the tray. Hugh stabs at Asha wildly with the broken whisky bottle. She lets go of the door and we both stagger back, but Hugh's foot kicks out, keeping the door open.

As we flinch away, Magnus muscles in, shielding us. The broken bottle smashes into his arm as he blocks his vulnerable throat, and Hugh swings a punch with his left hand.

Something cruel and sharp thrusts out from between his knuckles, and I realise he's palmed a corkscrew, its curling spear weaponised to brutal effect.

I leap, arms windmilling, to knock Hugh's fist from its trajectory, but I'm too slow. Magnus is faster, and his fist collides with Hugh's forearm, absorbing the force.

But the sharp point still nicks Asha's throat.

Through the blur of fighting, I see Kali and Uri rush along the walkway towards us.

Asha grips her throat and falls back, and Hugh attacks Magnus with lethal, lacerating blows. Magnus fends them off, but blood is streaming from his arms, streaking into his shirtsleeves. His eyes are wild with shock and pain – and determination to win this time.

As Kali wads up tissue against Asha's neck, I catch an evil flash of satisfaction in Hugh's face. He's only attacking Magnus to stop him defending Asha and me. If I'm not here, he won't go for anyone else. *Probably.*

I back away, scrambling to get out of the hall and to the walkway, my vision jolting as I break into the ungainly, uncontrolled run of someone panicking, with no bodily co-ordination, no plan, no idea of where to go. I feel like a terrified rabbit, zigzagging in desperation to outpace a cunning fox.

The last of the rapid sunset has sunk below the horizon and the purpling sky gives little light. Does that hinder me? Or help me?

I lurch over Olga's lawn as my legs wobble under me. I gasp like I can't breathe.

My heart feels like it will explode.

I burst through the shrubs, into the jungle, and onto the track, that cursed, bloody track.

My mind breaks through my feverish panic.

It's OK. I know this route. I know where it leads.

And Hugh won't.

I know that even if Hugh has been here before, one place he'll *never* have seen is the staff quarters. He won't be familiar with the building. I can secure myself somewhere, or I can arm myself. *I can be ready.*

I hear panting behind me, the pounding footsteps of someone with more stamina.

Terror spikes and I try to find some extra speed.

I don't have it in me. I feel weak, defeated, broken. I nearly sob.

And the hand on my shoulder makes me scream and *scream* in utter horror.

Chapter 31

Tuesday 8th April – 6.30 p.m.

'I T'S ME. IT'S ME.'
My legs liquify at Asha's voice.

'I know how much the jungle creeps you out, Thea. I had to come. We're in this together now.'

'You're injured.' I'm still shaking but my jangling nerves are calming a little. 'You need help.'

'Honestly, Thea, this is all I care about. We have to keep going. Magnus held him back for a while, but Hugh was doing his best to break free. And follow.'

'Oh, God.' I'm galvanised into action, and we hurry on together. I notice she keeps one hand on the improvised bandage at her throat. In the dusk, I can make out the bloom of blood. 'Seriously, Ash, go back and get medical help from Kali. Hugh won't come after you.'

'I'll find a first aid kit at the staff building. I'll be fine.'

We hurry on. I'm fearful of how far we have to go, that speed-walking isn't going to be enough. But I daren't ask her to run.

I'm terrified of the snakes that we can't see, but which I know are slithering between our feet. I'm scared of standing on one of them and getting a deadly bite to the ankle.

Even more, I dread the deadlier beasts that only emerge after nightfall. The secretive, silent creatures adapted to darkness.

And Hugh is the worst of them all.

I tug Asha's free hand, urging her along faster.

And then I see a beam of light and I hear the distant whine of an engine.

The quad bike.

Fuck. He's chasing us down in the bloody staff vehicle!

Turning, I'm blinded by the headlights.

But *he* might be able to see *us*.

With a desperate, despairing whimper, I pull Asha off the track and into the deep, unhacked jungle.

I hate to think what we're walking in, pushing through, of what's crawling on our skin as I power through the undergrowth, feeling branches scrape through my hair, the sinister caress of dangling vines.

My senses are uncomfortably heightened. My skin is crawling at every rustle, and my ears ring with the night chorus of chirruping, chirping insects or frogs, or something more dubious.

Over the jungle cacophony, I strain to hear the judder of the engine.

The halo of approaching headlights lets me see how much Asha has bled.

Shit. We're not going to make it to the building.

I rip off my shirt, sacrificing my arm coverage, and tie it as firmly as I can around her neck. This is a fine line between a torniquet and suffocation. But it's something.

'Can you carry on like this?' I ask. 'Try to get to the building? If we take it ... steady?' I wince. It's a horrific thought to be in this environment for one nanosecond longer than necessary.

'I ... I don't know.' She grips my arm, walks a few paces, then stops. 'In case I don't make it, let me just do something now.' She takes a folded photo from her pocket and kisses it. 'Love you, Samir.'

As she tucks it safely away again, I try to encourage her. 'Don't give in yet, Ash. We'll get there. Together.'

She takes my hand again and we thread through the awful obstacles, moving with as much purpose as possible. I'm terrified that every firecracker footstep, crackling on twigs and leaf litter, will give us away.

I feel Asha's grip loosening. I need to keep her with me. I need to keep her conscious and talking.

'Who's Samir?'

'My brother.'

Oh. I'd expected it to be a husband or lover, given the gesture. 'Older?'

'Yes. My big brother. He was the best.'

'Was?' A warning beat thuds in the back of my mind.

'He died.'

'Oh, Ash. I'm sorry.'

S-A-M-I-R.

And Asha's surname is S-A-N-I.

'Shit.'

'What?'

I hadn't realised I'd sworn out loud. 'I . . . I think I've just realised how he died, Ash. I think I've just realised everything.'

'Then you know what I need for justice to be done.'

The headlights are getting brighter, closer. I pull Asha sideways, further from the track and the beam. 'Would you show me his photo?'

'Sure.'

She hands it to me. In the half-light that's spilling this far into the undergrowth, I can make out the young man – the teenager – in the picture.

The memory stabs sharp and bright, making me gasp. Samir is the waiter, the young man who gave me water on the night of Hugh's millennium party. Who'd asked if I needed help. A good-looking boy, who Hugh probably propositioned, or who might have seen something ... And then had to be silenced.

A dispensable nobody, to Hugh.

Oh ... Oh God. This changes everything ...

I can imagine only too well the police enquiry that would have gone nowhere. The dead ends of evidence, despite maddening rumour. The lack of accountability.

As Asha pockets the picture, she bumps against me. 'I'm tired, Thea.'

'I know.' I pull her hand encouragingly. 'Just keep going.'

'I will. But will you?'

I know what she's asking. I swallow. 'Yes.'

As the light behind us gets brighter, closer, I pull us deeper into the jungle. Whole trees seem to move in the dark, winding with taut, serpentine bodies.

Chirrups and hisses and maddening buzzes are in full stereo surround sound.

I would be recoiling, but Asha has given me something else to focus on.

'Did you reach out to Olga because she'd crossed paths with both Hugh and Charles?'

'No. No, it didn't happen like that.'

'Tell me,' I invite.

Her breathing is becoming laboured. 'You ... tell *me*. If you're so smart.'

'OK ...' I let my brain refocus the pieces, like a blurred image sharpening up.

Oh, I see it now ...

'Your brother, Samir Sani, went missing after working at one of Hugh's parties. You investigated, relentlessly, I imagine. That search for answers probably shaped your whole career choice. But you hit dead end after dead end.'

Eyeing her, I see pure pain written across her face, and I don't think it's just because of the awful wound.

'I can envisage you assembling information, taking it to the police, yet it somehow gets shut down. Someone's flexing their influence. Magnus had done that for Hugh so many times, made sure he stayed untouchable. So . . . this time, was it Olga?'

Asha nods. 'Yes. She'd covered her tracks so thoroughly that it took a couple of years to find out who'd blocked the investigation. And then I had to find out everything about her.'

'Like her greenwashing?'

She nods again. 'I didn't even have to do the work for that. If you just make a couple of criticisms online about the report, the armchair experts do the rest. That takedown made her vulnerable. But I needed something deeper.'

'Like discovering she'd given up her child for adoption?'

'Yes. And, in the wake of her greenwashing failure, it was easy to reach out as a lone sympathetic journalist, offering her a voice. The ego boost of suggesting I ghostwrite her autobiography; the positive column inches and high-profile articles. *I* made *her* the phoenix.'

Ah. Of course. Asha had said that Olga had reached out to her. She had to make it seem that way, or her manipulation would have been obvious.

'The worst thing was, I realised how pally she'd become with Hugh. Then she started the affair with Charles. Yet I knew that she was aware of Samir. So there was only one conclusion. She hadn't used that information to get justice. She used that information, the death of my brother, for *leverage*.' A sob of anguish strangles the word.

'Once you knew about Zyra, you had your own leverage over Olga, though. If you knew she was distant yet involved, then it must have been *you* who asked her about her legacy? *You* sowed the seeds of the Pledge. You let it take root, then made a few suggestions about who she should invite from her select black book?'

I knew this retreat was an excuse for lining up the players for a reckoning.

'Yeah. I just suggested she cover political power and soft power to make sure Hugh and Charles would be part of a select cohort, at a totally private event. She joined the dots.'

'And Olga could only get the rest of the group together if she had leverage over them. Which is exactly what you needed, wasn't it? Olga to be surrounded – exclusively – with people who'd benefit from her death. And it couldn't have gone better, could it? With people going to her room to confront her about their grievances. Everyone so vocal about their motives.'

'Yeah, I can't complain. It did take a lot of careful planning. But you were different. No leverage on you, except for your ego, your desire to scale these heady heights. That, and the appeal to your intellect.'

I frown at her.

'Everyone else had a straightforward invite. But if we'd sent that to you, you'd have thrown it away! You needed something different, some cerebral challenge, to appeal to your sense of superiority. You *needed* the lure of the puzzle. And the push of the doxxing. That was easy to plan in advance, given the court case. If you'd lost, there was an invitation prepared in sympathy, to restore your reputation.'

'Oh, you covered all angles. I respect the thoroughness.' My voice, like my blood, has turned to ice at the manipulation. But I should have suspected that, shouldn't I? I don't like feeling like I'm a step behind. I wonder if I'm missing other steps. I do notice that her voice doesn't sound as weak now that she's critiquing me and crowing over her tactics.

Is she acting more injured than she really is?

'Was I invited because you thought I was involved in Samir's disappearance?'

'Yes.'

'I wasn't, Ash.'

'Yeah, I know that *now*.'

'Is that why you poisoned my rasul treatment?'

A scoffing laugh erupts from Asha. 'No. That was to make you scared. Same as when I tried to get into your room at night. I knew you'd be awake to hear it. I knew you'd barricaded the door, so I couldn't have got in and revealed my identity. And the rasul stunt was to make you believe I wasn't the killer.'

'Ah. Unlucky.'

'But you said—?'

'I lied. Of *course* I wasn't going to be convinced by a stunt like that. It's Marple 101. You only used it on your face. A classic attempt to appear that you were poisoned, while making sure you don't ingest enough for it to work. Then you scream the house down in a total overreaction to make sure someone – well, *me* – hears you and breaks in to find you. I'll give you commitment kudos for being naked, like you were going to use more of the treatment all over.'

'So that was pointless, then. *And* undignified.'

'Afraid so. What made you think of the poison?'

'Olga invited me out here for her autobiography research. That's how I got to know my way around. And when you're here, you see that everyone gets that rasul treatment. And you're invited to help yourself to anything from the spa. Which happens to be right by the herb garden. I'm no botanist, but I know monkshood when I see it. Aconitine. Deadly poisonous. Olga caught me staring at it, so I asked her why she had medicinal plants. She said was growing those for her own remedies. When I realised it has, amongst other things, anti-cancer benefits, well . . .'

'*Oh* . . . You wondered if she'd been cultivating it for her sister? Concocting her own treatments when Kali's wonder drug failed Freya?' I don't need her to confirm it. 'So getting Kali here was doubly convenient: she'd want to silence Olga, and she'd know all about the plant you used to poison the treatment.'

'When I discovered how little aconitine you need and how easily it can go undetected, the opportunity seemed . . . too easy.'

'That's why you angled for Kali to invite you and me along with her to the spa? You knew she'd give away her knowledge, and make herself a prime suspect.'

I think the rest of the case through. Everything is different now. Had Asha actually *found* the helicopter keys and hidden them? She certainly made sure she was the first person to check. She'd smashed all the communications. She'd been so avidly searching for clues because she'd needed to find the dossier on Hugh and Charles and Samir — then destroy it before anyone else saw it.

'Ah, that's why you talked to me in my room. To see if you could see where I'd left the information I'd taken about Samir.' She'd asked about the evidence I'd found, and hadn't been convinced that I hadn't taken it. I wonder if the attempt to break in later that night was really so that she could do a thorough search. Or maybe she would have killed me, if she thought I'd already — or was just about to — uncover her secret.

'I knew Olga had some physical evidence to use as leverage. I had to find it before anyone else did. And you were my witness to that discovery.'

I shudder, wondering if she'd planned for me to have an accident when we'd decided to take Olga's body to the staff quarters. After all, she'd believed I was involved in Samir's death then.

'Did Olga ever find out that you were Samir's sister?' I ask.

Another sob escapes Asha. 'No. But I did make sure I was right about her involvement. I didn't just kill her on a wild assumption. I told Olga I'd heard from colleagues about Charles being swept up in an awful investigation. That maybe she should think twice before getting involved with him.'

'What did she say?'

'She was so offhand about it – bearing in mind she didn't know that *I* knew everything. Said she was sure it was all blown out of proportion. That Charles's usefulness outweighed his liability. That confirmed it. Classic Olga. It's her attitude to everyone here, one way or another.'

I can hear Asha's outrage, how any hope for justice had been ripped from her and burned.

'So you killed Olga first. Was it symbolic, because she'd let you down?'

Asha snorts. 'I'd love to say it was. No, it was just practical. If I'd killed Hugh or Charles before her, Olga could have raised the alarm. It had to be her first, then all comms trashed, so that I could have a hope of getting to Hugh.'

Her breath is ragged. 'It all could have been so different, if Hugh didn't have that unbreachable, invisible shield around him, if Charles had had a backbone, if Olga had listened, or even just not been corrupt enough to use her power like that.'

I can hear her gulping back tears.

'So believe me when I say it's a big deal – a really big deal – that we are allies. *Now*.' She squeezes my hand. 'I think you're a lawyer who actually believes in justice. I saw what you were prepared to do.'

'Partners in crime, then.' My voice has a regretful edge. I'm not sure where I stand with my whole life view now. All my values are in chaos, they've slipped around like patterns in a kaleidoscope. Then again, they had already metamorphosised once, until they'd had no worth at all. So where does that leave me now?

'No. Partners in justice.' Asha seems to have no such doubts.

The light grows brighter still, and I pull us further off the path again. He'd be close enough to spot movement now. I pull Asha down so we're crouching under the cover of a banana plant, trying to hold still. The chug of the engine becomes louder as Hugh very steadily catches up with us.

And then I hear something else: his voice. Sing-song, taunting.

'Theeee-a?' My heart pounds as I realise he's enjoying this: he's a hunter playing with his prey.

I hold my breath as he tracks so … achingly … slo-o-o-wly … past us.

'Oh, *Theeee*-a …'

Chapter 32

Tuesday 8th April – 7 p.m.

Wᴇ sʜʀɪɴᴋ ᴅᴏᴡɴ ᴀs ʜᴇ passes. My heart is hammering like a trapped bird's.

'Holy shit!' Hugh leaps off the quad bike and peers at the path. I realise he must have found Olga's body – possibly a skeleton now, given the diabolical industriousness of the creatures in this hellish place.

'For the love of . . .!' He kicks at her ribs, bleached bright white in the headlights, and then he turns. 'Oh, Theeee-a! Come and join our friend Olga!'

He sounds deranged.

He turns again, this time in the direction of where we're cowering, and I see the lights dazzle off the awful thing he's holding: a machete.

Asha gasps, then holds her breath.

Hugh turns to us, lasering in on our location.

I grip Asha's hand. If we can just hold still, keep quiet, maybe he'll move along.

'Oh, Jesus!' He jumps, staring at the ground, and I realise he's seen a snake darting across his path. I pray it will make him reluctant to explore.

Maybe he'll accidentally drive over the cliff. That would be the best possible outcome, wouldn't it? Threat extinguished, but no one needs to actually kill anyone. *Else*.

But he paces, skipping occasionally to avoid another slithering reptile. And beside me, as my eyes widen and my panic skyrockets, Asha pulls a kitchen knife from her belt.

She grips it in front of her. 'It's going to need both of us to take him down if he's armed like that.' She breathes the words like they're weightless, as I grow heavy with dread.

'Or we could just get on the quad bike?'

'It's him or us, Thea. Whatever happens, I did it. OK? I did it for Sam. I'm not going to last much longer. I can feel it. You must say it was me.'

As Hugh paces forward, scanning the undergrowth, Asha creeps away, circling back to the path and emerging behind the quad bike – where Hugh can't see her approach.

I can't believe what I'm seeing as she heads towards him, her jaw clenched.

Through the clamour of frog song, a twig snaps under Asha's foot, and Hugh pivots.

Face to face, the two of them hold their blades out, their bodies rigid.

I hold my breath.

As Hugh and Asha square up, beyond them I see the shadows move: the liquid slink of the panther winding through the bushes on the far side of the track.

Before I can even think about yelling a warning, the panther's snarling, guttural roar echoes around us as it leaps, muscles rippling under velvet, claws outstretched.

At the sound of Asha's scream, Hugh twists round and shrinks back, hands covering his face as the panther pounces, pinning him down.

He yowls as claws rake his face, slicing skin. Long canines gleam in the dim light as the panther snarls. The putrid stench that suddenly fills the air tells me just how terrified Hugh is of the powerful beast looming over him.

Delighted schadenfreude blooms in my heart.

'No! No!' Asha lunges forward at the massive cat, waving her knife.

Freezing, the panther hunkers over Hugh. Its tail swishes, muzzle pulled back.

But Asha doesn't give any ground as she waves her arms. 'Away! Away!'

What the hell is she doing?

The animal's growl rumbles through my body, but Asha has a maniacal glint in her eye. I'm frozen to the spot, too afraid of spooking the big cat, of provoking attack, to move.

Its shoulders slink low, like it might pounce, as it snarls again, displaying its teeth. With its gaze fixed on Asha, it backs away, then evaporates into the jungle.

Asha staggers, like she'd been holding herself up with sheer bravado, and whips round to face Hugh. He's cringing as he scrambles to his feet, probably from his close encounter with the creatures of the jungle floor.

Before he can stand, Asha thrusts her knife at his kidneys.

'Arrgh!' He turns, swinging his long, curved blade at her.

Asha parries, drawing the energy from some deep well of rage. She stabs wildly as she pants, 'I'm not … letting a panther … do what I … came here to do.'

But Hugh's flashing blade swings too close to her, the deadly edge slicing nearer. I rush out and *shove* him.

Asha ducks, and his blade thuds into the tyre of the quad bike. She stabs him again, again, as he tries to pull the machete out, and I crash sidelong into him, making him let go and stagger into the undergrowth as I turn to pull out the awful weapon.

But he's too fast. He punches me in the jaw. My head *rings*. I can taste blood.

Then his hands are on my throat, clawing at me, crushing the breath out of me. My vision swims, swirling bright light fuzzed with black.

A blood-chilling screech rips from Asha and she rushes at him again. I feel the punch of her knife in his side. I see his eyes widen, then the familiar cruel flicker of his expression as he twists, releasing one hand from my neck, then the other, to swing his elbow back into her face.

As she staggers back, he clutches his side.

But Asha doesn't get up.

He turns to me again, but I drop to my knees and check on her. My shirt round her neck is soaked with pulsing blood. Her wound has ripped open with her head snapping back with the blow.

I hear Hugh move behind me and I grab the knife from Asha's hand.

I turn as Hugh runs towards me, about to give me that prissy little kick he gave Magnus on the first night here.

I hold still until the last second, then duck my head and stab the knife upwards with as much force as I can muster. It hits a fleshy barrier, and Hugh *howls*. Hot blood fountains from the femoral artery in his thigh.

He rolls on the ground, and a lime arrow-headed snake isn't deterred as it slithers across him. He screams again, and I know it's the last sound he'll make.

I return to Asha's side. *Oh God. There's so much blood.*

There's no pulse, no breath, no chance.

I'm not proud of what I do next, but I'm a pragmatist, plus I know I'd have her blessing. I hold the blade with a leaf, wipe the handle with Hugh's shirt – since he's been stabbed through it, any microfibres will match – press Asha's fingers back around the handle, then let it rest on the ground, on the leaf I carried it with.

I can't bring myself to go back to the main house after this. I don't want to explain, relive all this to the rest of them. And no one else followed me out to help. The staff quarters are closest, for a shower and a bed, and a drink. The quad bike might be useless now, with its stabbed, deflated tyre, but I can walk there, even in the dusk.

I'm so engrossed in checking the forensic scene and formulating a plan that I don't notice the silent approach.

A huff of hot breath behind me makes me jump. I turn slowly, fearfully, to find myself staring into the amber eyes of the midnight-black panther.

Its muzzle twitches, drawing back from the long canines, face contorting as it inhales my scent – and the stench of blood and death.

I itch to back away, to put distance between me and this deadly predator. Very, very cautiously, I take one step back and then another, moving inch by painful inch, so slowly that my thighs tremble. As I edge backwards I make myself as wide and as tall as I can, drawing myself up to my full six feet.

I'm willing the beast to understand: I'm too big to kill, and not enough of a threat to bother attacking.

Even so, I'm struggling to convince myself. Terror grips me and I try not to think about snakes, spiders and other nameless horrors that I could be reversing into.

The panther's eyes stay fixed on me, its body taut, shoulders low, poised to pounce. I move agonisingly slowly, skirting Asha's body.

But those amber eyes follow me, and the powerful body turns, keeping me in focus, as I move along the path. I daren't turn around and walk forwards. Don't big cats hunt you once you have your back to them? My steps are slow and careful: I can't afford to stumble.

I'm a few feet away from the panther now, and the bodies of Asha and Hugh are between us. I draw a shuddering inhale and keep moving, gradually, quietly.

The big cat lets out a huffing exhale. A growl rumbles. I can hear it snuffle at the corpses, and I close my eyes, trying to shut out the thought of it feasting on them. Not Asha, please not Asha.

Then the snarl becomes muffled, and I hear the rustle of something – I know it's a body – being dragged into the undergrowth. I don't look. I turn, and I force my shaking legs to propel me on.

I'm grateful for every step that takes me further away from the panther, but each one plunges me into deeper darkness, out of range of the quad bike's headlights. I manage to maintain a steady pace, despite being desperate to run – which isn't something I ever thought I'd say – but I know it will fire the panther's instinct. I may not be able to see it, but it will surely know exactly where I am.

My eyes are at least gradually adjusting, but the slithery, rustling jungle at night is otherworldly and disturbing. My skin is *crawling*.

I shiver, as I realise it's now pitch black. I push onwards – and am I imagining it? Is that … a blink of lights in the distance? I stare, heart pounding with hope.

Is that lights? At the staff quarters?

Are they back? Is help here?

I pick up my pace, then I speed-walk, then I run.

With a sudden shiver of familiarity, I realise I'm running *past* the building. Yet the lights are still ahead.

I run on further, wondering where they're coming from. The undergrowth thins out, then ends – and I skid, hearing rocks scatter below me. A breeze sweeps up from the sea to sting my hot, sweaty face, and I realise I've stopped at the precipice of a cliff.

As I back away, more stones crumble beneath my feet and bounce down the sheer drop.

The wind ruffles my hair. The lights are still blinking.

And then I know what I'm looking at.

It's the yacht!

It hadn't been here before, I know that. The staff must have returned, perhaps concerned that Olga hadn't summoned them. Maybe they were intending to slowly circumnavigate the island in case she called them in.

I cannot believe that help is right there ... yet out on the sodding ocean.

I can't tell how far away it is, but there's no way I can swim to it. Even if I could get to the sea from up here, which I can't ...

If I wait, maybe help will come to me. Maybe there's a flare in the staff quarters.

Maybe in the morning, it will be easier to see what we're dealing with.

But maybe in the morning, they'll be gone ...?

Just as I realise I can't let this chance slip away, and begin looking for the path down to the beach, the deciding factor announces itself.

With a roar.

I pick my way down the path, slipping on the scree. I panic about where I'm placing my feet in the dark, alongside a sheer drop down to jagged rock and churning sea.

I turn my ankle on an unexpected dip, and throw myself towards the cliff, clinging to the rock like a limpet, shaking in fear at what could have happened if my bottom wasn't such effective ballast.

I continue making my way down sideways, slipping as I grow tired.

And then the path runs out!

It's another few metres to the beach, but now it's a sheer drop.

I stare at the inky water. Do those idiots just jump in like crazy daredevils? The path is too well-worn to never be used.

I look out at the yacht. Towards hope. Rescue. There's no other way.

Another roar, closer this time, is the clincher.

Don't overthink it. I hold my nose, and jump.

The plunge sends a sick swoop up through me. A scream whooshes from my mouth, making my ears block up as my legs windmill in the air.

A sudden smack of ocean engulfs me in cold shock, and I sink, snorting briny water into my mouth and nose, panicking as I kick out.

My mind has me surrounded immediately with deadly sharks, sea snakes, jellyfish and those horrific tiny, spiky critters that want to swim up your personal areas.

I emerge, spluttering, kicking, splashing, swallowing salty gulps of revolting seawater. But I'm here. I'm alive. I made it this far.

The yacht looks impossibly far away. I strike out with my arms, trying to be purposeful about it. Trying to pretend I know how to do front crawl.

But I'm tired. And I'm not a swimmer.

Yet somehow, I just keep going. I get water up my nose and splutter, then swallow more and choke a few times. I turn and swim on my back when I need to rest my arms, but I keep making progress. Then I turn over again, and try harder.

It feels like I've swum and swum for a hundred years. And suddenly, the yacht seems ... larger. *Is that ...? Yes! I can hear music! And laughter.* And now it seems like it's just a swimming pool length away, looming up towards me.

Oh no ... Don't sharks follow big boats? Because food is often thrown overboard? Is that a Nat Geo fact, or has my panic-fevered brain made it up?

I freeze, scared of getting closer. I imagine wicked fins slicing through the dark water around me, the merciless gnashing of bone-stripping jaws, and I'm plagued by the adrenalin-spiking alert of imminent attack. Here I am again, the least well-adapted animal in any given natural environment.

And then the music stops. Someone peers over the side of the yacht.

'*Man overboard!*'

* * *

I'm swaddled in blankets, my teeth chattering so much from cold and shock that I can't speak for several minutes. I'm given warm – not hot, just warm – drinks to increase my body temperature.

Everyone is staring at me. There's a silence suggesting that they realise something awful must have happened, to make someone so desperate to leave that apparent paradise. Or perhaps they're just expecting to hear about a sea adventure gone awry. Drunken midnight japes.

Then Drew – the kind steward whom Hugh humiliated – steps forward. He tops up the tea in my mug from the pot.

'It's Ms Harrington, isn't it? Thea?'

I nod. I still can't speak.

He hunkers down to look me in the eyes. 'Can you tell me what happened?'

I nod again. I try to form words, but messy, spluttering sobs erupt through my chattering teeth instead. He rubs my arm, pulls the blanket around me, then rubs my back. It's soothing, warming, like I can feel the blood flow returning.

I manage a smile that doesn't wobble away.

'Are you warming up a bit?'

'Y-yes.'

'Good. Did you swim out here from the island? Or—?'

'Yes.'

His eyes widen. 'Bloody *hell*! Sorry. Why?'

Now I'm steadier, now that the wall of shock is disintegrating and I can feel most of my body coming back to life, I can ask for what I need.

'I n-need to speak to the police, Drew. Immediately. It's about Olga. It'll need to be the Chief Constable, or the island equivalent.'

'Oh . . . Sure.' He hesitates, worried, then strides to the wheel-house, returning with a chunky satellite phone that looks like a '90s mobile, and the concerned-looking Captain.

'She's here now, sir.' Drew says into the phone, then hands it to me. 'It's the Commissioner.'

I hear the greeting. 'Commissioner Cadogan speaking.'

'Hi, I'm Thea Harrington. There's been a serious incident involving Olga Helgesdotter and her guests at her villa on St Innocent. Multiple murders, including Olga herself. The remaining people are trapped on the island, in need of rescue – and at least one needs urgent medical help. And . . . any assistance heading there should also know that Olga's pet panther is loose.'

'One moment.'

I wait as the line is muted, knowing the Commissioner is deploying medics and forensic investigators. And maybe a vet. Seconds drag like centuries, and my teeth start to chatter. I take a deep breath, and the line crackles into life again.

'We'll need to take a full statement from you, but can you give me an outline, to help our investigation?'

'Olga was the first victim, found dead at around 6 a.m. on Sunday morning, in her pool, after contact poison had been added to her rasul body treatment.'

'I'm very sorry to hear that. Multiple deaths, you said? Who else?'

'Charles Harrington, my husband, was killed sometime during Sunday night, when the fixing for the massive glass sculpture chandelier above his bed was tampered with.'

'I'm sorry for your loss,' the Commissioner murmurs.

'I found . . . highly sensitive material that pointed to the killer . . . I'll specify where when I make my statement. The murderer was Prince Hubert, the Duke of Clarence.'

I'm not letting the blame for their deaths sit at Asha's door.

Olga, Charles, Hugh, they were all to blame, weren't they? Asha didn't get to ignore her loss, or her grief, or her pain.

Meanwhile, not only did Charles and Olga shrug their shoulders at the horrific crime, they also perverted the course of justice, prevented closure, then used the information to barter *even* more power, *even* more money, for themselves. When they already had so much.

Never enough. I feel sick. I want to distance myself from everyone like them, who treads on others just to scramble a little higher up that endless golden ladder.

'Hugh had been detained under room arrest. But he broke free earlier this evening. He attacked and injured Magnus Black and Asha Sani with a broken bottle and a corkscrew.'

I wonder what became of his supper tray, and feel a frisson of worry that the police might find the poison in his sandwich. Surely someone will have thrown it away. Hugh fleeing would have unsettled everyone, and they would have checked his room when he didn't come back.

At least we'd made the sandwich look unappetising enough that no one else was likely to eat it, especially as they'd all had dinner. Hugh's food will just have been tipped into the bin. It will probably be checked, but the chances of something that wasn't eaten being tested for poison, when that clearly isn't how Hugh died, is unlikely.

'Asha and I ran for the staff quarters via a jungle track, hoping to find a way to get help. But Hugh pursued us, and attacked us with a machete. Asha had grabbed a small knife and tried to fend him off. She caught him in the thigh, and severed his femoral artery, which killed him. His attack worsened Asha's injury, causing her to bleed out. I continued on to the staff quarters. I saw the lights of the yacht. And I managed to swim ... swim out.'

As I look across the inky ocean, I see a speedboat curving towards the enclosed bay.

'I can see your team arriving,' I say. 'I'll hand you back to the captain so he can advise how to gain access. Thank you, Commissioner.'

As the captain paces away with the phone, Drew approaches with more tea. *And my phone!*

He holds it out, and it's like having my whole life back in one tiny package.

'The captain says you're welcome to stay aboard or at a mainland hotel while you're helping the police with their enquiries. Anything you need will be taken care of.'

I wince. 'That's kind, and I appreciate the hospitality. But I'll take care of myself.' Looking around, I roll my eyes as I realise I'm still dependent on him for a little longer. 'At least, I will whenever you're able to take me to the mainland.'

'Of course.' He hesitates. 'I ... I listened to your phone call. Is he really ...?' Wide eyes and a nod of his head replace the word 'dead', and I note Drew doesn't dare utter the prince's name.

'Yes. And I suspect a few case files will also end up with the press. He'll be named as the perpetrator, even if the story is ultimately quashed, and even if the case goes nowhere.'

'That's ... something.' He blinks, hiding how his eyes are welling up at the suggestion that the prince might – just might – be called to account for something, even though reports will say 'suspected' and 'alleged' by the time they're published. 'Thank you.'

I stare after him as he leaves, recognising that's a glimmer of what justice feels like. And I haven't felt that for a very long time.

Chapter 33

Friday 11ᵗʰ April – London

IN THE BOUTIQUE HOLBORN COFFEE shop, I sip my espresso as I drink in the front-page news, noting the varying shades of scandal across the different papers. Like a barrister determining what parts of the crime to present to the jury, the details shared by the headlines reveal more than just the facts of the case:

Prince, CEO, Energy Minister and Journalist killed at private island retreat
Shocking murders at billionaire's playground
Pervy Prince fingered for murders on Island of Death

Kali is pictured, stating that she's returning to business as usual; Uri hints at his research and next big idea; but Magnus uses the press interest to announce that he's stepping back from party donations and instead focusing on non-profits. I can guess which charities will benefit. I do notice the interviewees' artful deflections of the avid interest in events at the island, stoked by Olga's social media hints at the Pledge.

I also side-stepped those questions from the journalists waiting for me at Arrivals, circling like sharks on the scent of a story, with a crisp, 'No comment.' Simple words said with a heavy heart. But as much as I was aching to, I couldn't possibly prejudice a trial, could I? The Commissioner has my statement and evidence against Hugh, and I'm prepared for the witness box. *That* will be a novelty.

The palace is studiously not explaining, not complaining, about the leaked video of Hugh's, well, *leak* on the yacht. A source close to the family stated, 'Video footage can't be trusted due to the widespread use of advanced AI deepfake technology.' Meanwhile the social media views and the column inches decrying it keep growing.

I applaud Zyra for releasing it, and I wonder if her social media team know. A picture of her and Estelle, now inseparable in New York, fills the other half of the front page. Rumours of a romance between them fill the gossip columns, but I suspect they're growing a business venture together. I'd bet on ethical fashion or sustainable events, or maybe both; they're not women who believe in limits. *And it's contagious ...*

The thought buoys me up as I finish my coffee and head into the street. It's a grey, mucky, mizzly day as I stride through a rainswept Lincoln's Inn. Yet I feel *light*.

I walk into the familiar office and my paralegal rushes over. 'Thea? I didn't think you were coming in today?'

'It's OK, Arthur is expecting me.'

'Oh. Well, how are you? I'm so sorry about Charles ...'

I'm saved from answering as Arthur opens the door to his stuffy, wood-panelled office.

'Thea! Good to have you back. How ... how are you?'

'Much changed, Arthur.' I hand him the slim envelope. 'Here's my written notice. Effective immediately. I'm setting up my own firm. I won't keep you today, but let's do lunch in a few weeks.'

I get the gape I'd hoped for, and then I can move on. I hurry along Chancery Lane in time to see 'Under Offer' being nailed across the 'For Sale' board.

In every way, this is a million miles from the luxurious lifestyle I've glimpsed first-hand.

In the space of less than a week, I've had activists protest my court victory, I've been trapped on an island with a killer, I've been attacked, I've been publicly humiliated by my philandering husband, who was then killed, making me the prime suspect for multiple murders. I believed I *was* a killer, and then I *had* to kill, in self-defence. I shudder.

I've survived the horrors of the jungle, handled corpses, escaped a panther – and faced my demons.

My idea of what justice looks like has been tested and found sorely wanting.

Now, a few thousand miles and a whole world away, I'm gazing up at this modest, drafty, leaky office on the third floor of the Georgian terrace – yet all I can see is *freedom*.

The building survey gave a list of complicated problems a mile long, all made lengthier and costlier for it being a listed building, naturally.

But it's entirely mine. My own practice, my own choices. Maybe . . . my own values.

I can choose my own cases. No high-profile glory, but maybe making a meaningful difference to people who really need it.

Genuine excitement flutters in my stomach, along with the fizzing nerves of leaping into the unknown: the challenge, and the chance. My heart soars with the sense of purpose, of having a real focus instead of the endless, empty, *never-enough* climb.

I laugh as I realise that something actually *has* climbed: if I took that Life Satisfaction survey again, my happiness score would be higher than it was mere days ago. Escaping death really does give you a new appreciation of life, it seems.

An email arrives about a pro-bono case I've taken on. The sound notification that accompanies the incoming message makes me smile: I've set it to be a panther's roar. It'll get old quickly, no doubt. But for now, it's my talisman.

My reminder that it's worth taking the leap.

Acknowledgements

IT HAS BEEN A TOTAL delight to work with the amazing team at Zaffre, and I owe huge thanks to Ben Willis for making this such a fun new adventure! I'm indebted to Isabella Boyne, Rianna Houghton and Anna Perkins for discussing storylines and polishing up my prose – you have added such fabulous extra sparkle to these pages, thank you!

I'm immensely grateful to the care and attention of Paris Ferguson. Huge thanks to Nick Stearn and Vishani Perera for lavishing this book with your talents to make Thea's world so atmospheric, and Chelsea Graham for working her magic with Adjoa Andoh to bring the book to life.

I'm so lucky to work with the most tremendous agent in the universe, Katie Fulford, at Bell Lomax Moreton. I just cannot imagine a more phenomenal partner to share this journey with!

One of the absolute joys of writing is learning from experts, and I've returned to two – who had previously advised on my Dr Nell Ward series – for this book: I'm enormously appreciative of the gory insights from Dr Julie Roberts, who isn't only a Chartered Forensic Anthropologist, she's a treasure trove of disgusting and brilliant suggestions and ideas. Her authoritative and exact assessments on how the poor victims' corpses in these pages would have fared in tropical climates – with and without air con, and with and without a pouncing panther – have been truly flavoursome. I'm always reminded that, underneath these consultations, is a specialist who uses these skills for very real, very traumatic work, and I'm full of admiration for the impactful and important work they do, when they're not helping to imagine fantastical scenarios for books.

Likewise, the poisoning expertise of Brian Price has been critical for this story – and I love that there doesn't seem to be a question that can faze him! The discussion of whether a poison that's deadly for a human would be also deadly for a panther has been one of the highlights of my research so far.

I'm really grateful to readers who gave their time to critique and provide feedback to help me improve the book: Rachel and Erin, thanks for your valued words of wisdom.

Mum and dad – thank you for always reading every draft and never worrying about how to sugar coat your opinions. ☺ Thanks also for the adventures and scrapes we've had over the years: our holidays and travels have provided an unusual set of near-death experiences that are surprisingly helpful to draw upon.

Jo, Rachel, Nick, Esther, Mark, Jay, Matt, Rajka, Lauren, Erin, Nigel and Julie – thank you for enforced cocktail and coffee breaks from the computer. Few could tempt me away from writing, and I'm lucky to have friends like you to do so.

My delicious husband, Ian – I adore you for the devious plotting, for reading all the drafts, for acting out the critical scenes and sharing this so wholeheartedly.

The inspiration for *The Pledge* has, of course, evolved from my career in ecology and sustainability. I've had the privilege of working with colleagues who haven't only had brilliant minds, they've also had that pure line of integrity that drives them along the tough path of continually growing challenges, and been stout enough of heart to not give up. This book is a salute to them – from whom I have learned, and continue to learn, so much about the complexity of how we take care of our planet – with ecology that is both fragile and ferocious, and people who can be both protective and destructive.

Sustainability is one of those areas where those working in it can be held to impossible standards, and picking at passion and progress can become a sport. In this book, Uri makes the observation that tinkering isn't the same as solving our climate issues, and he's right that significant shifts are needed. But few of us are in that position.

But, like the proverbial mosquito, every individual does contribute one way or another. Just like Thea, when she identifies what it is she can do to make a difference, we all have our own talents and abilities that we can use for good – if we so choose.

None of us can do everything; but each of us can do something.

And, for those who have taken the time to read – thank you, and I sincerely hope you've enjoyed reading this as much as I've enjoyed writing it.

Don't miss Sarah Yarwood-Lovett's next twisty psychological thriller

The Prospect

When pharmaceutical prospector Nathan is found dead in
the Amazon after uncovering a revolutionary new drug, his
widow, Cassie, is stunned to receive an invitation to the
lavish launch of Panacea Pharma's new Peruvian research
institute. Accepting means confronting danger –
but refusing could bury the truth about her
husband's death forever.

There, surrounded by ruthless colleagues battling over
the billions at stake, Cassie finds herself caught in a
web of greed and ambition as impenetrable and
deadly as the rainforest itself.

Undeterred, she begins to unearth the truth – until another
member of the team dies and Cassie is forced to retreat to
the safety of home. But peril and the laws of the jungle
follow her: hunted by a killer with secrets to keep,
Cassie realises the cost of discovering the truth
about her husband's death might be her own life.

COMING SOON